FINAL DESTINATION
DEAD RECKONING

"What's going on?" Jamie stepped up beside her and put a hand on her shoulder. Jess seized his arm like a lifeline.

"I had a vision! Like a kind of premonition... It was horrible, Jamie. The ceiling fell in and everybody died... It really happened! And now it's going to happen for real, and we have to get out of here before it does. Everyone dies, even me. You have to believe me!"

Jess fell silent, suddenly aware that she was raving. Slowly, she turned and looked around at a wall of stony expressions. With a horrible sinking feeling, she knew that she had lost them. She wouldn't believe anyone who sounded as crazy as she just did...

In the same series

FINAL DESTINATION #2:
DESTINATION ZERO
David McIntee

More New Line novels from Black Flame

BLADE: TRINITY
Natasha Rhodes

THE BUTTERFLY EFFECT
James Swallow

CELLULAR
Pat Cadigan

FREDDY vs JASON
Stephen Hand

JASON X
Pat Cadigan

JASON X#2: THE EXPERIMENT
Pat Cadigan

THE TEXAS CHAINSAW MASSACRE
Stephen Hand

THE TWILIGHT ZONE #1
MEMPHIS • THE POOL GUY
Jay Russell

THE TWILIGHT ZONE #2
UPGRADE • SENSUOUS CINDY
Pat Cadigan

THE TWILIGHT ZONE #3
INTO THE LIGHT • SUNRISE
Paul A Woods

FINAL DESTINATION
DEAD RECKONING

A NOVEL BY
NATASHA RHODES

BASED ON CHARACTERS FROM THE
MOTION PICTURE "FINAL DESTINATION"
CREATED BY JEFFREY REDDICK

BLACK FLAME

Thanks to my kick-ass editors Nozomi Goto &
Jay Slater, for making this book happen. Also
thanks to Powder, The Drills, and to all the great
guys & gals who put me up (and put up with
me!) this summer in LA. You guys rock!

A Black Flame Publication
www.blackflame.com

First published in 2005 by BL Publishing, Games Workshop Ltd.,
Willow Road, Nottingham NG7 2WS, UK.

Distributed in the US by Simon & Schuster, 1230 Avenue of the
Americas, New York, NY 10020, USA.

10 9 8 7 6 5 4 3 2 1

ISBN 1 84416 170 6

A CIP record for this book is available from the British Library.

Printed in the UK by Bookmarque, Surrey, UK.

ONE

If there was one thing Jess Golden had learned at school, it was this: never trust a guy who can run faster than you.

Not even if they're nice to you. Not even if they buy you dinner and drinks and tell you that they love you.

And certainly not if you think they'll ever have reason to chase you.

That thought was now at the forefront of Jess's mind as she tore across the lonely concrete parking lot towards the lights and safety of the buildings nearby. Her muscles burned with exhaustion and her lungs felt fit to burst, but she kept going. It wasn't as if she had any other choice. It was past midnight in downtown LA, and the empty streets were filled with the kind of shadows that moved when you looked at them. Orange sodium lamps did little more than accentuate the darkness and dogs barked as she flew past gated compounds strewn with razor wire.

From somewhere behind her came the sound of pounding footsteps, punctuated by heavy breathing and the occasional shouted obscenity. Jess ignored the sound and concentrated on running. Running was a really good thing to do right now.

The three-inch heels were a mistake, she saw it now. And the leather miniskirt? Just asking for trouble. She felt the heels of her expensive boots giving way as she ran and silently cursed herself. She'd spent a long time dressing up for dinner with this guy, and she'd got it wrong yet again. Why did looking good mean wearing stuff you couldn't run in?

She blamed men in general. She was sure they had something to do with it.

Still, she was nearly at the brightly lit cluster of buildings on the corner, which meant that she was almost safe.

Almost...

Jess skidded round a corner and nearly ran head-first into the fence that blocked the walkway. The sidewalk was completely cordoned off for road-works. Thick chicken wire was tied across it, strung in place with heavy ropes. A sign read "Diversion", and pointed back the way she had just come. There was no way around.

Jess swore loudly.

Glancing feverishly back over her shoulder, Jess began searching for a way around the blockade.

There had to be a way through. Fueled by adrenaline, she grabbed the barrier in both hands and yanked on it as hard as she could.

It stayed firmly in place.

There was only one thing for it. Jess kicked off her high heels, scooped them up in one hand and started climbing. There was no time to go around. Reaching the top, she threw herself over, feeling the edge of the fence draw blood from her bare stomach as she half climbed, half fell down the other side. She dropped heavily to the ground and then it was back to the running.

Seconds later, she heard her pursuer hit the fence with a sound like a shopping cart being dropped onto concrete. He gave a bellow of frustration and began shaking the fence in fury, yelling at Jess to come back.

Jess allowed herself a small smile. That would hold him for at least a minute, giving her precious time to escape.

She ran flat out for another couple of blocks, before slowing to a walk. She was wheezing. Boy, was she out of shape. She made a mental note to get her butt down to the gym after the weekend, instead of bitching to her friends that she looked obscene in Lycra.

Jess paused and stood for a moment with her hands on her knees, then took a deep breath and straightened, flicking her long dark hair out of her face. She leaned back on the wall and stole a glance behind her.

There was no sign of her pursuer.

Good.

Reaching into the pocket of her denim jacket, Jess carefully pulled out a large leather-bound wallet and regarded it with a great deal of satisfaction. She already knew what it contained—platinum credit cards, Diners Club card, a couple of hundred dollars in cash and a photo of Bill and his wife. Bill was the name of the irate man currently pursuing her, and he had good reason to do so. His illicit date had turned out to be very costly to him, in more ways than one.

Jess tucked the wallet back inside her jacket and patted it in a friendly fashion. There was easily enough money to pay a couple of months' rent in there, although she'd probably have to toss out the cards once Bill had reported them as "missing." Hell, the guy could sue her if he wanted the rest of his stuff back, although she was pretty sure that he wouldn't dare. If he wanted to mess around behind his wife's back, especially with her, then he deserved everything he got.

Jess gazed across the road, her eyes searching the street. *Ah—there.* On the roof of a derelict warehouse, a neon sign in the shape of a cat burned, lighting up the darkness with a deep crimson glow. Beneath it, a long line of clubgoers waited patiently outside the door, smoking and chatting.

Smoothing out her jacket, Jess took a deep breath and started making her way across the road towards the club. With everything she'd been through tonight, she could sure as hell use a drink.

The interior of Club Kitty was dark, dirty and loud. Jess yawned as she pushed her way through the heavy industrial doors and clanked down the metal steps in her high heeled boots.

There were countless such places in LA, clustered around the major intersections like flies on a corpse, attracting a diverse mix of tourists, high-lifers and even the odd celebrity. They were universally tacky and as transient as the town that housed them. What was Club X one week would be resprayed and turned into a pizza joint the next, leaving a lot of confused patrons scratching their heads and wondering what had happened to their favorite nightspot, and why on earth their pizza had glitter in it.

But in LA, the City of Angels, this was just how the game was played.

Out with the old, in with the new.

It didn't matter that the old had been new just a few days or hours ago. The constant ebb and flow of trade was the lifeblood of the city.

Jess looked around her in amusement as she reached the bottom of the steps. She'd not been wrong about this place. Everything about it screamed "cheap!" from the bare-board seating to the graffiti-covered brick walls. Judging by the state of it, the club owners had read somewhere that min-imalism was coming back in again, and had decided to decorate the place by, well, not decorating it at all. It was as stark and bare as the derelict warehouse above it. Tea light candles flickered on the rickety metal tables, filling the dank air with a jumping orange light, and the bar area was illuminated by a single bare bulb, which had been painted black in the mistaken belief that this made it look cool.

Over by the main stairway, a scruffy dog dozed peacefully on a pile of discarded jackets, occasionally awaking to snap at the ankles of those stepping over it.

But despite the air of general neglect, the place was packed to bursting. Dozens of too-cool-to-be-conscious teens and twenty-somethings jammed the place from wall to wall, all in various stages of inebriation and undress. Over by the far wall, a gaggle of girls burst into shrill peels of laughter over their ten-dollar apple martinis, eyeing up the guys in the designer jeans who were draped artfully over the sofas and chairs by the bar, pretending not to notice them. The general atmosphere was one of careless affluence, of seeing and being seen.

Toad the Wet Sprocket's "When Will We Fall Down?" was playing on the PA. A tall, willowy man in a tattered cowboy jacket was dancing to it all alone in a corner, lost in the music.

"This place really sucks, huh?"

Jess looked up to see a sandy-haired frat boy gazing at her appreciatively. She glanced around her, then shrugged, feeling expansive. "Nothing that a couple of hundred pounds of TNT wouldn't fix."

The boy snorted with laughter.

Jess walked past a handful of stoned-looking older guys dressed in black who were lounging against the wall, wearing leather jackets and eternally hopeful expressions, and entered the main bar area, trying to make herself look respectable. The room was dark and low ceilinged, lit only by the tangled neon display behind the bar. A giant disco ball lit the room with spinning red and blue reflections, further adding to the general air of tackiness. At the end of the room, a muffled thumping came from behind a heavy iron door labeled, "Enter Here". Above the sign, some wag had added, "Abandon hope all ye who..."

Jess's heel skidded on the floor. She looked down. The floor was scattered with heaps of glossy cards and band flyers. She peered down, trying to read the names of the bands listed on them.

"ID, please."

"Sure." Jess fished out her expertly doctored California driver's license and handed it over, taking care not to drop Bill's credit cards all over the floor. That would not be a good start to the evening. She paid the bouncer the six bucks cover charge and glanced behind her, hoping that Bill hadn't been so stupid as to follow her in here. He knew as well as she did that she could make a scene as well as anyone.

The scary-looking punk bouncer checked her card over carefully, paying particular attention to her date of birth. Jess surreptitiously studied him out of the corner of her eye.

She had been to this club once or twice before, and this particular doorman never failed to fascinate her. He always put Jess in mind of some primal and predatory beast forced to wear a suit and keep regular hours. He had a pierced eyebrow and a jaw like a piranha, and was so muscular that his arms no longer rested comfortably at his sides, hanging instead at an angle to his body. What was visible of his neck was covered in swirling tribal tattoos, and he had an impressive black and white striped Mohawk.

Jess wasn't afraid of the guy like some people around here were, but still, she made sure that she never went to the restrooms alone when he was on duty. It was just common sense. She always had the weirdest feeling that he was watching her...

The bouncer scratched a dirty thumbnail over Jess's license card, checking for telltale seams in the plastic, but couldn't find anything wrong with it. He gave Jess a sharp look and grudgingly handed it back. Then he took her hand and stamped it with the club logo, muttering something under his breath that she chose to ignore.

Moving on down the room as quickly as she could, Jess bought herself an overpriced drink at the bar, then picked up one of the scattered flyers. There were three bands on tonight—the Drills, the Vipers and some kind of rock-ska band named Mors Mortis.

Jess squinted at the fine print on the flyer. They'd spelt her name wrong again. Typical. Picking up her drink with a sigh, Jess smoothed down her hair and opened the main door onto a wall of sound.

The main dance floor of Club Kitty was packed, filled from wall to wall by a heaving throng of club-goers, all dressed up in glam rock gear. Jess frowned for a second, then remembered it was Friday. Friday meant Eighties Night. *Great*. Jess glanced down at her attire, and gave a smirk. At least she'd fit in here for once.

She shut the bar door behind her and peered into the crowd, trying to get her bearings. Strobe lighting flickered across the walls, making the clubbers look like badly animated puppets. The room was hot and the air thrummed with blast after blast of sound. The stage was book-ended by two enormous speakers, which pumped out arena-volume sound in the living room-sized club. Jess fished in her bag for earplugs.

Some local rock band was playing, presumably the Drills, a lively trio lead by a tough-looking guy with an eyebrow ring and skin-tight black jeans. His T-shirt bore the legend *"It Ain't Gonna Lick Itself,"* which for some reason Jess found highly amusing.

She paused in the doorway to watch as the band slammed into a crazy rock breakdown, the lead singer belting out a volley of insane high-speed licks on his guitar, jumping and spinning and expertly driving the crowd into a frenzy. Behind him, the tattooed drummer added a high-octane double bassdrum solo to the mix, his red-streaked hair whipping around him as he played.

The funky young bass player joined the others in an amp-smashing finale, stepping back hurriedly as the singer hurled his guitar into the air mid-solo as the final notes rang out. Then the lights went down and the audience went wild, applauding and cheering and shouting for an encore.

Jess shook her head in wonder, joining in the applause, then began pushing her way through the crowd, wiping her forehead as she walked. Empty bottles and soda cans clanked and crunched under her feet as she walked, and her heels stuck slightly to the floor with every step.

She grimaced. This place was pure class.

As the curtain closed and the filler music came on, Jess saw a familiar black-clad figure standing by the side of the stage, facing away from her, seemingly absorbed in the music. She squeezed her way through the throng and poked him in the ribs with a finger. "Hey."

The figure didn't turn round. Jess grinned and tugged on the end of his studded belt. "Aren't you glad I made it?"

The figure glanced over its shoulder, looked Jess up and down, and turned away again.

Jess pouted. "Oh, come on. I'm here, aren't I?"

The figure appeared to consider this. "Yes, you're here," he agreed. He daintily pulled back a black satin sleeve to reveal a Mickey Mouse watch. "You're here exactly one minute and thirty-two seconds before we are due to go onstage."

"Jamie. Baby. You know I'd never let you down." Jess beamed up at him, playfully trailing a white-painted fingernail down the muscle of his back.

Jamie reached around to catch her finger, then turned around fully. He was wearing a jeweled eyebrow-ring, which cast complicated highlights over his open, high-cheek boned face. His hair was spiked up with hair gel and he wore a black wireless headset over one ear. He did not look amused.

He stared at Jess for a couple of seconds, taking in her flushed appearance and sweat-streaked makeup. Then the corner of his mouth twitched up. "That's what you said last time."

Jess took his hand in hers. "You still have my word," she said.

Jamie gazed at her for a moment, then shook his head ruefully. "You know what? I'm not even going to ask." He winked at her. "Come on. Let's go wake up the others."

It was close to midnight, and the Vipers were rocking the joint. Jess strapped her trademark '79 Sunburst Gibson tighter around her neck and laid into the last few songs of her set with relish. All her tensions had evaporated under the harsh glare of the stage lights and she was just beginning to enjoy herself.

Damn, she loved being on stage. Sure, the rehearsals were a drag, but when she got up here in front of the crowd and the lights hit her, this was it. This is what it was all about. Her life might be going to hell, but while she was up here, nothing could touch her.

Jess paused in her playing and breathed in deeply, taking it all in. This was the place she truly belonged. The stage lights bathed her in a wash of flashing color, and the familiar smell of cigarette smoke and dry ice filled her nostrils. Jess drank the scent in like perfume, strumming a power chord on her guitar. She felt the note resonate through the body of the guitar into her own, buzzing behind her breastbone and filling her with a feeling of immense power and strength.

It was at moments like these when she really felt alive.

Jess grabbed the microphone and belted out a rapid-fire chorus as the crowd roared their approval, buoyed up by her enthusiasm. Out of the corner of her eye, she watched as Tony and Cassie, her two guitarists, drove the crowd wild with their patented leaps and jumps, playing like rock demons on fire. They were both shirtless, and wore combat pants and army boots with metal heels. Stylized snakes were painted around their bodies, which seemed to move and writhe as they played. Cassie wore a pink PVC bra studded with silver spikes, actually managing to make it look stylish, while Tony wore his trademark Union Jack belt strung with bronze bullets and a blue bandanna tied around his head.

Even Jamie had made an effort to smarten himself up for tonight's performance, Jess noticed. His black cotton shirt was unbuttoned to the waist to reveal the silver chain that connected his various piercings to the black leather dog collar around his throat. He was beating the hell out of the drums, sweat pouring down his face, his eyes closed in rapt concentration. High-pitched screams and camera flashes filled the air, and Jess glanced into the crowd with amusement.

They certainly had a lot of female fans here tonight.

Smirking, she slammed out a few more power chords, giving Tony a deliberately sultry look. He responded by poking his tongue out at her and pulling an equally lecherous face.

Jess laughed. She loved teasing the guys in the band. She *knew* she looked good. She'd spent a good few minutes backstage choosing a new outfit before the show, while the club manager shouted thinly-veiled death threats under the door in the hope of coaxing her out before the audience actually started killing one another. She'd gone for the black knee-length boots and leather miniskirt in the end, mainly for Tony's benefit.

She clicked her metal tongue-stud against her teeth and glanced at him with a grin. She could tell by the way he was choosing not to look at her that she was going to be featuring prominently in his dreams for a good number of nights.

Jess gazed out at the audience as she played, loving the attention. It was a good crowd tonight, very near capacity. There were a lot of familiar faces from the last show. Some of them were even singing along, and Jess smiled to herself.

She was starting to get actual fans. How cool was that?

As she played, Jess noticed one particular face in the crowd. Her heart gave a tiny flutter. It couldn't be... could it? She squinted against the glare of the spotlights, holding her breath. After a long moment, the face turned towards her. Jess made out the gleam of emerald eyes gazing up at her from a tanned, handsome face.

Jess stared for a moment, her mind frozen. Then she abruptly turned away, strumming harder on her guitar to quell the sudden hammering in her chest.

It *was*.

Charlie Delgado. The richest, most popular guy in class, and he was *here*.

At her show.

Watching her perform.

Holy cow.

This was a guy who had never said more than two words to her in the entire school year, and suddenly here he was, giving her one hundred percent of his attention.

Well, ninety-nine percent of his attention. Jess peeked quickly back at him, playing on autopilot. One glance confirmed the presence of two haughty looking girls at his side, draping themselves over his broad shoulders like smug Siamese cats. Charlie was ignoring both of them, and was gazing right at her, apparently liking what he saw.

Noticing her attention, he waved to her.

Despite herself, Jess felt herself blush. Her mind filled with images, most of them tinged with the red glow of embarrassment, of the few times she'd spoken to Charlie in class over the few years she'd known him.

Known *of* him, she quickly corrected herself. Nobody knew Charlie very well, not even himself. Jess was sure of that. He was a mystery, a tanned, toned enigma in scruffy blue jeans which, although faded and fashionably ripped, probably cost more than Jess's entire wardrobe. And God, was he popular. Although all the girls in class complained about him, about how he swanned around like he was God's gift, parked his SUV in the college flowerbeds and never, ever returned their calls, the moment he entered the room, they forgot all about that. They'd pose and preen as they watched him pass, pretending to ignore him. Then they'd start squealing and flapping their hands about like demented chickens, hissing *"Ohmy-GODhe'ssogorgeous!"* under their breath, in the way that only eighteen year-old girls can.

Jess delighted in making fun of them all, but at the same time, she understood why they acted the way they did. Charlie might be an arrogant son of a bitch, but then, he had a certain way of looking at you... that impassive, cool look breaking for a moment as he flashed you the biggest, warmest grin, those blue eyes creasing briefly in amusement as though sharing a personal joke that only you, of all the people in the world, would understand... and then he'd be gone, probably chasing after some cheerleader with a trust fund big enough to wipe out the national debt of a Third World country.

Maybe that was part of his charm, Jess reflected glumly as she slid her fingers down the fret board of her guitar. Charlie was a handsome devil, and he knew it. Hell, if she had the time and the money, maybe she'd try dating him herself. He was the most popular guy in class right? That should suit her down to the ground. She always went for the guys who were unobtainable, or who turned out to be unobtainable.

Such as Bill...

Jess quickly banished the thought of him from her mind. He was just the latest in a long line of unsuitable men, which her friends teased her about but couldn't stop her from perusing. There was something in her that needed that, the thrill of the chase, the constant challenge of it.

It was part of what made her who she was.

Her life right now was just so... well, it was boring. It was filled with boring people, who did boring things. She could sure use some excitement. Dating someone like Charlie was one of those things you just had to do when you were young, like going on a road-trip to Vegas or drinking so much alcohol that you wake up in hospital just as the doctor starts cutting off your bra...

Jess smiled to herself. She'd had a lot of fun in her time. At the tender age of nineteen, she'd done things that most girls only read about in the paper. She was rich in experience, if not rich in a monetary sense, but she knew that she needed to have actual cash if she was ever going to attract someone like Charlie.

A picture of herself pulling into his parents' driveway in her beaten-up Volkswagen Beetle flashed into her head, and she pulled a pained face. No, dating Charlie was a thing best left to the professionals.

And dammit, there were plenty of those around. Jess narrowed her eyes at the two girls flanking Charlie in the crowd, like two evil Barbie dolls from hell. Sorority girls, by the looks of them. Big hair, big boobs, plastic smiles. Eyebrows plucked to death and then spray-painted back on. Lips pouting and wet with lip-gloss. The kind of girl who'd check out your shoes, handbag and watch before she'd even look at your face to decide if she liked you.

Jess made eye-contact with Cassie, and nodded towards the girls in the crowd with a grimace. She was rewarded by Cassie's rich chuckle in her earpiece. Cassie was an ex of Charlie's, her waist-length black hair, exotic good looks and wicked bass-playing skills apparently not enough to keep Charlie's interest for longer than a week. She'd caught him making out with her sister just days after their first date, and after all the screaming and yelling had died down, that had been that.

Jess was aware that there might be some kind of politics involved in Charlie's appearance here tonight, but Cassie didn't seem too bothered. If she was, she was hiding it very well. Jess watched her friend play for a minute, striking pose after pose and tossing her hair around like a living whip, and saw why she didn't care. She was over him, and didn't care who he brought to the show. He could bring the whole cheerleading team if he felt like it, and the fact that he now got to see her on stage in six-inch heels and a PVC catsuit could only be a bonus.

Their wardrobe people had really done them proud tonight.

Jess grinned to herself and nodded to Jamie, making a small gesture in the air to indicate that he should speed up. Jamie cocked a pierced eyebrow at her and slammed into a bone-crunching power solo. The rest of the band swung in to join the tempo, tightening their sound around the pounding drumbeat. Jess's fingers flew over her strings, easily plucking an arpeggio of tumbling notes out of the air. The song gained speed, built to a crescendo, and then cut to silence.

Jess stepped up to the microphone.

A single spotlight clicked on high above, illuminating Jess as she began singing the bridge. It was a haunting little melody, one that she and Jamie had come up with after long hours of banging their heads together in the depths of his garage. The sounds from the audience died away to a respectful hush as the bridge washed over them, filling the room with echoes. Someone at the back cracked open a Zippo lighter and waved it above their head. There was a titter from the crowd around him.

Ignoring this, Jess closed her eyes against the harsh white light and let the melody spill from her throat, building the song in intensity as she neared the middle of the bridge. After a couple of bars she heard Jamie join in, tapping out an improvised accompaniment on his drums. They were soon joined by Cassie on the bass. Together, they wove a syncopated tapestry of sound that Jess filled in with the melody of the song, plucking ringing harmonic notes on her Gibson to complement the beat.

For a moment, the world stood still. Nothing else mattered, and Jess let herself be swept along by the flow of the music. In the back of her mind, she had to admit that for a band who typically rehearsed over a 3-way call on their cell phones, they were sounding pretty damn good. For a moment she found herself wishing that her parents were there to see her perform.

Then she shrugged. Hey, who needed them? They were probably at a party of their own about this time, or passed out in a gutter somewhere. Jess tossed her head, her eyes glinting. She was used to doing things on her own by now. If they never found the time to actually acknowledge her existence, that was their problem, not hers.

The band played on.

As the song built towards its crescendo, a thought nagged at Jess. She opened her eyes. She couldn't help herself. She had to see. She peeked casually into the crowd to make sure that Charlie was watching her—which of course he was.

Jess's heart swelled, and she felt a definite spark of satisfaction. By her calculations, she had now officially held his attention longer than any other girl in college.

Someone ought to give her a medal for that.

Greatly cheered by this thought, Jess's eyes left Charlie and casually roamed out over the audience as the band swung back into the final few verses of the song. It had been a great show. Even playing here in this dive of a club, this was probably one of their best gigs so far. Despite the fact that the place looked as if it was going to fall down any minute, and there were what looked like rusty girders sticking out of the wall in places.

Still, when they were all rich and famous they could all look back and laugh about it.

Jess thought this about a lot of things. Being rich and famous would make up for an awful lot of the crap in her life. Seen retrospectively, her various misfortunes would make great material for the eager biographers who would no doubt document her life in minute detail as soon as she hit the big time. She would be an inspiration to all those who hoped to follow in her footsteps, and her "rags-to-riches" story would make the front page of every newspaper.

She just hoped that she'd get rich and famous soon, as the whole "rags" part of her life was starting to wear a little thin.

Jess stepped back from the mike and glanced up at the ceiling as Tony went into an insane rock solo. Something caught her eye. One of the stage lights above them was glitching, fizzing on and off out of tempo with the rest of the lights. It seemed to be a bit loose in its mount too, hanging from the roof of the club at a slightly skewed angle.

Jess looked at it closely, strumming her guitar on the backbeat. The ceiling around it was covered in lumpy red paint, a tangled spiderweb of feed wires clearly visible in the gaps between the support beams, tied in place with leftover fuse wire. There was a small crack running down the center of the ceiling, which someone had tried to hide by applying a completely different shade of lumpy red paint.

Jess stared up at it, chewing on the inside of her lip. That crack didn't look good. She should really mention it to the manager after the show. The last thing she needed was a chunk of roof falling on her head when she was trying to do a B minor augmented ninth. That chord was tricky enough even without the concussion.

As Jess gazed upwards, some dust floated down into her eyes. She wiped at them, blinking in irritation. Her hand came away gritty and streaked with mascara, and Jess squinted accusingly at the rafters. Damn ceiling, messing up her makeup!

She saw Tony's curious look and strummed a few chords, then returned her gaze to the ceiling.

She frowned. Was it just her, or was that crack getting bigger?

She stared hard at it. It definitely did seem wider than it was a minute ago...

"What's up?" Cassie's voice came through her radio earphone above the noise of the music. Jess realized that she'd stopped playing. She covered the mike with a hand. "That crack," she shouted.

"What?"

"Up there," Jess pointed.

"What about it?"

"Doesn't it seem... well... kinda big?"

"Looks no bigger than that other crack," Cassie shouted back cheerfully, gesturing with the stock of her guitar.

Jess looked up. A second crack had appeared beside the first. It was at least an inch wide, and definitely hadn't been there a second ago. Or had it?

"This place is such a dump!" yelled Cassie happily. "Isn't it great?" She flexed her arms and grinned, then moved away from Jess to join Tony as he finished his guitar solo. The two of them started the lead-up to the final verse, leaning their backs against one another to share a microphone.

As they did so, they knocked Jamie's ever-present bottle of Jack Daniels off the stage into the photographers' pit, where it shattered with a strange sound. A small spray of orange sparks fizzled against the wall as the alcohol shorted out one of the lighting cables. Above them, the off-tempo light by the crack in the ceiling died, fading to black and starting to smoke.

Jess felt the hairs on the back of her neck stand up. This place was such a dump, and worse than that, it was seriously unsafe. She could feel it in her bones. If anything bad happened, the room would be a veritable deathtrap. She gripped the microphone, turning her gaze out at the cheering crowd. There must have been a hundred or so people packed into the small space—guys, gals, waitresses, staff. People out enjoying themselves, uncaring of anything else but getting drunk, getting high, getting laid.

A strange sense of foreboding thrummed through Jess, filling her mouth with a strange metallic taste. She strained her hearing over the thump of the music. Was it her imagination, or could she actually hear a low-pitched cracking sound coming from the ceiling?

As though drawn by a magnet, Jess's gaze was pulled upwards again. She gave a little gasp. It wasn't just her imagination. The crack had now reached the far wall, and was enlarging fast. She could actually see it moving, speeding out over the heads of the audience and reaching snake-like fingers across the damp plaster in all directions. A thin trickle of what looked like smoke spilled from the crack. Dust drifted down, lightly frosting the heads of the oblivious crowd.

Jess felt her mouth go dry. This did not look good. She had to warn somebody. But who, and how?

She looked at the microphone, and then took a hesitant step towards it, her mind racing. Was this really worth stopping the show for? Perhaps it was just the heat of the gathered crowd that was cracking the plaster. They would probably be fine until the end of the set, when she could discreetly step outside and have a few words with the stage manager. Perhaps he could put some filler on the crack before the next act?

"Um..." Jess began.

There was a loud noise behind her, accompanied by a rush of air and a spray of what felt like warm water. Then Cassie screamed, a long, loud sound that pierced the smoky atmosphere like a bandsaw.

The band thumped and plinked its way to a confused stop. In the ringing silence that followed, there was a collective gasp from the crowd.

Jess looked down at the stage floor by her feet. It was speckled with red.

Slowly, keeping her mind empty, Jess stepped back from the microphone and turned around.

Tony lay sprawled facedown on the stage. His guitar lay a short distance from him, smeared with what looked like red paint.

Jess blinked. A rusty girder was sticking out of Tony's back.

Jess frowned. She looked away from Tony, out at the Friday night crowd packing the joint. A sea of hushed faces stared back at her, clutching cans and bottles and glasses of soda. Some of them were wearing multicolored wigs. Down in the wings, the members of the next band were waiting to go on. At the back of the room, a young couple were making out on the sofa, heedless to those around them.

Everything looked perfectly normal.

Jess looked back at Tony. The girder was still sticking out of his back.

Jess studied Tony for a moment, feeling unreal, noticing in a detached way how the girder had punched through him at a perfect right angle to the stage, and how it now stood upright like a giant letter "I". Blood coated the last foot and a half of it, dripping down the metal sides to form a rapidly enlarging pool.

Her lead guitarist was stone cold dead.

As one, the eyes of the crowd turned upwards. Jess followed their collective gaze to see a jagged hole in the ceiling above Tony. Smoke was starting to pour through the hole. The ceiling around it seemed to be bulging downwards, like a rubber sheet with a weight in the middle. Dark cracks radiated out from the hole, reaching out in all directions to join up with the main crack that now bisected the center of the room...

Right above their heads...

Somebody screamed and the atmosphere shattered.

Suddenly, people were running. The dance floor became a confused mass of people pushing and shoving to get to the exits. The room filled with the sounds of a hundred people desperately trying to be anywhere other than where they were now. Bottles shattered on the ground, and a fight broke out over by the bar where ten people at once were trying to push their way through one of the "Staff Only" doors.

Jess stood on the stage and stared. Above the noise of the crowd, she could hear a dull rumbling, which nevertheless sounded as loud as a passing ocean liner in the tense atmosphere. She watched in horror as the bigger of the two cracks split open over the main exit door, raining brick dust onto the heads of those beneath. Bright flames started flickering through the cracks. At once people nearby started frantically backing up and ran into those behind them, who were still trying to get to the exit. Shouting and pushing erupted.

Jess saw the bouncer run forward. Pushing his way through the crowd, he started trying to separate the tangle by pulling people bodily out of the way, shoving them back towards the stairs that led to the fire escape. This didn't help matters, and people started yelling and kicking at him.

There was complete pandemonium.

"What the hell are you *doing*? Come on!"

Jess felt a hand grab hers and yank her away from the front of the stage. Her brain refocused, and she realized that this was happening for real. Her foot slipped on the bare wooden boards, and she saw to her horror that she had stepped in some of the blood that coated the stage.

Tony's blood...

Then she regained her feet and was running, keeping pace with Jamie and Cassie as they leapt over the tangled wires that criss-crossed the stage, her heart beating a tattoo of panic on her ribs.

Ducking behind the heavy velvet stage curtain, they shouldered their way past stacks of equipment and jumped down the steps that led to the back exit. The door was set way back in the room, covered by a curtain. Jess hoped to God that it was unlocked.

A loud *BOOM* came from behind her. Jess looked back just in time to see the entrance to the main doorway collapse, burying the bouncer and those around him in rubble. A cloud of dust billowed up and filled the room.

Shocked, Jess skidded to a halt and stared. All that was visible of the bouncer was his striped Mohawk, sticking up almost comically through the rubble. The main doorway had been completely blocked off by the collapse.

A moment later there was an explosion of glass as the windows in the partitioning wall blew out. Screams came from the crowd as people were hit by the flying shards. Then a second girder fell from the ceiling, burying itself in one of the giant stage speakers. There was an earsplitting bang as the mixing deck attached to the PA blew up, overloading in a burst of blue flame. A loud electrical zapping sound filled the air, and the wall-mounted speakers all round the room shrieked and spat fountains of white-hot sparks into the screaming crowd.

Above the noise, a metallic creaking became audible. The crowd stared around them in panic, trying to work out where the sound was coming from.

Then there was a burst of brick dust, and part of the ceiling started to cave in. People flowed away from the area like ripples in a pond, but there was nowhere left to go. The room was packed, and there was no space for them to run to.

They were trapped.

As Jess watched, the main crack sizzled down the far wall like black lightning. Big chunks of concrete rubble fell through the gaps. People began falling right, left, and center throughout the room as huge slabs of rubble fell on them. Thick black smoke belched through the holes, and the screams and shrieks of the dying filled the room.

A moment later, the room shook, and poles began dropping from the giant lighting rig, which was attached to the ceiling by a hanging scaffold. Clubbers underneath it scrambled over one another, trying to get to safety. Jess saw the metal chains that supported it begin to pull out of the plaster, one by one. The entire rig listed to one side, fizzing and sparking, then swung to the right and crashed downwards. There was an explosion of multi-colored light as the lamps hit the ground and shattered.

"Look out!"

Pain blossomed inside Jess's head as something struck her across the temple. The next thing she knew she was falling, then rolling as somebody tackled her and dragged her to the ground. She felt more points of pain erupt on her back and torso as she lay on the floor, arms wrapped over her head, and knew that bricks were falling on her.

Then the pain stopped. Jess waited a moment, but nothing more happened. She uncurled herself and cautiously raised her head.

Cassie lay just inches away, her upper body sticking out from under a large section of concrete. Her eyes were unfocussed, and blood ran in a thin line from her nose to her mouth.

She wasn't breathing.

The world blurred as Jess's eyes began to fill with tears. Someone—Jamie, she presumed—grabbed her by the shoulders and dragged her to her feet. Then she was running again, dodging and ducking as sections of red-painted plaster fell all around her.

Ducking backstage, she saw the welcome shape of the small green EXIT sign looming up ahead of her out of the darkness. She ran towards it, almost sobbing with relief. This door led straight out to the metal fire escape, which would take her away from the building right up onto the street. Nobody else was near it, as the main mass of the crowd tried to escape back out through the main doors, where they had come in. She was saved.

She reached the door a moment before Jamie, and yanked on the handle.

It was fucking locked.

Jess swore and kicked at the door in frustration. Turning around, she leaned back against the door and stared out at the room, breathing hard in panic. Thoughts chased themselves around and around her head like demented puppy dogs.

It had all happened so quickly. One minute she had been up there on stage, playing a guitar solo to Charlie Delgado, and everything in her life was wonderful.

Now she was living in this nightmare, and try as she might, she just couldn't wake up.

Taking a deep breath, Jess tried to think. She knew that she should calm down and come up with a plan, any plan, but she drew a complete blank. Her mind filled with a muddle of images from TV disaster movies, and she tried to focus, to visualize what the heroine would do in a situation like this, but it was no good. Her mind was a blur. This room was a slaughterhouse, and there was no escape.

She was going to die, right here, right now, and while wearing rubber underwear.

Jess let out a muffled sob.

As though in a dream, she saw a second section of the ceiling collapse with an earsplitting crash, dragging a giant girder down with it. For a second, she thought she caught sight of Charlie's tanned face in the crowd, turned upwards in alarm. Beside him, the two sorority girls shrieked in panic. Then the girder smacked lengthwise into the crowd, clearing a strip of living people like a human lawn-mower.

Moments later, an explosion rocked the joint as one of the giant Marshall amps blew up. There was a shriek from beside Jess. She looked to her left and saw a young female cop—presumably off-duty—reeling around and clutching at her chest. A bloody drumstick was sticking out of her ribcage, just above her heart, blasted through her body by the force of the explosion. Slowly, she toppled forward and fell face down onto the dance floor.

Then yet another girder fell across the bar in a cloud of white plaster dust, impaling the barman to the countertop and taking down a waitress who had been trying to make a call on the emergency pay-phone. There was a rain of blood, and then unused quarters clattered to the ground all around her.

The sounds of sobs and the screams of the injured filled the air. Plaster dust coated the room like ash from a volcanic eruption. The ceiling was bowing severely now, riddled with cracks and gaps through which fire belched.

There was an ominous creaking as the main support pillars started to buckle.

The survivors ran round the room like lab rats, trying to wrench open doors that were locked or buckled shut. But there was no way out.

This was it, Jess realized. Nineteen short years of life, and now it was all over. The thought of her own mortality had never once entered her head, and now here she was, looking up at several hundred tons of cold hard death, and she hadn't got a clue what to do.

"Don't move!"

Jess's eyes refocused, and she saw the black-clad form of Jamie leap back up onto the stage. He paused for a minute, his eyes scanning the crowd. Then he jumped down the other side and fought his way towards the metal fire escape. This door was also locked. A jock in a college letter jacket was trying to smash the corroded padlock with a metal fire extinguisher. A small huddle of people stood by him, including a hysterical girl who was obviously the boy's girlfriend. They were all yelling at him to hurry up.

Jamie pushed his way up the metal steps and grabbed the fire extinguisher from the boy. Raising it above his head, he used it to smash the Plexiglas window to the door. Then he reached through the splintered plastic with his bare hands, and made a grab for the sliding bolt on the other side of the door. But before his fingers touched the bolt, he was pushed aside by the jock, who scrambled past him and started trying to climb out of the room through the window.

As he scrabbled for freedom, Jess saw to her horror that something weird was happening to the doorframe around him. It seemed to be getting shorter, somehow. There was a hollow clanking sound, and the metal rivets started popping off the door. People nearby started backing away. She saw a look of alarm cross Jamie's face, and knew something bad was about to happen.

The next thing she knew, there was the scream of tortured metal and the doorway started to bend inwards. One of the jock's friends was taken down by a huge lump of concrete, which cracked his skull and knocked him to the ground. Then the door-frame collapsed, compacting the window and cutting the struggling jock in two as cleanly as cheese wire. His girlfriend shrieked as blood foun-tained over her dress. Then she was swept away in the stampede as the crowd on the gantry poured back down the stairs as bricks and mortar thudded down around them.

"Jamie! Look out!"

But it was too late. As though in slow motion, Jess saw a yard-wide chunk of concrete fall on Jamie, knocking him off the gantry and sending him plunging to the stone floor ten feet below.

He did not get up again.

Jess screamed.

Then a feeling of dread hit her, almost like a phys-ical blow. Jess froze as she felt something change inside her. It was as though the air pressure in the room was all wrong. A sense of darkness filled her mind. She leaped to her feet and clambered urgently back up onto the stage, heading towards where Jamie had landed.

Maybe he was still alive. Perhaps she could save him. He couldn't be dead, he just couldn't be...

She'd not gone more than ten feet before she real-ized that something else was wrong. The ceiling seemed to be getting closer, somehow...

There was a rushing sound from above her. Jess looked up to see a huge section of red-painted roof dropping down towards her at high speed. A soot-blackened girder was in the middle of it, pointed right at her head. There was no time to get out of the way.

This was it.

Jess closed her eyes and screamed...

TWO

An age ticked by.

Jess slowly became aware that she wasn't dead. She could feel her heart beating, hammering in her chest as though trying to burst through her ribcage and escape. Blood pounded in her ears and the echoes of her scream still hung in the air. There was a faint buzzing sound on the periphery of her hearing, like a small bee trapped in a long metal tube.

Other than that, the world was silent.

Jess slowly let out her breath, then, with some consideration, removed her hands from her head.

Nothing bad happened to her.

Taking this as a good sign, Jess opened her eyes.

A hundred puzzled faces stared up at her. Multi-colored stage lights played over the crowd, illuminating the packed club in staccato bursts. It was deathly quiet. Jess could hear the faint clicks of the stage lights as they moved in their mounts. A sea of people filled the dance floor in front of her, clutching their cans and bottles and glasses of soda. Some of them were wearing multicolored wigs. Down in the wings, the members of the next band were waiting to go on. At the back of the room, a young couple were making out on the sofa, heedless to those around them.

Everything looked perfectly normal.

Jess stood and stared, her heart pounding, fighting down an overwhelming sense of déjà vu.

A hand landed on Jess's shoulder, and she let out a small yip and spun around.

Cassie was standing behind her, looking at her in concern. Her bass hung forgotten from her neck, connected to an amp which was buzzing loudly in the silence. Behind her, Jamie sat behind his drums, staring at her and scratching his head with a drumstick.

"What's up?"

Jess yelped to see Tony standing in front of her, alive and well. She put her hand over her mouth and stared up at him.

He was alive.

"I..." she began. Then she looked off to her left, distracted. Jamie was waving a drumstick at her and mouthing, *"You freak!"*

Jess cleared her throat, trying to ignore him. "I had a..." She stopped. Had a what, she asked herself? Her heart was pounding as if she'd just run a marathon. What the hell had just happened to her? What *was* that?

A thought occurred to her, and she shakily picked up the bottle of water she had been drinking from on stage, and sniffed at it suspiciously. Was this a hallucination? Had somebody slipped something into her drink?

But even as the thought entered her head, she knew that this was not the case.

Terror raced through her, making her pulse pound afresh as the memories swamped her. The whole experience had been so *real*. She had been standing right here, and the ceiling had collapsed, and it had killed her. She could still hear the screams of the dying ringing in her ears. It hadn't just been a dream. Jess knew it with an unshakable certainty. She could still taste the blood in her mouth, feel the pain of her own broken bones piercing her skin as the rubble crushed her to oblivion...

A wave of goose bumps crashed over her, and Jess shivered despite the heat of the club.

"Er, Jess..." Jamie pointed over her shoulder. Turning slowly around, Jess saw that she was being stared at by over a hundred curious people.

Jess attempted a desperate smile, aware that some kind of explanation was called for. She adjusted the strap of her Gibson and tried to act casual. "There was a, um, a wasp."

The crowd tittered, although some of them looked less than amused. A buzz of conversation rose, punctuated by one or two shouts of "Off!"

Jess stepped back, her mind racing as she tried to adjust to this new reality. She felt as if she had just awakened from one bad dream straight into another.

But if *this* was real... had she really just screamed like that on stage?

Oh, the club manager was really going to kill her this time...

Outside the back of the club, Officer Marina Hewlett ducked into a shadow and waited. All was quiet in the streets around the place. It was approaching twelve-thirty, and the bars were just starting to turn out onto the street.

She straightened her cap wearily, trying not to yawn. It was late, and she was tired. This place was a hellhole, and the streets were filled with little devils. She knew that she'd almost certainly be needed out here tonight, to sort out some barroom brawl or scuffle.

But for now, she had a job to do.

Leaning in towards the door, she pressed her ear against the boarded-up top window. From within, she could hear a muffled rhythmic thumping, like some giant industrial machine.

That's what these places were really, she thought gloomily as she reached into her bag for her gun. Just giant machines for taking kids' money, getting them drunk, high, and occasionally, pregnant. All kinds of terrible things went on in these places. Marina knew that they did, because she was the one they called out whenever things got out of hand, which was often. She'd only been working this neighborhood for a month since her transfer from Chicago, and boy, was she missing home.

She sniffed loudly, glancing over her shoulder to check that no one was watching her. It was late, and she was yearning to go home to bed. The back lot of the club was completely deserted, which was good.

She glanced down at the ground, where the remains of a snapped metal bar taunted her, reminding her of her futile efforts to break into the club unseen. She rubbed the palm of her hand irritably, frowning at the door.

There was one other option... but no. It would never work. If she went in the front way, through the main entrance, her cover would be blown in about two seconds. It would be all over before it had even begun. She needed to get into this place unseen if she were going to do her job properly.

She smiled grimly to herself. Hell, if she pulled this one off, she might even get that bonus her superintendent had been going on about for the past three weeks.

She hoped that the guy who'd given her the tip-off knew what he was talking about.

She stared at the door, trying to gauge the strength and weight of the huge industrial lock cemented into place beneath the boarded-up window. What she was about to do was pretty risky, and she would no doubt get in trouble if anyone reported her.

But in a place like this, who was going to do that? It should be a simple job. She should be in and out in minutes, hopefully hauling out with her the miscreants who were allegedly using the club's backroom as a makeshift coke den.

Officer Hewlett cracked her knuckles pensively. Her entire day had already been wrecked by that jackass with the tow-truck this morning, so what was the harm in cutting a few corners? The sooner she got home and got to bed, the better. A whole morning of mopping up blood and wrestling with paperwork, just because some woman had been in the wrong place at the wrong time... It had not put her in a good mood.

Fate could be a bitch like that.

A graphic image entered her mind and she shook her head to dislodge it. She'd been pissed to lose her lunch break, but still, poor lady. What a way to go. There had been so much blood, she couldn't even finish her hot dog afterwards.

That in itself was a crime.

But it was just another typical day in the life of a LAPD cop. Things could be worse.

Banishing the thought from her mind, Officer Hewlett clicked the safety catch off her service-issue pistol and screwed a stubby silencer onto the barrel.

She had work to do.

She took one last peek through the gap in the boarding to ensure that nobody was in the room. The floor inside looked like it was made of pretty sturdy concrete. It should contain her shot nicely.

She aimed the gun at the lock, at an angle of 45 degrees.

Careful, now. Easy does it...

She moved her feet further apart so that her weight was distributed evenly on each foot, and took a careful breath. She held it, steadying her ribcage as she'd been taught.

Then she squeezed off a single shot.

Back onstage, Tony nodded curtly at Jess. "A wasp... sure," he said, trying to keep the irritation out of his voice. "You don't wanna get stung by one of them. That could really ruin your day." Giving Jess a strange look, he turned away from her and strummed a chord on his guitar. Then he nodded to the others and launched into the intro of the next song as though nothing had happened. Cassie joined him on the bass after a minute, then Jamie got the message and added his drums to the mix, breaking down after a minute into an energetic solo.

Together, the band played on.

Jess swallowed, trying to control the racing of her pulse. She was completely freaked out. It must have been a dream, but this feeling that she had... it was for real. It *had* to be. She knew in her gut that something was very wrong.

Jess reached towards the microphone, then stopped, her eyes scanning the mass of clubgoers.

Charlie Delgado was in the crowd. He saw her look over, and waved to her.

Unable to help herself, Jess glanced sharply up at the ceiling. But as she did so, the spotlights clicked on, blinding her. She squinted against the light, her vision filled with black halos in the glare. She couldn't see a thing.

Jamie finished his solo, and Jess realized that this was the bit where she was supposed to sing. Her mouth opened, then closed, but nothing came out. People were staring at her again. Her throat felt as dry as the desert. The crowd was starting to get restless, and as the silence lengthened she could hear mutters drifting up from the heaving throng.

"...last show was much better...."

"What's with that singer?"

"Bunch of amateurs..."

Jess swallowed, trying to get some moisture to her parched throat. Her heart was pounding again. She knew that it was ridiculous, but she couldn't shake the feeling that something terrible was about to happen. She squinted up at the ceiling again, but the lights were still shining into her eyes, completely blinding her.

Making a snap decision, Jess stepped away from the microphone and strode briskly to the side of the stage, ignoring the puzzled stares from the other band members. It was no good. She couldn't go on like this. She had to know. Outside the beam of the spotlight, she took a deep breath, then looked upward.

There was a crack in the center of the ceiling, badly covered with lumpy red paint.

In the room above her, Officer Hewlett's bullet drilled through the lock in a shower of sparks, then smacked into the wooden floor on the other side. In milliseconds, it traveled across the wire-packed space underneath the floorboards, and embedded itself in the ancient concrete support pillar just below it. The entire structure vibrated with the impact, dust jumping off the wall in the packed club-broom below.

And then everything was still again.

Outside the club, Officer Hewlett jumped back as the lock flew apart in a tangle of warped metal. A wisp of smoke drifted up from the lock.

The officer held her breath for a moment, her eyes ticking left and right. The neighborhood was silent.

Nobody in their right mind noticed another gunshot in a place like this, and the silencer had taken most of the sound out of the shot anyway.

Congratulating herself on a job well done, Officer Hewlett holstered her gun, then pushed the heavy door open with her foot and made her way into the club. She didn't even notice the small hole in the floor, where her bullet had passed through.

It was time to make those arrests.

In the space underneath the floor, a bundle of severed wires began to spark.

On the floor underneath, Jess began backing away from the front of the stage, staring upwards. A wave of dread rolled over her as she contemplated what she had just seen. This couldn't be a coincidence, could it? Maybe her subconscious had seen the state of the ceiling and incorporated it into her—hallucination, or whatever that was—but this was just plain scary.

She looked up again. She had to be sure.

There was one other thing...

On cue, one of the stage lights started flickering out of time with the rest.

Jess gave a small squeak.

Seeing that Jess wasn't going to sing, the band kicked into action to cover for her. Tony bounced to the front of the stage and went into a flamboyant rock break, trying to hide the fact that his lead singer had just gone AWOL. He bounced around the stage in front of her, trying to keep the audience's eyes off Jess for as long as possible. As he played, he knocked Jamie's bottle of Jack Daniels off the stage, which shattered and shorted out one of the stage's spotlights.

Behind him, he heard Jess gasp.

That did it. Snapping out of her trance, Jess ran across to center stage and seized the mike, making frantic "cut!" motions to Jamie. "Sorry, folks... that's all we have time for tonight." She announced. "We are the Vipers—we hope you liked our show. Thank you, and goodnight."

The band ground a halt for the second time that evening. The crowd stared at Jess, unbelieving.

"This club is now closed. Please make your way to the nearest exit," Jess said, in what she hoped was a firm voice. "Quickly, now," she added. Her hands began to tremble.

Nobody moved. A loud muttering rose from the throng.

Trying to move them along, Jess held out her arms like an airhostess. "The exits are to the back and to the left..." she said desperately.

Tony grabbed Jess's arm and spun her round. "What the hell?" he hissed. Jess started to reply, but Tony cut her off. "It was a wasp! Not a bomb! What are you, allergic?" He stared at her, his blue eyes blazing with fury. "Do you even care how long it took me to set this gig up? We're lucky to even have a show after last time!"

"Tony, listen to me. This club is unsafe!" Jess hissed back.

Tony started to reply, then saw that the people in the front row were watching him a little too closely. With a glare at the gawping crowd, he took Jess by the hand and hauled her to the back of the stage,

behind Jamie. "So, what, you've only just noticed?"
He ran a hand through his spiked hair, then took
Jess by the shoulders and gently shook her. "Jessie,
you can't keep doing this. I don't *care* what's not
right. You wanna play anywhere better, you *damn*
well take what we can afford to—"

"But the roof's going to fall in!" Jess hissed.

"What?"

"You heard me!" The words all came out in a rush.
"I had a... a vision of it happening. And I don't know
why or how, but I was *there*, not like in a dream, but
like it was real life, real life that was really happening
to me." She clutched desperately at Tony's hand.
"Tony, the whole fucking roof fell in, and it killed
everyone. It was horrible. I was there. I saw it
happen!"

Jess glanced feverishly out at the crowd, who were
craning their necks to get a better view of her. A loud
muttering filled the room. She felt tears start to
threaten, but carried on regardless. "Tony, you have
to believe me. Everything I saw is coming true
already. Everything is just like it was at the start of
my vision. Like when you broke that bottle... that
happened too! And now we're all going to die and
it'll be *your* fault for holding everyone up!"

Tony stared at her, his expression darkening. "Did
your 'vision' include the bit where I smack you one
and tell you to get over it?" He reached up and swept
the bandanna off his head. "For God's sake woman,
we have a show to do! The rent doesn't just pay
itself, you know!"

Jess stared at Tony, worlds colliding in her mind.
She realized in an instant that he would never

believe her, and that even now she was wasting precious time.

Before Tony could stop her, Jess pulled away from him and ran back across the stage to the mike. She had to get everyone out of the club, *right now,* or she knew that her horrific vision would somehow become reality.

She waved her hands urgently at the crowd, who responded with jeers and catcalls. "Come on, people. The show's over. We'll be closing in five—" An open bottle of water was thrown at her, bouncing off the end of her guitar. "—minutes." The speakers shrieked with feedback as the water splashed across her guitar pickups. The crowd started stamping its feet and chanting: "Off! Off! Off!"

As Jess stood there helplessly, a hand reached over her shoulder and plucked the mike from her. She looked back to see the club manager standing behind her, an imposing Mexican in a charcoal-gray suit and neon pink socks. He glared at Jess, his moustache quivering in anger.

"Hey!" Jess tried to grab the mike back, but the man held it up out of her reach as though she were a child. Turning away from her, he tapped the mike a couple of times, and then turned to face the crowd.

"Ladies and gentlemen," he began. To Jess it seemed like he took forever to get the sentence out. "We are having a few..." he glared again at Jess "...*technical* difficulties. Please bear with us for a couple of minutes. Mors Mortis is up next. Thank you."

He switched the mike off firmly, and made a gesture to one of the stagehands to close the curtain.

The boom of a pre-recorded dance tune filled the air as filler music was switched on.

Angry shouts came from the crowd and loud booing filled the air. They wanted a spectacle, not a blank curtain. Somebody threw a beer can at the stage, which clattered across the wooden flooring and hit Jess on the leg. Over by the bar, an off-duty female cop sipped slowly at her drink and watched Jess intently.

As the curtains closed, the manager folded his arms and scowled at Jess. "What's wrong with you?" he demanded.

"I had a vision! It was real, and I know it's gonna come true. The club fell down, and everyone died. We have to get these people out of here! I—" She stopped as she saw the expression on the club manager's face.

"Please leave."

"But I..."

"*Now.*"

"You don't get it, do you? This place is going to collapse! I saw it!" Jess was frantic. She knew that she sounded crazy, but she didn't care. "I know that it's true because of the crack in the ceiling, and the light broke when I knew it would, then Tony knocked the bottle off the stage at the exact same time as I saw him do it—"

"Okay, that's *enough.*" Tony took hold of Jess's hand and tried to pull her away from the manager, but Jess stood firm. She seized Tony's arm and gazed at him imploringly.

"They're all going to die! First you die, then *she* dies, then they all die! You've got to get them all out of here!"

"What's going on?" Jamie stepped up beside her and put a hand on her shoulder. Jess seized his arm like a lifeline.

"I had a vision! Like a kind of premonition... it was horrible, Jamie. The ceiling fell in and everybody died... It really happened! And now it's going to happen for real, and we have to get out of here before it does. Everyone dies, even me. You have to believe me!"

Jess fell silent, suddenly aware that she was raving. She realized how she must look. Slowly, she turned and looked around at a wall of stony expressions. With a horrible sinking feeling, she knew that she had lost them. She wouldn't believe anyone who sounded as crazy as she just did...

"This her?"

Jess looked over her shoulder to see the club bouncer step up behind her. He did not look happy. He folded his muscular arms, making that small gesture seem like the equivalent to jacking a round into a shotgun. Jess noticed that he had "FATE" tattooed on one arm, and "LOVE" on the other.

She swallowed.

"Mr Sebastian. Kindly show this young... lady... to the exit."

"Wait a minute. Just let me talk to the—"

"Now would be a good time, Mr Sebastian."

Jess found herself seized in a grip that could crush metal. She pulled at it ineffectually, then twisted around and dealt the bouncer a swift kick to the shins. All this succeeded in doing was making him grip her arm tighter. She winced and started slapping at his hand.

"Time to go, *miss*." The bouncer's voice could have ground down mountains.

"You gotta be kidding! Listen, there's no time for all this! In about two minutes, that roof's going to come down, and all those people are going to die!"

She saw the bouncer and the manager exchange looks. The manager pressed a button on his walkie talkie. "Ronnie, call someone from the squad up here. Suspected drug use." He clicked off the radio with a look of satisfaction and tucked it into his belt loop. Jess looked at him in horror.

"That's bullshit!"

"Sorry, Miss Golden. You know the policy."

"I'm not on drugs, you little... oh God, you've got to get those people out of here before..."

There was a crash from the dance floor, and Jess cried out in alarm, frantically trying to pull away from the bouncer. "It's started! You have to open up the exits! They're all locked, and we can't get out! We're all going to..."

She trailed off. The manager was holding aside the curtain to reveal a view of the room, where a waitress had just dropped a tray of glasses.

Jess fell silent. She looked up at the manager sheepishly.

"Goodnight, Miss Golden," he said.

Under the floor, the fiberglass around the severed wiring ignited with a *WHUMPH*. Small flames spread along the length of the cabling, melting the plastic coating. The bare copper wire sparked and jumped against the floorboards, tiny blue flames licking hungrily along its length.

Then a flame transferred itself to the fiberglass around it, and within seconds, the entire roll was ablaze. Above it, the ancient rotten floorboards began heating up, the dusty underside charring in the heat. One end caught fire, and soon flames were racing up and down the boards, feeding on the air coming up through the minute cracks in the ceiling below. The thick plaster of the ceiling began to dry out as the heat intensified, enlarging the cracks further.

Many years ago, when the warehouse's basement had been an actual basement rather than a club, there had been a wall dividing the room in two. That wall had taken some of the weight of the rooms above it, supporting the floor above and helping to spread the load. But now, that wall was gone, knocked out to enlarge the dance floor. It was safe to do so, the club owner had been informed by a pal of his, because the warehouse above was no longer used. The rooms were completely empty, and so it was safe.

And that would have been true, if the floor above had been solid.

But it wasn't. In fact, it was far from solid. It was a firetrap of moldering wood and flammable insulation covered in a thin concrete shell.

And right now, it was on fire.

With a low groan, one of the internal wooden struts gave way. A tremor ran along the roof as the weight of the rooms above redistributed itself onto the other five beams that ran crosswise across the ceiling.

They were on fire, too.

Slowly, the ceiling began to bow inwards.

* * *

Jess struggled furiously as the bouncer hauled her bodily out of the room. She knew that it was pointless, but she had to do it anyway, if only for the look of the thing. Jamie and Tony trailed after her, but at a respectful distance to indicate that she wasn't really with them, and that they were going that way anyway.

Catching her eye, Jamie gave her a little sad wave.

Marching her down the creaky backstage steps, the bouncer tried the back door, but it was locked. Jess groaned in disbelief as he started taking her the long way around, through the crowd to the main exit.

The young club-goers stared at her with interest as she passed by, some of them raising their drinks to her. "Get out of here! Now! The roof's gonna fall in!" she yelled at them. There was a wave of laughter, and the club bouncer gave her arm a warning shake that indicated that should he choose to do so, her entire arm could be quite easily removed to stop the flapping of her month. Jess glared back defiantly, kicking and struggling, all the time giving the ceiling sharp glances.

It stayed resolutely intact.

But a clock was counting down in her mind. She *knew* that she was right, she just knew it...

"Hey! That was a great little performance you gave up there. And I don't just mean the music."

Jess shut her eyes as two jocks materialized in front of her, expressions of mock seriousness on their faces. They were holding open beer cans, and their faces were flushed with drink. One of them was short and dark, and wore a tartan kilt. The other was taller and blond, and would have been passably good looking if it wasn't for the expression of smug arrogance on his face.

They both leered at her.

Jess gave them a Look, still trying to pull away from the bouncer. "Drop dead, freak show."

The jocks beamed back at her widely. "Seriously," said Kilt-boy. He looked her up and down, then waggled his eyebrows suggestively. "Me and Eric both thought you were great. Best thing we've seen in weeks. That scream you did? Amazing. You should go into opera."

Jess dug her heels in and swung round to face them, her eyes bright with anger. They stepped back, laughing. Jess glared at the taller of the two, the sandy-haired boy in a red and yellow letterman jacket, and a spark of recognition flared in her mind. She remembered him now—in her vision, he had been the one who had tried to escape through the window, "tried to" being the operative phrase. "What is *wrong* with you people? You have any sense of self-preservation at all? Then get out of here, right now!"

"Or what?" the jock sniggered.

"Or, this place is gonna collapse and kill everyone, idiot," spat Jess. The bouncer started trying to drag her away, but Jess stood firm. She stabbed a finger at the sandy-haired boy. "You wanna know how you die?"

"And what, like you're going to tell me?" The jock laughed, sharing a "What the fuck?" look with his friend.

"No." Jess tried to fold her arms, remembered that one of them was being gripped by the bouncer, and gave up. Rationality was pointless in dealing with these two. She may as well try to argue with a pair of monkeys at the zoo. "No, I won't. In fact, I'm going to let you find out for yourself."

"And when will that be, gorgeous?" Kilt-boy was having a great time. He sniggered.

Jess made a big show of checking her watch. "Not soon enough," she spat. She tapped the bouncer's meaty arm as though urging on a horse and carriage. "Fuck this. Come on, Jeeves, let's pick up the pace. I have a gala meeting at three."

Giving her an odd look, the bouncer pushed past the jocks and stomped towards the main door. The jocks tailed Jess like hounds, sniggering to one another. They knew quality entertainment when they saw it, and they weren't about to let her get away without making things far, far worse.

Jess groaned inwardly. At least they were going in the right direction. The sooner she got out of this place, the better. Then she could think more clearly, figure out exactly what she should do...

As they passed the bar, a shout of "Hey!" came from behind the counter. Jess looked over to see a young black-haired waitress throw down her order pad and start hurrying over towards them. She was dressed in a curious mix of official uniform and punk clothing, with bits of paper—presumably drinks orders—speared on her spiky wrist bands. The overall effect put Jess in mind of a teacher visiting the *Rocky Horror Show*. She watched her approach in alarm.

The waitress homed in on the two jocks like a guided missile. The milling crowd blocked her way, but she barged her way through, upsetting drinks and treading on feet. She shook a finger threateningly at the jocks. "Oh no you don't!"

"Shit! It's Macy! Run!"

As one, the jocks downed the remainder of their beers in one gulp and began hurrying towards the door, giggling like idiots. Macy the waitress tottered after them as fast as her high heels would allow, all the while pouring forth a stream of vitriol.

"I *told* them that lettin' you little horrors put stuff on tab was a bad idea, but did they listen? NO, they didn't. All I hear from them is blah blah blah, daily targets, customer service, client knows best, and it's all a load of *garbage*! An' then you little shits come in here with your fake IDs, trashin' the place and then expectin' everyone to bend over backwards for you..." She tripped over a hidden step in the darkness and nearly fell, but regained her feet with an energetic flail of arms and continued. "Well, this waitress has had *enough*! Eric Prescott, I KNOW that credit card expired three months ago. It's not coming out of my wages this time! *Come back here, you creeps!*"

They reached the outside door before Macy did, and the bouncer manhandled Jess out into the cool night air.

Outside, the city streets were quiet. Somewhere, a siren wailed.

The bouncer finally let go of Jess's arm. She rubbed her bicep, feeling a bruise start to form. "Did you have to train to do that?" she asked icily.

The bouncer didn't reply.

The jocks burst through the door behind her and ran out into the night, howling with laughter. They gave one another a high-five and danced off down the street, chanting, "Free drinks! Free drinks!"

Moments later, the door swung open again to reveal Jamie, tailed by the irate waitress. Officer Hewlett brought up the rear, anticipating trouble. Her big, important drug-bust had turned out to be nothing more than a sack of instant lemonade packets and a few ounces of cannabis, and the cannabis had been taken off a member of staff. She was feeling somewhat foolish, and hoped that helping out here would allay some of her guilt about breaking and entering.

It had *not* been a good day for her.

"Come back here, you little bastards..."

Macy set off in hot pursuit of the two jocks, who fled with loud whoops.

Ignoring the plight of the jocks, Jamie crossed the sidewalk and trotted over to Jess. "Ah, there she is," he said. He stopped in front of her, his arms folded against the chill night air. "Well, the show went marginally better than last time," he said, trying to be cheerful.

Jess dropped her eyes to the ground, a sense of foolishness creeping over her. "Where's Tony?" she asked quietly.

"He went to the restroom," said Jamie. "I think the excitement got to him." He gave a small smile, then reached out and tucked an errant curl behind Jess's ear. "Hey, c'mon, girl. Look on the bright side. At least you didn't break anything this—"

At that moment, the club collapsed.

THREE

There are times in your life when you've got to keep it together, no matter what, or you risk losing everything.

This was one of those times.

Jess slowly raised herself up on an elbow and looked behind her.

The club was completely gone.

Where it had used to stand, there was nothing but a U-shaped shell filled with rubble. The middle of derelict warehouse above it had completely caved in, leaving an empty skeleton of girders sticking up into the night air. A curtain of dust surrounded the ruins, billowing outwards like a miniature mushroom cloud.

Jess squeezed her eyes tight shut, her mind whirling. *This couldn't be happening. Any minute now, she would wake up, like she did last time...*

She coughed painfully. Her head hurt and her ribs were aching. The breath had been knocked out of her when she had flung herself to safety.

Carefully, she climbed to her feet on shaking legs and surveyed the remains of the building.

It was just... gone. There was nothing left to indicate this had once been a packed, thriving club. Even as Jess watched, the Club Kitty sign folded in on itself and plummeted down into the ruins with an air of finality. A few dangling power cables sparked and jumped, lighting up the dusty night air.

There were muted groans from around her. Jess took a step back and looked down. Jamie and the bouncer were lying flat on the ground, sprawled on the sidewalk with their hands over their heads. A short distance away, Eric and Ben, the two jocks, lay in the gutter, clinging together in fear. A shadow behind them suggested that Macy the waitress had dived for cover behind a dumpster at the last possible moment.

Jess took a deep breath. Her skin felt cold and clammy, and her entire body trembled with shock. A dark patch of blood slowly seeped through her sleeve where she had flung herself flat onto the hard concrete.

She stared at it in a daze. Her arm felt fine. There was no pain. Where was all that blood coming from?

This had to be a dream, Jess decided. The last time she'd seen this place collapse, it turned out to be just a dream, so it couldn't be real this time, could it?

Jess winced as her head started to throb. She reached up and rubbed at it, and her hand came away bright with blood. She frowned at it. You weren't supposed to bleed in dreams, were you?

She began walking across the road to the club, step by step, almost afraid to shatter the illusion. People were spilling out of the adjacent buildings and gazing at the wreckage of the club in horror. One or two were already starting to pick through the rubble, digging with their hands, searching for survivors. In the distance came the blare of an approaching fire truck and the whirr of police cars.

Stepping up to the wreckage, Jess pushed aside the remains of the main door and peered owlishly through. She felt very detached, as though this was some freaky alternative reality. In her mind, Tony was still in the restroom, and they were all outside, waiting for him so they could pack up their instruments and go home. Cassie was downstairs, probably trying to pry a few dollars from the manager to cover their costs. And Charlie was no doubt perched on a sofa somewhere, enjoying the affections of those two stupid sorority girls...

Jess stared fixedly at the rubble.

"You stupid crazy bitch... What have you done?"

Jess turned round to see the jock in the college sweatshirt standing behind her, his jaw hanging open. He had a hamburger wrapper stuck to his shirt, which he didn't seem to notice. His friend stood behind him, pale with fear.

"Nothing! I didn't do... this..."

"No? Then how the hell did you know what was about to happen?!"

Jess didn't reply.

"Answer me!" Eric took Jess by the shoulders and shook her. "You told me that I was going to die! What is this, some kind of crazy vengeance? Did someone put you up to this? Who else is involved? Hey!"

Eric found himself lifted off the ground by his collar. He hung there a moment, feet kicking in the air, then thought wisely and let go of Jess.

"What's with you, muscleman?" yelled Eric, twisting wildly. "You heard her say about the club, didn't you? You were there—you heard what she said!"

The bouncer was silent. The sounds of the fire truck were getting closer. To their left came the wail of approaching police cars.

"Hey, you son of a bitch! Put me down! Or I'll—"

"Or you'll what?" rumbled the bouncer.

"I'll... er..." Eric looked back at the enormous man, taking in the swirling Celtic tattoos and the deep scars that ran along the length of his arms. He paled slightly, then clenched his fists. "I'll sue your ass!"

"You will, or your daddy will?"

"We both will!" Eric was beside himself with rage.

"Go ahead. I work for *that* guy." The bouncer jerked a stubby finger at the pile of rubble. "Good luck." He deposited Eric in a furious heap on the sidewalk, then began striding over towards the remains of the building to lend a hand.

"Son of a bitch!" Eric straightened out his shirt, then turned a suspicious eye towards Jess, trying to regain his ruffled pride. He folded his arms defiantly. "I say we keep her here till the cops arrive."

"You know what? I don't think she's going any-where," said Jamie, who was helping Macy up. The poor woman had just been thoroughly sick on the sidewalk. He handed her a tissue and turned a thoughtful eye towards Jess. "If anyone knows what's going on, it's not her."

"Oh? And what makes you say that?"

"Because she..." Jamie hesitated. He wanted to say, *because she couldn't organize a carve-up in an abbatoir,* but decided to refrain. "Because she didn't do it," he said simply. He stared at Eric for a moment, and then frowned. "I know you," he said.

"Oh you do, do you?"

"Uh-huh. Stay away from Jess. She's innocent."

"Oh yeah?" Eric snorted. "What is she, your girl-friend?"

"No, of course—" Jamie stopped, aware that Eric was trying to rile him. "Jess didn't do it," he repeated firmly.

"So who did?"

"I don't know," said Jamie. He stared at the remains of Club Kitty.

"She saved our lives, that girl." Macy the waitress spoke up for the first time. She blew her nose loudly on her waitressing uniform.

"Yeah. We'd all be dead if it weren't for her," added Ben, the second jock. His kilt was streaked with engine oil from the sidewalk.

"But she didn't try to save us," snapped Eric, eye-balling Jess. "She just left us to die. We followed her out. We saved ourselves. She had nothing to do with it."

"Perhaps so, but we need to stay calm. Establish the facts," said Jamie.

Eric stuck a finger up at Jamie. "Establish *this*." He flung a hand wildly towards the rubble. "My goddamn girlfriend's in there!"

"Calm down, man. You're not helping."

"Calm down? How the hell can I calm down? My girlfriend's dead!"

"We don't know that," said Ben softly.

"He's right, you know." Jamie looked up at Eric, his expression unreadable. "And by the way, seeing as you mention it, Becci used to be *my* girlfriend. That was, before you—" He shook himself, unable to continue the thought. "There may be survivors. She might be still alive. Let's all keep our cool till we find out what happened."

"You can keep your cool. I'm going to keep on yelling," spat Eric. "My girlfriend's dead, and it's all her fault!"

"That's enough! A lot of people... were in there. You want to help? Go help those guys." Jamie gestured to the devastation behind him, where a big crowd of people was standing around in a hushed silence. "Perhaps there's someone left alive."

"In there? You've gotta be joking! Look at the place? Who could survive that?"

Jamie looked. A muscle in his jaw twitched. "There's always hope," he said simply. Then he turned away from them all, hiding his face and gazing up at the sky. Jess stepped up behind him and put a hand on his shoulder.

A loud crash came from behind him as the bouncer began lifting bits of fractured girder out of the rubble and heaving them aside. People were now crowded around the wreckage almost three deep. There was a flash of blue lights, and three cop cars zoomed to a halt beside them. The door swung open and a uniformed officer got out. The little group looked at him suspiciously.

"Did anyone see what happened?" he asked, pulling out a notebook.

"We all did. We were in there," said Macy, running forward.

"But we escaped," added Ben. Eric gave him a look as if to say, "*Oh, really?*"

Then his mouth dropped open. He pointed to Jess excitedly, hopping up and down on the spot. "I remember you! You talked to me before the show. You were talking about TNT... weren't you?"

"What? No! That was a joke!" said Jess, wishing desperately that he would shut the hell up. She smiled ingratiatingly at the policeman. "It was a joke," she explained through her teeth.

"I'm going to have to ask you all to come with me," said the policeman. "You're all witnesses." He opened the back door to his police cruiser and waited.

Eric bristled. "Me? Why should I come with you? It was *her* that did it." He pointed a defiant finger towards Jess.

"No! I didn't do it!" cried Jess, as the cop reached for his handcuffs. Then she mentally kicked herself, unable to believe what she'd just said.

The cop raised an eyebrow. "You'll have no problem in coming with me, then," he said. A second police cruiser pulled up alongside him. "You'll all be returned home afterwards."

"Who, me? No way. I'm not going in no cop car," said Eric, backing away. "What if someone sees me? What about my reputation?"

"Your reputation for what? Drinking too much and stealing other people's girlfriends?" asked Jamie, under his breath.

For a short guy, Eric moved surprisingly fast. He reached Jamie in under a second and pushed him backward, almost knocking him into the path of the first fire truck on the scene. The rig slewed to the side with a screech of brakes, before recovering and driving on down the street, blaring its horn. It headed around towards the back of the club.

Growling, Jamie regained his balance, seized Eric by the shoulders and pushed him backwards, away from the road. Eric awkwardly blocked his charge with a knee and then head-butted Jamie, sending him reeling.

"Guys! Stop it!"

"He started it." Jamie grabbed Eric in a headlock and kicked his legs out from under him. Eric fell spinning to the ground, collapsing in a heap on the foul-smelling sidewalk.

As the cops rushed forwards to separate the pair, Jamie stepped back in triumph, and gave Jess a little bow. She turned away from him in disgust.

Glancing at one another with raised eyebrows, the two cops stepped in to make their arrests.

It was just coming up to two o'clock in the morning. The survivors sat in a glum circle in the waiting room at the local police station, rubbing their eyes, while the sheriff questioned them one by one. The room was dark and depressing, and smelled of damp paint and old cigarette smoke. A yellow neon light crackled on and off on the ceiling.

Apart from that, the room was quiet.

Jess sat silently, twisting the ends of a broken plastic coffee stirrer between her fingers. Jamie sat beside her, trying to warm himself up as the freezing cold air conditioning blasted through his damp shirt. Every so often, he rubbed at the blossoming bruise on the side of his head and gave Eric a dirty look.

Macy sat on the opposite sofa with Ben, as far away from him as possible without actually sitting up on the armrest. Every so often, she would dart little glances at Jess, and dab at her eyes. She looked exhausted.

Sebastian the bouncer sat with his back to them all, on a wooden chair by the window. He hadn't spoken at all since he came in, apart from to give his name to the sheriff when it had been his turn for questioning. It was clear that he wanted as little to do with them all as possible. Jess thought that it was strange seeing him away from the context of the club. In her mind, he'd been born there.

They all glanced up as the door to the next room opened. Eric stepped out, managing to look smug despite his impressive black eye and disheveled appearance. He turned to Jamie and made a flamboyant gesture back towards the sheriff's office. "Your turn, dickwad."

Jamie got up and made his way with exaggerated care towards the door. As he passed Eric, he paused and stepped hard on his foot with his steel-heeled army boot.

Eric howled.

Jamie slammed the door before Eric could retaliate, giving them just a flash of a Cheshire Cat grin.

The injured jock limped across to the threadbare green sofas, muttering obscenities under his breath. He sat down heavily. "Did you just see that? Did you see what he just did?"

"What, when he stamped on your foot? No, we didn't see that," said Jess primly.

Ignoring her, Eric reached down and rubbed at his foot. "These are genuine 1970s British Doc Martens," he grumbled. "Cost me a wad on Ebay. Now look. They're all scuffed."

"My heart is breaking," said Jess sourly.

Eric gave her a glare. "D'you know how hard it is to find original Seventies gear?"

"My grandma seems to do pretty well at the local thrift store."

"Like you know about fashion?" Eric snorted. "Just look at you. Who dressed you this morning—your pimp?"

"At least I don't look like a Prep Boys catalogue reject," said Jess smoothly. "Look at the size of your collar. You could go hang-gliding."

"Excuse me—" said a voice.

"At least I can *afford* to go hang-gliding," said Eric smugly. "You, on the other hand, would be lucky to afford a communal skateboard for you and your loser band friends to ride on." He sniggered. "I can just see you now, wobbling down Main Street with all your gear packed on the back, dogs chasing you..."

"If I could just have your attention for one—"

"You could rope Nancy Boy over there to the front, and he could pull you along like a dog sled." Eric snorted with mirth. "Maybe then you'd show up to a gig on time, for once in your sad little lives..."

"Meaning what?" Jess's voice was soft, but there was a dangerous edge to it. The bouncer turned around, watching her with interest.

"Meaning that you guys suck. Your music's crap, you look like crap, and you always go on late. Oh, and your hair looks particularly stupid tonight."

Eric settled back on to the sofa with a flourish, like a grand champion chess player making the decisive move.

Ben shuffled along the sofa so that his mouth was right next to his friend's ear. "You really want her, don't you, dude?" he whispered, his eyes fixed on Jess.

"Shut up!" Eric hissed. He crossed his legs defiantly.

"You know what? You have a very big mouth for such a small guy," said Jess, leaning forward. "And..." A thought struck her. She smiled for the first time that night. "*And*, how do you know we always go on late if you've only ever seen one show?"

"I wonder if I might interrupt you for just a—"

"Well, it's obvious, isn't it?" said Eric, but he knew he was trapped. "Word—like you—gets around."

"Guys, is this even important right now—"

"Hey! *Dudes!*"

They all looked up. A handsome young man standing in the doorway. He had a plaster cast on one arm, and a dazed-looking sorority girl on the other.

Jess gasped. It was Charlie Delgado.

"How's it going, guys?" he asked brightly, swaying slightly.

Jess rose to her feet, unable to believe that he was real. "What...?" she began.

"Charlie, man, I can't believe you made it!" said Eric, as though he had just turned up to a barbeque as opposed to having recently escaped death. He leapt up and bounced over to Charlie, crushing him in a giant bear hug.

Charlie yelped. "Dude, watch the arm!"

"Sorry, man," Eric patted his cast, causing Charlie to yelp again.

Jess rolled her eyes. If it wasn't bad enough being stuck with Eric, now she had two frat boys to deal with. And to add to her worries, now she was in the same room as Charlie Delgado, and she knew she looked like death warmed up.

She furtively glanced around, searching for some kind of reflective surface to check her hair in. There was nothing. Giving up with a shrug, she waved at Charlie, trying to refrain from running up and hugging him. *He was alive.*

"What happened? We thought you were dead," she said, trying to keep her voice casual.

"Dude, you are not going to believe this," said Charlie, his voice bright with excitement. "I was dancing with these girls, right, and the next thing I know the band stops playing. Just like that. Lead singer had some kind of fit or something."

"I know. That was me," said Jess, trying not to sound hurt.

Charlie stared at her a moment, as though trying to place her. His eyes were slightly unfocussed. "No, I don't think it was. It was this other chick. She was much taller than you. Anyway," he went on, ignoring Jess. "The music just stops, and my friend Amber here, she was like, 'Man, I'm dying for a cigarette.' So I take her outside the back for a smoke. Next thing I know, *ka-blam!* The whole freaking place falls down! Man, did we have a close call."

"What happened to your arm?" asked Eric.

"This? Oh." Charlie grimaced. "Fire truck hit me."

"So you got out of the club no problem, only to get hit by a fire truck?"

"Yeah."

"Man, that sucks," said Eric.

Charlie nodded. "Doctor said that if it'd been going just a tiny bit faster it would've given me some serious brain damage. Lucky, that." He scratched his head, then brightened. "Still, I'll have the cast off in a couple of weeks. You wanna sign it?" He began hunting around the room for a pen.

Jess scratched her head. There was cocaine at frat parties, she remembered. Charlie went to a lot of frat parties. She gazed at him, trying to take in the irrefutable fact of his continued existence.

She watched him limp over to the sofa and sit down between Ben and Macy. The sorority girl—Amber, she presumed—tried to perch on his knee. Charlie pushed her off absent-mindedly and resumed his excited conversation with Eric.

Across the room, Macy cleared her throat. "Who's that?" she mouthed, pointing to Charlie.

Jess waved at her to come over. Macy did so, sniffing loudly. Her eyes were red with unshed tears. "That's Charlie," said Jess. She looked at Macy. The waitress couldn't have been more than twenty-six years old. Jess detected a subtle change in her demeanor, a slight straightening of her shoulders and a faint glint in her eye. She realized that Macy was already starting to fall under Charlie's spell.

Yeah, her and half the world, she added wryly to herself, gazing at Charlie wistfully. She sighed. Even dog-tired and covered in engine oil, there was just something about him...

There was a small noise behind her. It took Jess a moment to realize that Jamie was standing next to her, clearing his throat pointedly. She looked up, her expression slightly dazed. "Oh, hi," she said. "Are they all finished with you?"

"Yup. Your turn," said Jamie. There was something odd about his voice. He was staring fixedly at Charlie.

"What did they want to know?" asked Jess, distracted.

"Oh, this and that. Cake recipes. Nuclear secrets. I'm not allowed to tell you." Jamie gave a half smile which completely failed to reach his eyes. He jerked his head towards the door. "Go on in, girl. They're waiting for you."

Nodding, Jess stood up and made her way across the green linoleum to the door of the sheriff's office. She had been dreading this. This was worse than waiting for the dentist. She hoped that the others had the sense to keep their mouths shut about her little outburst back at the club.

It was much, much later. Jess emerged from the sheriff's office looking haggard and bemused. A uniformed cop trailed after her. All the lights were out in the room, save for one small desk light on the sheriff's desk by the door.

Jamie was sitting at the front desk, reading through an issue of *LAPD Times* without much enthusiasm. The desk in front of him was covered in clutter and stacks of unfinished paperwork. There was a heavy-looking gold award at the back, a golden statue of a policeman with an inscribed base. It was currently being used as a hat-stand.

Eric sat on the opposite side of the room, as far away from Jamie as possible. There was a general atmosphere of belligerence in the room, and the faint smell of cigarette smoke.

Jamie rose to his feet at the sight of Jess. Eric glanced round, then firmly turned his back on her.

Jess looked around her, blinking. "Where did all the others go?"

"Home. They were released," said Jamie. He glanced over at Eric.

"And you're still here because...?"

"I was waiting for you." Jamie looked at Jess. "And they said they need *him* to make a second statement." He gave Eric a cheerful little wave, then turned back to Jess, his expression becoming serious. "Why did you take so long in there? What's wrong?"

"Everything." Jess rubbed her hand over her eyes. "They think that I did it."

"Did what?"

"Knocked the place down."

"But that's crazy! You were on stage when it—"

"I wasn't onstage. I left just before it happened."

"Surely they can't blame you for..." Jamie's expression changed. "What did you say to them?"

"It wasn't what I said to them. It was what they already knew."

"Eric." It wasn't a question. Jamie's eyes lit up with anger.

"What?" Eric looked around. "Are you starting on me again, creep?"

"That depends on what you said, jerk."

"Guys! Enough!" Jess rolled her eyes, and glanced back at the uniformed officer standing behind her. He was staring at them both with a look of infinite suspicion on his face. "You're not helping."

"Fine. Let's get you home." Jamie reached out for Jess's hand, but she snatched it away.

"I can't go home, can I? They want to keep me here." Jess was practically in tears. "They say they want to take me to a different station for more questioning."

"More questions? But you were in there for hours! It's practically morning! What could they possibly have left to ask you?"

"I don't know. I don't care. I just want to sleep."

"That's crazy. Don't they need a warrant or something?" Jamie stared accusingly at the officer, who yawned widely.

"I don't know." Jess shook her head in irritation, rubbing her eyes. "You should go. It's late."

"I'm not leaving you here, Jess. Where did that guy go—the sheriff? Maybe I can talk to him, make him listen..."

"Jamie..."

"No. This is crazy. You've been through so much crap tonight. They can't just keep you here indefinitely... What about your parents?"

"My parents don't give a shit. They're probably off at some rave somewhere." Jess rubbed at her eyes again, then stared fixedly at the gold statue on the desk. It seemed to be winking at her. She looked up at the officer, a plan starting to form in her head. There was no way in hell that she was going to that other station. Not tonight.

Jamie marched up to the officer guarding Jess. "Who's in charge here?"

"I am." The officer managed to speak without appearing to move his mouth.

"No, I mean that sheriff guy. I'd like a word with him."

"The sheriff's gone home already. I have instructions to take Miss Golden to a secure holding facility."

"That's a load of crap! Look at the state of her—she's exhausted. The poor thing's been through hell tonight."

"That may be the case, but I have my orders." The officer sighed and glanced at the clock. "And a wife, waiting at home in bed for me. A nice warm wife, if my memory serves me correctly." He shook his head, giving Jamie a dark look. "Do me a favor. You don't like it? Lodge a formal complaint. The address is on our website."

He marched over to the desk and pulled a pair of handcuffs from the drawer. He turned to Jess and held them up, having the decency to look faintly apologetic. "Sorry, ma'm. Company policy."

Jess hesitated a moment, then sighed. "Just get it over with." She watched tiredly as the officer cuffed her hands together. She stretched out her arms, testing the strength of the cuffs.

"This is bullshit."

"Go home, Jamie."

"But..."

"No buts. I'll call you in the morning."

"No way. There's no way I'm leaving you here with—" Jamie looked hard at Jess. She was a stubborn girl, but he liked to think he knew her better than anyone else. He noticed a faint spark in her eye, and saw her shake her head fractionally.

He raised an eyebrow. The girl was up to something. "Well, if you're sure..."

"I'm sure."

"Fine. Just call me as soon as you know what's going on, okay?"

"Sure." Jess stopped and sniffed. Behind her, the officer stated walking round the room, turning off lights and setting the alarms. She leaned back against the desk and lowered her voice. "What's that smell? Have you been smoking?"

"I... um..." Jamie scratched at his ear, looking embarrassed. He picked up an apple from a nearby fruit bowl and buffed it on the leg of his jeans. "Smoking is such a strong word..."

"I thought you quit!" Jess hissed. "You were so proud!"

"I know, I know!" Jamie looked genuinely distressed. "I guess I just lost it for a minute there. I was stressed. That prick over there was bitching at me, and he wouldn't shut the hell up. I had to smoke, or I'd have beaten him to death with his own severed leg by now."

A thought occurred to Jess. "Where did you get cigarettes from? It's so late."

"Swiped them from the doorman."

"Jamie!

"What? He'll never miss them." Jamie tried to smile. "If you don't see me again, you'll know he's found out and butchered me in my bed."

Jess gave a small jerk of her head. "You're crazy. Go home and sleep."

"Fine, have it your own way." Jamie stepped towards Jess and gave her a quick hug. Jess pulled away after a second, leaving Jamie floundering. He opened his mouth to say something, then thought better of it. He settled for ruffling her hair instead, then turned and walked out through the open door.

As he vanished into the night, the wind blew his shirt up at the back. Jess saw the *LAPD Times* magazine sticking out of the back of his jeans.

She smiled ruefully. The boy just couldn't help himself.

Then her smile faded. She glanced at the police officer. He gazed back at her, unblinking, and pulled the main door open. "After you," he said, with exaggerated politeness. He turned to Eric. "And you."

"Oh, goody, I thought you'd never ask," said Eric. He stood up deliberately slowly, stretched, and made his way towards the door. "I'll get you for this, bitch," he whispered as he passed Jess.

"You promise?" Jess fluttered her eyelashes at him. Eric growled at her.

Jess straightened, moving away from the desk. She started breathing harder. As she drew level with Eric and the officer, she smiled sweetly and nodded back towards the waiting area. "Oh, I think someone left their bag behind," she said offhandedly.

"Did they?" The officer glanced back towards the chairs. "Where?"

Jess swung around and cracked the officer across the kneecaps with the statue from the desk. She was slightly hampered by the fact that she had her hands cuffed together, but she had a decent grip on the statue, and managed to get up a good bit of momentum with it before it hit him.

The officer fell forwards, crying out in pain and surprise. Before he could react, Jess dropped the statue and ran forward as fast as her tired legs could carry her. The officer had let go of the door, but she barged through it just before it closed, taking the impact on one shoulder and throwing it wide open.

Then she was out, haring across the car park outside the station, running towards freedom...

FOUR

Police Officer Andy Adams was not having a good night. Most days, he enjoyed working in the police department, but sometimes things happened to him that made him wish he'd gone for a quieter option job-wise, for instance, nuclear testing.

It was the lack of respect that got to him the most. Take tonight, for instance. Routine patrol. Some jerk had tried to smash his partner's head in with a beer bottle, just because he was wearing a police uniform. The night before that, someone had stuck a lit firecracker up his tailpipe outside Fat Johnny's. He'd not noticed it until he'd got right up to the car, and then he'd been forced to grab it with his bare hands and hurl it into a nearby hedge, because there was no time left to run. He'd only stopped for a coffee.

Well, okay, there had been a donut involved too, but it was late at night, and it was the only place open on his beat.

Go figure.

A colleague had not reported in for work tonight, and so Officer Adams had been put on a double shift as a result. It was nearly three in the morning, and he'd been working for almost twenty-four hours straight tonight, blowing any chance he had of making it home to his family before dawn. He had been looking forward to a nice beer down at the Irish pub after work, followed by a hearty helping of steak-and-gravy pie and a sedate smoke with his co-workers.

Now that was all gone, and he was not happy about it.

His stomach rumbled at the thought. Officer Adams liked his food. If given the choice between food and sex with a beautiful woman, he would without hesitation take the food, and tell the woman to make herself useful and wash up afterwards. He spent most of his working hours thinking about food, pulling over at various seedy fast-food restaurants whenever work was a little slow, and secreting rolls and pastries about his person to munch behind his desk whenever he thought nobody was looking. Although approaching twenty-eight years of age, Officer Adams was already beginning to develop a paunch worthy of a man many years his senior.

However, tonight, there had been no food, and Officer Adams was a man on the edge, his habitual grumpiness deepened by the lack of savory meat products lining his stomach. His foul mood had been further encouraged by the fact that his last job of the day—escorting a young girl to the next office in the precinct—had just gone horribly wrong, and the girl had now escaped after hitting him in his trick knee with the sheriff's prized gold statue.

He wasn't sure which he'd get in the most trouble for—letting the girl escape or wrecking police property—but he just knew that there would be trouble with a capital "T" as soon as the sheriff found out about tonight's little incident.

And now he had to run on an empty stomach.

Life just wasn't fair, he decided, as he hared across the parking lot after the girl. He cursed to himself. She was halfway across the lot already, moving incredibly fast for someone with both hands tied behind her.

He assumed she'd had a lot of practice.

"Stop!" he cried. The girl kept on running.

Yeah, like that one was really going to work, he thought irritably. Drawing his nightstick, he set off after her, wondering vaguely whether there would be any food places open this time of night. His stomach growled at the thought.

Across the lot, Jess had just disappeared into a 24-hour drive-through Chinese restaurant, trying to throw him off her trail. Officer Adams pulled out his badge. There was no hiding from the law, especially when the law was hungry.

Damn, that place smelled good...

On the other side of the outlet, Jess burst through the back door and darted off down the back alley, trailing the smell of cooking after her. She was slowing down. This had seemed like such a good idea when she'd first thought of it, but now she was starting to doubt the merit of what she had just done. Run first, think about it later—it was just her way of doing things. She couldn't believe she'd pulled it off.

Now what?

Jess sped up, ducking down behind a line of parked cars as she ran. She had to get away, she knew that much. The so-called charges against her were ludicrous, any fool could see that. But now, the uneasy thought was creeping into her head that running away probably wasn't going to help her case.

She hurtled towards the edge of the car park, then changed direction and began pounding up a side alley.

And she'd hit that cop...

Stupid, stupid, stupid...

The alley turned out to lead to a busy street. Jess stopped, the sound of footsteps ringing in her ears.

"I'm getting too old for this," she puffed. Her head was starting to throb again.

She ran forward a little way, to where a dozen cars were parked by the side of the road alongside an anti-smoking billboard. Selecting a car at random, she dropped to her knees and quickly slid herself beneath the car. Pulling in her legs, she lay still and waited breathlessly.

She felt a wave of tiredness swamp her as she lay there, and cursed herself. She hadn't even begun to get to grips with the events of the night, and she had just gone and made things worse. Why did she never think things through properly?

She held her breath as booted feet marched along-side the car, paused, and then doubled back. As quietly as she could, she ran her hand over the road surface, trying to gather up enough gravel to throw in the officer's face if he caught her.

The boots walked a short distance beyond the end of her car, then stopped again. Jess tensed, getting ready to throw the gravel.

Then someone grabbed her foot. Jess shrieked in fright, banging her head on the car's axle and reflex-ively throwing the gravel with all the might she could muster. It pinged and plinked off the under-side of the car, and Jess kicked hard at the hand, trying to dislodge it. It let go almost immediately, and Jess began frantically wriggling away from it, out the other side of the car. She scooted her body out, then lifted up her head to see...

"Jamie!"

"One and the same."

Jess lifted up her head. "You idiot! You scared the shit outta me! What the hell are you doing here?"

"Same as you. Wondering what on earth you're up to."

Jess rolled awkwardly to one side and sat up on her third attempt. She motioned frantically with her head. "Get out of here. Go on!"

Jamie looked hurt. "Why?"

"Because that cop's after me, idiot!"

"Of course he is. That's what cops do. They're not happy unless they're after someone." Jamie gave Jess a lopsided look. "You're just getting yourself into more trouble, you realize?"

"Bite me."

Jamie laughed. "Gladly. But first we should run, don't you think?" He held out his hand to her.

Jess just looked at him, rattling her handcuffs.

"What? Oh, sorry." Jamie dropped his hand. "Get up, then. We've got some serious legwork to do."

Jess got awkwardly to her feet. She felt her relief rapidly turning to anger. She glanced around, a hunted look on her face. "Let's get one thing straight," she said. "There is no 'we'. You're no longer involved. I got myself into this, I'll get myself out."

"But—"

"No buts." Jess shook her head, all trace of humor gone. "You're always doing this. I need to fight my own battles. What were you thinking, following me like that? He'll arrest us both!"

"Well, I'm sorry! What did you want me to do—just leave you here?"

"It would've made things a lot..." Jess froze, listening. "Where's he gone?" she hissed.

"Who, the cop?" Jamie shrugged. "Followed you into that Chinese food place. Didn't come out again. I think it threw him off your scent. Speaking of which..." Jamie waved a hand theatrically in front of his nose.

"Don't be cheeky. I knocked some stuff over in the kitchens, that's all. The staff people had a good yell at me, and I don't blame them." Jess flexed her shoulders, pulling on her cuffs. The metal didn't even flex. She sagged. "Jamie. You have to get out of here. I don't know what I've done."

"You haven't done anything. Well, besides breaking out of a police station and terrorizing some Chinese people..."

"They weren't Chinese. They were American. Oh, and I hit the nice policeman."

"And assaulting an officer of the law. No, you haven't done anything at all." Jamie gave Jess a quizzical look. "Come on. I ordered a cab about five minutes ago. Let's see if we can catch it."

"She's over here!" someone yelled.

Jess groaned inwardly as Eric's blond head popped around the edge of the alleyway. *That meddling little...*

"Eric, you dick! Get lost," hissed Jamie.

"Why should I?" said Eric smugly. "*I* haven't done anything wrong." Cupping his hands around his mouth, he turned and bellowed back down the alleyway. "I said, she's over... *mmphh!*"

"Jessica, dahling," said Jamie, his hand clamped around the struggling Eric's mouth. "I don't suppose you happen to have any gaffer tape on you, by any chance?"

"I wish I did." Jess glared at Eric. *Nails would be a preferable option,* she thought.

"What should we do with him, do you think?"

Jess's thoughts turned back to the nails again. She pried them away with difficulty. "We could make a bonfire," she suggested, glancing nervously over her shoulder. There was no sign of pursuit.

"MMMmphh!!" Eric kicked and struggled in Jamie's powerful grip.

"A bonfire... I like that idea," said Jamie, ignoring him. "But where would we get enough wood this time of night?"

"There's enough of that in his head," said Jess. "All that dorky hair-gel would go up a treat. We won't even need to buy firelighters."

"You think? Well, I don't know, honey. We should stop by the 7/11 anyway, pick up some burgers to cook on the fire. Might as well make a night of it—"

"Hold it right there!"

Jess spun around. The police officer burst out of the alleyway and started jogging towards them. He was panting, and was covered in bits of food and garbage.

Jess's feet were moving before her brain had even decided on a plan of action. The cop came after her like a guided missile, wiping his face on his sleeve. He did not look amused.

Despite her exhaustion, Jess mentally punched the air as she ran. It looked like her little booby trap had worked a treat. She had pushed some garbage cans against the back door of the kitchen, and it looked like the cop had fallen right into them. If he'd been dumb enough to fall for that one, then she didn't know what it said about the state of the police department.

Still, it had slowed him down a bit, although she wasn't out of the woods yet. Not by a long shot. In fact, she had the distinct feeling that she hadn't even entered the woods yet.

It wasn't a good feeling.

Jamie ran alongside her, easily keeping pace with her. He dragged Eric along with him, one hand locked immovably on his forearm.

"Let go of me, you big freak!" yelled Eric, trying to dig his heels into the sidewalk.

"No chance," said Jamie. "If we're in trouble, then so are you. You just earned yourself an express ticket to freak city."

"You *what*?"

"You're coming with us," Jamie translated. "Move it!"

"Guys! Over here!" Jess tore up the road towards a taxi rank. A yellow cab had just pulled in. Jess yanked open the back door and leaped inside, while Jamie opened the front door and shoved Eric into the passenger seat. As he started to protest, Jamie thumped the lock down and slammed the door, trapping him. Eric tried the handle, then banged furiously on the window.

Unfazed, the cab driver adjusted his mirror. "Where to, folks?"

"Nowhere. Just hit the gas!" yelled Jess.

"Sure." The driver paused and jerked a thumb out of the window. "Is your friend coming with us?"

Jamie opened the back door and leaned inside the vehicle. "You guys get going. I'll keep him busy."

"What? No!" Jess sat up in her seat as Jamie slammed the door and banged twice on the side of the cab. The driver accelerated out of the stop with a screech of tires.

Jess watched in alarm through the back windshield as the rapidly shrinking figure of Jamie ran back towards the cop... then they turned a corner, and she lost sight of them both.

She slumped back in the seat, her eyes shut. "That stupid son of a... Oh! I give up!"

"Where to, miss?"

"Anywhere. Just drive."

The cab driver floored the gas pedal. Living in LA meant that he was more than used to such requests. He didn't even bother to look into the rear view mirror to see who was chasing them. He'd decided a long time ago that taking an interest in his late night customers might cost him a lot more than he had bargained for.

"Stop the cab! Let me out!" Eric tried to unlock the door, panicking.

"Don't listen to him. He's sick. I'm taking him home."

The bearded cab driver shrugged in the mirror. "You're the boss."

Jess leaned forward in her seat so that she could whisper in Eric's ear. "Listen, you little creep. You're not getting out. You're not going home. You're not doing anything. We're all in this together now." She lowered her voice as the driver glanced at her with mild curiosity. "Why do you think they kept you back for questioning? You're a suspect too."

It was a lie, but she knew that Eric was stupid enough to swallow it. He had gotten her into this, and she was damned if she was going to let him just waltz off home.

Even in the dim light, Eric noticeably paled. "What? Why?"

"You were there, weren't you, dumbass? And you accused me of doing it. In cop-speak, that's practically an admission of your own guilt."

"That's a load of crap," said Eric. But he didn't sound convinced.

"You wanna clear your name? You keep your mouth shut and stay out of sight. There'll be an investigation. They'll find out that we didn't do it, and then we can go home."

"And what if they don't? Huh? You planning on running forever?"

"If need be, yes," said Jess. "But it won't come to that. I'll give it a day, two days tops. They'll send in their experts, do some tests. They'll find out the reason the place came down, then we can go home, face the music. Maybe get some trauma therapy."

Eric was silent for a moment. "So you didn't blow the place up?"

Beside him, the cab driver clicked on the radio, humming desperately.

"No, you idiot! Why on earth would I do that? Half my friends died in there tonight!" Jess whispered savagely.

And they did die, didn't they, thought Jess? That really happened. They were really dead.

A picture of Cassie and Tony playing their guitars together swam unbidden into her head. The show had been going so well...

She swung round to Eric, a new ferocity sparking in her eyes. "I had nothing to do with it," she hissed. "*Nothing*. And if I hear one more word out of you, I'm going to open that door and throw you out myself. If I'm going to be accused of murder, I might as well enjoy doing it."

Eric opened his mouth to argue, then thought better of it. He sat back on his seat, all the fight going out of him. He began chewing on his manicured thumbnail, staring through the front windscreen with a worried look on his face.

Jess glanced fitfully over her shoulder, but there was nothing there save speeding buildings, palm trees and cars. They weren't being followed.

An overwhelming waved of tiredness washed over her, and she rubbed again at her eyes. It felt like years since she last slept. She felt tired and cold and dirty, like the whole of LA was stuck to her skin. She thought longingly of the hot shower in her room.

She turned to the driver, her face carefully guarded. "Do you know anywhere we can stay for the night?" she asked.

"I know a lot of places. How much do you wanna spend?"

With an effort, Jess twisted around so that she could get a hand into the pocket in her skirt. She rifled through her pockets, and cursed. She'd left Bill's wallet in her jacket, back at the club. It was gone now, buried under the rubble. She sorted through the various loose notes in her pocket and winced. "You. Spud boy. You got any cash on you?"

"Left my plastic behind the bar," said Eric helplessly.

Jess groaned. She turned back to the driver. "Er... as little as possible?"

The cab driver thought for a minute, running his hands through his hair. "Sure thing, honey. There's this great little place, just south of downtown... all the backpackers go stay there. It ain't the Ritz, but it's clean."

"Downtown?" Jess pulled a face. "Isn't that place a bit... you know?"

"Yeah, it is." The driver shrugged. "Or I could drop you off at the Beverly Hills Hilton. I'll ring ahead and make you a reservation. Your call."

Jess settled back in her seat. "Downtown it is then."

Two miles away, Sebastian the bouncer gunned the engine on his red and white Kawasaki motorcycle and accelerated through the darkness, heading home.

What a night it had been! Sebastian normally looked forward to Monday nights at the club—the crazy, noisy weekend was past, and there were four gloriously quiet days until Friday night, the busiest night of the week.

Sebastian liked the peace and quiet. It made it all the more fun when something nasty happened.

Sebastian was not by nature a man who liked violence. In fact, he actively enjoyed it. Some of his happiest memories from the past involved violence. He was never happier than when there was something bad happening, or about to happen. He'd had a good long innings as far as violence was concerned, riding around with the big boys and shaking things up on a regular basis.

It had been *fun*.

However, that was all over now, and the only thing to remind him of those colorful, fun-filled days was a faint twinge in his left leg, where they had removed the police officer's bullet from his calf muscle. The dirty sons of bitches had taken down ten of his best buddies on that day, and now he was on his own. All he had now were memories, and the brightly colored bandana he wore around his neck, under his jacket where no one could see it.

He reached up and stroked it with a finger. There were rules against wearing those particular colors around here, he knew, but Sebastian didn't care. If they wanted him to take it off, they could remove them themselves. He'd even give them a plastic bag to take their fingers home in afterwards.

After his release, he'd got a job at a club on Sunset Strip. He was eight years older now, and had eight years worth of anger to expend. Being a doorman wasn't exactly the most glamorous job in the world, but on the plus side, he got paid for beating people up, which suited him down to the ground. If a day or two went by without some punk getting his face, he would quite happily give someone something to be angry about.

For instance, there was the "banned items" thing. That one always got to people. All the other clubs on the strip had metal detectors, but Club Kitty didn't need one. Oh no. It had Sebastian. Here was a man who could sense a camera concealed in a clubgoer's padded bra at thirty paces. His stare could freeze alcohol in the bottle, and he could make the word "NO" mean thirty-seven different things. Hardly a day went by without patrons hearing the trademark cry of, "Now look here, you big stupid... *arrggghhh!*" as Sebastian bodily ejected yet another skinny teenage Goth for trying to smuggle some kind of recording device into a show.

At the Kitty Club, his confiscated items box was second to none. It was a regular topic of awed conversation amongst staff, and sometimes even the manager would swing by to take a look. As well as the usual smuggled cameras, Sebastian had confiscated picture phones, iPods, dictaphones, miniature tape recorders, MP3 players, Walkmans, nail files, laser pointers, Swiss army knives, screwdrivers, bike chains, nail scissors, tweezers and an assortment of other items that would make any airport security official proud.

It was his job, and he loved every minute of it.

But as of now, Sebastian had no job. The club had gone, taking his boss and his beloved bouncer position with it.

And if it wasn't for that screaming young skeeze, he thought, he probably would have gone down with it.

He shrugged off the thought, accelerating around a blind bend. Screw it, he could find another job. He was still alive, wasn't he?

Then he swerved as a cop car sped by in the opposite direction, zooming over the center line and shooting past way too close to him. Sebastian gripped the handlebars tightly and swore as the whoosh of air in its wake made his bike wobble.

He swore explosively. *Damn cops*. No matter where he went, no matter what he did, they were always there. He was convinced that they were watching him, just waiting for him to slip up so that they could throw him straight back in the slammer. Hell, when they'd taken him in earlier in the night, he'd been convinced that they were going to try to pin the club's collapse on him. He didn't know how, but he was sure that they were going to arrest him for something.

He was almost disappointed when they didn't.

Sebastian checked his watch as he slowed and pulled over to the side of the road. It was nearly 3am, and he was dying for a smoke. Yawning, he unzipped his thick leather motorcycle jacket and reached into his breast pocket, hunting for his pack of cigarettes.

His fingers met empty air.

Sebastian ground his teeth together. This was the last thing he needed. His head was thumping with tiredness, and he was starting to get jittery. What the hell had happened to his smokes? He was sure he'd put them in his pocket after his lunch break.

Thumping his heel on the kick start, Sebastian peeled away from the roadside and roared off up the street. The welcome sight of a gas station loomed ahead, and Sebastian headed thankfully towards it. He wound his way into the forecourt and pulled up in front of one of the gas pumps.

He glanced at his fuel gauge. Hmm. Getting a little low... he may as well fill up while he was here.

Dismounting, he rocked the bike back on its kick-stand and unscrewed the cap from his gas tank, putting it safely on top of the pump. He began filling his tank.

As the gas began to flow, Sebastian noticed two eyes watching him from the darkness. They weren't friendly eyes. He tensed, peering into the night, then relaxed. It was just some homeless guy.

Sebastian began humming tunelessly under his breath as he filled his tank. The homeless round here were pretty harmless, but if it ever came down to it, Sebastian knew that they would have to be foolish to try and take him on. Even a normal, healthy man would have difficulty in beating him in a fight. And this guy was haggard and thin, malnourished from eating leftover fast food crap out of trash cans... just look at him. Poor guy. He'd have no chance.

Sebastian realized that he always thought of new people in terms of whether he could beat them in a fight. He wondered briefly what this meant, and whether he should see somebody about it.

Then his tank was full, and he withdrew the nozzle, still peering at the homeless guy, who stared back intently. Sebastian's feet started to feel damp, and took him a second to realize that a thin trickle of gas was still running from the nozzle, tricking down the lever and splashing on his boots. Already, a small puddle surrounded him.

Muttering oaths under his breath, Sebastian shook off his boots the best he could and marched over to the gas station's store. At the counter, he paid for his gas and asked for two next packs of cigarettes. He blew on his hands to warm them. It was late at night, and his body temperature was dropping.

Sebastian shivered.

Below him on the floor, a decrepit electrical heater hummed. Sebastian felt its warmth through the leather of his motorcycle pants, and stepped closer, trying to absorb this small amount of heat. It sure was cold out tonight. Fall must be on the way.

Directly behind him, light from the heater glinted off the long rows of barbeque products. Bags of charcoal, skewers, knives and firelighters were arranged all along the top display shelf. A big sign announced "Explosive Summer Sale—50% Off!" The bottom shelf was groaning with a fresh delivery of kerosene lighter fuel and camping gas, which the store owners were trying to shift while there was still a market for them.

As Sebastian moved closer, trying to read the price on one of the knives, he accidentally kicked the heater. The fan inside made a grating noise. A moment later, a small shower of sparks flew out, bouncing on the carpet. A second shower joined it a moment later, landing perilously close to Sebastian's diesel-soaked boot.

Unaware of the danger he was in, Sebastian was debating over the thirty different flavors of chewing gum on the stand by the counter. An Eighties tune came onto the radio, and he hummed along with it under his breath while he decided, trying to remember the name of the band. "Hmm... hmmm hmmm... Don't fear the reaper..." He knew this song. These guys were called the Blue Oyster something or other... Cart? Cult? Something like that.

Whatever. He liked this song. He started humming again.

Down on the floor, the fan sparked for a third time and cut out, caught on the wire frame inside the unit. Without a supply of fresh air to cool it, the heating element glowed brighter and hotter, heating up to a dangerous temperature. Tiny white sparks danced across the surface as the diesel fumes from Sebastian's boots were sucked towards it.

Sebastian picked a packet of gum off the wire stand, hesitated, and then replaced it again, bewildered at the choice. His head was starting to ache. He just wanted a pack of Juicy Fruit, but there was no Juicy Fruit. Instead, he had a bewildering number of different kinds of mint gum, spearmint and fresh mint and double mint, whatever the hell that was, some types sugar-free, some not, others with sweetener...

Sebastian sniffed and squinted at the tiny labels. Which was the one that was supposed to be better for your teeth? He ran his tongue around the inside of his mouth, pondering his options. Maybe he should get one of those, for a change.

Out on the boulevard, the cab had not gone more than ten more blocks before Jess heard the sound she'd been dreading—the whirr of a police siren. Waving to Eric to duck down, Jess scooted down low in her seat, hoping that it would pass her by. Then red and blue lights flashed through her window as the police cruiser drew alongside. She peeked through the window, and saw the officer making sharp "pull over" gestures to the cab driver.

It was the officer from the station. He did not look friendly.

"So, what sort of trouble are you folks in, then?" asked the driver, in a conversational tone.

"Nothing! We didn't do anything!" protested Jess.

"So you didn't rob a bank or anything?

"No! We were just in the wrong place at the wrong time."

"Ah, one of those. I see." The driver touched the brake with his foot, locked the doors with a click of a switch and began to pull over.

Jess's heart sank. She reached into her pocket again. "I have... um... thirty-eight dollars. I know it's not much, but..."

"Don't worry about it."

"What?"

"Put your money away." The driver crossed his hands over the wheel as he pulled up to the curb. He put the car into neutral, and waited, whistling a little ditty as his engine idled.

"But we have to..."

"I said, don't worry about it." The driver adjusted the mirror so that he could see Jess's face. It could have been Jess's overtired imagination, but for a moment she thought that he winked at her.

She watched with a heavy heart as the police officer got out of the patrol car and walked alongside the cab. He knocked on the window. Eric shrank down in the front seat, making little bubbling noises.

The bearded cab driver beamed at the officer, starting to wind the window down.

Then he hit the gas, screeching away from the curb. The outraged officer was left standing in a cloud of dust.

Jess stared at the driver as he rode up through the gears, careering over into the middle lane. He chortled and thumped on the wheel. "Gets 'em every time." He readjusted his mirror again and floored the gas pedal, making the engine scream. "You were saying?"

Jess was momentarily speechless. She looked behind her, watching as the rapidly shrinking cop ran back to his car and leapt in. He pulled out after them, siren wailing.

"You do this a lot?"

"When I can, lass, when I can." The driver looked modest. "Used to be a stunt driver up in Hollywood till I bust my knee. They laid me off, the bastards."

"That was some pretty neat driving." Jess threw a glance over her shoulder. "Think you can keep it up?"

"No problem." The driver yanked the wheel violently to the right, cutting the car across the road almost at right angles. The car flew up a small side street like a yellow arrow. Behind them, Jess heard the screech of the officer's tires as he fought to keep up with them. The cab bounced once as it ran over a pothole, then began climbing rapidly up the steep hill. At the top, the driver swung the cab around and began accelerating along a wide stretch of open road. Illuminated billboards and neon signs flashed past, blurring as the cab picked up speed.

"I'm Steve, by the way," said the cab driver. He extended his hand to Eric, who shook it gingerly, as thought it might explode.

"Nice to meet you. I'm Jess. And that's..." Jess stopped. She frowned. "What was your name again?"

"Eric."

"This is Eric," said Jess. "Don't let him touch anything."

She sat back in her seat, then yelped as the cab bounced again, her head knocking against the canvas roof. She heard the back of the car scrape sharply on the asphalt.

"Crappy roads round here," said Steve mildly. "Still, it adds to the fun." He thought for a moment, head on one side as though listening to some internal monolog. Then he touched the brake, slowing the car. "Fasten your seat belt, little lady."

"Why?" Jess sat up in the back seat, feeling helpless. Her hands were still cuffed behind her.

"Watch." Steve waited until the cop car was almost level with them. Then he hit the brakes hard. Jess's head whipped forward as the cab decelerated rapidly, then fell sideways as Steve pulled on the wheel, sending the car into a spin.

Jess screwed her eyes tight shut, pressing her face into the vinyl of the seat as the streets whirled around them. When she opened them again, they were heading back in the opposite direction, picking up speed again.

Jess grimaced and tried to hold on. This was going to be a rough ride.

Back at the gas station, Sebastian was still trying to decide which pack of gum he should buy. At his feet, the fan heater glowed red hot, reaching maximum brightness. The power cable overheated and started to melt at the base, spitting tiny globules of molten copper into the nylon carpet. Smoke started to creep out from beneath the unit.

At the counter, Sebastian reached a decision. He'd go with the double mint. He'd had some once and remembered that it was good.

He plucked a pack off the rack and stepped up to the counter, just as the fan heater exploded at his feet. He jumped back as it blew up with a loud bang, jumping and sparking across the carpet for a couple of seconds before shorting out with an electrical zapping sound. Beneath it, a patch of blackened carpet smoked. Sebastian landed on the wire, kicking it and inadvertently dragging the sparking fire away from the rows of lighter fuel. He swore and stepped off the wire immediately, glad of his thick rubber biker boots.

Moving backwards, he pulled out an oily rag and mopped at his brow, his heart thumping.

Christ, that had made him jump. He'd thought someone was shooting at him.

He looked down at the exploded fan at his feet, then his gaze slid sideways to take in the rows of camping gas stored just feet away. His brow furrowed as his brain did the math. Boy, that could have been nasty. The world was really out to get him tonight.

The shop assistant came running round the edge of the counter, wearing an apron and a look of sleepy concern. "I'm so sorry... are you all right?"

"I'll live." Sebastian gave a short barking laugh. "Although I think your heater's had it." He opened his hand and peered inside. A look of sorrow came over his face. "Oh, and I squashed your gum."

"Keep it." The assistant was flustered, anticipating possible lawsuits. He wiped his forehead and plucked a second pack of gum off the rack. "And here's a fresh one. On me." He shook his head, looking down at the charred patch on the floor. "It's been one of those nights."

"Tell me about it."

Sebastian paid the man for his cigarettes, then strode outside, lighting up as he walked.

He took a long, deep drag.

Ah, that was better. He felt the warm rush of nicotine flood his brain, and relaxed for the first time that evening.

Damn, he loved smoking.

Striding back towards the pumps, he put away his cigarettes and reached for his keys, then paused. "Hey!" he said. The homeless man was standing by his bike, inspecting it with great interest. "You! Get away from there!"

He strode over to the man, who backed off, holding up his hands as if to say, "No worries."

Sebastian put his hand protectively on the bike. "You got a problem?"

"Not me, no sir. But you do, you do."

"And what's my problem?"

"Not going to tell you, tell you." The man smiled a small bright mad smile, and pointed dramatically at the sky. "Beware the moon!" he said, and burst out laughing.

"Whatever." Sebastian took a drag on his cigarette, and swung a leg over his motorcycle. He put the key in the ignition and peered suspiciously up into the sky. "There isn't even any freakin' moon," he snapped.

"No moon, no moon," sang the man. "Don't forget to cover up before you go."

"Okay...I will..." ...*you goddamn freaky little man*, he added to himself. What was it, open house at the crazy farm today?

Zipping up his jacket against the cold of the night, Sebastian gunned his bike's engine and slowly coasted out of the forecourt towards the road. All he

wanted to do now was get back to his apartment and
hit the sack. He couldn't even remember when he
last slept. The nicotine would keep him going
throughout the twenty minute ride home, but then it
was definitely bedtime.

He'd had enough excitement for one night.

He stopped the bike at the edge of the gas station
forecourt, and took one last, long drag on his cigarette, watching the end glow like a tiny bonfire in the
night. With his other hand, he reached for his cycle
helmet.

It was time to blow this joint and head for home.

Back at the pumps, the homeless man reached out a
grimy hand and stroked the shiny silver disk the
bike man had left on top of the pump. It was so
pretty and so shiny, like a little silver dish for mice to
eat out of.

He thought that he might like to keep it.

Cautiously, he picked it up and turned it over in
his hands, then bit it experimentally. It tasted bad,
but he didn't mind. He held it up to the light bulb
that illuminated the area, so that it blotted out the
light. Closing one eye, he moved it slowly back and
forth. "Moon there, moon gone," he said in a
singsong voice.

Then he turned so that the red glow of Sebastian's
tail lights were visible, and covered them up with
the disk. "Man there, man gone."

He lowered the disk, a look of dismay on his face.
"Man gone...?" He tilted his head for a moment, as
though listening to silent music. Then he stuffed the
silver fuel cap into his pocket and began backing

away rapidly. "Time to go now, I think," he said, and fled into the night.

Over on the concrete ramp, Sebastian finished his cigarette and strapped his motorcycle helmet on. He didn't notice that he'd left the cap off his tank. Yawning, he twisted the accelerator and roared out into the LA night, carelessly tossing the still-lit stub of his cigarette behind him as he did so...

"Piece of cake." Steve whooped as the car bounced hard at the end of his 360-degree spin and straightened out. He gave it some more gas, then reached into the glove compartment and fumbled around, driving one-handed. Beside him in the passenger seat, Eric was in the process of turning an interesting shade of green.

Steve pulled out a pack of cigarettes, and lit one up. "So," he said, puffing away. "Where d'you wanna be dropped?"

"I don't know." Jess's mind was a mess. "Some-where safe. If there is such a place." She risked sitting up in her seat and glanced over her shoulder again. The sound of the siren was beginning to recede into the distance. "What if they catch you? she asked nervously.

"They won't," said Steve. He reached back into the glove compartment, and pulled out two metal plates. He held them up for Jess's inspection.

"You took off your license plates. Isn't that against the..." Jess stopped. "Oh," she said.

"I find it helps business," said Steve, stuffing the plate back into his glove compartment.

"Hey, if I ever getting round to robbing that bank, you'll be the first person I'll call," said Jess.

Struggling to reach with her bound hands, she counted her money out by the light of an approaching gas station, splitting it in two. Then she sighed and put it back into one pile. She passed the lot through to Steve. "Take it," she said. "I think you lost your hubcap back there."

Steve took the money and stuffed it carelessly into his pocket. "I'm not worried. It's not my cab."

"Oh." Jess looked confused. "Then whose is it?"

"My friend Vladi's," said Steve with a smirk. "I work nights, he works days. But he always leaves his cab in the station with the keys in. I always take his cab out in case mine gets damaged. You know they charge you for that?"

Jess thought about this. "Doesn't he get suspicious?"

"Nah. He's convinced that these guys break into the station a couple times a week and steal the gas from his car. It's costing him a fortune." He snorted with laughter.

"That's not very nice," said Eric, who had now recovered somewhat.

"I didn't say I was nice," said Steve. "And speaking of not-nice things, did you hear about what happened tonight at the—*holy shit!*"

Up ahead, a blinding white light blossomed. An intense burst of heat washed over the cab, like the blast from a miniature atom bomb. Even through the closed windows, Jess could feel it singe her face.

"What the...?" Jess was thrown forward, bumping her head on the seat rest in front of her as the cab skidded across the road. Steve swore as he wrestled with the wheel, fighting to regain control of the vehicle. There was a loud cracking sound as the front windshield splintered in the heat. The smell of smoke and burning rubber filled the car, and a thumping noise came from under the tires as the cab ran over something.

Jess prized her head away from the seat rest and tried to stay down as the car jerked that way and this, engine revving. Eric shrieked, holding onto his seat belt for dear life.

"Hang on!" Steve pumped the brakes, trying to slow the car enough to steer. The engine made an ugly sound, and something crunched inside the stick shift lever. The car slowed fractionally, but kept on going.

A piece of burning metal struck the front of the car, bouncing off with a loud *SHRING*! Then another struck. And another. Jess yelled as the opposite side window shattered and glass spilled onto the seat next to her.

"Son of a bitch!" Steve managed to straighten the car on the road. Pumping the brakes, he squinted through the fractured windshield and steered carefully over to the side of the road.

As the car slowed, Jess pulled herself upright and peeped through the blackened side window. She saw that the cab's yellow paintwork was on fire. She watched it burn, flames licking up the side of the window. *That's not entirely normal*, she thought, and someone giggled shrilly.

It took Jess a moment to realize that it was her.

The car limped up to the curb and stalled, coasting gently to a stop. The lights faded and died as the engine cut out. Then all was still, save the gentle popping sound of flames licking across the cab's hood.

"Shiiiiit!" Steve kicked the driver's door open and half-climbed, half-fell out of the cab. Brushing the glass out of his clothes, he straightened up and surveyed the devastation around him. Eric scrambled out of the cab after him and collapsed on the grass at the side of the road, hyperventilating.

The road was littered with flaming debris for a hundred yards in either direction. Several of the stubby palm trees beside the road had caught fire, and were now blazing away merrily. The wreckage of what looked like a motorbike lay just beyond the gas station.

Steve squinted. There was a dark figure lying crumpled on the side of the road, about ten feet away.

Steve automatically started towards it, then stopped. The figure's helmet was smashed open, and what was visible of the man's face wasn't pretty to look at. Steve gave a low whistle and shook his head sadly, pursing his lips. Nobody who looked like that was about to get up again.

Eric staggered to his feet behind him and stared at the body. "Dude! Look at that dude. Oh, man..."

"I'm looking." Steve gave Eric the thumbs down. "He's had it, for sure."

"This night sucks. It really, really sucks," whimpered Eric.

Steve glanced over at him. The kid looked like he was about to burst into tears. "You don't say," he said, his eyes still on the body.

Beyond it, at the nearby gas station, he could see the solitary pump attendant speaking rapidly into the phone through the brightly lit window of the shop.

Steve turned and cast a rueful eye over the remains of the cab. The yellow paintwork had been completely burned away from the upper chassis, leaving a blackened, pitted surface that wouldn't have looked out of place during a street riot. One of the cab's silver hubcaps was missing, and two of the windows were smashed in. Steve sighed. He sure as hell wasn't going to be able to leave this cab for Vladi, back at the station.

This was going to be expensive...

His roving gaze settled on Jess, who was trying to pull herself upright in the back seat. He hurried towards her, his face creasing in concern. "Damn, girl! Are you all right?"

"I'm still alive, if that's what you mean," said Jess, coughing. She managed to hook a foot beneath the seat in front of her, and with an effort, levered herself into a sitting position. She gazed at the door handle, seemingly wrestling with herself, then cleared her throat sheepishly. "Er.. I might need a hand with these." Slowly, she swiveled around in her seat so that Steve could see the shiny glint of her handcuffs.

"Good grief, girl!" said Steve. "What have you been up to tonight?"

"I told you. Nothing. It was all a big misunderstanding."

"Uh-huh. I see." Steve took off his shirt. Carefully, he wrapped it around his hand, and pulled open the smoking back door. Jess clambered out and stood there swaying, feeling slightly foolish. She saw the body lying by the side of the road, and drew back in horror.

"Shouldn't we go help him?" she said in a hushed voice.

"Nah." Steve shook his head. "He's gone. Just look at him."

Jess looked. She looked again. Then she frowned. There was something very familiar about the fallen motorcyclist...

Seemingly without instruction from her brain, her legs started walking, taking her forwards, towards the body. In the distance came the wail of multiple police sirens, but she paid them no heed.

She stopped when she was ten feet away and gave a little gasp. The body of the man was sprawled on its side, its head bent back at an unnatural angle. The man was wearing bulky motorcycle leathers, which were torn, charred and burned through all along one side. Blood oozed through the gaps, pouring from torn and singed flesh. The corpse was still smoking slightly. There was a strong smell of burnt rubber and gasoline.

There was something familiar about the body...

Gingerly, Jess walked around the other side of the man. Hardly daring to look, she steeled herself, then peered through the shattered glass of the motorcyclist's helmet. The man's face was unrecognizable. Sightless blue eyes stared back at her from a cut and bloodied face. His teeth had been smashed, and one cheek was torn open. Bone shone whitely through the tattered mess of blood and flesh, and a large chunk of skin was missing from his forehead. The inside of his motorcycle helmet was coated in red blood.

Jess averted her gaze. Her eyes traveled down his torso. The entire left sleeve of the man's leather jacket had been ripped to shreds, revealing a burnt and bloodied arm.

Jess tilted her head. The man had a distinctive tattoo on his forearm, the swirling black letters visible through the blood.

Jess gasped in recognition, feeling a terrible chill go through her.

The tattoo read "FATE."

FIVE

Jamie sat on the hard wooden bench in the police cell, his head in his hands. It was cold in the cell, and kind of draughty. His head ached and his jaw was starting to swell.

He rubbed his eyes, then rolled his head around to loosen the stiffness in his neck and shoulders. He was beyond tired now. His mind was all fuzzy and warm, and it felt like forever since he had last eaten.

He licked his dry lips and looked around without enthusiasm, taking in the bare concrete floor, the white-painted breezeblock walls and, most importantly, the thick steel bars separating him from the world. There was no sign of food anywhere, not even a suggestion that some might be served at some point—no table or chair, no little metal hatch through which a bowl of gruel or bread might be shoved, not even a mangy dog on the floor chewing a bone thrown by a previous prisoner, like there was in the cartoons.

This, as Jess would so eloquently put it, sucked the butts of a thousand hairy monkeys.

Jamie settled back on the bench and tried to make himself comfortable. Through the bars he could see a door with a window in, through which the sheriff's office was visible. The office was filled with all kinds of things—a desk with a telephone, a hat stand, a filing cabinet with a dying potted plant on top. There was even a stuffed fish on the wall.

Normal things, in a normal room.

Jamie glanced at the bars again and sighed.

Across the room, the station clock ticked up to 6am. It was quiet in the cell. Everyone had gone now and left him alone, which was far preferable to the shouting and yelling that had gone on for the past half hour.

He couldn't believe that this was the same night that the club had come down. In fact, this night felt like about a half dozen different nights, none of which had been good. What had happened to his rights? He'd thought that disaster victims like him should be treated, well, nicely, given hot sweet tea and little leaflets about trauma counseling, preferably ones with pages you could color in.

Jamie sat back, shrugging to himself. It wasn't his fault that he'd gone a bit off the rails. He was obviously in shock. He'd insisted to the cop who'd brought him in that pulling down his trousers and flashing passing motorists was an obvious sign that he was in shock. He wasn't trying to distract the nice policemen from doing their job and chasing after their suspect. No sir. Not him. Nor was stuffing an apple into the tail pipe of the aforementioned police officer's car, and then running off in the opposite direction. That was crazy behavior, obviously associated with people who'd just been through a tough time and weren't really aware of what they were doing.

People should realize that.

But they hadn't. They'd treated him like a common criminal—shock, horror!—and treated Jess far worse.

And now he was in an actual police cell, and Jess was on the run.

Jamie pulled his thin shirt tighter around himself, wishing for the hundredth time that he'd chosen something more substantial to wear that night. Even a leather jacket would have helped matters.

And where was his jacket, exactly? Buried beneath a hundred tons of rubble, that's where it was. Jamie shivered at the thought. Along with his drum kit, his sound gear and several of his best mates. And a hundred or so other people who he hadn't known, but who had showed up for one of his gigs, and so unknowingly condemned themselves to death.

Poor bastards.

Jamie rubbed at his eyes, still unable to take this in. No matter which angle he approached it from, it still seemed unreal. It was like some half-remembered dream that hits you with full Technicolor force as you wake up, but fades so quickly that by the time you're fully awake, you've almost completely forgotten it.

He hoped that it would stay that way for as long as possible.

Tiring of staring at the door, Jamie swiveled around on the hard wooden bench and lay down, hoping to get some kind of rest before morning. Wincing, he shifted around, trying to find a comfortable position. Was this bench naturally splintery, he wondered, or had they put the splinters in after it had arrived here, just to make it extra uncomfortable?

Jamie shifted again, picturing the sheriff kneeling in front of the bench in a surgical apron and mask, surrounded by anxious onlookers as he glued splinter after splinter into position, every so often cackling madly to himself.

Jamie grinned hollowly. It could well be true, judging by what he had seen of this sheriff so far. The man was so twisted, they could stick a handle in his ass and use his head to turn screws.

The phone rang in the next room, shrill and insistent. Nobody answered it. Jamie half-opened one eye and peered out of the door. After a dozen rings he heard it click to the answerphone. Everybody must have gone home for the night.

He was alone.

Lying back, he looked up at the ceiling. Above him, someone had written, *"There is no justice— There is just us"* on the bare plaster, in what looked like red crayon.

Jamie reflected on that for a moment. Then he closed his eyes and tried to rest.

His brain was shouting something urgent at him.
He ignored it.

God, what a night. He'd been worried when Jess
was late for the performance. Ha! Right now, lying
here in this cold cell, he thought that he'd give anything to have such a simple and uncomplicated
worry. He could handle the crazy intricacies of Jess's
timekeeping skills, no problem. But now, things
were just horrible.

Jamie sighed. There was no more avoiding the
thought any longer.

Tony and Cassie were dead.

*And the club was gone, and Jess was being blamed
for it.*

He hadn't really known anyone in the crowd, but
they were all dead too, and nothing that he could say
or do would bring them back.

Jamie knew he ought to feel upset about this, but
he didn't. He just felt... tired. He knew that all those
people were dead, but he didn't feel like it was really
true. It couldn't be true, could it? The last he'd seen
of Tony was his chain-draped back, disappearing
into the men's room. He'd asked him if he should
wait for him outside, but Tony had shrugged and
told him to go on ahead. He remembered how he
had hung around outside for a moment, debating
whether or not he should use the restroom too. But
he had decided against it in the end, and had gone
up the steps to check on Jess instead.

What if he'd waited for Tony? Would he now be
dead, along with the rest of them, lying in a morgue
somewhere while some creepy alien doctor picked
bits of brick out of his brain?

Jamie shivered.

Once again, a thought niggled at the back of his mind, like a mosquito in a tin. It was a worrying thought, and he ignored it.

It niggled again, loud and angry-sounding.

Jamie sighed and squeezed his eyes tight shut.

Then there was that other thing.

Jess had said that the place was going to collapse— before it actually happened.

There, he'd let himself think it. That was what had been bugging him all evening.

Jamie shifted uncomfortably on the bench, his eyes flickering beneath his closed lids. If he'd listened to Jess, would he have been able to save all those people?

He just didn't know.

And how had Jess known what was going to happen? It was just too much of a coincidence to be a... well, a coincidence. Could she have had anything to do with it?

But even as the thought entered his head, Jamie knew that it was the wrong thing to be thinking. For all her assorted craziness, Jess was not a killer. Jamie could feel it in his bones. She would never do anything to physically hurt anyone.

But he'd ignored her warning, if that's what it had been. He'd thought that she was tripping, or possibly just trying to get attention. Perhaps something was wrong with their performance, or that she'd spotted someone in the crowd she didn't want to play to. Or maybe she'd asked her crazy mother to come to the gig, and she hadn't shown up. Again.

Jamie rolled over on the bench. Hell, it could have been one of any number of reasons. The girl was notoriously skittish about her stage performances. She'd once blown off an entire show because she thought that the lighting made her look fat, then refused to go back on stage until they'd hauled a mirror out of the dressing room to prove to her that it didn't. And then she'd refused to go on anyway because she said that she hadn't realized that her skirt clashed with her top.

Jamie smiled at the memory. It had taken him an hour of very fast talking to prevent the venue manager from taking his drum kit to pay for the gap in the listing.

He'd been *so* mad at her that night.

And yet... and yet... when she was there, with them, she really got it *right*. She had a voice like nothing else he'd ever heard, and when she got going up there on the stage, you couldn't take your eyes off her.

She just had... what was it she had? Jamie didn't know, but he knew that it was great. It was what the fans paid their six bucks to watch. It was what got them into club after club, despite the fact that they had to cancel every third gig because of Jess's regular disappearing acts.

And hell, it was what made him...

Jamie's eyes snapped open, then flicked to the side. From the next room came the sound of a door opening.

Jamie rose to his feet, his tiredness forgotten, and moved soundlessly across to the bars. Pressing his forehead against the cool metal, he listened intently.

Muted voices came from the next room, raised in argument. Jamie strained his hearing, cursing the years of band practice that had left him with a faint ringing in his ears. There was a man's voice, deep and rumbling—a police officer, he assumed. And then there was a woman's voice.

It sounded kind of familiar.

"Jess?" Jamie called out before he could stop himself.

Next door, the speakers paused. There were the sound of footsteps, and then the door to his cell swung open. A moody-looking cop stuck his head around the edge. He had dark rings under his eyes, and he did not look amused. His cap had a big piece of fried egg on it. "What?" he said irritably.

"Is... is Jess out there?" asked Jamie. He considered commenting on the egg, but decided against it.

The officer considered this. "Who, that girl you came in with?"

"Yeah." Jamie tried not to look hopeful.

"No. It's not her."

"Then who's out there?" Jamie pointed through the door.

"A friend of yours. You should consider yourself very lucky," said the officer.

Jamie frowned. A friend? Who even knew that he was...

"Hey, you!"

"Oh... hey." Jamie stepped back as Macy the waitress pushed open the door and waved at him. She still looked tired, but she had obviously been home and had a shower since the last time he'd seen her. She was wearing light-colored cotton pants with a retro fluffy yellow sweater, and her hair was up in a ponytail.

"I thought you went home," he said.

"I forgot my bag." Macy blushed and dropped her gaze to the floor. "Isn't that silly of me? I only realized it when I got in. I must've been in some kind of a daze after everything that happened, because I was in the shower, right, and then I thought, jeepers, wasn't I carrying something when I went out tonight? Then I realized that I'd put my purse down while that man with the hat was asking me questions, so I called the sheriff, and he said that I could come by and pick it up at my convenience. Imagine! At my convenience! What a nice man!" She glanced up at Jamie to check his reaction.

"I guess that was nice of him," said Jamie helplessly.

"I know, it was, wasn't it?" Macy went on. She took a deep breath, chewing her gum thoughtfully. "So I went to bed and I tried to sleep, thinking I'd pick it up in the morning, but I couldn't sleep, you know, knowing that all my stuff was on some guy's desk somewhere? You know, my *personal* stuff? So, I decided to hop in the car and drop by the station, 'cause I just live a couple of blocks away, and I need my credit card for the morning when I go for breakfast at that little green coffee shop, you know, Pete's."

"I like that place," said the officer. The egg on his cap had now worked its way to the side, and was

now hanging down like a fried Rastafarian dread-
lock. It wobbled when he talked.

Jamie tried hard to keep a straight face.

"I wouldn't get coffee anywhere else," said Macy
solemnly. "So anyway, I get here and see that
everyone's all running around like crazy, and then I
see *you* going back into the police station with three
officers holding on to you, fighting like mad. So I
asked myself, what's going on? Then I asked the
officer, what's going on? And *he* said, that band girl's
run off and her friend tried to help her escape but
had been caught. So I thought I'd come in here and
see if I could help y'all out at all."

"Macy's putting up some money for your release,"
said the officer.

"Really? That's very... kind of you," said Jamie.
"But why...?"

"No reason," said Macy, a little too quickly for
Jamie's liking. She smiled shyly, gazing up into
Jamie's eyes. He dropped her gaze almost immediately, but it was too late. He'd seen a little spark of
something in her eyes, and he knew what that
meant.

Oh no, not *that*...

Macy brushed her hair out of her eyes, stepping
closer to the bars. "I just like to help out where I can.
I had a bit of money saved up for a weekend away,
but then I thought, who needs this money most, me
or him?"

"Oh, right. Thank you." Jamie moved quickly
away from the bars and turned to the officer,
scarcely daring to hope. "So, does this mean I can go
now?"

"I guess it does." The officer did not look pleased. Unconsciously, he reached up to fiddle with his cap. His fingers encountered the egg, and his expression grew thunderous. He swept it off onto the floor and stared accusingly at Jamie.

"Cool. Er."

Jamie stopped, a nasty little thought swimming to the surface of his mind. It was late, and he knew without looking that he didn't have any money on him. His house was a good hour's drive away.

That just left him with one option.

He looked at Macy. She smiled back at him.

Ah, great. She was *expecting* him to ask.

Jamie closed his eyes briefly, uttering a silent prayer to whatever deity happened to be nearby and awake. "Macy, can I ask one small favor..."

"Of course, silly," she gushed.

"Well..." Jamie gritted his teeth. "I live a long way away, and it's kind of late... and I'm kind of broke..."

"Why, you must stay with me tonight!" said Macy, as though the thought had never occurred to her before.

"I was only going to ask for a ride—"

"Nonsense. I have a spare bed, and I just live round the corner." Macy held up a hand. "I won't have it any other way. Now come on, before you catch your death in this place."

Great, thought Jamie sourly, as the police officer unlocked his cell and let him out. It would be nice to have a shower and a clean bed for the night, but why did it have to be at Macy's? She was a pleasant enough girl, but she was just a bit... well...

Jamie toyed with words like *vapid* and *vacuous* for a moment, then settled on *odd*. Although young and pretty, Macy acted like somebody's mother. More specifically, she acted like somebody's mother who was in their late fifties, and had never married. Jamie had only talked to her a couple of times before, at previous gigs at the Kitty Club, but he remembered his conversations with her because she had always served his drinks to him with admonishments to wrap up warm, or to make sure that someone else was driving if he kept on drinking that way, or to get a wallet rather than just stuffing his change into his back pocket like that, in case somebody tried to steal it.

What she was saying made perfect sense, but he had a strong feeling that her own mother used to talk to her in that way, and that she had hated it. She probably wasn't even aware that she was now doing it herself, but he'd still found it annoying. Just by talking to her, he knew without a doubt that she lived alone, maybe with a pedigree cat or two, and that at least one room in her house was painted pink. And that she still had all her childhood toys, arranged neatly in a cardboard box under the bed.

She just seemed like that kind of person.

He arranged his features into a hesitant smile as Macy bore down on him, taking his arm and propelling him from the room before he could protest.

Behind him, the police officer pocketed Macy's check and smiled.

Jess only stopped running when she ran out of light to run by.

Panting, she bent over and put her hands on her knees, dispelling the stitch that had cramped her side for the past twelve blocks. She breathed in deeply, and let the air out of her lungs in a controlled breath. She had no idea where she was. She couldn't remember when she had last run that fast, and that far. The streetlights had run out half a block away, and now she was in the darkness.

Straightening up, she looked around her. She was standing at a crossroads in the middle of nowhere. Nondescript houses surrounded her, most of them either gated or boarded up. The grass in front of them was yellow and patchy, like desert stubble, indicating that their sprinklers were either non-existent, or had dried up a long time ago due to non-payment of bills. It was sometimes easy to forget that LA was built in the middle of the desert. Litter filled the gutters, and the air stank of garbage and stale urine.

"Nice. Really, really nice."

Jess closed her eyes as Eric jogged up beside her, puffing. She'd been hoping that he hadn't followed her. She wiped her forehead and spoke without looking at him. "Can it, frat boy. I'm not in the mood."

"No, really, I'm serious. I was thinking of buying a condo here." Eric pretended to breathe in deeply. "Ah! That smell!" He pointed to a house at random. "I think I'll take that place. I'll come down here when I get bored of living on the beach." Eric mopped his forehead. "Those darn ocean views... all that sand and blue sky... very stressful, you know. Some days I get so depressed I can hardly put on my sun block."

"You're funny," said Jess. "You're a very funny person. Now go be funny someplace else." She began walking away.

Eric hurried after her. "You mean you're just going to leave me here?"

"Yup. That's about the size of it."

"But I don't know where I am!"

"That makes two of us. Now hop it."

Jess pushed her hair out of her eyes, peering warily into the darkness. She must be somewhere in the outskirts of Downtown, she thought, but where, exactly? Glancing up, she sought out a street sign to place herself by, but the only one visible was covered in a wild tangle of graffiti. The street was lit by one solitary nightlight that hung from the window of a boarded-up shop. A black stream of cockroaches scuttled in and out through a gap in the metal doorplate, busying themselves with cockroach errands. On the stone wall of the shop, a colorful mural of the Virgin Mary had been painted. A sign reading, "Cerrado" was nailed to its outstretched palms.

Jess looked up and down the street, her skin crawling. Every house had bars on the window. That was generally not a good sign.

"So... do you have any brothers or sisters?"

"Shhh... quiet!" Jess glared at Eric.

"What?"

"You'll attract attention."

"And what if I want to attract attention?" Eric jammed his hands into his pockets, perplexed. "We need help. We need to find someone and ask directions."

"Yeah, that's right. If you want to get out of here in a body bag."

"Don't be ridiculous. It's just downtown... where are we? Southside? It's not Beirut," said Eric, but some of his confidence had drained away. He looked around him, seeming to shrink inside himself a little.

The streets *were* very quiet...

"You ever been here before?" asked Jess, making him jump.

"Sure. There's this great little Mexican restaurant just off Hoover—"

"I mean, to somewhere that's not near college?"

"Well... no... But I've driven through places like this a lot. I've never had any trouble, or seen anything bad."

"Apart from the hobos..." prompted Jess.

"The hobos... and the... what? I can't lip-read, you know."

"The gangs... and the car-jackings... and the shootings... and the muggings... and the—"

"Okay, okay! I get the picture. Give it a rest, will ya?" Eric spread his arms. "There's nobody here!"

His voice echoed down the street ominously. Eric glanced around him, listening. Jess noticed that his face was very pale.

"So you don't think it's quiet round here for a reason?" asked Jess, trying to keep the sarcasm out of her voice. Despite her bravado, a bolt of fear went through her at the thought. Steve had managed to cut the chain joining her handcuffs, cracking it open using the industrial-style bolt-cutters he kept in his trunk for when he got towed, but this hadn't calmed her nerves at all. She still felt just as vulnerable.

Jess shivered, hugging herself. The streets really were dead around here, with not even a breath of wind disturbing the thick ivy that grew over everything. There was no traffic noise, no chirping of crickets, not even the sound of passing aircraft to break the silence. It was warmer here than it had been down by the ocean, and there was the general smell of things rotting. The atmosphere was as still and as close as the air in a coffin.

Eric touched her arm in a half-hearted way. "It's late, you silly thing," he said. "That's why this place is so quiet. Everyone's in bed."

"Or dead," muttered Jess, staring at something in the gutter.

"Oh, grow up." Eric stuck out his chest. "You're such a wimp. There's nothing to be afraid of. You've just got to look like you... *what was that?*"

"That was me, throwing a stone at that rat. Listen. We can't stay here. We have to leave. Right now."

"You're telling me. Just point me in the direction of the taxi stop, and I'll be on my way."

"Like a cab's gonna stop here?" Jess gave a hollow laugh. "We might get a bus if we're lucky. I'm told that the 333 runs through the night." *I hope,* Jess added to herself. She gave Eric a flat stare. "Just... follow me. And *don't* make any more noise."

Before Eric could argue, Jess began moving, trotting back in the direction from which she had come. There was no point in escaping from the police if she just ended up getting mugged or picked up by some gang. Being stuck out here, especially with that preppy idiot bumbling along behind her, was not her idea of a good time. Couple of white college kids, stranded in Southside? That ought to give someone a laugh. Even if it wasn't so late at night, they'd still stick out a mile.

Stupid, stupid...

Jess walked a couple of blocks then stopped, casting around to try and get her bearings. She had a horrible feeling that she hadn't come here in a straight line. She'd dodged and ducked and changed directions more than once, anticipating being followed by a cop who never came. She was amazed that Eric was still with her. He must have had a good set of legs on him to have kept up with her.

Jess scuffed her feet as she walked along the road, trying not to look behind her. Had she made a right on this road, or a left? A sinking feeling in her stomach told her that she hadn't a clue.

She wished that Charlie was here. He was so brave. He'd know what to do...

"So where're we heading?"

"That way." Jess pointed straight ahead, hoping she sounded more confident than she felt. "And quit bugging me."

"Bugging you? Hello? You're lucky I'm here."

"Excuse me?" Jess stopped walking and stared at him.

"If I weren't here, you'd have no one to protect you," said Eric. He folded his arms smugly.

Jess actually laughed, although there was no humor in her eyes. "You think that you're protecting me?"

"Well, yeah." Eric shrugged. "You're just a girl. If you were out here by yourself you'd be dead by now. Especially dressed like that."

Jess spun around. "You think I planned on being here tonight?" she snapped, trying to keep her voice down. "What do you think, that I was standing in front of my wardrobe earlier on and thinking, hey, I know! The club we're playing at tonight is gonna collapse and kill all my friends, then I'll get accused of doing it, then I'll run away from the police and get involved in a car accident, and then I'll get stranded overnight in downtown Southside with no money and some stupid jerk from class who won't *shut the hell up*... I know, I think I'll wear a miniskirt and high heels tonight? Is that what you think?"

"Whoa, girl, take a chill pill! All I was saying was—"

"You know what? I don't care what you're saying. It's *your* fault that we're both here. If you hadn't gone raving to the police with your petty little accusations, we'd both be home in bed by now. Did you even think before you opened your mouth?"

"Of course I—"

"No, you didn't, did you? And now you're stuck here with me. Well, I'm sorry, but this is all your fault, and if you wanna get through tonight then you'd better stick with me and keep your mouth shut. Cause if you open it again, I'm leaving you here. I'm sure the cockroaches could use the company."

Jess span around on her heel and flounced off towards the nearest set of traffic lights. She was livid. That idiot. How dare he? What did he think he was playing at?

Then her brow furrowed as something else filtered through. She turned around. "And I'm not 'just a girl'!" she yelled back at Eric.

That didn't make any sense, she thought, as she stomped off. But hell, she couldn't just let that one ride. It wasn't her fault that she was tired.

Jess hadn't gone far before she realized that she was going the wrong way. There still weren't any signs, but there was a general thinning of houses and street lamps that told her she was definitely heading away from town. If anything, it seemed to be getting darker. There was a feeling of airlessness here, as though the streets were holding their breath. Her ears hummed in the silence.

Slowing down, Jess looked around anxiously for something that looked familiar. Hadn't she passed that pile of overflowing garbage bags before?

"Sp're'nych'nge?"

Jess nearly jumped out of her skin. She spun around, bringing her arms up into a boxing position, but there was no one behind her. She paused a moment, frozen to the spot, then looked down.

A skinny homeless man was lying at her feet in a doorway, wrapped in a threadbare blue blanket. His face and hands were sunburned, and he was wearing a tatty old cowboy jacket. He squinted up at her sleepily, and repeated his question.

"Sorry... no." Jess backed up a couple of paces and started walking away as quickly as she could. Adding creepy homeless people to the mix would not do wonders for her state of mind.

She came to a junction and paused, trying to mentally retrace her steps. She completely ignored Eric, who was following her at a distance, dragging his feet and muttering under his breath. She looked right, then left. Both routes looked the same. Perhaps she could navigate by the stars...

"One dime will show you the way."

Jess looked over her shoulder. The cowboy man was standing right behind her, looking at her in a hopeful fashion. His blanket was slung over one arm.

Jess made a show of patting her pockets to calm the thumping of her heart. She hadn't even heard the guy approach her. He didn't look dangerous, but you never knew, especially around these parts. "Sorry... I don't have a dime," she said truthfully.

"No dime—no time." The cowboy held up a finger and wagged it at her disapprovingly. "Man had no time. Now man gone."

"Look, I don't have any cash on me. Honest." said Jess, holding out her hands. What would it take to get rid of this guy? If she *did* have cash, would she be standing in this dump that smelt like a public toilet, talking to a madman? She glanced around surreptitiously, looking for an escape route.

"Hey, bozo. Take a hike." Eric stepped up beside Jess, his arms folded. He jerked a thumb over his shoulder. "You heard me, buddy. Beat it."

"What are you, my mother?" snapped Jess. Then she flinched as the homeless guy tapped her on the head with his knuckles. She turned round to face him. "What?"

"Girl going the wrong way," the cowboy admonished. "Girl must look out for signs. Signs will show the way."

"But there are no signs..." Jess stopped, struck with an idea. This guy lived around here. He had to know where they were. "Hey—can *you* show us the right way?"

"Show? No. Tell? Yes," said the cowboy. He stuck his thumbs into his worn belt, looking pensive. The wind blew through the holes in his blanket, making the frayed threads dance.

In the backyard behind him, a cat started yowling.

"Okay... okay, good." Jess backed away, thinking rapidly. "I need to get back to Main Street. Do you know where Main Street is?" Jess thought for a moment, trying to remember the layout of the city's grid system. She turned to Eric. "Help me out here. What roads hit Main Street?"

"Er..." Eric thought for a moment, regarding the cowboy with a look of deep distrust. "Pico... Venice... Rose... they all go the same way down to the ocean, as far as I know. But this guy won't have a clue—"

"Cool." Jess cut him off and looked up at the cowboy, hardly daring to ask. "Am I far?"

"Far? Yes. Very very far. Girl very lost."

"Shit." Jess blew out her cheeks in frustration. "Okay, think... Do you know if there's a cab firm round here? Or a motel?"

"Motel? No tell." The man grinned impishly and put his finger to his lips. "Shhh! The mice are sleeping."

"Okay, that's great." Jess rapidly ran her hand through her hair. "Look," she said. "You tell me how to get home, I'll bring you money tomorrow. *Lots* of money. I'll come back here. I promise."

"Yeah. Lots of money," added Eric. "We *promise*." He winced as Jess kicked him.

"Promise no good," said the cowboy, a look of sorrow in his eyes. "I *told* you. Girl want to get home safe? Girl follow the signs. Not got much time left."

"Are you even listening to me? I said there *are* no... Hey, where are you going?" Jess ran down the street after the man, and then stopped as he swung around to face her, excitement lighting up his sunburnt face.

"I know, I know!" he cried, hopping from foot to foot.

"You do?"

"Yes!"

"Tell me, then. Which way is home?"

He stepped up to her, shockingly close, and whispered in her ear: "There is no home. There is only death." He put a calloused hand on her shoulder and nodded grimly. "Soon."

"What?" Jess shook her head, pushing him away from her. He smelt like rum and old tobacco. "No. No death. Look, I just need to get home..." She shook herself, panic rising in her like a swarm of black flies. The dude was quite obviously crazy.

She waved to Eric, motioning for him to come over and join her. It was time to go.

"But girl died tonight. I *saw* you. *You* saw you."

Jess froze. "What?" she said, carefully.

"You heard. You died. He died. They all died." The cowboy flung out his arms in a sweeping motion. "Bang, crash! It all came tumbling down." He tilted his head and stared at her, curiosity sparking in his bright black eyes. "You're all dead, but still you walk. Pitter patter, pitter patter, like teeny tiny feet in the churchyard..." He cocked his head on one side, looking puzzled. "Tell me—how can that be?"

"Okay. That does it. You're crazy," said Jess, but she didn't walk away. The guy was actually making a horrible kind of sense, and he was creeping her out, big time. His mad ramblings had to be a coincidence, but at the same time, she wanted to hear more. "I'm not dead," she told him. "I'm here. I'm alive."

"Yes. Alive now, dead later. That's life. You all fall down." The cowboy looked at her sideways, then glanced back at Eric. "Girl next, then boy. You'll see. *I* see." He tapped the side of his nose meaningfully.

"Are you fucking with me?"

"Fucking with who?" Eric walked up to her, hands in pockets. "Come on. I'm bored. And I need the bathroom. Can we go now?"

"Shhh! What are you, twelve?" Jess scolded him. "Wait a minute."

"Why?"

"I don't know. He knows... something..." Jess said desperately. "Hey..." She touched the cowboy's shoulder as he started to walk away from her. "Could you tell my friend what you just said?"

The cowboy frowned, scratching at his sunburned face. "Girl said I was crazy. *Not* crazy. Just hot. Sun hot, moon cold." He glanced up at the sky. "Moon *good*..." He stared fixedly upwards for a moment, his eyes scanning the sky. Then his face crumpled, and he began to cry.

Jess looked up, drawn against her will. There was nothing but a streetlight above them. The stars were blotted out by the smog and the light pollution. There was no moon.

"That's great intel, Jess." Eric gave her a strange look. "Do you want a pen so you can write that down? Seriously. I'll radio Scully, get them to send in a chopper."

"But he said..." Jess stopped, biting her tongue. What was she thinking? They were miles from the club. There was no way this guy could know anything about what had happened to her tonight. Her brain was making connections where there were none. She was obviously over-tired.

She turned back to the cowboy, making a decision. "Look, I'm sorry. We've gotta head out now. It's late."

The cowboy looked up at her mournfully. "Yes. Girl go," he said, wiping at his eyes. "But I *told* you. Follow the signs. Signs are *everywhere*. Maybe then girl won't die."

"Yeah, that's great, cheers," said Jess. She turned around and began walking away from the cowboy. Perhaps if they walked far enough and fast enough, they'd come to somewhere recognizable before the gangs got them.

"Don't take the stairs," the cowboy called after her. "You tell him that!"

"I will."

Jess walked away as fast as she could, shaking her head. All she wanted to do was to get back to civilization. And light. And food. And warmth. And *bed*. All those lovely things she normally took for granted, which were now decidedly lacking in her life.

"Well. He was a regular barrel of laughs, wasn't he?"

"Shut up."

They reached the end of the street. The road ended in the car park of some kind of industrial packing facility, a low concrete building surrounded by enormous wooden packing crates. There was a high chain-link fence surrounding it, topped by barbed wire.

Jess stared through the wire, an idea popping into her head. It was late, and she was too tired to walk much further. She could feel it in her bones. Too much had happened tonight and she was exhausted. She had an overpowering urge to just lie down on the sidewalk and sleep, but she fought against it. They were miles from anywhere, and the further they walked, the more likely they were to bump into scary people.

Maybe if she could get into this place, she could find somewhere reasonably clean to lie down, just to rest her eyes for a bit? Perhaps there would even be a phone inside.

Jess's eyes brightened at the thought. She looked at the building afresh. There was no sign of human activity—no light on, no cars in the lot. Even if there wasn't a phone, the place looked reasonably safe. No one would bother them in there. They could crash here for the night, then figure out how to get home in the morning, when it was light and there were non-crazy people around.

It was a plan, of sorts.

Jess took hold of the fence and peered through. It was doubtful that she could break into the actual building itself, but there seemed to be a lot of packing crates and general junk lying around. Surely there would be some place for them to sleep? With a bit of ingenuity, she was sure they'd be just fine. And quite frankly, anyplace that didn't smell like dog pee would do nicely right now.

There was just one small obstacle to overcome, and it wasn't the fence.

"Eric?"

"Yes?"

"You ever been rock climbing?"

"Why do you ask?"

Jess gave him a small smile, one hand on the fence. She beckoned.

Eric shook his head violently. "You've gotta be kidding me!" He looked at her in horror. "I'm not climbing that! The wire's all dirty. What if I cut myself? I'll get blood poisoning and die horribly in the gutter! I'll never live it down!"

"I'm not asking you to climb anything. Just stay out here and stand guard. I'll be back soon—I promise." Jess gave an impish grin.

"Oh, no you won't!" snapped Eric. "You're not gonna leave me out... I mean, you're not going in there. Look, that sign says 'Keep Out'—it's private property!"

Jess reached out and ripped the sign down. "What sign?" She said sweetly. "Come on. There might be a phone."

"What if there's not? Then you've only gotta climb back out..." He stopped as he saw the look on her face. "Oh no! No way! I'm not sleeping in there tonight!"

"Fine. Suit yourself." Jess put a hand on the wire.

"You're crazy! It's a warehouse! You're not supposed to sleep in warehouses!"

"No. I'm right. You're the crazy one, hanging around out here."

Jess looked around her, then reached down and gingerly pulled an inch-thick pile of old newspapers out of a nearby garbage bag. A cockroach scurried urgently out of the pile. Jess pulled a face, ignoring Eric's look of utter disgust. She shook out the papers thoroughly, making sure they contained no more nasty surprises, and then tucked them into the waistband of her skirt and began expertly shinning up the fence. Her eyes burned with exhaustion, but she kept going. The sooner she got through this, the sooner she could get to sleep.

As she reached the top, she held on with one hand and pulled the thick wad of newspapers out of her belt. Carefully, she laid them on top of the barbed wire, and pressed down on them so that the sharp metal barbs dug into the first couple of layers, holding the papers in place. Then she cautiously took hold of the wire through the protective padding of the papers. Quickly, she pulled herself up and over the top of the fence. Her arms shook with the effort, but she ignored them and concentrated on climbing down the other side of the fence without falling on her head.

She landed safely on the sawdust-covered ground inside the yard, and gave a little nod of satisfaction back up at the fence.

"I can't believe you just did that," said a voice.

"I can't believe you're still out there."

"I can. And I just totally saw up your skirt." Eric grinned, safe behind the fence.

Without a word, Jess took hold of the fence and briskly shook it so that the papers fell off the top. She picked them up. "Now you're definitely not coming over."

"Suits me just fine."

Turning, Jess swept the loading yard with a glance, evaluating it for potential places to sleep. She'd done this before a couple of times down by the beach, usually obscenely late at night when she'd been too wasted or out-of-it to deal with the intricacies of cab-finding or walking home. She was even a little bit proud of her ability to find somewhere to crash where others wouldn't even think of venturing. It was part of her independent streak. She liked to think that she was a survivor. Hell, growing up on *that* side of town with *those* parents, she'd had to be.

But beside that, she also knew that she was taking a risk. And only an idiot would try to sleep outside Downtown. She wasn't completely stupid. If the crackheads didn't get you, the roaches would. She hoped that the ten-foot fence would keep her safe. If Eric wanted to stay outside then that was his problem.

An open packing crate to her left beckoned to her, and she walked over and glanced inside. Her face fell. She'd been hoping to find something she could use as bedding—maybe some packing paper or thick bubble-wrap—but instead the crate was filled with rectangular closed boxes. Annoyed, Jess reached in and pulled one out, slitting the top with a fingernail. Inside was a newly published safety manual.

Jess snorted. "A lot of good that's going to do me." Idly, she flicked it open at a random page, reading by the orange light of a nearby streetlamp. "Common work-related accidents... How to escape from a stopped elevator," Jess read. "Hmmm—handy." She tossed the book back into the box and began walking towards the building.

Perhaps there would be a way in. You never knew until you tried.

The main entrance to the building was locked and double-barred. Jess made her way around the building, one hand on the brickwork, until she came to the side door. She examined it carefully. It was made out of thin wooden planking reinforced with sheet metal. She saw that one side of the metal sheeting was coming away from the wood, and was struck by an idea.

Walking back over to the crates, she picked up a thick plank of wood that was lying on the ground nearby and levered the end into the gap at about waist-height. She leant back on it, twisting with all her might. After a moment's concerted effort, there was a loud snap. A piece of the door cracked away from the frame. Jess dropped the plank and pushed her hand through the gap she'd just made. Groping around, her fingers found the sliding deadbolt and she pulled it across.

The door swung open.

Damn, she was just too good at this. Jess bowed to an imaginary crowd of cheering onlookers and made her way into the building.

It was dark and damp inside, and smelled strongly of engine oil. Jess made her way along the dusty corridor. Pushing her way into the first room she came to, she groped for the light switch. The room was low ceilinged and cluttered, but that didn't matter, because there was a telephone on the desk.

Her tiredness forgotten, Jess darted across the room, picked up the receiver and quickly dialed the number of her parents' house. She leaned on the desk and listened while it rang two, three, four times. She cleared her throat. What could she say? Hello Mom, sorry to wake you up, guess what I've been up to tonight?

After the third ring, the line was answered. "This number is out of service. Your call could not be completed as—"

Jess hung up the handset with a clatter. Shit! Damn him, damn her dad for letting them get cut off again.

Could this night get any worse?

Even as the thought entered Jess's head, a voice inside told her not to think it, but it was too late. She froze, listening intently, but things seemed quiet enough.

She pushed the phone back on the desk, vowing fervently not to think such stupid thoughts ever again. Now, who else could she try calling?

Then a sixth sense twinged. After a moment, Jess turned around.

There was a dog standing behind her.

Normally, Jess liked dogs. She had fond childhood memories of running along the beach and throwing sticks into the sea for Saffy, her pet boxer.

She even had a fond spot for Mojo, Jamie's evil-smelling little Jack Russell, who had a dastardly tendency to curl up and fall asleep inside his bass drum, then scare the living bejesus out of them all by waking up and barking the place down when Jamie started playing.

But this was not a nice-looking dog.

In fact, it looked distinctly unpleasant.

It was huge, at least waist height, and was covered in thick, black, greasy fur. Jess had no idea what breed it was, but it had the definite look of something that had been bred for taking down some large, vicious wild animal. And worse, it looked half-starved. Its ribs stood out prominently along its powerful flank, and its head seemed too big for it. The animal's barrel-like chest was matted with a mixture of wood shavings and drool, as though it had been trying to eat the sawdust.

It wasn't wearing a collar.

Jess held up her hands, backing away. "Er... nice doggy..."

The dog stared at her fixedly, every muscle in its body quivering with alertness. Its head was almost unnaturally still, as it regarded her with every particle of its being.

Moving as slowly as she dared, Jess stretched out a hand towards the heavy desk lamp behind her. It wouldn't kill the animal, but thrown properly, it would probably slow it down for a minute, which was all the time she needed to escape.

She gritted her teeth, getting ready to make her move.

Talk about out of the frying pan...

Jess's fingers touched the thick power cord of the lamp. She began pulling it towards her, inch by careful inch. It hadn't moved more than half a foot when the ceramic base caught on something on the metal desk. Then the lamp tipped over with a loud clang.

"*BWUUFFF!*"

Jess froze, her ears ringing. The dog still hadn't moved, but she knew that sound. That wasn't just a bark. That was a threat. It meant, *This is my home, and you're in it, bitch.*

She tried to stay as still as possible. Perhaps if she didn't move, the dog would get bored and go away. After all, it wasn't like she was actively threatening it, was she?

The dog lifted its head and snuffed at the air, slobber hanging from its meaty jowls. Then slowly, its lips drew back. Jess watched as the hackles rose along its spine. It growled deep in its throat, hitting several different tones of fury before settling on what Jess guessed was a low D minor.

I guess that's what sleep deprivation will do to you, thought Jess, as she rapidly backpedaled across the room, trying to put as much space between herself and the dog as possible. She just wanted to keep out of range of those teeth.

The dog still didn't move. It just stood there, growling at her.

What now, dumbass, Jess asked herself, her back pressed up against the wall? It was uncanny how still that mutt was standing. She almost wished that it would try something, just to break the tension. She wished more than anything else that she had a tennis ball to throw. No dog could resist a tennis ball.

She glanced behind her, taking note of the small window set back into the wall. It was slightly ajar. It would be a tight fit, but if she could just jump up onto the desk, then maybe she could fit through the window.

Without breaking eye contact with the dog, she reached out and put a hand on the edge of the table, getting ready to make her move.

And the dog lunged.

SIX

Afterwards, the memories came back to Jess one at a time, like drops of blood falling from an arterial wound. She remembered the dog lunging—that had been the worst bit—but she couldn't remember exactly how she had escaped.

She remembered it in bits. One part of her mind held the perfect memory of the way her foot slipped in the sawdust as she tried to leap for the safety of the table. Her ankle had twisted, and it had hurt. A lot.

She'd yelled out, and the next moment she'd been jumping, scrambling for purchase on the smoothness of the table, as the dog barked at her in a frenzy. It had jumped up after her, and without even thinking she'd turned around and kicked it in the throat with all her might, sending it spinning off the table with a yelp and a slide of claws.

Another part of her remembered with icy clarity how the dog had bounced right back like a jack-in-the-box. It had come at her again an instant later as though it was on a spring, its teeth snapping shut an inch from her thigh, so close that she could feel the heat of its breath on her skin. Her kick had done little more than wind it.

It was a big dog, heavily muscled, and the fact that it was half-starved only made it more determined to get to her. The animal managed to get its front paws back up on the table, and it had stood there on its hind legs, snapping and snarling at her, while Jess hammered on the window with the heel of her hand, trying to force it open.

The window, of course, was stuck. She'd seen straight away that it had been painted open, the hard paint sealing it immovably in place.

This was just her luck, she remembered thinking. She'd come this far, only to be eaten by someone's pet pooch. And a decidedly mangy one at that. The smell coming off it had been appalling, reminding her of rotting meat. She hoped desperately that it wasn't the remains of the last intruder.

As she banged futilely on the window, she had suddenly heard the dog yelp. Its claws had scraped once on the table, then it had turned away from her and started baying in the direction of the door. Whirling around, Jess had caught a glimpse of Eric's face, looking very pale and very determined. Then he had vanished underneath the dog as it leapt at him.

Without thinking, Jess had snatched up the heavy metal desk lamp and jumped down off the table.

Raising it high above her head, she'd brought it down with all her might on the top of the dog's head. The animal had given a kind of high-pitched bark, and had slowly toppled over. It didn't get up again. There'd been a dent in the dog's skull where she had hit it, right in the middle of its powerful, wedge-shaped head. One paw had twitched, as though waving at her. Then it had been still.

Just for that one moment, Jess had felt sorry for the dog. She'd run a hand over its coarse fur as she dragged the massive carcass off Eric, and found herself wondering what its name was. She doubted that it even had one.

Eric had been bitten quite badly, but he was all right. Jess had known he was all right because he was still breathing, but it had been a while before he'd stopped hyperventilating long enough to tell Jess to stop asking him if he was okay.

The next thing she'd known, there'd been a bang on the front door and a team of five policemen had burst into the warehouse. Aiming an incredible number of guns at them, they'd informed them that they were trespassing, and that they had the right to remain silent.

And that had been the end of that. There had been a lot of banging around and shouting while the police sorted out the whole business of the dead dog, which seemed to cause them a great deal of excitement, more so than their discovery of trespassers in the warehouse. There was a lot of talk about animal rights, and a search had been conducted of the facility, leading to the discovery of two more equally battered hounds, which were found wandering loose in the boxing plant. One of them had bitten the police chief on the leg, and had earned itself a swift kick in the head for its troubles.

Their night had been further enlivened when the warehouse owner himself had shown up, woken by all the cop cars zooming past his corner house onto his lot. He was currently in the back of a second police cruiser, protesting to all that would listen to him that the dogs weren't his, and even if they were, they weren't really attack dogs, they were just defending themselves, and anyway, the reason the dogs didn't have collars or licenses was because they weren't his anyway, so why should the fact that they were in his warehouse with no food or water automatically mean that he knew anything about them?

Jess settled back into the seat of the police cruiser. It was surprisingly comfortable for a cop car. There was air conditioning, and the inside had a delightful new car smell to it.

Jess stretched lightly, wriggling down into the leather of the seat. This time, her hands were cuffed in front of her. For some reason, this made her inordinately happy.

For the first time that night, she was almost comfortable.

And she felt... safe.

She couldn't stop yawning as the car rocked and bumped its way up the 10 freeway. Compared to the assorted horrors that lurked outside in the night, an express trip back to the police station sounded almost cozy. Outside the window, the sky was the greeny-gray color of dawn.

Eric sat beside her, holding a blood-soaked handkerchief to his ear and wincing. He removed it and examined the blood. There was a lot of it.

"So, you wanna go out again tomorrow night?" he asked, after a little time had passed.

Jess was quiet for a moment. "I'd rather die," she said, with some consideration.

She gazed out of the window for a long moment. "No, I take that back. I'd rather *you* die. I've got a lot of sleep to catch up on."

"No? You sure?" Eric tried to smile. "Hey, we can both keep the handcuffs on. It'll be twice as kinky." He winked at her.

Jess looked at him blankly for a moment, then the corner of her mouth twitched as she was reminded inescapably of Jamie.

"Aha! I saw that! You smiled."

"I wasn't smiling at you. I was just smiling in general." Jess paused, struck by a thought. "And what is it with men and the handcuff thing?"

Eric shrugged, dabbing the blood out of his sandy hair. "So I'm a man now, am I? Not a jerk, or a dipshit or a dumbass?"

"I didn't say you were a dipshit." Jess rubbed her throat thoughtfully. "But a jerk and a dumbass? Definitely. That's not a reputation you can just throw off by saving someone's life, you know."

Eric thought about this. "But I did."

"What?"

"Save your life," said Eric. He leaned forward in his seat, rubbing his hands together. "You owe me big time, little lady." He licked his lips. "I'm thinking, maybe a couple of cinema dates, night at the theatre, perhaps some dinner somewhere, before we—"

"But I saved your life first. That cancels it out." Jess sat back smugly.

Eric's mouth opened and closed a couple of times while he tried to work this one out. "My life? You mean, when you hit that pup on the head with the desk lamp?" He shook his head. "There was no need for you to do that. I could've got away, no probs. I was just about to do this incredible martial arts move where you grab—"

"No, back at the club."

"The club?" Eric frowned. "How did you save my life at the club?"

"You followed me out. Just before it collapsed. Remember?"

Eric shook his head. "Now you're really tripping. I *told* you—I was going to leave anyway. That whole thing with the waitress? Big coincidence. I would've got out in time."

"If that's what you believe." Jess stretched her legs out in front of her, and gave a sigh that seemed to come from the very depths of her soul. "It's been one of those nights."

Jess slid down in her seat and tried to relax, listening to the deep bass rumble of the car's engine. It flowed up through her body, seeming to vibrate in her bones. Jess closed her eyes in concentration. The note of the engine was pitched in... what was that? B minor, she guessed, shifting down to a solid G whenever the driver changed down a gear.

That was the one problem with being in a band, Jess thought. Everything came to sound like music.

She hadn't even known the names of the notes until Tony had painstakingly taught her to read music, a year and a half ago.

Now, she saw music in everything. One of her first exercises had been transcribing the conversations of her friends onto sheet music. It was as silly exercise, but it had taught her to differentiate between subtle tones, an important skill for a lead singer. Her mother's calls had provided her with the most amusement, her morning cry of, "Jessie! Get the fuck u-up!" translating nicely onto the page as E-C, G-G-G E-C.

For a Sixties flower child, her mother would have been proud to know that she called her daughter out of bed using the three most dominant chords in rock.

Not that she would have cared, of course, but it was still nice to know.

Then Jess frowned. The rumble of the engine was shaking something loose in her mind. There was something stuck at the very back of her consciousness, like a Christmas decoration discovered whilst redecorating in mid July.

Jess concentrated hard. What was it? Just for amusement value, she tried to identify the key of her thoughts. A moment later, she shivered. Her thoughts were all pitched in a very definite, and very menacing, F sharp.

In the front, the cop driver idly clicked on the radio. AC/DC's "Hell's Bells" filled the car. Jess winced, dragged out of her trance. The cop hurriedly turned down the radio, but left it on, playing quietly in the background. He started nodding his head to the beat.

Suddenly, Jess knew what was wrong. Her eyes snapped open and she gasped. "This isn't over."

"Well," said Eric. "I'm sure there'll be a court case, and we'll get fined, and you'll probably face a whole shitload of charges for what you did to that cop—"

"No, I don't mean that. I mean, this. Us."

Eric's eyebrows zoomed to the top of his head. "There's an 'us' now?" He started to smile.

"No, you jerk. It's not all about you. Get over it. I just have this feeling..."

"You and me both, baby."

"Zip it. I'm talking about this whole situation." Jess lowered her voice to a bare whisper. "I told you. I *knew* what was going to happen back at the club."

"That's because you planned it with all your psycho mafia friends... Ow!"

"Shut up. It's *because*, I had this really strong feeling about what was going to happen. And I'm having it again, now. I think what happened tonight is going to have repercussions for all of us, for a long time."

"And you say that because...?"

Jess didn't even bother to reply. Instead, she angled her body away from Eric, gazing out of the window at the speeding landscape. They were closer to the coast now, and the sky was filled with an orange haze as the streetlights lit up the rolling night-time fog.

Jess spoke softly, almost as if she were afraid of what she was saying. "It's like, when you go on a rollercoaster—it's scary going up the big hill, then you get a little respite at the top, and you think, hey, this isn't going to be so bad." She stared out of the window, her expression fixed. "Then you look down at the drop and you start screaming. But you know that no matter how loud you scream, there's no way you can stop it."

"I hate rollercoasters." Eric shuddered. "They scare the crap outta me."

"That's because you're a big baby. Anyway, that's how I feel at the moment. I can't explain it. I just feel so... powerless."

Eric thought for a moment. "Is this all about that bouncer guy?"

"Yes. Maybe. I don't know." Jess twisted her cuffed hands around in her lap helplessly, staring at her feet.

Eric shrugged. "Ah, that was just a coincidence. Dude was tired, probably going too fast. Who else was awake but us, at that time of night?" He spread his hands. "It could've happened to anybody."

"But it didn't happen to anybody. Don't you see? It happened to *him*." Jess sat forward in her seat, her eyes lighting up with worry. "He escaped death because of me, then got killed anyway. It was like, fate stepped in and took him back."

"You think that this is all about you? Please!"

"No." Jess chewed fretfully on her lip. "I think it's all about *us*. I think that we should all be careful for a while, take it easy, you know, stay out of harm's way."

"Or what?"

"I'm not sure. It could be bad. I just have this... this feeling..."

"You mean, you think the old Grim Reaper's going to come charging after us with his great big scythe, shouting, 'Get back here, you pesky kids'?" Eric grinned.

"That's about the size of it."

Eric looked at Jess for a moment, and his grin faded a little. Psycho-girl seemed deadly serious for once.

Eric rubbed a hand across his mouth and looked at Jess earnestly. Despite her exhaustion and her smudged makeup, he thought that she was still quite beautiful.

And at this time of night, and then only because it was this time of night, what she was saying made sense. Perfect sense. And if they were all doomed to die, then there was only one thing he had left to do.

He cleared his throat.

"So about that date..." he said.

The next morning, Jess awoke to the sound of bird-song. For a delicious slice of time she lay there, eyes shut, luxuriating in the feeling of the sunlight shining across her face. It was very bright sunlight, so intense that it made the insides of her eyelids glow red. She pictured a beautiful summer's day out-side—blue sky, green grass, bees buzzing through the flowers, the whole works

A feeling of timeless contentment filled her.

Jess stretched, then yawned hugely. It had to be quite late in the day for the sun to be up that high, she thought. That must mean it was the weekend.

Jess smiled, her eyes moving beneath her closed lids. Weekends were *good*. Weekends meant two whole solid, blissful days of not-working, of doing what she wanted when she wanted, of shopping and friends and fun. It meant days out on Melrose Avenue with Cassie and the others, window-shopping for punk gear in all the cool little boutiques and outlets, having dinner in some funky café with an outdoor patio and local artists' work on the walls. It meant hitting a club on Sunset Strip at night, seeing some cool new band, and hanging out on the beach all day beforehand, maybe getting a new bikini, a bit of a tan, and maybe a henna tattoo.

Jess loved the beaches. She loved everything about them, from the quirky little shops and rides on the Santa Monica pier, to the colorful craziness of Venice. She loved to bodysurf in the strong waves, and to maybe check out a hunky lifeguard or two in the process...

Ahh, the lifeguards. Jess's mouth curved into a lazy smile. There was this one older guy, who was just sooo cute... he was new on the lifeguard station just past Ocean Park, and always winked at her whenever she went past in her bikini. He had a body to die for, bright green eyes, and such an honest smile. What was his name, Bill something-or-rather...?

Jess's carefree smile faded, and a few seconds later she frowned, her eyes still closed. Bill... Bill... That name reminded her of something. Something bad. She didn't know what it was, but the echoes of the thought sliced through her happiness like a cold knife through warm jelly.

Jess coughed, running her tongue thoughtfully round the inside of her lips while she tried to catch hold of it. Her mouth tasted like she'd been sucking on an old sock all night. Sleepily, she reached out a hand towards her bedside cabinet for the big glass of water she kept there.

"Ow."

Jess reeled in her arm and sucked groggily on her fingers. Then she stretched out her other hand and groped around in front of her, her brow creasing in confusion. She traced her fingers over the rough concrete wall just a foot from her face. What was that doing in her bedroom?

Her consciousness slowly expanded to take in the information from her other senses. For starters, her back ached. She felt as if she'd been lying on a log all night. She rolled over and was rewarded with a series of clicks and pops from her back as her spine straightened. Jess winced. That wasn't good, she thought, shivering. It was surprisingly cold in her bedroom. Odd—she didn't remember leaving the bedroom window open. And then there was that dull buzzing in her ears, like a distant swarm of bees heard through a mattress.

There was no escaping the fact that something didn't add up here.

Jess fought against the urge to open her eyes, some long-buried part of her brain screaming at her to keep them closed, to hold onto this feeling of happy ignorance for as long as possible.

But it was no good. She had to wake up some time. It might as well be now.

Sleepily, and with great reluctance, Jess opened her eyes.

The first thing she saw was a face, hovering right above hers.

It was a very familiar face.

"Morning," said Charlie Delgado.

"Yargh," replied Jess, rolling over and falling off her bunk. She landed on her knees on the concrete floor of the police cell.

She stayed there for a moment, frozen in place, while assorted parts of her brain whirred and clicked and tried to protect themselves from this new and distressing reality. There was a wooden bench in front of her. And bars.

She was in a police cell.

Why the hell was she in a police cell?

It was no good. Memory after memory slammed into her head. Jess squeezed her eyes tight shut, groaning, as the full horror of it hit her.

She remembered.

Opening her eyes a crack, Jess stared at the floor in front of her. It was made of sanded concrete, clinically bare and cheaply constructed. She blinked, trying to focus. A big black spider scuttled away from her in alarm, vanishing into a crack in the wall. Above her, the bright strip lighting buzzed.

Her assessment of the room finished, Jess looked up at Charlie. He smiled down at her, his head on one side, then reached out a hand towards her.

"Sorry. I didn't mean to startle you."

"Yeargh?"

"I thought that you were asleep. You looked so peaceful. Here, let me help you."

Jess hesitantly took hold of Charlie's hand. It was warm and dry, and his grip felt wonderfully firm. She let him pull her to her feet. She stood there for a minute, swaying, then sat back down heavily on the wooden bench.

She stared at Charlie. Of all the nights she dreamed of waking up and seeing his face first thing in the morning, this wasn't quite how she'd pictured it.

There had been a definite lack of bars, for one thing.

"Where... What...?"

"Eric called me. Said you guys needed a hand."

"Who?"

"Eric. That dude." Charlie pointed. In the next cell, Eric paused in his dressing and gave her a little wave. Despite his less-than-ideal surroundings, she saw that he'd folded all his clothes neatly and arranged them in little piles according to size.

Weirdo.

The next thing she noticed was that the door to his cell was open, as was her own.

What was going on? Was this another dream?

Jess cleared her throat, her mind informing her gleefully that dream or not, her hair was sticking up in seventeen different directions at once, and that she was in the same room as Charlie Delgado. She patted at it desperately with a hand.

Charlie beamed down at her. The stresses and strains of the night had obviously taken their toll on him, as they had on everyone, but he was still, well... he was still Charlie. He still had the same amiable, thousand megawatt grin, the same bright and breezy demeanor, the same floppy, glossy hair. Even the fact that one arm was wrapped in a white bandage didn't detract from the picture. It was like a little badge of vulnerability that made Jess's heart melt, while she told her brain, shut up, shut up! You *know* what he's like, really. *Everyone* knows what he's like...

But somehow, she just didn't care. She smiled wanly up at him, and he grinned back. His blue eyes were a little bloodshot and crumpled with lack of sleep, but otherwise, he was looking good.

And in her newly-woken-and-vulnerable state, Jess couldn't help but look. Charlie was dressed casually in expensive-looking khaki pants and combat top, with a woven leather belt and matching wristbands. He looked as though he was just on his way to a hip-hop slam rather than visiting a friend in a police cell. If anything, the fact that he was in a police cell made him even better looking. Charlie was the kind of person who instantly made their surroundings look like a backdrop at a model shoot.

And here she was, looking like a cheap date the morning after. Jess started self-consciously combing her fingers through her tangled hair. She felt entirely gross. Her skin was cold and damp, and her hair felt greasy. She wasn't even going to think about what her makeup might be doing. "So," she said, trying to get her brain into gear and wishing desperately for a hot shower. "What's happening...?" She tried to refrain from adding, "Dude."

"We've got some news for you," said Eric.

"News?" Jess sat up in alarm, all her senses swinging into full scale alert. "Is this the kind of news I'm going to want to hear, or should I cover my ears and start screaming right now?"

She saw Eric and Charlie exchange looks. "Well, it's kind of—interesting—news. You might want to wait for the sheriff to tell you," said Charlie, scratching at the bandage on his arm.

"Sheriff? No. Tell me now. I want to know."

"Don't you want to wake up a bit first?" Charlie looked concerned.

"I said, tell me now." Jess sat forward on the bench, trying to keep the tremor out of her voice. "What is it? Is it about last night?"

"Well, yes and no..."

"Don't tell her. I'm still pissed at her. Do you know what she called me last night?"

"Eric!"

"I was only asking you out. A lot of girls would be glad to have—"

"Oh my God! I don't care!"

"Eric, man. Come on. I think she needs to know this." Charlie sat down on the bench next to Jess. "It *is* about last night." He said carefully. He took hold of Jess's hand and looked at her earnestly. "They think they've found out why the club fell down."

"They have?" Jess squeaked. She cleared her throat and tried again. "They have? What caused it?" she said in a more normal sounding voice.

With immaculate timing, the door swung open and the sheriff walked in. Jess sat back on the bench, narrowing her eyes at him. She was starting to associate him with Bad Things. She watched as he pulled out a sheaf of paperwork and leafed through it, his face grim.

He turned to Jess. "Congratulations. You made bail."

"I did?" Jess turned to Charlie. "How?"

In reply, the sheriff wordlessly tossed her the morning paper. Jess looked at it blankly, then unfolded it with a gasp. Pictures of the club were plastered all over the front page. Someone had obviously been working through the night to get this edition out in time. She looked up at the sheriff and tapped the page, licking her dry lips. She had to know. "Do they know yet what caused it?" she asked nervously.

The sheriff's lined face crumpled even further. "We have our suspicions." He nodded to the end cell. "One of them's sitting over there."

Jess turned to see a young female police officer sitting on the bench in the cell. She was sitting so still that Jess hadn't even noticed her before now. She was staring straight ahead out of the window, wearing a sorrowful expression.

She immediately recognized her as the officer from the club. "Her? What did she do?"

"What *didn't* she do?" The sheriff pulled out another sheet of paper and squinted at it. "Says a lot of curious stuff here. Incorrect police procedure. Discharging a firearm without due care. Failure to obtain correct search warrants before breaking and entering."

"What's that got to do with anything?" asked Jess.

"Could be everything. Could be nothing. We don't know yet. Preliminary reports suggest that the collapse of the warehouse into the club was caused by a fire under the floor."

"And how is that her fault?"

"That's just it." The sheriff ran a hand along his moustache, narrowing his eyes at the officer. "Somebody called the station in the middle of the night to report hearing a gunshot. We checked out the remains of the building and found a bullet hole in the back door and the remains of the floor matching the specs of a Colt 45 round exactly. Officer Hewlett here is field equipped with a Colt 45. She was picked up in the vicinity of the club following its collapse. Upon questioning, she admitted to discharging her weapon illegally to gain entry to the club via the back door. The fire is thought to have started in the same area."

"Why didn't she just come in round the front, like everybody else?"

"Officer Hewlett was under the impression that she is special and that police work should be like it is in the movies." The sheriff held up his hand to silence the officer, who started to protest. "However, that is not the case, and now, she has now come to understand that." The sheriff's expression hardened. "The disaster site is currently under forensic investigation to establish the exact cause of the fire, but in the meantime, I'll hazard a guess that young Marina here could be looking at some very steep penalties indeed."

In her cell over by the window, Officer Hewlett hung her head.

Jess felt an enormous weight lift off her shoulders. She knew that she should feel bad for the police officer, but for the moment, all she felt was relief that the blame had been removed from her. "So... can I go home now?"

"Bail has been granted, yes," said the sheriff. "We have been unable to contact your parents, so this young man has kindly offered to pay the two thousand dollar bail and take both of you home."

Jess blinked. She was going home with Charlie.

He thought that she was worth two thousand dollars...

"However," the sheriff went on. "You are still guilty of a number of lesser offenses, for which you shall stand trial at a later date. I am going to recommend community service." He picked up his hat. "However, for now, we have work to do. I must get going." He gave Jess an old fashioned look. "You do remember where the door is, don't you?"

It was later. Jess was warm again.

"You sure you're all right in there?"

"Yeah—I'm fine!" Jess called out, sliding down further in the bath and reaching for the soap. It was incredible how the simplest of things—soap and hot water—could seem so wonderfully luxurious. She worked the soap into a rich lather on her arms and ducked them under the water, washing off the grime of the night. A rubber duck floated nearby, bobbing up and down in the foamy water and giving her a look of plastic amusement.

"Okay, then. I'll be out in the garage if you need anything."

"Thanks!"

The world turns, then turns again, thought Jess, settling back into the water and glancing around her appreciatively. A few short hours ago she had been on the run from the police, wanted for suspected manslaughter.

Now she was at Charlie Delgado's house, taking a bath.

She thought about that.

She was in his actual house, in his actual bathtub. The same bathtub that he was naked in on a regular basis.

Jess did her very best not to squeak.

Charlie had such a cool bathroom, she thought lazily, looking around through half-closed eyes. It was tastefully decorated with white tiled walls and chrome fittings that wouldn't have looked out of place in a five-star hotel. There was a predominance of marble in the décor, a hairdryer hanging from a hook by the bath, and an abundance of fluffy white towels hanging from heated towel rails. Jess knew that they were heated because she'd backed into one while she was getting undressed. Her shriek had bought Charlie and half the household running to the door. He'd laughed and told her that it happened a lot.

Jess winced as she remembered the bathrooms of the guys she normally hung out with. The last time she'd been round Jamie's house for rehearsals, she'd felt compelled to run out to the supermarket, even at ten-to-midnight, to buy toilet cleaner, disinfectant wipes, a laundry basket, a screwdriver to fix the broken lock, and most importantly, toilet paper.

Why did guys never ever have toilet paper in their bathrooms? Jess scratched her head and shrugged to herself. It was one of the eternal mysteries of guyhood. It was as though there was some kind of unwritten agreement between all men aged eighteen to thirty, specifying that if they wanted to use each other's bathrooms, they should bring their own toilet paper. And more importantly, that they should never, under any circumstances, tell any women about this agreement. This would ensure that any women visiting would be forced to buy them toilet paper, which they'd then remove from the bathroom and squirrel away under lock and key, so saving them from ever having to buy any themselves.

Jess shook her head, casting her eye over the artistically arranged cactus plants on Charlie's windowsill. This guy not only had toilet paper, but he had pot plants. And colorful little bottles of conditioner. And a shower curtain that wasn't even semi-pornographic.

That fact alone meant that she was probably going to have to marry him.

The water lapped around her ears, and Jess closed her eyes and slid under the water for a moment, holding her breath in the clanging depths as she washed the shampoo out of her hair. Suds billowed out around her, turning the water cloudy. Emerging, Jess squeezed herself out a second handful of fruit-scented shampoo and reapplied it, massaging it vigorously into her scalp. She couldn't believe how good it felt to be clean again. It was as though she was washing away the events of the last twenty-four hours away, emerging clean and new with a fresh chance at life.

Lying back, she closed her eyes and felt the warmth of the water surround her, soothing her tired muscles and soaking the grime off her skin.

The water felt so good...

Slowly, she began to drift off to sleep.

A breeze blew in through the open bathroom window. Above her, the hairdryer started to swing on its hook.

* * *

Outside, Charlie slung his bag of tools over his shoulder and clanked up the steps towards his garage. He needed to do something while that chick took a bath, or he'd start thinking about last night again. Eric had fled home, leaving him alone with his thoughts, which were not something that Charlie wanted to face right now.

Clicking "Open" on his remote control, he waited while the garage doors hummed smoothly open.

And there she was. The love of his life.

Tossing his keys onto the back bench, Charlie gazed adoringly at the sleek black car inside, finding himself growing misty-eyed with pride. At twenty-one, not only was he lucky enough to have his own bachelor apartment in the prestigious Westwood, paid for by his doting father, but he'd also recently acquired a mint condition 1970 Chevy Camaro. He'd even got a bar job and paid for some of it, although in the back of his head, he realized that the part he'd paid for with his entire summer's labors had probably been one of the hubcaps.

This car sure was a beauty. It was midnight black, with leather bucket seats and chromed white-walled wheels. Ever since he had taken ownership of it three weeks ago, it had been all Charlie had thought about. It occupied his thoughts like a beautiful woman, and called to him just as often. Whenever he had a spare moment, he found his feet automatically carrying him down to the garage, just to sit and look at it, to make sure that it was real. He felt like if he didn't, it would evaporate like so much gold dust, leaving him with nothing but an empty parking spot.

He was *so* proud of that car. He'd spent a week reorganizing the garage so that everything was away from the car, so it didn't get scratched. He'd recently installed shelves along all four side of the garage, stacking them high with all the boxes of junk that seemed to accumulate in the corners of the garage. Anything sharp or potentially scratchy—shears, gardening tools and so on—had gone up in big wooden boxes on those shelves. He'd wanted a Chevy ever since he was a little boy, and now he finally had one, he was damn well making sure that nothing could possibly happen to damage it.

However, as with all vintage cars, it was seriously high-maintenance. Charlie had quickly grown used to coming down here with his bag of tools, tuning this and tightening that, just to make sure his baby was kept in tip-top condition. He enjoyed it more than anything else he could think of.

Well, *almost* anything else he could think of...

Right now he was adjusting the fan belt, which seemed to be slipping. Tomorrow's job was oiling the hand brake, which had taken to sticking from time to time. It wasn't too serious. It was one of those vaguely annoying things that could wait a day or two while he attended to more important things.

Charlie smiled. Funny old car. He loved its little quirks.

Dumping his tools down on the work surface, Charlie popped the hood. Ducking his head inside, he began work, pausing every so often to mop his brow. It was coming up to five in the afternoon, and the temperature was still well in the eighties.

Man, was it hot. Charlie straightened up, wiping
his forehead on a sleeve. Working with one arm in
a sling was seriously cramping his style. His arm
was feeling a lot better today, but it still ached like
hell where the muscle was bruised. Damn fire
truck. He still couldn't feel one of his fingers. The
doctor had assured him that feeling would return
soon when the bruising went down, but for now, it
was just another little annoying thing he had to deal
with.

After a minute or so of work, Charlie turned and
pulled a large bottle of iced water out of the nearby
cooler. It was just too hot, but he didn't want to stop
working. Pulling the cap off the bottle, he took a
deep draught as he regarded the car, mopping his
forehead with a polishing rag as he gazed down at
the car lovingly.

She really was a beauty. Perhaps he'd take that
chick for a spin in her later. What was her name
again? Tess?

Charlie swished the water around his mouth
reflectively, then swallowed and opened the passenger door, tossing his jacket inside. Yeah. He'd
take the girl for a drive. It was a nice evening for it,
and it'd take his mind off the unpleasant events of
last night. He'd cruise up the Pacific Coast highway,
maybe stop off at the Malibu Inn for a cocktail and a
romantic sunset on the beach... it could be a very
entertaining evening.

Charlie gave a half smile. She was an odd one, that
Tess, but she was kind of pretty, in a scruffy kind of
way. He remembered what Eric had told him about
her escapades last night, and was now curious to

find out more about her. Apparently, she'd had, like, a vision of what was going to happen. That was seriously strange.

Charlie wondered vaguely whether or not she'd sleep with him.

"Halloo-oo!" Charlie!"

Charlie rolled his eyes and tossed the rag up onto a shelf. *Amber.*

He watched her come up the garden path, staggering slightly in her hot pink miniskirt and high heels. Her handbag was pink, as was the dangling cord of the headphones she constantly wore.

Charlie sighed. The girl had a great figure, true, but in spite of that, he was starting to get a little tired of her, if the truth be told. He remembered how she'd clung to him like a frightened puppy all the way home from the police station last night, refusing to leave his side until he'd told her to go home and get some rest. He had to actually order her a taxi to get her to leave so he could get a little shut-eye. She'd kept blubbering about the fact that her friend Heather was dead, and he couldn't sleep with her crying in his ear all night.

It was understandable that she should be so upset about Heather, he supposed. But it was just a little strange considering the fact that the two of them usually couldn't stand one another.

Funny thing, that, he thought. He knew that he was the most popular boy in class, and he also knew that Amber and Heather had long vied with one another for his affections. Each one knew that the other one wanted him like crazy, but rather than admit that they hated each other, they had instead pretended to be the very best of friends, just so that if one was invited out by him, the other could come along too without feeling the slightest trace of guilt.

That was the trouble with girls, Charlie thought. They kept their friends close, and their enemies even closer. It could make for some really interesting nights.

But Charlie didn't mind their little games. In fact, he actively encouraged them. It suited him down to the ground to have two girls rather than just one as a date, and he had the added perk of knowing that they'd do just about anything to out-do one another and claim Charlie's heart as their prize.

Well, Charlie reflected wryly, it wasn't his heart that they each regularly claimed, but as far as he was concerned, any other part of his body was just as good. In fact, he'd invited both of them out with him to the club last night, intending to leave with whichever one of them put out first, but his plans had been seriously scuppered by the roof falling in on their heads.

Charlie took a moment to reflect on that. *Jeez. That was one close call.* If that Tess girl hadn't stopped the show when she did, he supposed that they would all be dead right now. That would seriously suck.

And worse, if he'd died, he wouldn't be able to drive this beautiful car any more.

He shuddered at the thought.

Amber reached the top of the path and ducked her head around the edge of the garage. "Knock knock! Charlie? Oh! There you are! I didn't know if you were in or not."

"Hey, girl," Charlie worked up what he hoped was a genuine-looking smile. He was doing car stuff right now. He didn't particularly want to be disturbed. He hoped that Amber wasn't staying long. He picked up a wrench and swung it idly. "What's up, kiddo?"

"Nothing much. I just thought I'd swing by to check on how you were doing."

"I'm doing fine, pumpkin," said Charlie, shrugging. He *was* doing fine. Working on his car was his way of dealing with stuff, of taking all the stressful crap out of his mind and turning it into a fixed carburetor or a newly oiled bearing. The way he saw things, shit happened, and you could choose to either deal with it and move on, or drag it out, feeling sorry for yourself until everyone around you got sick of you.

Charlie put down his wrench as Amber slipped round the side of his car. He saw her metal belt buckle make contact with the paintwork as she slid around towards him, and suppressed a grimace of genuine pain. Some people just didn't think...

Despite this, he hugged her, then kissed her passionately as she pressed herself up against him. She held onto him for a long time. When she pulled away, he saw to his dismay that her cheeks were wet with tears. "I just can't believe she's dead," whispered Amber. Her body started to shake.

Oh, Christ, here we go again, thought Charlie, as he stroked her hair in what he hoped was a comforting fashion. This was going to take time, more specifically, his time. Didn't she have any girlfriends available to work this stuff out with?

Out loud he said: "I know. I can't believe it either. It seems just like yesterday that Heather was here with us..."

"It *was* yesterday that she was here!" wailed Amber. "It's just so unfair!" Sniffing, she reached up and dabbed primly at her eyes, being careful not to smudge her mascara. Then she stepped away from Charlie, reaching into her purse for a tissue.

As she did so, she knocked over an open carton of engine oil that was sitting beside the car. Dark brown oil gushed out, running beneath the wheels of the Corvette and pooling on the garage floor.

"Oh! I'm sorry." Amber bent down to try to pick it up.

"Here, let me." Charlie bent down and rescued the carton. Most of it had spilled, running away in a thin oily line down under the car and out through the door.

He shook the carton, then peered in. It was nearly empty. *That was just great.* "Not to worry," he lied. "There wasn't much left anyway. I'll stop by at the gas station later and get some more."

"You're going out later?" Amber's tears immediately stopped and she perked up, looking hopeful. She hooked her fingers into Charlie's belt and pulled him towards her. "Can I come? Where are you going?"

"Nowhere, sweetie." Charlie carefully unhooked her fingers, trying not to let his irritation show. "I didn't have any plans to go out."

"But your jacket's in the car." Amber pointed.

Charlie looked. His jacket was indeed in the car. "So?"

"So, you always put your jacket in the car if you're going out later, silly. You forget it otherwise, and then you get cold when the sun goes down." She fluttered her eyelashes at him.

Charlie shrugged, irritation rising within him like steam. What was with Amber today? She was never normally this observant.

Turning, he cupped her face in his hands, trying to inject some warmth into his voice. "I'm sorry, sugar. I just don't feel like going out this evening. I'm kind of tired, you know, after last night and everything. But hey, thanks for dropping round." Pecking her on the cheek, he turned away and picked up his wrench.

"Perhaps we can stay in together, then." Amber stepped up behind Charlie as he began working, and pressed a suggestive kiss on his neck. She smelt like coffee and lip-gloss. "I could go to the store, get a bottle of wine, maybe some strawberries..."

"You know, I'd love to, cupcake, but let's do it some other time. I'm really not in the mood." Charlie shrugged, idly picturing Jess up in his bathtub. She'd been in there for hours. Perhaps she was waiting for him to join her? He should go up there as soon as he'd finished fixing the car. It could be really worth his while...

"Why not?"

"What?"

"Why don't you want to hang out tonight?"

"I do!" Charlie was still thinking about Jess naked. He blinked, trying to focus through the swirling images of his internal porno show. "I'm just... not in the mood right now, you know." He thought for a minute, then brightened. "Can you drop by tomorrow?"

"What if I don't feel like dropping by tomorrow?" Amber looked away from Charlie. Her bottom lip began to quiver.

"C'mon, Amber baby, don't be like that." Charlie reached out for her, but she pulled away from him angrily.

"Heather's dead! Do you even care?"

"Don't be silly. Of course I care."

"Then why don't you want to be with me?" Amber blew her nose loudly. "We should be going through this together."

"But we are, honey," *Unfortunately*, Charlie added to himself. He pulled out a tissue and smiled winningly. "Look, I'll spend all tomorrow with you. How's that? We'll go to the pier, go on that big old wheel she liked so much... maybe throw some rose petals off the top for her, into the sea. Heather loved her roses, remember? And then we can... what? Why are you looking at me like that?"

"Heather hated roses! She said they smelt like her grandmother's mothballs! *I'm* the one that loves roses!" Amber's face crumpled. "I like the pink ones. Not that you've ever remembered..." She began to cry.

"That's what I meant! I—"

"Do you even care about me?"

"Of course I do! Look, Heather, sweetheart..."

"My name is Amber! And don't you dare 'sweetheart' me, Charlie Delgado! Not now. Not ever. My friends were right. You're just a big loser and you're mean, and you don't love me. You never did love me. You don't even care if I live or die."

Spinning on her heel, Amber turned and flounced off down the pathway.

"Amber!" Charlie called after her.

Amber's only reply was to raise a perfectly manicured middle finger in his direction.

"Oh... to hell with it."

Charlie turned back to his Chevy. He stroked a
hand soothingly along its chromed wing mirror.
"You still love me, baby, don't you?"

With a put-upon sigh, he opened the door of the
car and leaned across the passenger sear, reaching
for his jacket. He supposed he should go after her.
After all, when all was said and done, she was still
a good lay. And she'd stuck around a lot longer
than most girls did, almost two months at the last
count.

Hell, that practically made her his girlfriend.

He tugged on his jacket, but it seemed to be stuck
on something. Charlie saw that the sleeve was
caught in the door on the passenger side. Feeling too
lazy to walk all the way around the car to free it,
Charlie put a knee on the driver's seat and crawled
through the car, awkwardly balancing on his bad
arm while he opened the far door to free his jacket.
Mission accomplished, he pulled the door shut and
crawled back through the car.

Suddenly, his wrist buckled and slipped down
between the seats, sending a stab of pain shooting
up his arm. Charlie swore and toppled sideways.
Instinctively he jammed his other hand down to support his weight, and quickly jerked his injured limb
out from between the seats.

As he did so, the full weight of his body came to
rest against the ancient handbrake. With a quiet
click, it disengaged.

The car began rolling forwards.

Charlie's head whipped up like a prairie dog as he felt the car begin to move.

"*Fuck!*"

Scrambling backwards as fast as he could, Charlie clambered back into the driver's seat. Grabbing the handbrake, he tried to pull it back, but now, of all times, it chose to stick.

Usually he solved this problem by pumping the foot brake a couple of times until it released with a loud clunk. This time, the car didn't seem to want to respond. After a couple of attempts, the foot brake locked up too, along with the steering wheel.

Cursing freely, Charlie grabbed the handbrake and pulled on it with all his might. The brake moved upwards by half an inch before jamming completely.

Try as he might, he couldn't budge it.

"*Fuck, fuck, fuck!*"

Daylight filled the car is it slowly rolled forwards out of the garage, heading towards the driveway that ran steeply downwards towards the busy street. Between the driveway and the road, a concrete wall loomed. If the car got onto the forty-five degree slope, it would smack into that wall in about three seconds.

Charlie couldn't let that happen. He'd spent a fortune importing that chromed headlight and bumper set. His daddy's insurance people would never forgive him.

A crazy idea shot through his head. Leaping out of the driver's side, he grabbed hold of the Chevy's doorpost with one hand. With the other, he seized the garage doorframe. He wasn't letting the car get out of that door.

He braced himself. This was going to hurt...

In the warmth of the bath, Jess dreamed.

It was a strange dream, filled with shouting voices, broken thoughts and confusion. Out of the hubbub, Jess found herself walking down a narrow pathway hewn from bare rock, surrounded on both sides by a deep chasm of darkness.

The crazy voices died away as she walked, and soon she was surrounded by nothing but golden silence. She peered downwards, and immediately her head swum with vertigo. The chasm was so deep that the bottom faded into nothingness, as though she were walking above a black, shimmering void. A faint hint of blue was visible at the very bottom, so far down that it might have been a trick of the eyes.

Jess thought that it was very beautiful.

She looked on ahead up the path. At the other side, there was the dark shape of a majestic mountain range. The scale of the mountains was beyond belief, soaring way up into the night sky and towering over the path like ancient stone gods. The mountains appeared to be made out of a translucent kind of crystal, lit from within by a benevolent glow. Tiny twinkling lights were dotted about all over them, as though they were covered in habitations of some kind.

Jess knew instinctively that she would be safe there.

She glanced behind her. All she could see was darkness.

Steeling herself, she started walking up the long path towards the mountains, trying not to look down.

After a little while, she became aware that the path in front of her was getting narrower. Soon, it had tapered down to little more than a foot across. Jess paused, looked down and shivered. She was so high up.

She looked across to the other side, and saw that the path behind her was evaporating like so much smoke, blowing up into the air. She couldn't go back, only forwards. She craned her neck, looking far above her, and saw that the smoke was billowing and twisting over her head, forming a complicated double-helix shape before looping over and joining up with the path far in front of her, where it became solid ground.

Jess stopped, uneasiness creeping over her like a blanket of marching spiders. A breeze kicked up, blowing leaves and newspaper over her head. A double-page spread wrapped itself around her mid-section, blown by the wind.

Jess reached down and pulled it away from herself. Holding it up to the light between her thumb and finger, she saw that the club disaster had made front-page news, even down here in this strange place, wherever she was. There was a picture of the smoking ruins, a long list of the names of the victims, and, bizarrely, a photograph of herself underneath, stark naked and holding a platter of cheese.

How weird, thought Jess. She turned the newspaper over in her hands. On the back was nothing but an advert for engine oil. She dropped the newspaper page and the wind whipped it away from her, spinning off into the void.

Then she stopped. Up ahead of her, a figure formed out of the mist and began walking towards her. Jess screwed up her eyes against the light, trying to make out the figure's face. She knew in her gut that it was someone important.

As it approached, Jess saw that it was her mother. "Mom! Over here!" Jess yelled, excitement filling her like helium. She hadn't seen her mom in ages. She started to run towards the figure.

Then she slowed and stopped.

Then she broke into a run again, then for a second time, she stopped.

She frowned.

The figure of her mother was still walking steadily towards her, but every time Jess took a step forwards, the path before seemed to lengthen, carrying her mother further away. Jess looked down at her feet. Beneath her, the path was less than eight inches wide.

Jess stood very still. She couldn't risk falling. She would wait for her mother to come to her.

As her mother approached, Jess saw that something was wrong. Her mom was dressed all in black, and her face was shrouded by a thin veil. She was crying.

"Mom? What the matter?" Jess's voice sounded like it was stretched thin, coming from a great distance away. She cleared her throat and tried again, but her voice came out the same. She waited for her mom to reply, but she didn't. Instead, she pulled a lacy handkerchief from her pocket, daintily blew her nose, and then carried on walking.

She stopped opposite Jess, and seemed to pause, her worried green eyes meeting Jess's behind her veil.

Jess swallowed a lump in her throat. There was so much history in those eyes. Her mom had never cared much for her, acting as though motherhood had been dumped on her, like some crappy waitressing job that she couldn't wait to quit. Sure, she went through the motions, but Jess knew that secretly, she couldn't wait for her and her sister to hit twenty so she could turn them out of the house and get on with the life of partying, drink and drugs she left behind. Everyone in the family knew that it was true.

But now her mother seemed different, uncertain. Jess saw her mouth twitch, as though she was trying to work out what to say to her. It was as though she finally understood what it was to be a mother, faced with the thought of losing Jess. She must have heard about that club disaster on the news. As Jess watched, a tear slowly slid its way down her cheek, and her mother opened her mouth to speak, but no words came out.

Scarcely daring to breathe, Jess reached out to hug her mother, to brush her tears away and tell her that it was all right, she understood, she still loved her.

Her hands went straight through her.

Jess was left holding empty air while her mother continued on her way, walking down the path away from her, weeping and wailing.

Jess froze, feeling a dagger of ice work its way into her heart.

"Mom?" she said. Her voice raised weird echoes from the landscape.

There was no reply. She turned around to see that the dark figure of her mother was several hundred yards from her, already vanishing into the mist.

"Mom!"

She began running after her mother, but the faster she ran, the quicker her mother moved away. Soon, she had disappeared into the darkness of the night.

Jess slowed and stopped, staring after her mom. She had completely vanished. Panic set in. The night seemed to be pressing in around her like thick, black molasses, working its way into her skin and filling her bloodstream with darkness. Jess strove to breathe, panic gripping her heart and squeezing her ribcage. She knew that she had to carry on across the chasm, but she didn't want to leave her mother behind. She couldn't. She knew instinctively that if she did, she would never see her again.

Jess began running back down the path, as fast and as hard as she could. She didn't dare look down. After a few minutes, she stopped, panting for breath.

Something caught her eye, and Jess looked downwards. Something had fallen out of her mother's pocket when she'd taken out her handkerchief.

Jess stooped down and picked it up.

It was a pink rose.

It was pretty. Jess sniffed at it, but it had no scent. She tucked it behind her ear.

As she did, one of the thorns snagged her hand with a sharp pain. Jess winced and sucked at her hand as blood started to flow. She looked at her finger. Three drops of blood fell from it, splashing onto the path beneath her.

Damn rose. Jess sucked on her finger and stared in anguish into the darkness. She couldn't go back now. It was too dangerous. She knew, somehow, that her mother was lost forever.

Turning around, she began walking, and tripped over something lying on the path.

She looked down.

It was a body.

More specifically, it was Charlie's body.

Jess looked down at him. He was still dressed in his smart combats and white arm sling, but his head was missing. The bloody stump at the top of his neck glistened wetly, soaking his crisp white shirt with red. A fountain of blood poured from him, gushing towards her down the path, spilling over the sides and raining down into the abyss.

Jess screamed.

Outside, in the garage, the car was proving to be much heavier than Charlie had originally thought. His grip tightened as the car rolled forward another few inches, then slowed. He swore loudly as he took the strain, the full weight of the car stretching his bruised muscles to their limits. He gave a gasp of pain, his arms quivering with the tension.

But his grip held, and slowly, the car drifted to a halt.

Charlie breathed a sigh of relief.

Now, all he had to do was secure it with something. Then he could get the key from the bench at the back of the garage and reverse back up the slope.

Idiot. He couldn't believe he'd nearly dented his beautiful car.

His eyes narrowed as he did a couple of calculations. If he let go of the car again, he'd have about ten seconds to grab some rope and secure the car before it hit the slope. That was more than enough time to loop the rope round the metal doorpost of the garage. That would hold it, no problem.

Grunting, he reached out with one foot towards the dangling loops of blue nylon tow rope that was hanging from the shelf just behind the garage door.

He couldn't quite reach it.

Charlie thought for a moment, running through the various options currently open to him. Then he sighed and hollered, "Amber!"

There was no reply. If Amber was there, she was ignoring him.

He tried again. "Amber! Get up here!"

No response.

"Shit!" Charlie's bad arm began to shake with the effort of holding on. He cast around frantically for a backup plan, but his brain seemed to have frozen at the thought of his beloved car getting damaged. Even one scratch would be too much. He looked back at the rope, hanging tantalizingly just inches out of reach.

There was nothing else for it. He'd have to make a grab for the rope.

Steeling himself, Charlie let go of the car. It immediately started drifting forwards. Charlie lunged towards the dangling rope and yanked down on it. Half the reel flopped down towards him. The other half stayed resolutely on the shelf.

It must be caught on something, Charlie thought frantically. He tugged on it as hard as he could, but it didn't even budge.

There was a sliding, grating sound from above him.

Charlie looked up. His eyes widened.

"Oh, crap..."

He flung himself aside as a big box of tools tipped over up on the shelf. Power tools and gardening implements came sliding down towards him, pouring off the shelf like rain. Charlie yelped in pain as a pair of garden shears bounced off his shoulder, then hurriedly ducked as the entire box came crashing down, missing him by inches and clattering down all around him.

And then all was still. A spare hubcap revolved slowly on the garage floor, in accordance with the ancient rules governing such a situation, then came to rest. The coil of rope stayed resolutely on the shelf, snarled on a jutting nail just behind where the box had been.

The car, Charlie thought desperately! Clutching the end of the rope, he ran towards the Chevy and looped it through the circular tow bar beneath the rear bumper, just as it rolled past him out of the garage door. He pulled the rope taut, looping the free end tightly around the doorpost and praying that the shelf would hold.

In less than a second, the rope sprang taut. Charlie braced himself and held tightly onto the loose end, taking the strain like a one-ended tug-of-war contest.

The car stopped rolling.

Charlie breathed a sigh of relief, cocking an eyebrow at the bizarre cat's cradle of rope he'd created. He couldn't believe what a mess he'd got himself into in such a short space of time.

But the car was safe, which was the main thing. Now all he had to do was tie up the free end of the rope, and that was that. He bowed his head to an imaginary cheering crowd. He was *so* clever. Anyone else would have just accepted their fate and let the car roll, but not him. No sir. He'd saved the car, and saved the day.

Fate could go hang.

There was a creaking sound from behind him. What now, Charlie thought irritably? He didn't dare look over his shoulder to locate the source of the sound, concentrating on holding onto the rope. His shoulder felt uncomfortably warm and it took him a moment to notice that he was bleeding.

"Oh, great." He craned his head around, trying to see the injury. The shears had grazed his shoulder, slitting open his expensive Armani sweater and gashing his skin. Blood welled slowly from the shallow wound.

There was another creak, louder this time. Behind him, the shelf slowly began to pull away from the wall.

At the bottom of the driveway, Amber sat down on the wall and sniffled to herself. She heard Charlie call out to her, and pouted. There was no way in heaven or hell that she was going back to him. He'd called her Heather! That bitch! She *knew* that he loved her the most, so what was he doing even thinking about that little slut?

It just wasn't fair.

What was *with* Charlie today? Last night he'd been so nice to her, kissing her forehead and holding her protectively as she cried. She'd felt so good, wrapped up in his strong arms, safe and warm and protected from the horrors of the night. He'd been incredibly sweet, and had even gone to the trouble of ordering her a taxi so she wouldn't have to walk the three blocks home from his house.

It was almost as if they were actually dating.

But today, something had changed in him. He'd shut himself off to her again, as though yesterday had never happened.

He did that, sometimes. It was as though there was a switch inside him that clicked on and off at random. When the switch was on, he was the most loving, caring person ever.

But when it was off...

Amber wiped her eyes on the back of her hand, noting with a sob that her makeup had streaked. She'd spent hours in the bathroom getting ready so that she could "just drop by" on Charlie. She'd taken a long shower, using five different kinds of hair product to get her hair just so, then spent a good hour wrestling with rollers and pins, blow-drying her long blonde hair into big bouncy waves. Then she'd painted her nails a pretty shade of pink, done her makeup impeccably, tried on twelve different outfits before settling on the one she was originally wearing, chosen matching shoes, and finally spritzed herself all over with sparkly perfume dust before heading out towards Charlie's house.

She'd known from long experience that five in the afternoon was an optimum time to drop in on him at the weekends, just after he woke up from his after-dinner nap and before he headed out to football practice.

More often than not, he'd invite her along with him, and she'd spend a blissful afternoon watching him play, watching from the sidelines and pointedly ignoring the other six blondes on the bench who were also cheering him on. He was hers. Didn't they see that? The fact that he hugged them all when he came to sit with her at half time did nothing to dampen Amber's enthusiasm. She knew he appreciated all the effort she went to in order to attend the games, and that deep down, he loved her for it.

He never said it out loud of course, but she could just tell by the way he looked at her.

Really, she could...

But today, it had been all for nothing. Charlie didn't want to see her tonight. He hadn't even noticed what she was wearing, or how prettily she'd done her makeup.

She sniffed, wiping her eyes as her mascara started to run.

That boy was a waste of perfectly good eyeliner.

As she reached for a tissue, a trickle of gravel rolled down the steep driveway behind her...

Up in the garage, Charlie stepped towards the light, pulling up his sleeve so that he could see the wound on his shoulder better. He winced. That had better not leave a scar,

The creaking behind him began again.

Charlie glanced behind him. Dammit, what *was* that?

Several things happened at once. The first thing that happened was that Charlie's foot slipped on a patch of the motor oil Amber had spilled. He stumbled and started to fall. As he did so, the shelf gave up its brief struggle with the laws of friction and came away from the wall, unable to take the strain of the entire car pulling on it. It flew spinning across the room, whistling at high speed through the space Charlie's head had been occupying just a split second before he slipped on the oil.

The next thing that happened was that Charlie hit the ground. A second later, the coiled end of the rope whizzed towards his head, looped like a lasso...

"CHARLIE!"

Charlie's head whipped around at the sound of his name. It had come from the house, and it sounded like Tess's voice. It was followed a second later by a loud splash, a bang, then a scream. Then all was silent.

An instant later, the coiled rope landed in the exact spot his head had been a moment before Tess's yell. It shot onwards over the concrete and disappeared out through the garage door, dragged off behind the car.

Charlie watched as his beloved Chevy rolled away from him and vanished down the steep driveway. He let out a small sob.

At the bottom of the driveway, Amber came to a decision. She'd had enough. She would get herself a proper boyfriend, one who was just hers, who actually got her name right two times out of three and didn't spend all his time chasing after cheerleaders.

She took a deep breath, intrigued by this new thought. Yes. That's what she'd do. Charlie could go screw himself as far as she cared. Her friends had been right. She could do so much better than him.

Amber ran her fingers thoughtfully through the long grass in the flowerbed behind her. She touched the pretty flowers planted amongst the grass, and bent over to inhale their scent.

They were miniature roses.

Amber picked herself a pink one, breathing in its perfume while she came up with a plan. She would go home, pick up her keys, and then drive into school to see if that cute quarterback was still out on the field. She knew that he'd had a crush on her since third grade, but she'd never even given him a chance while Charlie was around.

Hell, Amber thought wryly, *nobody* got a chance when Charlie was around.

She would ask him out, and go from there. It would be the start of a whole new life for her.

Standing up with a flourish, Amber brushed off her skirt and popped her earphones into her ears. Clicking on her MP3 player, she scrolled through until she found her current favorite song, Aerosmith's "Angel." She cranked it up loud, then started walking across the driveway, heading home.

Above her, a midnight black Chevy rolled silently out of the garage and began speeding down the slope towards her.

Jess saw the car heading down towards Amber, and her fingers tightened on the bathroom window ledge. "Amber! Look out!" she yelled, as loudly as she could. Behind her, the hairdryer fizzed and bubbled in the tub. Jess was so, so glad that her dream had woken her up when it did. Five more seconds, and she would have been toast.

But for now, she had more important things to deal with.

She yelled out of the window again. She saw Amber stop and half turn towards the house, her brow creasing with puzzlement as she strove to hear over the blare of her MP3 player. Then her face dissolved into a look of panic as she saw the driverless Chevy heading towards her. She clutched her purse to her and started to run.

Jess's hand flew to her mouth as she saw the girl's foot slip on the thin trickle of motor oil running down the driveway from the garage, forming a small but deadly puddle at the bottom of the slope. Next thing she knew, Amber had come crashing down on her back, winding herself.

The car picked up speed as it shot towards her. Amber tried to roll to one side, but she wasn't quick enough.

There was nothing Jess could do but watch in horror as the car carried on over the top of Amber, rocking slightly to the side as it rolled over her. A spray of blood spattered out from beneath it, mingling with the motor oil on the driveway.

Then the car was still, its front half sticking out onto the road, its downwards plunge halted by the human wheel jam. An arm stuck out from under the side of the car, still holding a pink rose.

Jess felt the world swim in front of her eyes as she stared at the second body she'd seen in twenty-four hours. She backed away from the window, and then slowly sat down on the edge of the bath, staring at a point beyond the floor. Outside, she heard running footsteps, then the sound of yelling.

In her head, an unavoidable countdown had begun.

The eight survivors were down to six.

SEVEN

"What the *hell*?"

Ben stood by the side of the pool and looked in bemusement at the crazy scene before him. It was just coming up to seven in the evening at the college campus, a time normally associated with exam revision and long conversations at the coffee shop. But not tonight. The streets around Ben's lodgings were packed with a colorful throng of people, making their way to and from the various sorority and fraternity houses, which were decked out in colored streamers. Scantily clad girls prowled the sidewalk in packs, dressed in fascinatingly short miniskirts and high heels. They were watched by the groups of guys sitting up on the concrete walls, some of them shirtless, most of them drinking beer from red and blue paper cups. Beside one of the classier houses, a gang of giggling boys was busy hoisting someone's bicycle up a telegraph pole on a piece of rope.

Ben stood and stared as people pushed their way past him, laughing and chatting. There was one major-looking party going on here. How come he hadn't been invited?

He reached into his pocket for his cell phone. If Eric had known about this party and not invited him, the dude was seriously dead.

Ring.

Ring-ring.

Ring-ring-CLICK.

Dammit! Answerphone.

Ben listened to the message, waited for the beep, then belched loudly into the phone and hung up. Feeling infinitely satisfied, he stowed his phone in his jeans pocket and gazed around him with interest. A white marquee tent had been set up on the grass beside one of the bigger fraternity houses and the overflow from the tent spilled out onto the surrounding grounds. Tables were set up around it, groaning under the weight of barrels of cheap imported wine. Shiny black SUVs cruised slowly up and down the street, disgorging fresh groups of partygoers, who all headed straight to the wine tent. The entrance was guarded by two stern-looking bouncers, checking people's IDs as they walked in.

Ben shook his head wonderingly. Freaky country. You could go buy a gun from a shop on any main street, but you couldn't get a drink until you were twenty-one.

There was a slightly hushed air to the revelry, but Ben didn't notice that. He was still concentrating on the girls in the miniskirts.

And there were so many of them...

He gazed at the nearest girl, who was standing with her back to him, flirting with some muscle-bound meathead in a lettermen sweater. At twenty, Ben had never been laid, and it was currently one of the biggest thoughts occupying his mind, besides football and a strange craving for a really, really good Chinese meal. He unconsciously licked his lips as he studied the girl's rear profile, marveling at how tiny her waist was and how well her miniskirt hung on her, barely skimming her full behind, and yet still managing to hide it infuriatingly well. Ben stared hard at the drink in her hands, psychically willing her to drop it so that she would bend over for just a second, which was all that he needed...

"It ain't gonna happen, bro."

Ben tore his eyes away from the girl in the miniskirt. Eric was standing beside him, his arms folded. His bright orange shirt was open to the waist, and he was wearing a garland of bottle tops around his neck. From the expression on his face, Armani himself couldn't have dressed him better.

He winked at Ben. "Watch," he mouthed, then gave a long, low whistle. The girl in the miniskirt glanced over her shoulder. Eric stuck out his tongue and waggled it around obscenely. The girl curled her lip and gave him a look of pure disdain before turning back round, pulling the hem of her skirt further down. The meathead gave Eric a warning look, then put his arm around the girl's shoulders and walked her away towards the wine tent.

Eric laughed in delight. "Strike one!" He punched the air in triumph, bouncing on the balls of his feet.

"I think she wants me. Whaddya think?" He pulled a fresh bottle of beer out of his backpack and opened it up with his Swiss army knife.

"I think you shoulda told me there was a party tonight, dude," said Ben. He sounded hurt. "I've been sitting up there in my room all night long, stressing about shit. Nobody told me there was something happening." He looked at Eric meaningfully.

"Party? What party?" Eric looked around him, all innocence, sipping on his beer. "Oh, you mean this?" he smiled, waving his hands around airily. "These are just my bitches. They've come here for the express pleasure of hanging out with yours truly."

"You mean this isn't a party?"

"Hell no. But I can see how you might be confused."

"By what? All the food and the skirts and the drinking?"

"Correct. But still not a party."

"Then what is it, for Chrissakes?"

"It's a wake." Eric looked smug.

"A what?"

"A wake. To celebrate the lives of the, er, the deceased." Even Eric had the decency to look a little abashed. He ripped a colorful flyer off a nearby tree and handed it to Ben. "Here."

Ben inspected the flyer. It had a picture of a skull on it, superimposed over an old picture of Club Kitty. The writing beneath read, "Come Celebrate our Lives." The whole thing was extremely tacky, and the pink neon paper it was printed on certainly wasn't helping matters.

Life went on, thought Ben wryly. It didn't matter who'd just died. As long as at least two human beings were left alive on the face of the planet, somewhere, there'd be a party. It was one of the few certainties in life.

Eric took the flyer back, answering Ben's unspoken question. "One of the dudes who died left some money. I'm told he asked his folks once that if anything ever happened to him, they should throw a party. So they did."

Ben wasn't surprised. A lot of students had been in that club when it collapsed. The memorial service was in ten days' time, and he hadn't a clue what to wear. The only black clothes he owned had band logos on them, and he was sure that attending a funeral in a top that had "Slayer" printed on it in big bloody letters wouldn't be very appropriate, even for him.

"Cool idea, about the party"

"Yeah." Eric thought for a moment. "Poor sons of bitches."

"Yeah."

They stood for a moment in silence while people drank and boozed and laughed around them. When Ben judged that a suitably respectful amount of time had passed, he cleared his throat hopefully. "So... any of that beer left, then?"

"That depends," said Eric, a malicious gleam coming into his eyes.

"On what?"

"On what you'll do to get it."

It was much, much later. Ben sat on a low stone wall, watching the floor intently. It was pitching from side to side, like the deck of a ship on the high seas. He was sure it wasn't supposed to be doing that.

"Funny floor!" he giggled, pointing an unsteady finger at the ground as it dipped and swayed past him. He hiccupped loudly, then shook his head like a dog. His stomach felt as if someone had poured an entire ocean of fizzy water into him, then put a cork in his throat and shaken him up for about a half hour.

He smacked his lips loudly, looking woozily around him. Somehow, after ten pints of beer, he was still incredibly thirsty. He wondered vaguely whether there was any drink left anywhere, or whether he'd drunk it all.

Beer was *good*...

Right on cue, someone walked past and kicked a beer bottle over towards him. It rolled across the sidewalk with a glassy clanking sound before coming to rest against his outstretched boot. Ben tipped his head on one side and gave it a look of intense scrutiny, his eyebrows weaving around like mating caterpillars as he strove to focus. His face fell.

"S'empty," he announced, then slowly fell off the wall.

The ground was surprisingly comfortable. Ben lay on his side and congratulated himself on this new discovery. The concrete was still warm from the heat of the day, and it smelled strongly of alcohol. Or maybe it was him that smelled strongly of alcohol. He tried to move his head to determine the source of the smell, but discovered that he was too comfortable to even move.

But that was all right with him. He lay still, grinning happily.

The ground was so warm! It was just like some big, flat, warm woman, he thought, snuggling up to it happily. What was that phrase... Mother Earth? Ben smiled at his own cleverness. Mother Earth. What a wonderful, wonderful woman she was. He reached out an arm and patted the ground fondly.

Then he threw up.

"Hey, jerkoff!"

"Mmph?" Ben wiped his mouth and rolled over, groaning. Someone blurry was talking to him, backlit by a strong light. He tried to shield his eyes with his hand and missed, poking himself in the eye instead.

He lay still, deciding that movement wasn't good.

"Get up. We need you." Eric poked Ben in the ribs with his boot.

"Hey! Don'do... that."

"Come on. You can't lie there, you great doofus. You're blocking the sidewalk." Eric grabbed hold of Ben's outflung arms, and half-lifted, half-dragged him onto the grass, away from the road.

Ben rolled over and looked up at the sky, wishing heartily that he had something to eat to get the horrible taste out of his mouth. He wished heartily for some Chinese food. There were no stars above him, and this made him feel oddly sad.

"Are you going to get up, or am I going to have to get you up?" Eric sounded far too bright and bouncy for someone who had just consumed almost an entire keg of beer by himself. Ben wondered whether he had been cheating. He certainly wouldn't put it past him.

"No... 'm getting' up..." Ben burped and squeezed his eyes tight shut while his brain spun around violently inside his skull. Oh, this wasn't good. "...Annyminiutenow..."

"Loser!" Eric grabbed Ben's arms again, heaving him up into a sitting position against the wall.

Ben blearily opened his eyes to see a semicircle of blurry strangers watching him. Some of them were girls. Very pretty girls. Very pretty blurry girls all looking at him. His brow creased in puzzlement.

"Who...?" he asked the world in general.

"Friends. Nice friends. Come on. Drink this." Eric pushed a glass of cold water into Ben's hands. "And try not to puke on me."

Ben drank the water down in one gulp, wondering vaguely why his front was starting to feel cold and wet. Was it raining? He looked up at the sky, and almost fell over again. He was pretty sure it wasn't raining, so why was his front getting wet?

He sighed. It was just another one of those mysteries that he didn't have the answers to.

He finished the water surprisingly quickly and handed the empty glass back to one of the Eric-shaped blurs hovering in front of him.

"Here. Up you come." Eric pulled Ben bodily to his feet, supporting him on one muscular arm. Ben stood there, groaning and swaying gently. The ground seemed like it was a very long way away, like his legs had stretched and grown until they were the length of a tree-trunk. He waved muzzily down at the ground, which was doing its swaying-from-side-to-side thing again.

"Ready to rock?" Eric whooped, punching the air and making Ben jump.

"Yeah!" yelled the watching crowd.

"Yea...!" Ben hiccupped, a preoccupied expression on his face.

"All right then! Let's go, people. You know what you have to do."

The crowd dispersed, marching off in twos and threes across the grass.

"Wassappening?" asked Ben, focusing on the central Eric-blur on his third attempt.

"We're doing dares," said Eric, his eyes glinting. "First one to complete their dare for the evening gets this." He swept his hand behind him to reveal an entire barrel of beer, propped up against his red pickup truck.

"S'that beer?" Ben's eyes lit up.

"Yup. But it's not for you, buddy. Took me a long time to get hold of this."

"D'you steal it?"

"Nah. I *requisitioned* it." Eric smiled and punched Ben on the arm. "Gotta get your terminology right if you're gonna be a college student. Now. This is our dare." He reached into his bag and pulled out a piece of paper. There was a diagram drawn on it in blue biro. "This is the security building. All the security guards live there. This," he stabbed a finger at the map. "...is the elevator. What we're going to do, is stop it from working."

"Why?"

"Because, my friend, we want to have a good night. I have a lot of... plans... for tonight, but there's some stuff I have to do first. Alcohol-related stuff. If security comes snooping around my block in the next hour, we will not have a good night. Comprende?"

Ben's face pulled five different conflicting expressions before settling on one of bemused stupidity. "Not really," he hiccuped.

"That's because you're drunk," said Eric, so patiently that Ben wanted to hit him. "Focus. This is the plan. If we can stop the elevator working, we can keep security holed up for an hour. They're all up there right now, having a meeting about how to deal with us guys tonight. Assigning shifts and whatnot." Eric glanced behind him, lowering his voice. "All we have to do is keep them in there for an hour. If they can't leave the building, they can't fuck things up for me, I mean, us."

Ben rubbed his forehead with the effort of thought. "Won't they... 'scuse me... take the stairs instead? Iffyou break... theelevator?"

"Thought of that. That's Lou and Sharon's job. Blocking the fire escape. They're off over there right now with the police tape and the crazy glue for the door handles. The guards'll figure it out eventually, but in the meantime..." Eric waved a hand at the party in front of him, taking in the food, the drink and more importantly, the girls. "All of this is ours."

Ben nodded, impressed in a faraway, distant way. His stomach was empty, and he realized that he was starting to feel hungry.

Very hungry.

He turned to Eric hopefully. "You got any Chinese food?"

It was later. Food had been had.

Ben was starting to feel a whole lot better, although the four extra beers he'd drunk on his way through the parking lot hadn't helped matters so much.

"So... what's the plan, Batman?"

"Shhhh!"

"Sorry." Ben giggled. His voice seemed to come from a long way away. He ducked back down behind the hedge and watched the last of the security guys disappear into the tall brick security building, closing the door behind them. He was feeling a little bit more sober now, thanks to the three big cups of coffee Eric had forced him to drink, but he still had enough alcohol surging through his bloodstream to kill a small horse. Everything seemed very funny indeed, for some obscure reason. His head was still spinning, and despite the huge portion of fries he'd just consumed, he was still starving. His stomach growled, and he patted his belly to quiet it. "You *sure* there's no more food?"

"Nope. I ate it all."

"What, all of it?"

"Yup." Eric was straight-faced. "Everything on campus. And for the love of God, *will you be quiet?*"

"Why? There's no one out here."

"There's windows open up there! They could hear us!"

"Ooh! I'm really, really scared." Ben rocked back on his heels and peered up at the building. All the lights were out, save the ones on the topmost floor, eight stories up. The windows were indeed open.

He snorted in mirth. "They won't hear us from all the way up there."

"Are you kidding? Remember what happened in the cafeteria last week?"

Ben scrunched up his face with the effort of remembering. A light dawned. "You mean, when you were in the lunch line, and you said, 'Hey! I wonder what'll happen if I drop my fork in the fruit smoothie mixer tank?' And then the security guard threw you out?"

"Yeah. That's exactly what I mean. That dude was standing across the other side of the room. *Nobody* has hearing that good. Nobody."

"It was kinda scary," Ben admitted. He ducked further down behind the hedge, looking worried. "Here, do you think he heard that thing I said about his gay little hat?"

"Dude, why do you think I ran?" Eric shook his head. "You've got *no* idea. I don't even know why I let you hang with me sometimes. Now zip it and hand me that bag."

Ben obliged, muttering under his breath. He passed Eric the big bag of tools that they'd purloined from the janitor's closet.

Purloined. That was another good word he'd learned today. Hell, if he kept learning new words at this rate, he'd know the whole goddamn dictionary by the end of the year.

Eric had told him that it didn't mean "steal", as he'd thought it had. In Eric's idiosyncratic vocabulary, it merely meant "borrowed indefinitely."

Ben broke off a long stem of grass and chewed fitfully on the end. Eric borrowed a lot of things indefinitely. He said that it wasn't wrong. After all, he'd reasoned, most people "borrowed" things from school or work, like office supplies or those little sachets of sugar they gave out for free in restaurants. It was just one of those things that people did. It didn't make them bad people, it just made them... well, people.

But not Eric. He only went for the good stuff. Most of the things he owned were permanently on lease from other people. Ben knew that Eric's CD collection alone was "borrowed" from at least sixty different people, all of whom were currently driving themselves crazy wondering where in the blazes they'd put their limited-edition Megadeth CD box set.

Eric was an old pro. He reasoned that since students were *supposed* to stea... borrow stuff—traffic signals, street signs and whatnot—he may as well go ahead and have himself a ball. Since he got his job at the bar last month, they'd never been out of alcohol, shot glasses, bar towels or cutlery. And as an added bonus, they now had enough giant industrial-sized reels of bathroom tissue to last them pretty much indefinitely.

Eric said it was "perks". Ben privately called it something else, although he wouldn't dare say it out loud for fear of getting his head kicked in.

And besides which, he really, really hated buying bathroom tissue.

He kept his mouth shut as Eric rifled through the bag, pulling out various monkey wrenches and hammers before finally settling on a miniature crowbar, which he stashed inside his shirt. He dropped the bag behind the bush and motioned to Ben. "All set? Let's go."

Ben followed Eric, crouching low as they ran across the manicured grass, heading towards the security building as fast as they could.

That was the great thing about being drunk, thought Ben happily, as he bounced and skipped along behind Eric. He may not be able to see straight, but his legs felt like they could go on running for hours, all on their own. It was like they were supercharged or something. It was hugely entertaining to find that he could run as fast as he liked without getting tired or falling ove... Oh.

Eric ran back and held out his hand. "Get up. Quick. C'mon, someone'll see us."

"Okay, okay!" Ben flopped over into the flowerbed and levered himself to his feet. "Gimme a break. I tripped."

"On what? We're on grass!"

"On... er... yeah, I tripped on the grass." Ben broke into a shrill giggling fit, and then subsided with a cough.

"You're stupid."

"But it's very long grass!"

"And you're very, very stupid."

Shaking his head, Eric started trotting towards the security building. Jerk. Dusk was falling, and the security building's lamps were starting to come on, one by one, bathing them in an orange glow.

He prayed that nobody had seen them.

The pair of them ran over to the back door. It was locked.

"Ah, crap." Eric looked around him, searching for a way in. His eyes lit upon a half-open window on the first floor, and he made a snap decision. "Stay right here. Yell out if anyone comes."

The window was a good twelve feet up off the ground. Eric tightened the straps on his backpack, then rolled up his sleeves. This should only take a second.

There was a big square iron grille over the ground floor window. It was about six feet long and was topped with sharp points, presumably to discourage students from climbing on it. There was a low stubby tree underneath it, surrounded by a bed of ivy and nasty-looking cactus plants.

Eric remembered how easily that Jess girl had got over that fence last night. He wasn't a big fan of climbing things, but now, needs must, and all that.

He put one hand on the lowest branch of the tree, testing to see how strong it was. A fall into that patch of cactus plants would not put him in a good mood. The tree seemed strong enough, so he began climbing it, as quickly as he dared.

"What are you doing?"

"I'm climbing the damn tree. What does it look like I'm doing?"

Ben sniggered. "You look really stupid. You climb like a girl."

"You think I care?"

Eric drew level with the metal window grille, and cautiously reached out a hand towards it. Getting a firm grip, he swung himself out of the tree, so he was hanging by both hands from the top of the grille, dangling six feet above the ground. He kicked upwards with his feet, getting his boot on the bottom rung of the grille, wedging it firmly in between the bars. A small shower of plaster dust trickled down the wall, as the nails that held the grille to the wall pulled out slightly under his weight.

Oblivious to this, Eric got his other foot on the grille and slowly pulled himself upright.

A second trickle of dust later, the grille slid out slightly further.

Eric craned his neck upwards. The ledge of the open window was an arm's length above him. He checked the distance. It was easily reachable.

Something made his nose itch, and Eric sniffed. Dammit! He always got an itch when he had no hands available to scratch it with. Leaning to the side, he ducked his head down level with one of the wicked-looking metal spikes that topped the grille, and carefully rubbed his nose against it.

A further shower of brick dust fell out of the wall, trickling unnoticed into the cactus bed below. The grille shook slightly.

Itch satisfied, Eric straightened up and pulled himself upright. Now, this should be fairly simple...

Trying not to look down, Eric reached up with one hand and got a firm grip on the window ledge above him. Transferring his other hand up, he freed his first foot from the grille...

Which finally gave way under his weight, the nails sliding out of the crumbling brick. The whole thing plunged down towards the ground.

Then halted.

Eric cried out in pain, clinging desperately onto the window ledge above him. His foot was still jammed through the bars of the fallen grille, which now dangled from his leg, the weight of it slowly pulling him off the ledge. Eric spun around like a rabbit caught in a trap, kicking frantically.

Ben ran forwards. "You all right?" he called up.

"Do I look like I'm all right?" Eric yelped. The grille weighed a ton, and his leg felt as if it was being pulled out of its socket. He felt his grip starting to slip and clutched frantically at the ancient brickwork, which was starting to crumble beneath his fingers. He tried to kick the grille off with his other foot, but it was stuck fast. "Gimme a hand here!"

Ben reached up and caught the dangling grille, supporting it with both hands. "Heavy," he commented.

"Really? I hadn't... noticed," said Eric, as his biceps screamed in pain. "Just get it off me, for the love of God!"

Staggering slightly, Ben pushed the grille upwards, twisting it back and forth to disengage Eric's boot, which finally came free. Ben jumped back as the grille plunged to the ground, the metal spikes driving deeply into the flowerbed.

"Shit." Eric flexed his leg with a wince, then began swinging his body back and forth, trying to get up enough momentum to reach the window. The weight of the grille had badly wrenched his muscles, and he knew he didn't have long before his arms gave out.

After a couple of swings he went for it, straightening his arms into a push-up and arcing his body upwards with all the power he could muster. To his relief, one of his flailing feet caught the window ledge. He scissored his legs, propelling himself upwards and scrambled through the window, jumping lightly down on the other side.

He walked over to the main door and flipped the catch to let Ben in.

The interior of the building was brightly lit. The two of them gazed around them for a minute, getting their bearings. Then Eric sauntered casually over to the elevator and pressed the call button. He leaned against the wall, whistling under his breath. To his relief, there were no security cameras inside the lobby.

"Okay," he dropped his voice and clicked his fingers in front of Ben, who was gazing owlishly at the brightly lit floor buttons. "Pay attention. This is what we're gonna do. I'm going to go in there and cut the power to that thing. If I really mess it up, it should keep those goofs upstairs a good couple of hours."

"What do I do?" asked Ben, one of nature's little helpers.

"Ah. You, my friend, have a very important job."

"Which is...?"

"You're my lookout. Just stay here, and tell me if you see anyone coming."

"Yessir!" Ben straightened up and saluted. Then he turned and walked over to the door, somehow managing to trip over his own foot before he got there. He had another giggling fit.

"Oh, God help me." Eric pressed the elevator call

button. The lift dinged open, and Eric stepped inside
and hit the "Door Close" switch.

Inside, he took a deep breath, hearing the hum of
the air conditioning kick in. His heartbeat started
pounding in his temples.

This was it.

If they pulled this one off, he was home dry for the
year.

He reached into his pocket, checking that his CB
radio was switched on. Then he reached inside his
shirt and pulled out three bags of white powder,
stashing them more securely inside the small blue
backpack he was carrying. His mouth felt dry with
anticipation. He hoped that Ben had swallowed his line
about wanting to drink more freely at the party. He
hadn't seen the need to come up with a more elaborate
story. Ben was... well, he was Ben. He was stupid.

Eric liked stupid. It meant a definite lack of questions, which suited Eric down to the ground.

There were three guys waiting outside the campus
with a truck. One of the guys had enough money for
Eric to live on comfortably for a year.

Once again, Eric blessed his good luck in finding
things. The big party he'd gatecrashed at that dude's
house last Thursday had provided him with a lot
more than the free coasters he'd shown to Ben. A
random snoop through the guy's CD collection in
his room upstairs, and he'd left with three sealed
containers of what he guessed was something very
naughty indeed, hidden inside several double
albums labeled "80's Party Mix."

A short walk later, and his chemistry student
buddy Kevin had confirmed that it was indeed grade

"A" cocaine. There was enough there to get more than enough booze money to last him well past the end of term.

There were so many stupid people in the world. Eric hoped that he'd meet more of them soon.

He wasn't afraid of getting caught, but he knew he had to move fast. Eric doubted that anyone had seen him come into the party, but knew that he had to get rid of the drugs quickly. The last thing he wanted was to get spot-checked by a campus security guard. If they caught him, they'd have a field day.

Reaching into his jacket, he took out his little crowbar and studied the lift's control panel with interest. He knew he had to work fast. There were twelve assorted buttons under the main panel, marked with obscure phrases like "Lighn Ctrl" and "Opp Assis." Eric cursed to himself. He'd been hoping there'd be an obvious power switch somewhere, but he couldn't see one.

Putting his backpack on the floor, he ran his hand down the panel, then grunted in satisfaction as his fingers traced an almost invisible seam on one side. There was a hidden compartment under there.

This was where the crowbar came in. Eric jammed one end into the seam, expertly wiggling it back and forth to dig it into the metal, which buckled and bent around the edges. When he judged it had gone in far enough, Eric tensed his arms and pried the crowbar backwards as hard as he could. It took a couple of yanks, but on his third try, the panel popped open.

Eric's face fell. Instead of the big red STOP button he'd been expecting, the inside of the hatch was filled with a confusing tangle of wires and fuses. There was a circuit board on the left, covered in little blinking lights, and what looked like a small black transformer box, wired to the central circuit board. It was obviously a control unit of some kind, but controlling what, Eric didn't know. It had to be something pretty major for it to be so well hidden.

Frowning in concentration, Eric reached into the hatch and took hold of a couple of the thickest wires at random. They were on the ground floor, he knew, so if he pulled out the wrong wires he wouldn't end up plummeting to his death. The elevator door was open, and he felt fairly sure that he could get out in time if it started to close.

Bracing himself, he yanked the wires out of the circuit board.

Nothing happened.

Eric glanced casually back through the elevator doors, but everything was quiet outside. Perhaps he needed to pull the lot out to have an effect?

He poked the hooked end of his crowbar into the hatch, sliding it underneath the main bundle of wires, making sure he got hold of a big loop of them. It was more damage than he wanted to do, but with any luck it would be chalked down by the security people as a student prank.

Leaning back, he tugged on his crowbar. The wires came free with a snap and crackle of electricity, and Eric made a leap for the door as the lights in the elevator went out.

He stood outside in the corridor for a couple of seconds, waiting, but nothing else happened.

Hardly daring to hope, Eric stepped forward, leaned inside the lift, and experimentally pressed the "First Floor" button. The lights on the control panel were out. The lift remained motionless. The doors didn't so much as even twitch.

"Yes!" Eric punched the air, then danced across the lobby to where Ben was waiting. "I did it! I am the greatest," he announced, spinning his crowbar on one finger.

Ben looked him up and down. "You took your time."

"I know." Eric pocketed his crowbar. "Stupid lift didn't have a 'Stop' button."

"That's no excuse," Ben said, then he stopped. He frowned, studying Eric. "Dude. You look different. Why do you look different?"

"I don't know," said Eric patiently. "Why do I look different?"

"Because—" Ben stared at Eric.

Eric fancied that he could hear the cogwheels turning in his friend's brain.

"Because... something's missing from you. You had something. And now it's gone..."

"My bag!" Eric's eyes widened with realization. "Shit! I left it in the elevator!" Turning around, he ran back towards the open door.

Then he stopped dead. The elevator's call button was flashing orange. Someone was summoning the elevator, and it was responding.

As Eric watched in horror, the doors started to slide closed—with his bag full of drugs still inside it.

* * *

Three floors up, security guard Chris Latshaw was getting a cup of coffee from the corridor drinks machine while he waited for the elevator to arrive. He was a little late for the nightly meeting, but he figured that it would take at least fifteen minutes to get started, as any gathering of more than five people usually did. There would be a lot of swapping seats, bickering and chatting, followed by the ritual of the getting out of pens and making coffee while they waited for the last person to arrive.

Security guards were good at procrastination. Some of them made it into an art form. The smarter ones learnt that it meant a lot less standing around in the cold.

Tonight, however, the last person to arrive was him. Chris yawned and rubbed his eyes, hoping that the meeting would be over quickly. There were a couple of hundred unsupervised brats running around down there, and the sooner they got the evening shift sorted out, the better. The last thing he needed was to have to stay up all night, waiting for the paramedics to come and pump lighter fuel from some kid's stomach.

Chris inserted a coffee cartridge and stood by the machine, staring blankly at the wall while the coffee machine fizzed and burped, then poured a stream of hot black coffee into his styrofoam cup.

He scratched his stubble absently. He knew that the coffee would taste like shit, as it always did, but at the same time, it was strangely addictive shit. He and the other guys couldn't stop drinking it.

He glanced at his watch. The elevator was taking its time.

Opening a little pot of half-and-half, he stirred it thoughtfully into his coffee, then on impulse gathered a handful of sugar sachets from the overflowing pot and stuffed them into the back pocket of his uniform. There was so much of the stuff here—no one would miss it. That would save him from having to buy any sugar for a fortnight.

The thought made him feel strangely satisfied, and almost justified his trip down here.

"Come on, come on," he muttered, pressing the elevator call button again. He knew on some level that this wouldn't make it come any quicker, but a part of him insisted that the more times he pressed the button, the quicker the damn thing would arrive.

Turning back to the coffee machine, he started sorting through the little milk cartons. Now, wasn't he out of milk too?

Pockets bulging, he idly reached out and punched the elevator call button yet again.

Downstairs, Eric tore across the lobby, arriving at the elevator just as the door was closing. Performing a heroic leap, he dived between the closing doors just as they slid shut with a clunk.

Relieved, he picked up his backpack from the floor and slung it safely over his shoulder.

Man, that was close!

He patted his bag fondly. No way was he losing all that beer money.

Turning round with a sigh of relief, he pressed the "Door Open" button.

Nothing happened.

He pushed it again, harder this time.

Still nothing.

Ah, crap...

Without warning, the lift jolted under his feet and started moving upwards, its lights flickering errati-cally off and on as it climbed up the building.

Eric's eyes swiveled in their sockets towards the control panel. The eighth floor button was lit, glowing a steady orange.

"Shit!" Eric swore and pounded on the button for the next floor, hoping that it would light up. The button stayed determinedly dark.

Moving back across to the open hatch, Eric stared hopelessly inside at the tangle of wiring. What the hell wires had he cut? Perhaps he'd just taken out the lighting circuit. All the wires looked the same to him. He couldn't even tell which ones he'd pulled out.

He stretched out a hand towards the panel, then stopped. What if one of them was live? Perhaps he shouldn't touch them. The last thing he needed was an electric shock.

He ran a hand through his hair, thinking rapidly. The irony of his situation didn't escape him. Here he was, on his way up to a room full of security guards, with several thousand dollars worth of cocaine in his backpack.

That alone had to be worth several million idiot points.

He pressed a couple of elevator buttons at random, then punched the panel in frustration and flopped back against the wall, breathing heavily.

Son of a bitch!

He felt like the guy who had decided to rob the ATM at a police convention. He pictured the elevator door sliding open onto a roomful of uniformed officials, aiming big ugly guns at his head. All the alcohol dancing through his bloodstream was making him paranoid.

Okay, think. There had to be a way to stop the elevator. What would Bond do?

Probably cut through the doors with a diamond cutter, then rappel out of there with a semi-naked woman on each arm, he thought.

But in the real world...

Eric watched warily as the "Second Floor" light lit up. He hit the "Open Door" button as hard as he could, followed by the floor button labeled "2".

Still nothing happened. The lift resolutely carried on towards the third floor.

Maybe there was nothing on the eighth floor, Eric thought desperately. Perhaps it was just the janitor, calling the elevator to clean it for the night.

He held his breath as the elevator bumped to a halt on the seventh floor. He waited for the doors to open, but they stayed reassuringly closed. That was a relief. Perhaps he'd get away after all.

Then he almost fell forward as the elevator stopped in its tracks with a thump.

What the...?

There was a loud crackling sound from the vandalized control panel. As Eric watched in dismay, all the floor button lights lit up and started flashing. The whine of the air conditioning died away to a pregnant hum, and the lift shuddered for a moment, then jerked upwards a couple of feet. It stopped again with a loud banging noise.

Then, all the lights went out.

And the elevator started to drop. Fast.

Downstairs in the lobby, Ben leaned against the wall and yawned, waiting for Eric to come back down in the elevator. He felt as if he'd been standing here forever. What was taking him so long? Maybe he'd stopped to chat up some cute young security girl.

Ah, girls...

Ben smiled to himself

He liked girls. They were nice.

Preoccupied with such thoughts, Ben didn't notice the elevator call button start flashing madly. Nor did he notice the elevator doors slide part way open, pause, and then jerk closed again. There was a muffled clang from the floor above him. A small spray of sparks trickled out of the gap in the door, vanishing with a snap.

What he did notice, however, was the uniformed security guard. He was standing with his back to Ben, reading an official-looking notice pinned to the fire escape, which was sealed off with striped yellow police tape.

Ben blinked. He was sure that the dude hadn't been there a minute ago.

"Hey, you." The guard called to Ben. "Do you know what's up with the stairs?"

"Me, sir? No, sir. No, very definitely not, sir," said Ben. He tried not to hiccup.

The security guard stared at him in an odd way. "You from around here?" he asked.

"Who, me? No, not at all. In fact, I live..." Ben gestured helplessly with one hand. He was aware that he was moving far too fast. He didn't want the guard to think that he was in the slightest bit drunk. He tried to slow down his arm movements, and ended up with a kind of controlled flail. "Oooh, miles away. In that direction." He pointed at random, and nearly fell over.

"Huh." The security guard was still looking fixedly at Ben. "I thought you looked familiar."

"No. Not familiar at all. Really just passing through. I..." Ben stopped and stared at the guard's head.

Oh no.

That hat.

It was so...

Ben's face twitched a couple of times while he fought to regain control of his facial muscles. It took him a moment. When he dared, he looked again at the hat.

It was round and slightly floppy and it had a shiny silver star on it, like the ones they gave out in kindergarten. It was also about three sizes too small, perched on the guard's balding head like a sailor's cap on the high seas.

A single giggle forced its way out past Ben's not-so-iron control. His eyes widened and he clamped his mouth tight shut, a tiny bubble of mirth escaping from between his lips. The security guard gave him a sharp look, but Ben avoided his gaze, concentrating furiously on not looking at the hat.

It wasn't the size or shape of it, he knew, or the fact that it was gold.

He snuck a quick peek.

No, it was the single tassel that got him. It hung down at the back, like the tail of a horse. It was also gold, and fluttered wildly whenever the guard moved.

The security guard frowned, noticing Ben's frantic expression. "Are you... are you looking at my hat?"

"Nossir," said Ben, tight lipped.

"Are you sure?"

"No. Of course not, sir."

But now he was looking. And by God...

That hat!

It was so.

Incredibly.

Gay!

The security guard raised his eyebrow as Ben doubled up, howling with laughter. What now, he thought bitterly? "What's so funny?" he asked, sounding hurt.

Ben slapped his hand on the wall, shaking his head frantically.

The guard self-consciously straightened his hat. *I* like it, he thought defensively. Out loud he said, "So, you're in here... why, exactly?" He was proud of the exactly measured amount of menace he managed to inject into his voice. He watched as the student's eyes widened.

Ah-hah! Up to no good. He *knew* it...

Ben sobered up slightly, although little spasms of laughter still shook his shoulders. "I, er," he said. "We were just leaving."

"We?"

"I mean me. I was just leaving."

"I suggest you get going then. This building is off-limits tonight."

"Right."

"Right."

There was a pause. "So, you'll be going then," said the guard.

"Yessir. Any minute now." Ben said.

There was another pause.

The security guard raised his eyebrows expectantly.

"Okay, okay!" Ben turned and started walking towards the door, dragging his feet. The security guard watched him all the way.

Weird kid, he thought, turning to press the elevator call button.

Then he flew across the room as a giant arc of electricity from the elevator panel earthed itself through his body. He crashed into the far wall and slumped to the ground, groaning.

Ben stared at the fallen guard stupidly.

Then he turned and looked at the elevator call button. It was flashing and sparking.

"Eric!" He shouted.

There was no reply.

After a moment, Ben sighed and reached into his pocket for his cell phone. His brow creased in drunken confusion.

Now, what was the number of the emergency services, again?

"Oh, fuck..."

Eric crouched down in the elevator in the dark, clutching at the wall, his heart hammering. The elevator had dropped about ten feet before the emergency brakes had cut in, slamming him to a halt.

Eric wiped the sweat from his brow. He had to get out of here, and quickly, in case the elevator dropped again. He couldn't believe what he'd done. He'd only cut a few tiny wires...

A few tiny wires behind a big thick fuck-off panel, he reminded himself grimly. *Moron!*

Eric stepped forwards cautiously in the dark, his hands stretched out in front of him like a sleepwalker. His fingertips brushed the cold metal of the elevator door and he jerked them back as if stung, visualizing the doors opening and sending him plunging downwards to a grisly, gear-filled death in the guts of the elevator shaft.

That wouldn't be cool. Not cool at all, in fact.

Eric stayed absolutely still, hoping against hope that the lights would come back on. Maybe this was just a temporary power glitch?

A minute dragged past. It got noticably warmer inside the elevator.

Nope, definitely not just a temporary power glitch. This baby was out of service for good.

Eric started to sweat. Pictures of the emergency services arriving and having to cut the elevator doors open raced through his mind. There would be no escape for him and his little bag of drugs. He could see the headlines now.

There was only one thing for it.

"Er... hello?" Eric called out, steeling himself. He really, really didn't want to be doing this. He felt like such a loser, but knew that he had no other choice. He hammered on the door, then waited.

There was no reply. He hadn't really been expecting one. The metallic echoes of his voice rang back, as though taunting him.

Eric drew in his breath, ready to call out again.

Then he stopped. Was it just him, or was the elevator moving?

He held his breath, listening intently. There was a very slight sensation of movement, although he couldn't tell if it was moving up or down. The elevator was definitely creeping in one direction or the other.

Hey, this might be good. If the thing was moving, then it still had power, which meant he might be able to make it work again.

Moving carefully across to the far wall, Eric ran his hand downwards until his fingers brushed the recessed call buttons. He pressed them all, one by one, but nothing happened.

He was well and truly stuck. Stupid elevator!

Frustrated, Eric lifted his hand and gave the panel a hefty smack.

The vibrations of the impact traveled up and down the wall. Inside the service hatch, one of the wires moved a fraction of an inch and touched one of the other wires.

It was not a good wire for it to touch.

With a fizz of electricity, the power to the emergency brakes cut out. Before Eric had a chance to draw breath to cry out, they released with a clunk.

The elevator dropped like a boulder.

EIGHT

Back at Charlie's house, Jess sat on the sofa, her head propped up on her hands. Charlie sat next to her, at a slight distance. They watched through the dining room window as paramedics and police swarmed around in the front yard, speaking urgently into walkie-talkies and fussing around with yellow police cordon tape.

The silence stretched between them like an invisible spider web, the air filled with unspoken thoughts. Jess fancied that she could see them buzzing around Charlie's head like angry mosquitoes. She rubbed her eyes, sunken too deeply into her own misery to bother with platitudes.

She wondered how Charlie was coping. There were no words to describe how she was feeling. When she was little, Jess remembered that her dad had always told her that when bad stuff happened, she should visualize a big empty box in her mind, then gather everything about the bad event up and put it in the box, then close the lid on it. He said it would get everything together in the same place. That way, you could put the box away in a corner of your head, and free up the rest of your mind to carry on with your day.

That was bullshit, Jess decided. No one with as many problems as her father could give her advice on how to deal with stuff.

Besides which, there was no way in hell she could visualize a box that big.

Charlie was the first one to speak. "I didn't mean to do it."

"Nobody said you did," said Jess. She was staring blankly at the carpet. "It was an accident. Just an accident."

Charlie just shook his head. He looked dazed.

"Do you think..." he began.

"What?"

"Nothing. It's just..." Charlie appeared to be on the verge of tears. "She saved me. From the club, I mean."

"I know." Jess reached out and patted Charlie awkwardly on the knee.

"Wasn't for her needing a cigarette, I'd be dead."

"You don't know that," Jess soothed.

"Yes I do. She saved my life. Now she's dead." Charlie thought for a moment. "Like it's payback or something." He thought for a moment. "Is God punishing me?"

"That's ridiculous. There *is* no g... I mean, don't say that."

"I can't help it," said Charlie, looking anguished. "I keep thinking about what happened. I could have saved her."

"You didn't know she was still down there," said Jess.

At the back of her mind, an evil little voice whispered, *"Charlie's single now."* She mentally threw a rock at the voice, shocked at the thought. That was the last thing she needed to be thinking about right now.

But if Charlie really was single...

Shut up, shut up, she told the voice. She'd had it with dating. Men bad, ice cream good, she reminded herself. She didn't need the stress in her life. She tried to think of other things, things that didn't involve Charlie.

She had a really, really hard time of it.

After a minute had grated past, Jess decided that she'd had enough. Her thoughts were going in circles, and she was getting nowhere. She got abruptly to her feet, then strode over to the window and stared out at the scene. "I can't just sit here. I need to go and... do something. I don't know what. Sitting here is making me crazy." She turned and studied a poster on the wall, a chart of spider species. Above it was a box of preserved butterflies, mounted on pins. She pulled a face. *Creepy.* "Can't we go out and help?"

"Police chief said to stay here." Charlie tapped his fingers on the leather of the sofa, his face pale with worry. "Do you think they'll press charges?"

Jess looked at him. "What do you think?"

"I don't know." Charlie wrung his hands together.

"I told you: it was an accident. It wasn't your fault." She put a hand on Charlie's shoulder. He didn't seem to notice.

She decided to leave her hand there, just for a moment.

A thought struck her. She had to ask him something. She turned towards him, her eyes lowered. "Charlie, um. I don't know if now is the time, but there was something I wanted to—"

She stopped as the door handle turned. But instead of the sheriff she was expecting, it was someone very familiar.

"Jamie!" Jess jumped up and threw her arms around him.

"I came as soon as I heard. What the hell happened?"

Jess turned her face inwards, pressing her cheek against Jamie's chest. "It was horrible. Just horrible," she said. Pulling away, she looked up at Jamie. He was freshly shaven, but looked like he hadn't slept in days. He was wearing his black gas attendant's uniform, complete with shiny gold name tag.

"I tried to go to work," he said, by way of explanation. He shook his head ruefully, starting to unzip his top. "*That* lasted a long time. I just couldn't..."

"Jamie, man. Good to see you." Charlie stood up and solemnly clapped Jamie on the back.

Jamie blinked at the sight of Charlie. "Yeah... yeah. Good to see you too." Jamie's voice sounded a little odd, but Jess didn't notice. She had never seen him in his work clothes before. He looked kinda cute, which was weird, because she saw him go topless on stage every night, and had never really paid much attention to the way he looked before.

It must be the shock, she thought to herself. Shock does funny things to a person.

"How did you hear?" she asked, sitting back down on the sofa.

"The sheriff called me. Said that you'd been involved in an accident." Jamie paused, gazing at Jess. There was a strange look on his face. "I thought he meant that—"

"Involved? No. She wasn't involved." Charlie sat down beside Jess and put a protective arm around her shoulders. He nodded to Jamie. "Come on in. Sit down."

"No thanks. I'll stand."

An uncomfortable second ticked by. Jamie stared at Charlie's arm for a moment, then looked at Jess, a question in his eyes. She avoided his gaze expertly.

"Jess had nothing to do with it," Charlie said. "It was me who did it. I killed Amber."

"Charlie! You gotta stop saying that!"

"But it's true. One minute she was alive, talking to me. Just like we're talking now. Next minute she was dead. All because of me."

"Come, now. It wasn't your fault—"

"Would you stop saying that? Of course it was my fault. I didn't mean to do it, but it happened, and now she's dead." Charlie's fists clenched on his lap, his eyes fixed to the scene outside the window. For once in his life, his cheeky demeanor was gone. "Do you know what the last thing she said to me was?"

"Charlie, you don't have to—"

"We had an argument. When she was leaving, she told me that I was mean and that I didn't care if she lived or died. She said that to me."

"Well, I'm sure she didn't mean it."

"Of course she meant it. I *was* mean to her. She came over to see me and I blew her off. Just 'cause I—" Charlie glanced at Jess and shook his head. "She was wearing her pink nail varnish. She only wears that on really special occasions..." Charlie's voice choked up. He bowed his head, staring at the floor.

"Come on now. It wasn't your fault. It was just a dumb accident."

"I know it was. I know that." Charlie swallowed, his voice tight. "But I made it happen. So it was still me who killed her."

"Come on, now. If you think like that, you're gonna go crazy." Jess thought for a moment. "Hell, if you wanna blame anyone, blame me."

"You? Why should I blame you?"

"Because I was in the bath."

Charlie stared at her. "How does that make it your fault?"

"Well, if I got out of the bath just fifteen minutes earlier, I would've been downstairs with you guys. I could've done something... talked to Amber, kept her here a couple more minutes. Kept her away from that driveway."

"That's stupid."

"No it's not. Or I could've helped you with the car. Stopped it from rolling. If I'd been there with you, Amber might still be alive now."

"But you *weren't there*," sniffed Charlie. "You didn't know."

"But neither did you." Jess glanced outside the window again. "It was just a dumb accident." She gestured helplessly. "A million things could have saved her. She could have stopped to tie her shoelaces before crossing the drive. But she didn't. She could have gone straight home instead of stopping to pick that rose. But she didn't. Hell, a duck could have hit an airplane in the sky and fallen down on her head. But it didn't. That's what makes it so dumb."

"But..." Charlie stopped, a tiny glimmer of hope in his eyes. "She didn't know what was going to happen. So she didn't do any of those things."

"That's my point." Jess sat forwards in her seat, bitterness sounding for the first time in her voice. "Shit happens. We can't control everything that happens to us. We can control some of it, but not all." She gave a hollow laugh. "That bit we can't control? It's called fate. It sucks. Get used to it."

Charlie was quiet for a moment. "I did everything I could," he said.

"I know you did," said Jess. She squeezed Charlie's hand. "You did your best. It's all any of us can do."

Jess gazed up at Charlie. He didn't let go of her hand and she felt her mouth go dry. His eyes were even more blue than usual at close quarters. She wondered hazily whether he wore contact lenses to make them so blue.

She peered closer, trying to see if there was a tell-tale ring of a contact lens around the edge of his iris.

"'Scuse me, guys? Not to break up the party or anything, but shouldn't we be out there, I don't know, filling in reports or something?"

Charlie and Jess looked up at Jamie. He was hovering awkwardly in the doorway. She had forgotten that he was there. Some part of her recognized that she should feel bad about this.

"Well, isn't that what you do when someone dies?" Jamie prompted, scuffing a boot on the floor. He stared down at the floorboards, a fixed expression on his face.

"Are you all right?" said Jess, after a moment.

"I'm fine. Of course I'm fine." Jamie sounded irritated. "I just had a... stressful... night. That's all. But I'm perfectly fine." He looked her in the eye. "How are you?"

"I'm just dandy," said Jess, frowning at Jamie. What was up with him? He was acting weird.

"You look tired," said Jamie, then stopped, as though he had said too much. He shifted from foot to foot, his eyes flicking nervously between Jess and Charlie.

"Yeah. I am a little sleep deprived."

"You both look tired," said Jamie, carefully.

"Me? No. I slept fine," said Charlie. He was still holding onto Jess's hand.

"Oh, really? That's good to know. And where did you sleep last night?"

"I slept here. I live here." Now Charlie was staring at Jamie. He frowned, as though seeing him for the first time, and sat up a little straighter. "Why do you ask?"

"That's good," said Jamie, ignoring Charlie's question. "And where did Jess sleep?"

"Who?"

"Jess." Jamie pointed.

"Oh, *Jess*." Charlie paused for a moment, glancing up as though filing something away in his head. "She slept... well, I don't know. In the police station, I guess." He met Jamie's eyes, a challenge on his face.

"I see." Jamie turned to Jess. "Did you?"

"Of course I did. What—don't you believe him?"

"Should I?"

"Yes! He's telling the truth!" Jess started to feel uncomfortable holding Charlie's hand. She squeezed it briefly, then let go. "What's up with you?"

A muscle clenched briefly in Jamie's jaw. He turned away from her to look out of the window. "Nothing," he said tensely. "I'm just tired." He pointed outside, where a covered stretcher was being loaded into the back of a paramedic van. "And she's dead. Kind of destroys the mood, don't you think?" He glanced pointedly back at Charlie.

That did it. Anger sparked in Charlie's eyes. He started to get up, but Jess put a hand on his knee and shook her head slightly. She got up from her seat and walked up behind Jamie. "Hey," she said softly.

There was no reply.

Jess reached out and touched Jamie's elbow enquiringly, but he pulled away from her. "Excuse me," he muttered. "I've gotta go." He pushed past her roughly and headed towards the door, zipping up his uniform as he walked.

"Where're you going?"

"Work. I'm late. Have fun."

A second later, the door banged shut.

Charlie was the first one to speak. "What's *his* problem?"

"Beats me." Jess stared after the retreating figure marching away down the path.

"Let me go after him. I'll talk to him." He started towards the door, but Jess stood in his way.

"Let him go. He'll be fine. He doesn't need to be here."

"Why is he even here?" Charlie demanded. "He didn't know Amber. Why did the sheriff call him?"

Jess shrugged, her eyes still on Jamie. He had stopped by the ambulance, and was talking to one of the medics, gesturing back towards the house. Jess felt a strange feeling in the pit of her stomach. "The sheriff saw me here. I guess he thought that we were... together."

"Why on earth would he think that?"

"We came in together last night, to the police station. Some stuff happened. Jamie got caught up in it. I guess the sheriff just assumed that we were, like, a couple or something."

"And are you?"

"No! Of course not. Jamie's..." Jess stopped, searching through her mind for a way or describing Jamie. "Well, he's Jamie. He's a nice guy." She shrugged, unable to think of anything else to say.

"So he's a nice guy. What else?"

"Nothing else. We're friends. That's all. Although we once had a..." Jess stopped, conflicting expressions chasing themselves across her face.

"Had a what?" prompted Charlie.

"Er, a drink. Together. Once. A long time ago." Jess cleared her throat nervously. "Since then, he, er, well... he's been kind of hanging around me. I like him a lot, I really do, but just as a friend. I think he thinks there's more to it than that, but I haven't the heart to tell him otherwise." She paused, shrugging helplessly. "He's a really nice guy, but well, he's got no car, no money, no real job prospects... but he's a kick-ass drummer. We really needed him in the band. D'you know how hard it is to get a decent drummer, these days?"

"All that after just one drink? Wow."

"Yeah." Jess shrugged. "It was a good, er, drink. But that's all it was." She heartily wished that Charlie would drop the subject. She was in no mood to deal with this right now. She yawned hugely, feeling a wave of tiredness sweep over her. Her little sleep in the bath hadn't done much to refresh her. "Hey, do you mind if I lie down for a little while? I'm about ready to fall down."

"Sure." Charlie tossed a pile of newspapers off the sofa, then pulled a couple of cushions together, heaping them up at one end. He patted them with a hand. "Here you go."

"Thanks." Jess lay down slightly self-consciously on the sofa, aware that Charlie was watching her every move. She glanced down at the newspapers on the floor in front of them. The top one had a cover story about a guy from Topanga Canyon who'd got trapped in an elevator for three days. That's news, she thought?

Shrugging to herself, she closed her eyes and tried to shut the horrors of the last twenty-four hours out of her mind. She tried to concentrate on nice things. She was warm. She wasn't in any immediate danger. Charlie was there.

She heard a chair creak at the end of the room as Charlie sat down. She opened her eyes for a moment and saw that he was gazing fixedly out of the window, his eyebrows drawn together in worry. Feeling her gaze on him, he glanced over and smiled briefly, before returning his gaze to the window.

Jess smiled back, feeling herself blush. *He was so cute.* Then she rolled over and tried to relax. The cushions were soft under her head, and she was so sleepy...

After a couple of minutes, she frowned, eyes still closed. Despite the fact that she was exhausted, her mind was revving. Something had just clicked into place.

What was it that the homeless guy had said to her the other night? Something about falling down? She wished she could remember. She knew it was important...

Then she froze, the memory hitting her with crystal clarity.

You're all dead, but still you walk, he'd said. She remembered, because it had creeped her out totally when he'd said it. The hairs on the back of her neck stood up at the memory. What else had he said?

Then, she remembered.

"*You all fall down,*" she mouthed. "*Girl next, then boy. You'll see...*"

Jess's hand flew to her mouth. She'd had no idea at the time what he meant by "girl", but he'd definitely been looking at Eric when he'd said "boy".

And now, a girl was dead.

Which meant...

Swallowing hard, Jess turned to Charlie. "Where's your phone?" she asked.

* * *

Eric only stopped screaming when he ran out of breath to scream with. He lay on the floor, hands over his head, his eyes screwed tight shut. He didn't dare open his eyes for fear of what he might see. All was still again, which was just fine by him.

This really, really wasn't his day.

He was reasonably sure that he wasn't dead. He knew this because his head hurt, and his mouth tasted like blood where he had bitten through his tongue. It was dark, but all his senses seemed to be working, which was always a good start.

Groaning, Eric shifted on the floor and lifted his head groggily. At least the elevator had stopped moving now. He wasn't sure whether this was a bad or a good thing. He spat the blood out of his mouth and pushed himself up into a sitting position, moving carefully, just in case. He groaned, feeling a wave of dizziness hit him.

What the fuck had happened to the elevator? All he'd done was break a couple of wires. There was no way he could have known that *this* was going to happen.

Moving infinitely slowly and carefully, Eric rubbed his head, feeling a big lump start to come up where his forehead had hit the floor on the way down.

Oh, this so, *so* wasn't good.

He had an idea. Groping in the darkness, he reached into his pocket, feeling for his cell phone.

It wasn't there.

"Shit!"

Eric knew that he had to get out of here. He remembered with a shudder that brief, horrible moment in the darkness when the elevator had dropped, leaving his stomach a dozen feet above him. He remembered thinking very clearly, *"This is it."* He hadn't even been aware that he'd been screaming.

Then an explosion of sparks had filled the elevator as the emergency brakes locked back into place, fizzing and glitching, bringing the elevator to a halt and knocking him to the floor.

Now the elevator was still, but for how long? What if the brakes gave way again?

Eric realized that he had to do something, and quickly. Someone would probably come along to rescue him sooner or later, but what if he didn't have that long left? He had to get out himself. He was too young and too pretty to end up as a pancake. All those years at the gym would be wasted, for starters.

Above him, something metallic creaked and he froze, a stab of white-hot fear shooting through him. As he watched, the lights in the control panel flared up brightly then exploded with a bang, leaving glowing after-images dancing on the insides of his eyelids. Eric flinched, preparing himself for the worst. A loud clunking sound rang out, then something struck the top of the elevator and rolled off. There was a creaking noise from the cable above him.

And then all was ominously quiet...

Eric gave a small scream as the elevator suddenly dropped again, just a short distance of several feet, but it was enough to set his heart pounding. He clutched at the floor, swearing uncontrollably, his pulse thundering in his ears. The brakes must be on the way out, he decided, with a thrill of horror. They were working now, but how much longer would they hold?

He knew he had to move fast.

Moving as quickly as he dared, Eric got to his feet and stood up in the blackness, swaying like a drunken surfer. Was it just his imagination, or was the floor sloping a little under his feet? The thought sent a fresh chill of fear through him.

He stepped forwards cautiously, all the while listening out for any warning sounds from the elevator. Nothing happened, so he moved to the front of the elevator and reached out his hand, groping urgently for the control panel.

He shut his eyes in the darkness, trying to visualize where the "Door Open" button was located. Third one down... two to the right... was that it? Eric's fingers traced over the raised buttons cautiously. There was Braille on the buttons, and Eric found himself thinking guiltily about all those after-school classes he'd skipped. He wished desperately that he could wind back time and go to just one...

But it was too late now. He had to sort this one out himself. There was one button that was bigger than the others. That had to be the one.

There was only one way to find out.

Eric held his breath, and pressed the button.

"Can't you drive any faster?" Jess snapped, reaching down into the seat well of the car for her Thomas Guide map.

"Faster? Are you kidding? This is as fast as she'll go!" lied Charlie. He gripped the steering wheel of his father's prized Jaguar tighter, praying that he wouldn't get pulled over. Palm trees and low-rise prefab buildings whizzed past his window at blinding speed.

"You're kidding, right? Please tell me you're kidding."

"I wish I was! Look!" Charlie pointed to a wood-inlaid dial aboard the Jaguar. "See? This is her top speed."

Jess squinted at the little dial. "That's the gas gauge!"

"Oh... really?" Charlie gave a nervous little laugh. "Silly me. Must've got confused. Which is the...?"

"*That's* the speedometer," said Jess "And look! It goes all the way up to..."

"Yes, I know how fast she goes," said Charlie desperately. "It's just... she's an old car, you know? We have to take it easy on her."

"Screw the car. Eric could be dead by now," snapped Jess. "Don't you care?"

"Of course I care," said Charlie, trying to come to terms with this new side of Jess. When he'd talked to the girl before, she'd been so different, so calm and eager to please. She looked good, she smelled good, and she looked at him like he was some kind of rock star.

He really dug that. She was just his kind of girl.

Now, she'd apparently turned into some kind of lunatic. She was still cute, but now she was scary-cute. He wasn't too sure that he could handle that.

He cleared his throat timidly. "It's just... don't you think you're taking this a little seriously? I mean, I'm sure it was a good dream, but maybe that's all it was. Just a dream. And that whole thing with the homeless guy..." He stopped as he saw the look on Jess's face. "What?"

Jess put down her map and stared at Charlie. "Do you think I'm making this up?"

"I didn't say that. I just think that rushing over there might not be the right thing to do. Can't you try calling him again?"

"I did. He's still not answering." Jess tossed her cell phone into the back seat. She folded her arms and sat back, jiggling one leg. The change of clothes she'd borrowed from Charlie fitted her quite well, but she wished heartily that the sweater wasn't pink. Charlie had assured her that it hadn't been Amber's, but she wasn't too sure that she believed him.

"So he's not answering his phone. Big deal. He's a guy. That could mean anything. He could be in the shower, out at a party, having a nap..."

"Lying dead in a ditch somewhere..." Jess shook her head. "Something's wrong. Something's happened to him. I can just feel it."

"What do you care, all of a sudden? I thought you said you didn't like this guy."

"I don't. I just feel... responsible. If anything happens to him, it'll be my fault."

"Jess," Charlie cleared his throat, tapping the wheel. "I know that the last couple of days have been tough on all of us. And this morning? With Amber? I still can't believe—"

"I know, I know!" said Jess brusquely. "She's dead. And Eric's going to be next."

"You don't know that," said Charlie, thinking, I wish everybody would stop saying that. He tightened his grip on the wheel, trying to block the images of Amber from his mind. "But running away like that— before the police chief even got back—just because you had a dream... Don't you think it looks a little, you know, incriminating?"

"It was an accident. Everyone said it was," said Jess dismissively, her nose buried in the map. "You'll be fine. Just tell them you ran out of hair gel and had to make an urgent trip to the store."

Charlie unconsciously reached up and patted his hair down, unsure whether this was a compliment or not. "You think they'll believe me?"

"No, but it's always worth a try. Crap! Turn here!"

"What, here?" Charlie hauled on the wheel in panic as the exit flew towards them, nearly blind-siding an expensive-looking BMW. The car blared its horn at him, and Charlie hit the brakes and swerved away to let it pass before turning. The driver yelled at them out of his window as they passed. Jess shouted something back at him that made Charlie blush.

This wasn't at all the ride he'd expected to have with her. Not by a long shot.

"Are you all right in the back, there?" Jess called over her shoulder.

"I'm fine," said Jamie, clinging desperately onto the door handle as the car righted itself. He was starting to regret coming along with them, but he would be damned if he was going to let Jess ride off in a car with that bleached bozo. He should never have answered his cell phone when she'd called to tell him what they were doing, but after all, it *was* Jess...

He rubbed his head where he had bumped it on the window. "Hey, don't worry. I'm in a band. I didn't need those brain cells anyway."

"That's cool. Hang on in there. We're nearly there." She turned back to Charlie. "Where the hell are we?" she said. Charlie shrugged.

Jess opened up the map fully and ran her finger across it. "Dammit! We missed the Hoover junction!" She stabbed a finger out of the window. "What road was that?"

"I don't know. We're going too fast. I can't see the signs."

"What are you, blind?" Jess stopped as something filtered through. *Charlie Delgado.* She smoothed down her hair and attempted a smile. "Sorry. I mean, perhaps we could afford to slow down a bit. Just a little bit," she added, as Charlie gratefully let off the gas pedal.

"So," Charlie said, still trying to get his head around what Jess had told him. "What you told me— I'm still trying to understand. You think that, what? Because this hobo guy said something about a girl dying, you think he meant Amber?"

"And Eric." Jess nodded vigorously. "I know it sounds crazy. Like, psycho-crazy. But I just have this terrible feeling..." She closed her eyes and struck her chest with her fist. "...right in here, that he knew what he was talking about. Two people who survived from the club are dead. That's more than a coincidence."

"And you don't think that he was drunk, or high?"

"Probably both. It doesn't matter. I believe him. I was right about the club thing. This... I don't know.

It just feels the same." She looked at Charlie mean-ingfully, holding his gaze just a second too long. "You've gotta trust your feelings, you know?"

"Right. Fine. If that's what you believe." Charlie spun the wheel and pulled over into the outside lane, slowing down as a traffic light approached. In front of him was a ridiculous-looking stretch HumVee, with a bumper sticker that read, "Elevate your Expectations." The picture on the sticker showed a HumVee driving out of an elevator.

He pointed it out to Jess and got a small smile out of her.

It was a start, he thought.

"So what about the bouncer?"

"What about him?"

"Did this guy mention him at all?"

Jess thought for a minute. "I don't know. I don't remember."

"Well, there you go. If this guy was so great, he would've mentioned the bouncer too."

"Maybe he did. I was just so tired..." Jess scratched her head irritably. "Perhaps I should go find him again."

"What, the homeless guy?"

"Uh-huh."

Charlie gave a hollow laugh. "Good luck with that one. There are only, like, fifty thousand homeless folk living around here. It should be easy to find him."

"Don't be cheeky. If I'm meant to find him, then I will."

Charlie shrugged. "It's your call. Do you even remember what this guy looked like?"

Jess thought for a moment. "He had an old cowboy jacket on. With tassels on it. And he smelled very bad. That's about all I remember."

"That narrows it down a bit."

"Well, it's a start. No, don't stop!" Jess knocked Charlie's hand away from the stick shift.

"But the light's about to change!"

"So? This is LA. Green means go. Yellow means go faster."

"Whatever you say." Charlie slammed his foot down on the gas pedal, speeding past the changing light and rocketing across the intersection, accompanied by the traditional blast of horns from the waiting traffic. A pedestrian with one foot on the crosswalk jumped out of the way, hurling abuse.

"Whee... that was fun," said Jess absently. The car bounced over a pothole, scraping its front end on the ground and making the suspension creak alarmingly. Charlie muttered an oath under his breath.

"Now, this guy," continued Jess. "He was downtown, probably around the middle of South Central." She thought for a moment. "Could you take me there later?"

"Sure. As long as I don't have to stop or get out of the car at any point," said Charlie, putting a protective hand on the dashboard of the Jag. "If anything happens to this car, my dad'll kill me. He only lent it to me for the weekend."

Jess looked at him blankly. "Does it matter? This is someone's life at stake here."

"Or not."

"Look, if you don't believe me then that's fine."

"I didn't say I didn't believe you. It's just... I don't know. I just think that we're going on a wild goose chase. Some terrible shit's happened, but I don't think that chasing after some random madman is gonna help matters."

"It'll help me," said Jess quietly.

"But will it? What if he's just been drinking wind-shield cleaner and tells you that you're going to die next? What then? Are you going to spend the next ten years of your life locked up in a padded cell somewhere?"

"You don't understand." Jess put down her map and turned to face Charlie. "I need to know this. All those people died, and it was my fault. I should've warned them, and I didn't." She paused and gazed out of the window, choosing her words carefully. "This has just blown everything else out of the water. It's changed everything. Who I am, where, I'm going—everything." She broke off and waved a hand at the SUV in front of her. "C'mon, go! The light doesn't get any greener than that! What *is* it with these people today?" She stamped her foot in frustration.

"Don't worry about it. You're probably still in shock. Just try to stay calm. We'll get through this. I promise you. Everything will be fine." Charlie put a hand on her shoulder and gently rubbed her back, thinking, Crazy chick, but I bet she's great in bed...

"You promise?" Jess bit her lip anxiously, her eyes searching Charlie's face.

"I promise." Charlie ran his hand up Jess's back and brushed her hair out of her face. "Just stick with me, and you'll be fine."

"And what if I'm not? What if I'm next? The guy told me to look out for signs... What if I'm seeing signs right now, and not realizing that they're signs?" Jess shifted restlessly in her seat. "Look! There's a hot dog stand. What if I'm about to be killed by a giant hot dog?" She bit her nails anxiously.

"You won't be. Just trust me on that one. I'll look after you. Nothing bad can happen to you while I'm around, scout's honor."

Jess looked sidelong at Charlie. She couldn't help feeling like something terrible was about to happen. But he was so adorable, and she wanted to believe him so badly.

But that look in his eyes... it was as though he could read her mind. He looked so sweet and caring, as if he would go to the ends of the world to protect her...

"Er, guys?"

"What?"

"Can you throw me a sick bag?"

"Shut up, Jamie."

"Come on! Open, damn you!"

A low-pitched whirr filled the air inside the elevator. Eric stepped back from the door, nearly dancing with impatience. He assumed that he'd killed the doors when he'd ripped out the control panel, but now they seemed to be responding, albeit slowly.

Closing his eyes, Eric made a silent oath. He'd pulled some crazy shit in his life, but this was pretty much taking the cookie. If he made it out of here alive, he vowed to lay off the drinking for at least a month...

As the thought crossed his mind, there was a clunk and a hum, and the "Door Open" light lit up, flashing a pregnant orange. Eric's eyes flew open and he watched with baited breath, scarcely daring to hope.

A thin slit of light appeared in front of him as the doors slowly began to open.

"Yes!"

Eric moved swiftly towards the light, hope flaring in him like a beacon. But as he did so, the sound of the motors died away and the doors creaked to a halt. Eric groaned. Stepping forwards, he jammed a hand through the tiny gap in the doors and tried to lever them open, but try as he might, he couldn't shift them. The motor had frozen, locking the door firmly into place. He might as well have tried to pull apart solid concrete.

Eric thumped the door in frustration and put an eye to the crack, peering feverishly outside. The elevator had stopped between floors, and he could just see the edge of the floor, with its green linoleum and dirty metal joints. It was just above chest height. Below it was a complicated tangle of piping and wiring, and below that, about a foot of the room underneath was visible. There was nobody there, either.

Eric yelled, "Help!" through the door for a minute, but there was no response.

He stepped back from the door, thinking rapidly. He had to get that door open, and quickly. The brakes might give way any minute.

Eric stretched his arms, cracking his joints, and pushed both hands through the gap. It was now or never. With a Herculean effort, he started levering the doors apart. The door motor whined in protest, pulling against him as he grunted and strained, heaving for all that he was worth.

Slowly, inch by precious inch, the doors came open, the motor whining shrilly in protest. When they were about a foot apart, Eric carefully reached behind him with his foot. He snagged his backpack, and maneuvered it into the gap at the bottom of the doors, wedging them open. Then he let go of the doors and quickly began climbing out of the elevator, squeezing through the gap like a cat and hauling himself up onto the lip of the third floor.

At that moment, the elevator creaked again. Whimpering in panic, Eric kicked his legs out behind him, pulling himself through the gap as fast as he could. He saw in his mind's eye the elevator dropping again, cutting him into two gory halves.

Damn. He watched *way* too many horror films to be pulling this shit...

Then he was free. Almost sobbing with relief, Eric flung himself forwards and rolled clear of the elevator. He lay curled on the floor for a moment, breathing deeply.

He'd made it. He was alive.

Then his eyes flew open as he remembered his bag. He rolled over and peered down inside the elevator, his whole body vibrating with adrenaline. He could clearly see his bag in the shadows, wedged between the doors. Perhaps he could find something to fish it out with...?

He jumped as the sound of a siren blared through the open window behind him. His eyebrows flew to the top of his head. What were the cops doing here? How had they known?

Then rationality descended. Perhaps the cops didn't know about his little drugs stash, but they'd probably been called by some kind of automatic elevator alarm thing. Eric realized that he had to get his bag back, and fast.

Scrambling to his feet, Eric made a quick decision. He would go to the next floor and try to grab his bag back from there. It would be a heck of a lot easier than trying to get hold of it from where he was.

There was a door at the end of the room. Eric jogged towards it, picking up speed as the siren continued to blare outside. He shouldered his way through it and ran out into the darkened stairwell. It was so dark that he could barely see, but he didn't have time to stop and hunt for a light switch.

He began pounding down the stairs, two at a time. He was vaguely aware that there was something he should be remembering, but his mind was so clouded with panic that he couldn't think straight.

His head throbbed as he pounded his way downwards, flying around the corner at breakneck speed. As he did, his foot caught on something stretched across the stairwell. He threw out his arms to try to grab the rail, but it was too late. With a feeling of disbelief, he felt himself start to fall, plunging forwards at full speed down the stairwell. A second later, he ploughed into what looked like a wall of yellow police tape, stuck across the top of the stairs between the floors. The tape pulled away and wrapped itself around him as he continued his fall, hitting the stairs hard and bouncing downwards in a flail of limbs.

What the fuck? Eric thought hazily. His head cracked against the first step with bone-splitting force, then he saw nothing but darkness.

NINE

"Dude... dude... Are you okay, dude?"

The security guard groaned as he slowly swam back to consciousness. Some kid was peering down at him, shaking him by the shoulders. "Gerrroff," he muttered groggily. He tried to get up, but found that he couldn't move. Every cell in his body was throbbing. His whole body as if like it had been squeezed for about a year in a giant vice.

He moaned and rolled over, clutching his head. His hand come away red with blood. He stared at it stupidly. "Bleeding," he said. "Why am I bleeding?" He looked around him, aware that something important was missing. "And where's my hat?"

The kid backed off and was replaced by a worried-looking paramedic, who loomed above him. "Try to relax, sir. We'll be moving you into the ambulance in a minute."

"Ambulance..." The guard struggled to keep his eyes open. "Where... what...?"

"Dude, that was fuckin' awesome." Now the kid was back, looking down at him and grinning like a goon. "You should have seen yourself. You went flyin' across the room like Superman. It was so neat. Does your head hurt? 'Cause I think you hit it."

"Stand back, guys. Coming through," said the paramedic. He put a collapsible gurney down next to the guard and folded it out. "Places, people." A team of five other medics surrounded the guard, rolling up their sleeves and readying equipment. "One, two, three... lift." They lifted the groaning security guard up onto the gurney and started to wheel him towards the door.

The guard gazed down at his boots from his horizontal position.

They were smoking.

He was sure that that wasn't entirely normal.

Then he heard the door crash open. Footsteps ran into the room and a female voice yelled, "Eric... Eric!"

"No... It's Jason, actually..." said the guard, trying to be helpful. He heard the footsteps move over towards him and tried to sit up, but some invisible guy bashed him on the head with a red-hot poker. He subsided, grimacing.

Then a face was peering down at him, some girl in a pink sweater. The guard screwed up his eyes, trying to focus on her. He thought she looked a little familiar. She certainly looked very worried. Could this be his girlfriend?

He couldn't remember, but he hoped it was. She was kind of pretty.

"What happened?" the girl asked the paramedic.

"Yeah... what happened?" asked Jason.

"Electric shock," said the medic. "I'm gonna have to ask you to stand back. We need to get this guy to hospital." He kicked the brakes off the gurney and started wheeling it towards the door.

"How did he get shocked?" asked the girl, trotting alongside. Boy, she was persistent.

"Ask this guy. He said he touched something in the wall. We're looking into it."

There was a pause, then a male voice said, "Holy cow—it's you!"

"Yeah, it's me," said the girl, sounding anxious. "Where's Eric?"

"I'm here," said the guard pathetically. "And I told you—my name's not Eric, it's Jason." *Or is it?* Asked a voice in his head. *What if I really am Eric? Would I remember?*

He gazed up at the ceiling, a wave of existential confusion washing over him. He turned his head and reached out to the girl. "Honey? Could you find my hat? It's got my name in it."

There was a snigger from the boy.

"What?" asked the guard, as they wheeled him out.

As the paramedics disappeared out of the door, Jess turned back to Ben tensely. "I saw the ambulances parked outside. I knew I'd find you here. I just knew it."

"Did Eric call you?"

"No. That's just it. I need to find him. It's urgent. Where is he?"

"Dunno." Ben shrugged. "He went up in that elevator like, ten minutes ago."

"And he hasn't come down yet?"

"Not that I know of. Hey, don't touch that!"

"Why?" said Jess, her hand frozen halfway to the elevator call button.

"I think that's what that guy touched that gave him a shock."

"Fine. I'll take the stairs. And you should tell that guy," said Jess, pointing over her shoulder as she headed towards the fire escape.

"I will," said Ben, gazing at the stern-looking officer who was kneeling by the wall. The man was examining it carefully, looking at it like it might bite him. "Eventually."

Ben giggled to himself and settled down to watch. Today was proving to be hugely entertaining. He hoped that Eric would be back soon. He had so much to tell him.

"So," said Charlie. He glanced in the rear-view mirror, then reached down and fiddled with the seat adjuster.

"So," replied Jamie.

The two of them sat in the car, waiting for Jess. Outside, partying students walked by, glancing with curiosity at the ambulance parked outside the security block.

"You wanna go in after her?" asked Jamie, after a while.

"There's no point. She's a big girl. She'll be fine."

The silence in the car was almost deafening. Jamie slouched down in his seat, drumming a little solo on his denim-clad thigh with his index fingers.

"Nice night," said Charlie, sounding strained.

"Yeah," said Jamie. "Good weather we've been having lately."

"Uh-huh. This is California. Good weather's pretty much a given."

"Indeed." Jamie nodded to himself, thinking, Come on, Jess, get back here...

Charlie whistled a little song to himself, then clicked on the radio and fiddled with it, trying to find a good station. There was no real signal here. For a moment, he caught the strains of what sounded like Aerosmith's "Love in an Elevator", but the song was swamped by static at the end of the first chorus.

He clicked the radio off and sat back in his seat.

Amber loved Aerosmith, Charlie remembered. His mind swam with guilt. For a moment, he almost hoped that Jess knew what she was talking about.

"So... you don't believe Jess?" he said to Jamie, trying to break the ice. He fancied he could almost see frost forming on the windows of the car, despite the evening heat outside.

"Why should I?" Jamie sat up in his seat, peering glumly out of the window. "Last Thursday she was convinced that mice had stolen her boots. She was dead serious about it." He gave a wan smile. "Jess ain't exactly a poster-girl for sanity."

Well, *that* was a conversation-killer, thought Charlie.

Three leggy girls in miniskirts walked by the car, peering in at Charlie and giggling. They walked off, whispering to each other and glancing back at him. Charlie watched them pass, giving them a little salute.

In the back seat, Jamie resumed his drum solo.

"Do you have to do that?" said Charlie, after a while.

"What? Oh, sorry." Jamie stopped his drumming. He folded his arms and stared moodily out of the window. Then he pulled some gum out of his pocket and popped a stick in his mouth. He started chewing loudly and was gratified to see Charlie wince in irritation.

"Do you think..." said Charlie, then stopped.

Jamie sighed. "Do I think what?" he asked, blowing a careless bubble with his gum.

"It's just that... well, how long have you known her for?"

"By 'her', I presume you mean Jess," said Jamie. The temperature in the car seemed to drop even lower. "And I've known her since she was twelve. And your point is...?"

"My point is," said Charlie carefully. "I think you need to let go of her."

Jamie stopped chewing. He blinked, unable to believe what he had just heard. "What the fuck do you mean by that?"

"I mean," said Charlie determinedly, "she doesn't think about you in that way. I talked to her about you. I was curious. She told me what happened between you guys."

"She told you? What the...?" Jamie stared at Charlie, slack-jawed.

"Yeah. She told me everything. All the nasty little details," said Charlie with relish. He pulled what he hoped was an innocent face. "But she didn't give me any indication that you guys were anything more than just friends."

"We *are* friends. We've been friends a hell of a long time. And where the fuck do you get off, asking her about me?" Jamie removed his gum from his mouth and stuck it under the leather-upholstered seat, somehow managing to make the move threatening. He sat forward in his seat, glaring at Charlie.

Charlie shrugged. "I just wanted to know. I care about Jess. I didn't want to see her getting hurt in any way."

Jamie's eyes flashed. "Okay. Number one—you don't care about Jess. You've known her for, what? All of three hours? Come off it." He glared at Charlie in the rear-view mirror. "I know your type. You just want to screw her. You're all about the sex with the pretty girls, and you don't give a damn who gets hurt in the process."

Charlie snorted. "Is that what you believe?"

"No. It's what I know." Jamie dropped his voice. "You think I don't see you? Waltzing around like you're God's gift or somethin'? You and all your tough-guy friends." Jamie shook his head, clenching his fists in his lap. "You have no idea how lucky you are, getting to go to university. No crappy dead-end job for you, slogging your guts out for a lousy couple of bucks an hour. No, just a nice car and a nice allowance and a nice apartment that you never even fuckin' *earned...*"

Jamie put a hand on the seat rest in front of him, glaring at it as though it was personally responsible. He let out his breath through his teeth. "All you are is just a big waste of your daddy's money. Some people would kill to do what you're... oh, never mind." He transferred his heated gaze to Charlie.

"But you don't go to college to learn—you go to get laid. That's all you give a damn about."

"And you're in a band because..."

Jamie stared at Eric for a moment, his mouth working. "That's different!" he spluttered.

"Is it?"

"Of course it is! I'm a musician!" He stopped. "What? What's so funny?"

"I've heard you play."

"And?"

"And, you were... very musical. All that yelling and jumping around with your shirt off— Tchaikovsky himself couldn't have done better."

"Name three works."

"What—by you or Tchaikovsky?"

"Good stalling. Were you going somewhere with that point?"

"Hey, buddy, I'm just saying—it *just* so happens that you get to spend a lot of time with Jess, being 'musical' together, because you're in this band?"

"She's our lead singer. Of course we spend time together. We're a team."

"Are you, now?" Charlie gave an annoying little smile that Jamie wanted to hit.

"Yes! We look out for each other. That's what friends do. She said once that I—"

"She told me that you were a nice guy."

Jamie stared, his expression frozen. "She said *what* about me?"

"You heard."

Jamie turned away from Charlie and looked out of the window towards the security block. He couldn't believe it.

"I'm sorry, man," said Charlie, not sounding sorry at all.

Jamie reached up and slowly rubbed at his shoulder. Why the hell had Jess said that about him? Being called a nice guy was like a deathblow to any man alive. He'd teased Jess for saying that about all the guys who hit on her in class. He knew what it meant—*nice guy, wouldn't wanna date him.* He would add the second bit himself whenever Jess said that about someone, which she did a lot. It was like their private joke. A lot of the guys who flirted with her *were* nice, she'd said, but that's all they were. They didn't have that spark to them, that indefinable thing that meant the difference between a best friend and a lover.

Jamie had hoped, someday, that he would fit into the second category.

And now, what? Jess had started saying that about *him*? After everything they'd been through together—when did *that* happen? Had he really been that switched off lately?

Jamie sighed. "I have to go talk to her," he said. He reached over and unlocked the side door. "Wait here."

"Do I have to?"

Jamie reached into his pocket and pulled something out. He waved it in front of Charlie. "Now you have to."

"Hey—that's my cell phone! Where did you get that?"

"A little birdie gave it to me. If you're still here in ten minutes, you'll get it back."

With that, Jamie slammed the car door and began trotting away towards the entrance to the security block.

Charlie watched him go. Then he grinned and thumped the steering wheel. "Damn, I'm good!" Opening the car door, he jumped out and hurried off after Jamie, tailing him at a distance. If this guy was going to get humiliated, he wanted to be there to watch. It was too good an opportunity to miss.

"So, this door was locked a couple of minutes ago?"

"Yes. No. I don't know," squealed Ben, holding up his hands. Jess had practically backed him into a corner, and was holding him up by his collar. "Get off me, you madwoman! I don't know anything!"

"Well, which is it?"

"Don't ask me. All he told me to do was to watch that door." Ben pointed frantically.

"Why did he ask you to do that?"

"No reason."

Jess dropped Ben onto the floor. He backed away from her, rubbing his neck and looking bewildered. Jess crossed her arms and fixed him with a stern look. "What was your name again?"

"Ben," said Ben meekly.

"Okay, Ben. I'm going to give you thirty seconds to tell me what's going on with you two."

"What if I don't?"

"Then, I'm going to press that elevator button with your head."

"You wouldn't!"

"Try me," said Jess levelly.

"Well," said Ben, his eyes flicking towards the exit like a trapped mouse. "It's like this." He took a deep breath, opened his mouth as if to speak, then bolted towards the door at top speed, vanishing before Jess could stop him.

Two seconds later, he reappeared, moving backwards at high speed. Jess watched as Jamie strode in through the door, his eyes fixed on Ben. "Hey, Jess!" Jamie called. "Is this the guy who was hanging around with Eric?"

"Yeah, that's a safe bet," said Jess.

"Oh, come on guys! I don't know anything! What do you want me to say?"

"I want you to tell me what's going on," said Jess.

"What *is* going on?" asked Jamie. "Is Eric okay?"

"That's what I've been trying to find out. Oh, hello Charlie. Do come and join us."

"Hey, Jess. What's happening?"

"We're all talking to Ben," said Jamie. "Come join the party."

"What's he done?"

"Nothing! It was all Eric's idea!"

"What was all Eric's idea?"

"The thing!"

"What thing?"

"The thing with the party, and with the, er..."

"With the what?"

"With the elevator. Um." Ben wished heartily that he could keep secrets. He hiccupped, then rubbed again at his neck.

"You mean Eric did something to the elevator?"

"No! That thing with the guard just kind of... happened. It wasn't anything to do with Eric. He *was* going to do something, but then he vanished upstairs and left me all alone down here." Ben backed up a couple of steps as they all stared at him.

"Hey! Here's an idea! Why don't you go all go find him and let me go home? Because I'm tired, and oh my God, you people are scary."

"Because we're here now, and so are you," said Jess, taking hold of Ben by the shoulders and propelling him across the room. "You're not leaving. Come on. Help me get that door open. Then we can get some answers."

She walked across to the fire escape door and began pulling on it, then bent down and peered through the keyhole. "Ah," she said. "Here's your problem. Glue in the lock. Haven't seen that one for a while. Jamie, hand me that knife of yours."

"Knife?" Ben paled slightly as Jamie obligingly reached into his boot and pulled out a wickedly curved street knife.

"Here you go."

"Thanks." Jess poked the end into the keyhole and began prying it back and forth, carving the glue out of the lock.

Jamie sidled up to her. "Um, Jess? How did you know I had a knife?" he whispered.

"I didn't. But I do now," Jess said. "You're from the other side of Venice, right, down past Rose?"

"Right. But how did you...?"

"I've seen the street you live on."

"Ah. I see. Clever."

"One and the same." Jess got to work with the knife. "Could be worse. At least you're not stupid enough to carry a gun."

Beside her, Ben became suddenly and intensely interested in inspecting the ceiling. He rocked back on his heels, whistling quietly to himself.

"Okay, that'll do the trick." Jess handed the knife back to Jamie. She tugged on the door handle. "Hmm. It's opening now, but it's caught on something." She pushed and pulled on it a couple of times, but it repeatedly thumped on something on the other side of the door. "It's stuck. Could someone help me out with this? I need to get upstairs and find Eric."

"Why don't you just use the elevator?" said Charlie.

"Ben says it's broken. Here, Ben, help me get this door open."

"Do I have to?"

"If you wanna live, you do."

Charlie watched as Ben helped Jess struggling with the door for a moment, then shrugged to himself and wandered towards the main exit. He peered out into the crisp night air, watching as they loaded a security guard on a gurney into the back of an ambulance. "Hey, Jess," he called out. "What happened to that dude?"

"Tell you in a minute," puffed Jess, heaving on the door.

"Huh," said Charlie. He shrugged, then wandered back to the elevator and gave it a cursory glance. The call button was flashing.

Hey, maybe it wasn't broken after all.

Charlie reached down and pressed the call button with his thumb a couple of times, then stood back expectantly. There was a weird humming sound from the elevator, then the doors whined and started to open.

He turned and faced the others as the doors swung open behind him. "Hey guys, elevator's working."

He gave a little bow to Jess. "No autographs, please. I'll hold the door for you."

Jess looked up. Her eyes widened in alarm. "Charlie! Wait!" she yelled.

"Don't worry, my sweet, I'll wait. I'm not going anywhere without you." Charlie gave Jess one of his patented glowing smiles. Then he stepped backwards through the elevator doors and plunged ten feet to the ground.

There was no elevator in the shaft.

"Charlie!" Jess and the others rushed to the elevator door and peered frantically down into the dark bowels of the elevator shaft. At first she couldn't see anything, but then as her eyes adjusted to the dark, she could just make out the prone form of Charlie lying sprawled on the floor beneath the elevator mechanism. To Jess's relief, he seemed to be moving. A weak groan echoed up towards her.

"Oh my God—everyone stand back." Jess stepped away from the elevator doors and turned to the main exit. "Somebody help!" she yelled. "We need help in here!" She grabbed Ben by the shoulders. "You! Go get a paramedic in here. NOW!"

"Okay, okay! But I think he's all right." Ben inched towards the elevator shaft and peered down. "Charlie, man," he called. "Are you okay?"

"Don't worry about me," called Charlie feebly. "I'll be fi..."

There was a warning creak from the elevator shaft above their heads.

As one, they all looked up.

"Ah..." muttered Charlie.

With a scream of severed brakes, the elevator fell on him.

TEN

Jess gazed into her frying pan, watching dazedly as her eggs and bacon popped and fizzled in the oil. A delicious smell of frying food filled the apartment, but for once in her life, she wasn't hungry.

She reached automatically for the pepper and sprinkled it liberally into the pan, her eyes fixed on a point somewhere beyond the far wall.

Charlie was dead. She couldn't believe it. This amazing, wonderful, sweet man had just been completely erased from the world, and there was nothing she could do about it. She was still waiting to wake up and find out that this was all some horrible nightmare.

What had happened to her life? Jess was shocked at how much her priorities had changed in less than forty-eight hours. They'd done a complete one-eighty, in fact. Two days ago, the biggest dilemma in her life had been deciding whether to wear rubber or leather for Friday's show. It had seemed like a huge thing at the time, affecting so many things—the band's image, Tony's opinion of her, her ability to both dance and breathe simultaneously... everything.

Now, all those people were dead. And people were still dying. Jess felt like she had somehow stumbled into someone else's life, and now couldn't get back out again. This didn't seem real. How could this be happening to her?

The signs. The cowboy had said that there'd be signs. Jess tried to think back. What signs had there been that Charlie was about to die?

She thought hard for a moment. He'd been killed by an elevator... Had she seen anything warning her about it? Well, there had been that bumper sticker on the HumVee, but that was surely just a coincidence. And, thinking about it, that story in the paper at Charlie's place had been about some guy getting trapped in an elevator... but that was hardly an obvious warning.

Jess stopped, her spoon poised over the frying pan. She remembered the book she'd picked up at the downtown warehouse the other night. She'd picked it up completely at random, and it had opened on a page about how to escape from a stopped elevator...

The smell of burning reached her nostrils and Jess blinked, reaching for a knife. Deep in thought, she scraped the burning bacon loose from the frying pan and added another couple of eggs, flipping the charred remains of the first two into the trashcan.

She lit a scented candle on top of the stove and switched on the ceiling-mounted air conditioning unit to get rid of the smell of burnt meat.

Had those been real signs? Jess rubbed her eyes tiredly. If they had been, how the hell was she supposed to have picked up on them? Maybe if she'd been looking *specifically* for stuff about elevators she would have noticed them, but how could she have known? It was crazy. She couldn't see *everything* as a sign. A person could go mad living their life like that...

Jess looked down. Her hands were shaking again. Even in her shell-shocked state, Jess realized that her body was close to exhaustion. She was far too wired to eat, but she knew that she should probably have something, if only to keep her system going. She hadn't really slept or eaten in almost two whole days. She was too tired to cry, too tired to grieve. The only thing that was keeping her going was the thought that when she finally got to go to sleep, she'd wake up and find that none of this had really happened.

If Cassie were here, she'd be given such a scolding.

Jess tried to shut her mind to the thought. Cassie was dead, just like the rest of them.

She leaned back and reached for a plate to distract herself, wiping her eyes with a hand. "Dad! Would you like anything?" she called above the noise of the fan.

There was no reply. Jess sighed and took a couple of steps backwards, peering around the edge of the kitchen doorway.

In the living room next door, a scruffy, balding man slept on the sofa in front of the TV, snoring loudly.

Jess turned down the stove and silently padded through into the next room. "Dad!" she called again, shaking the man's shoulder. She noticed that her father had a couple of new tattoos on his forearm, joining the others that already covered most of his body, forming a kind of second skin.

Jess snorted. How long had it been since she'd last seen her dad? Must have been a while if he'd had two more tattoos done. Her father collected tattoos like most people collected stamps. Rumor had it that he single-handedly kept afloat many of the eclectic tattoo parlors on Venice Beach, and several of the less eclectic ones.

"Wha...?" said her dad, stirring. He opened one bloodshot eye and blinked at her. Jess noticed a small platoon of empty whiskey bottles on the floor next to his chair. He'd hardly stirred when the cops had dropped her off, but then, with her lifestyle, that was nothing unusual.

"You want food?" asked Jess softly.

"Food... wha' time is it?"

Jess glanced at the cat-shaped clock on the wall. "Oh... I'm sorry. It's after midnight. I didn't realize..."

"What!"

"I was just hungry, and thought you might like someth—"

"At this hour? I'm fuckin' sleeping. Can't you see that?" Mr Golden raised himself up on an elbow and peered at his daughter through bloodshot eyes. "Cops were bangin' on the door for you all day. Couldn't get me no sleep. Had to lock the gate in the end." He sniffed, wiping his nose on the back of his hand. "Can't have them fuckers comin' in here, poking their big noses around. It was bad enough last night. I had to shift all me stuff around. Took me ages, thanks to you."

"Sorry, I just thought that that you—"

"Don't think. Push off. I've got a big job tomorrow." Her dad rolled over and grabbed a pillow, dragging it up under his head. "Little brat," he muttered, curling up in the chair.

"Suit yourself," Jess said, adding, "*and I'm nearly twenty, you asshole,*" under her breath. She grabbed a couple of the empty bottles off the floor and started walking back towards the kitchen. She stopped as a thought struck her. "Where's mom?" she asked, trying to keep her voice level.

"Dunno. Prob'ly dead, or off bangin' that bastard lawyer of hers. I ain't seen 'er in days. Now clear off."

"Fine." Jess stalked back into the kitchen, hurling the whiskey bottles into the trash as she did so. A half-dozen flies buzzed up in alarm. Jess grabbed a nearby canister of bug spray and angrily doused them in spray, killing most of them before the spray can ran out. She tossed that into the trash, too.

Switching off the stove, she slid the steaming bacon and eggs onto a plate and cleared a space on the rickety kitchen table. She sat down heavily and stared at her food.

The food stared back at her, the bacon and eggs appearing to be two eyes and a grinning mouth on her plate.

"What're you so happy about?" she asked the bacon, prodding it with a fork. "You're dead too, right? What's so good about being dead?"

She cut off a chunk and chewed it, wincing as bits of charcoal cracked between her teeth. "On second thoughts, guess you don't have to worry about dying any more. Lucky pig."

"Are you talking to your bacon?" said a voice.

Jess looked up as the kitchen door swung open. "Hey, Macy," she said, rising to her feet. "What're you doing here?"

"I saw the light on and thought I'd swing by. Couldn't sleep. You know me, nightshift and all." Macy gave a half smile. Then her expression changed. "Well... not any more, I guess..."

Macy was without makeup for once, and looked drawn and pale. She took a hesitant step into the kitchen, hanging back, not sure if she was disturbing Jess. "Jamie called me and told me about what happened." She shook her head, making her silver hoop earrings swing back and forth. "It's horrible, just horrible."

"I know," said Jess. She didn't trust herself to say more than that.

"Why is this happening to us?"

"I don't know." Jess grabbed the back of a wooden chair and tipped several hundredweight of newspapers and unpaid bills off onto the floor. "Here. Sit down."

Macy sat primly on the edge of the chair, glancing around her at the room.

"Sorry about the mess," Jess said, after a moment. "I think I cleaned this place once, when I was ten."

Macy flapped a hand. "Pssh, don't worry about it. You should see the state of my apartment. Oh—" she pointed, covering her mouth. "I think your cat's died."

Jess looked. "No, he's fine. That's what he always looks like." Jess got up and scooped up J-Bo, her scarred tortoiseshell tom, removing him from his upside-down position on top of a beer crate. He meowed in protest, then settled back in her arms, the deep bass rumble of his purr filling the room.

Jess smiled, rubbing the cat's ears. "He sits on anything new in the room. Dad's always telling him off for making his beer all warm. Hey, if you stay here for long enough, he'll probably come sit on you."

"Does he bite?" Macy stretched her arm out towards J-Bo, who opened his eyes and regarded her hand with a look of haughty contempt.

"Only if you smell like food. His eyesight's a bit crap."

"Hey... sweet kitty..." Macy gingerly stroked J-Bo's head with a finger, grateful for the temporary change of subject. "What happened to his eye?"

"He got in a fight."

"And his ears?"

"Another fight."

"And his side?"

"Yet another... oh no, that's chewing gum." Jess ran her hand up the cat's back, feeling the sticky mess attached to his flank. "J-Bo, I thought I told you not to sleep in the trash," she scolded him. "Come here." Jess hoisted the cat up over one shoulder, then reached for the scissors and started clipping away at his fur. J-Bo regarded Macy steadily over Jess's shoulder, a self-satisfied look on his face as he lapped up the attention.

"There. That's better." Jess threw the matted mess of fur and gum into the trash. "Go on, be off with you." She pulled up a chair and sat next to Macy, while J-Bo purred and rubbed around her ankles.

"Charlie was the good-looking one, right?" asked Macy, unable to put off the topic any longer. She put her cell phone down on the edge of the table.

"Yeah. He was, kind of," said Jess. She swallowed a lump in her throat, her mind filling with glowing pictures of Charlie.

It was his smile that she was going to miss the most...

"Did you know him very well?"

"We used to go to school together. He was in the grade above me." Jess stopped, thinking. "We were kind of friends, but he never really talked to me. We had this little understanding, you see? He would say hi to me once a month or so, and I would refrain from stalking him. Most nights." Jess gave a sad little laugh and then sobered up. "But the way he looked at me... there was definite potential there, if you know what I mean." She scratched her nose reflectively. "Of course, then he went and died on me. That kind of put a dampener on our relationship."

The bright kitchen light stung her eyes, and Jess reached out and clicked off the main bulb. She gazed sadly at the kitchen rug under her feet.

Above her, a large fly that had been endlessly circling the light bulb buzzed away from it and zipped downwards, attracted to the secondary light of the scented candle. It zoomed through the flame in a state of great excitement, setting itself alight, and fell downwards before expiring quietly on top of the stove. If flies could think, it would have thought something along the lines of, "*Typical.*" A gust of air from the open door caught its tiny burning body, sending it tumbling onto the pile of receipts stacked up next to the oven.

After a moment, a small flame flickered in the depths of the pile.

Over by the kitchen table, Macy reached down and stroked J-Bo, who promptly snapped his teeth at her hand before resuming his innocent purring. She sat back up on her seat, tittering nervously. "Oh, so you didn't know Charlie that well? I thought that you guys were pretty tight, from what I heard. Jamie said..."

"I did know him. I know... *knew*... a lot about him," said Jess defensively, thinking, *Yeah... his favorite color, where he liked to go for dinner, where he hung out practically every night of the week...*

Macy shrugged. "He never paid his tab," she said matter-of-factly. "In fact, I was going to ask, well... you wouldn't happen to have three hundred and fifty bucks on you, would you? He still owes me from last month's tab."

"Do I look like I do?"

Macy swept the small apartment with a glance. Then she reached for her purse, looking awkward. "Do you... would you like to..."

"I don't need to borrow any money," said Jess automatically. She tried to smile. "But thanks for asking."

She pictured Bill's leather-bound wallet, lying buried under three hundred tons of rubble, and cursed herself again. Maybe she'd go back over there tomorrow, make a few enquiries. The electricity bill was due in about ten days, and she had about as much faith in her dad's "jobs" as she did in Santa Claus.

"You're welcome," said Macy. "Jess?"

"Yes?"

"I'm scared. Why is everyone dying?"

"I don't know." Jess shrugged helplessly. "It's just a coincidence—I think."

"But four people have died now, and they were all people who escaped from the club disaster. That's one big coincidence."

"Macy, I really don't know what's going on." Jess stood up, sniffing. "Do you smell something burning?"

"But you said that you knew what was going to happen, back at the club," insisted Macy. "You said you saw it all in a vision—like some kind of message from God or somethin'."

"I'm not religious. But I did see something." Jess glanced distractedly around the apartment, trying to locate the source of the burning smell. Then she stopped, staring at Macy. "Wait a moment—did you say *four* people had died?"

"Yeah. It's just so tragic..."

Jess glanced up at the ceiling, counting on her fingers. "Who's the fourth?" she asked sharply. A thought hit her. "Please tell me Eric's okay. Not that I care..."

"Eric's fine. I heard that he's been released from the hospital already." Macy tutted under her breath. "He was so silly, falling down the stairs like that. He was lucky he didn't break anything." Macy looked up at Jess, a girlish grin on her face. "He never pays his tab either, but—he's kind of cute too, don't you think?"

"Absolutely not, but go on." Jess gripped the back of her chair. "What about number four?"

"Oh—didn't you hear?" Macy reached into her pocket for a tissue and dabbed at her nose. "That police officer? The one who they arrested? She's dead."

"You're kidding! No way! What happened?"

"Spider got her."

"What?"

"She was bitten by a spider. A poisonous one. They say it must've been a black widow for it to have affected her so quick."

Jess put a hand on the table to steady herself. Black specks danced in front of her eyes. This couldn't be real. "When? When did this happen?"

"This morning. She was still in the police cell, waiting for bail, the poor thing. Her partner never showed up to get her. Cops all went to get lunch, and when they got back, she was dead. Her leg was all swelled up like a balloon where she got bit. They say her heart just stopped."

"I can't believe it. How—" Jess stopped, her mind flicking back to the morning, when she'd been woken up by Charlie in the police cell. It seemed so very long ago, but now, a nasty little memory was jumping up and down, waving its hands.

Hadn't she seen a spider in her cell? A big black one, crawling into a crack in the wall? She'd only seen it for a second, but it *had* been kinda big...

Oh, it couldn't be. Please tell her that it hadn't been a black widow. There were a lot of them around in LA, Jess knew, but she hadn't heard of anyone dying of a bite in a long time. She'd known the drill since childhood: stay calm, don't rush around or do anything that'll spread the poison through you, and get your ass to a hospital straight away. You had about an hour to get to the emergency room before it was too late, and ambulance response times were pretty quick these days, even with the LA traffic.

But if the officer had been left alone in a locked room for longer than that... Jess closed her eyes and bowed her head.

Nasty.

Macy took out her handkerchief again and blew her nose. "It's just—I don't know what to think any more. What if there's some kind of crazy killer out there, bumping off everyone who got out of the club? He could've put the spider in the cell, cut the elevator cable that got poor old Charlie, pushed that girl under the car..."

"Macy, that's crazy. Who would do such a thing?"

"I don't know," sniffed Macy. "But that's what I think is happening. It's just too much of a coincidence. I had this horrible dream last night where some monster dressed in robes was chasing after me. He was all made of bones, and there was this terrible noise... I probably shouldn't have had that double pepperoni pizza before going to bed, but still. It was really scary. I had to put the light on for the rest of the night. My kitty cats thought I'd gone crazy."

"Pizza before bed is never a good idea," said Jess thoughtfully. At her feet, J-Bo gave a plaintive meow. Jess reached down and picked him up, hugging him to her chest and burying her face in his warm fur.

Then J-Bo's whiskers twitched. He twisted in her arms and began struggling to get down. "Make up your mind, cat," Jess said mildly. She put him down and watched as he bounded away from her towards the back door. He reared up on his hind legs and began scratching on it, begging to be let out.

"That's odd." Jess watched the cat. Then she sniffed again. This time she definitely smelled something burning. She turned around, her eyes scanning the room.

"Oh, crap!"

Behind her, the pile of paperwork next to the stove was on fire.

"What *is* it with the world this week?" cried Jess. She ran towards the stove.

As she did so, one of the burning papers drifted down off the work surface and landed in the trashcan. The mixture of alcohol-soaked newspaper and sugary cat hair flared up instantly. Jess jumped back as two-foot flames shot up. Glancing around her wildly, she grabbed the frying pan off the stove, filled it with water and tossed it towards the fire. "Dad! Fire!" she yelled towards the next room, as though this were a regular occurrence.

"Fuck off!" came the sleepy bellow from the next room.

"Fine. I'll just deal with it, then."

There was no reply.

Macy rose to her feet and ran over to help Jess as she refilled her pan from the faucet. The water she had thrown hadn't made much of an impact. Macy wrenched open a cupboard, then another, searching for something to put water in. "Where's your fire extinguisher?" she gasped, yanking open the pantry door.

Jess pulled an apologetic face. "Dad pawned it last Wednesday." She tossed a kitchen towel into the washing up, soaking it with water, and held it up, ready to throw it over the fire.

At that moment, the flames reached the can of bug spray in the trashcan. It fizzed briefly as the flames heated the pressurized contents, then exploded with a bang, sending a rain of flaming trash all over the kitchen. Jess was thrown backwards, crashing into the kitchen table and tumbling to the ground as it collapsed beneath her. She rolled over, dazed, clutching her head.

Across the room, Macy closed the pantry door slowly as the echoes of the explosion died away. The ripped-open remains of the aerosol canister were projecting out of the door at about head height, driven almost completely through the wood.

Macy gulped and glanced fearfully around the room. Several small fires had started up here and there, burning merrily amid the heaped mountains of discarded paperwork. Above her, the ancient A/C unit whined, starting to suck up the smoke. A piece of whiskey-bottle glass tinkled merrily around inside it, bouncing off the blades.

"What in the *blazes* is going on?"

Jess's father stood in the doorway, his hair sticking up in all directions, blinking at the scene. His kitchen was on fire, and his daughter was lying on the collapsed remains of his brand-new poker table. There was some slut in a skirt standing over by his beer cupboard, looking shocked.

None of this was good.

"Jessica?" he growled.

"I don't... I... er..." muttered Jess, trying to get to her feet. Her legs gave way, then she tried again, with similar results.

Jess's father scowled, his face like thunder. "You— girl! Hand me the fire extinguisher."

"Er... Jess said you sold it."

"I did no such thing!" The man paused while his face readjusted itself. A touch of self-righteousness entered his eyes. "Pass me the phone, then."

Jess stumbled to her feet and lurched across the room towards the sink. Her clothes were smoking. "The phone was cut off two weeks ago, dad. Don't worry. It's just a little fire. I'll put it out." She broke into a fit of coughing. "Where's that saucepan?"

Macy silently pointed. Jess looked down to see it stuck to the floor, melted into the linoleum.

"Oh," said Jess, looking up at her father guiltily, who glowered at her.

There was a grinding sound from the ceiling.

Jess looked up.

Everything seemed to go into slow motion. It was as though she were watching herself from a distance. Jess cried out and sprinted towards Macy, shoving her away from the stove. A fraction of a second later, the elderly A/C unit gave a creak and plunged downwards, jarred from its rusty ceiling-mounts by the force of the explosion. Jess and Macy landed in a breathless heap as the heavy unit hit the floor with a crash, right where Macy had been standing.

A clicking buzz came from the wreckage as the fan blade started to slow, still attached to the ceiling by a long length of wire.

"Hey! I paid good money for that thing!"

"Then you'll just have to buy another one, won't you?" said Jess, disentangling herself from an ashen Macy and helping her to her feet. "Perhaps you can sell the cat this time. That should about cover it."

"Just you *wait* till your mother gets back." Mr Golden strode over to the sink and picked up the wet cloth, then marched around the room, beating at the flames and muttering under his breath.

"And that's likely to happen—when?"

"Watch your mouth." Jess's father put out the last of the fires and hurled the charred towel down onto the floor. "You've been living here rent-free for sixteen years—"

"Nineteen years."

"Whatever. It ain't gonna happen for much longer. As soon as your mother gets back, she an' I are gonna have Words."

"Good luck with that one," Jess said sweetly. She turned to Macy and tried to smile as her father stamped out of the room, slamming the kitchen door behind him. "I think you'd better get going. I'm sorry about all this."

Macy nodded silently, glancing back towards the fallen A/C unit. "That was close! I thought I was a goner. Did you have another vision?" she whispered.

"Nah. I just have very good hearing," said Jess. She listened to the spinning fan blade as it jumped and hummed, caught on the linoleum. "And I think

I should switch that off before it does any further damage."

She walked across the room to the wall switches. She glanced back over towards the humming unit and waved a hand. "Hey, J-Bo! Get away from that!" She turned back to the wall, hunting for the "off" switch.

Ignoring her, J-Bo paused in his exploratory circle around the unit, then bunched his muscles and jumped up onto it, sniffing it experimentally. His weight tilted the unit to one side and he leapt down again with a meow.

The unit started to pitch forwards, its whirling blades plummeting towards the floor.

At that moment, Macy's cell phone went off. Macy turned her head sharply to see where the noise was coming from, then felt a gust of air hit her ear as something whizzed past her head at high speed. There was a *clang* from behind her. She spun around to see Jess staring fixedly at the wall behind her, where a fan blade was buried in the thin plaster.

"Um," said Jess. "I think you'd better go home now."

Macy put a hand to the side of her head, checking that her ear was still attached, then shook herself and trotted over to the collapsed table, looking dazed. She picked up her cell phone and clicked it open. "Hello?"

Jess switched off the power and studied the blade sticking out of the wall. Then she turned and surveyed the mess that filled the kitchen—the fallen unit, the broken table, the little smoking piles of embers dotted here and there.

It was almost as if something *wanted* Macy to get hurt. But there hadn't been any signs... or had there?

She jumped as Macy tapped her on the shoulder, her hand over her phone. "It's the sheriff," she whispered. "Says he's been trying to ring you all night."

"What does he want?"

"He says he needs you to come to the station tomorrow morning. He wants you to make a statement about Charlie." She paused. "He sounded kind of weird."

"That's fine. Tell him I'll be there."

Macy glanced at her. "Are you all right?"

"I'm just dandy," said Jess, pulling the fan blade out of the wall. "Go on. Talk to the man."

Macy shrugged. "Okay."

Jess looked down at the blade in her hands. This was seriously creeping her out. Maybe she had somehow been cursed? She didn't believe in such things, but since Friday night, everyone who came near her seemed to be having horrible things happen to them.

She did a swift mental calculation. Out of the nine people who'd made it out of the club, now only five of them were left, including herself.

A shiver ran up Jess's spine as she watched Macy talk on the phone. The sheriff may be old-fashioned, but he wasn't stupid. She may have been temporarily cleared of suspicion over the club disaster, but now his chief suspect was dead, what if he and his goons decided to come after her, instead? If anything happened to the other four survivors from the club, she had a strong feeling that she could soon be back in that police cell, facing some very tricky questions.

She put the fan blade down carefully on the worktop, and started methodically picking up the strewn papers and cutlery from the remains of the table. Tomorrow, after she'd finished at the station, she'd get everyone together for a talk. The deaths of the other four may have been genuine accidents, but perhaps that was because their brush with death had made them careless. This whole "sign" thing was crazy, but at the moment, it was all she had to go on. She needed to talk to the others, make sure they were taking extra care until they'd recovered from the effects of the club disaster. They all needed to watch every step they took in the next few weeks, for their own sakes as much as hers.

Jess looked down at her feet, where J-Bo was enthusiastically polishing off the spilled remains of her dinner. He lifted his head, licking his lips, and fixed her with a bright-eyed gaze. He began to purr.

Jess considered everything that had happened that night, and came to a very definite conclusion. "I think I need some sleep," she said.

It was quiet in Jess's bedroom. The numbers on her bedside clock glowed *10:38 pm*. Her door was locked and barred, with a sturdy chair pushed up under the doorknob. On the bed, J-Bo stretched and curled up tighter at Jess's feet as she slumbered, a small puddle of happy warm cat protecting her from the darkness.

And as Jess slept, she dreamed...

* * *

Darkness.

Nothingness.

And then...

This time, the voices in her head were louder. Jess had to put her hands over her ears in order to hear herself think. There were shouts and screams, bellows of rage, and the occasional peel of hysterical laughter echoing through the void. The voices weren't friendly or unfriendly. They just *were*.

But they weren't important. This time, Jess knew what she was looking for.

Concentrate...

Just beyond the edges of her perception, she heard a different sound, an older one, a noise that harked way back to the very beginnings of man's evolution.

Straight away, she knew what it was.

It was the sound of death.

It didn't have a tone, exactly. It was more a kind of feeling in the air, a sensation of *wrongness* that you couldn't quite shake, as though your skin were suddenly turned inside out on your body and all your nerves were exposed to the air. It was as soft as silence and as all pervading as the night, and when you got right close up to it, it was cold enough to freeze your thoughts, turning them into icy and intricate patterns in your brain.

In the grayness of the void, Jess turned her head this way and that, seeking out the source of the feeling like someone trying to get a signal on a cheap cell phone. Every nerve screamed at her to leave, to run away before it was too late and save herself from the unspeakable horror of what she knew lay before her.

But she had to go onwards. She took a step forward, then another. With each step, the pressure of terror inside her head increased, until she felt as though the next step would cause her mind to explode.

Just when it got unbearable, she stopped.

There.

Jess opened her eyes and looked down, seeing the familiar rocky pathway beneath her feet. The pathway appeared to be old and freshly hewn, both at once, as though she were seeing the path's entire history in one glance. A sense of déjà vu swept through her, and she glanced sharply downwards, into the abyss beside her. She knew she'd been here before, but that didn't concern her.

This time, there was something different.

Jess glanced up and down the path, but it was utterly empty. Smoke swirled overhead. The night pressed in all around her, and it seemed to be growing darker with the passing of each second. Ahead of her, the lights on the hilltop glowed temptingly bright, but she ignored them, concentrating on the job in hand.

She knew what she had to do.

Closing her eyes, Jess took a moment to concentrate her mind.

Then she screwed up her nerves and stepped off the path.

There was a brief sensation of weightlessness, then a rushing feeling. When Jess opened her eyes again, she was standing on thin air.

She looked down beside her. The path had gone. In its place was a long, narrow, horizontal ladder, that seemed to move and squirm under her gaze.

But there was something wrong here. Jess peered more closely at the ladder. The perspective was all wrong. Her brain lurched as she suddenly realized that it wasn't right in front of her, but in fact it was quite a distance away. It was like looking at one of those Escher paintings, which look perfectly fine so long as you keep your eye in one place, and then kick you in the brain as soon as you try to follow any of the lines. It was like getting an ice-cream headache in your soul.

Jess followed the ladder with her eyes, tracking along it until it reached the mountains ahead of her. There was something wrong here, too, a nagging sensation she couldn't quite put her finger on.

Then she worked out what it was. The ladder was pointing downwards, not along.

Jess's mind gave a second squeal of complaint as the world spun around her, her sense of balance informing her that she was now the wrong way up. Acting on some long-buried instinct, she closed her eyes again and counted to ten. When she opened them again, she was facing the right way up. She looked down, and found that she was now standing on the narrow rocky ledge at the end of the ladder, set back into the mountainside. Above her, the dark mountain loomed. Now she was looking down at the ladder rather than across at it.

Above her, the lights of the hilltop glowed, casting their ghostly light downwards.

Jess looked down, then gasped, unable to believe what she was seeing.

Close-up, she could see that the ladder was made up of living human bodies. They twisted and writhed as she watched in horror, bound together by what looked like bloody cords, standing on each other's shoulders to make up the length of the ladder. Some of them were relatively normal-looking, but others were the stuff of nightmares, naked and disease-ridden, crawling with maggots. The stench was appalling. Some had missing limbs, others had huge holes where their internal organs should have been, revealing gaping cavities, their bodies crushed and mangled.

One guy with only half a head waved to Jess, his brain clearly visible inside his skull, which had been cracked neatly in half like two halves of an orange. He reached out to her as she backed away, pressing herself back against the rock.

Then Jess felt a creeping sensation run up the back of her neck, a feeling so deeply buried and primal that it took her a moment to figure out what it was.

Then, she knew what it meant.

Somebody was watching her.

Hardly daring to look, Jess inched along the edge of the rock until she was a mere couple of yards away from the top of the grisly human ladder. The ledge was so narrow that she couldn't get much further away and still see down, but for now, it was enough. The people on the ladder didn't seem to be threatening her in any way, but she still wanted to keep her distance, if only because of the smell.

Carefully, she crept to the edge of the rock and peered over the side.

At first she saw nothing. Just an endless infinity of darkness, stretching down and down forever.

Then, as her eyes adjusted to the gloom, she began to make out a dark, ominous shape, moving slowly towards her up the human ladder. It was still at a great distance to her. Jess guessed that it must be pretty big to be visible from this far away.

Gradually, she became aware of a strange sound. It was quiet at first, barely more than an oscillating whisper, but then gained in intensity as the dark shape crawled up the ladder towards her. It was kind of a rushing sound, like sand being poured onto a tin tray, getting louder and louder until it sounded like a thousand birds taking flight all at once, filling the air around her with the sound of their wing beats. The randomness of the noise began to slow, slow, slow down, until it sounded as if the wing beats were perfectly synchronizing with each other, as though the unseen birds were all, impossibly, flying to the same beat.

Jess backed away as the sound slowed down still further, dropping in pitch until it seemed to pass into the subsonic range. Jess listened, her skin trying to crawl off her body and run away to hide, all by itself. She suddenly became aware of how alone she was, out here on this ledge in the darkness.

She peeped back over the edge again, and a bolt of fear shot through her The thing, whatever it was, was closer now. She could already start to make out its shape. It was vaguely human in form, but there was something inherently *wrong* about it, as though she was seeing the memory of a human shape rather than an actual physical presence. It seemed to be simultaneously taking its time and moving astonishingly quickly, although Jess couldn't see how this could be.

As it drew near, details became visible. Jess drew in her breath sharply. The only frame of reference she could come up with to describe the creature was *skeletal*, but this didn't even come close to describing it.

Not even close.

It didn't just have one set of bones. It had, Jess decided, all the bones that had ever existed. Every species, every shape, every twisted mutation—they were all there, picked out by the sickly glow from the mountain. The creature flickered and fluctuated as it moved, its bones stretching and evolving and forming new and wild shapes and connections, the ghostly bones appearing to be brand new and crumbling at the same time. It was like looking at the living embodiment of an infinitely long time-lapse photograph, every second made physical and represented by the bones of the creatures that lived at that moment, all at the same time.

Peering closer, Jess saw that the creature was dressed in the blackened and charred skins from a thousand different animals and humans, forming a kind of robe that hung from its bones in oily tatters. Some of the skins appeared to be still alive, twitching and bunching up as the creature moved. Beneath the robe, the creature's arms and legs were spattered in blood from its victims, adding a splash of terrible color to the gleaming white bone.

As the creature climbed up each living rung of the human ladder, the people—and Jess used that word loosely—it touched cried out and began to age at an astonishing rate, their flesh withering and cracking until their bones looked almost shrink-wrapped. As the creature moved on, their bodies decayed at high speed and then burst into dust, showering the night air around them with floating particles.

Jess started to back away as the creature drew close. The white-noise sound it gave off became louder and more intense, filling her head with its buzzing like a swarm of angry, radioactive wasps. She knew instinctively that the sound was somehow dangerous, and that she should try to shield herself from it. She tried putting her fingers in her ears, but that only seemed to concentrate the sound. A strange sensation made her look down at her hands. She saw that the skin on them was withering, aging weeks, months, years in a matter of seconds.

That did it. Her nerve cracked, and she ran back across the ledge to the side of the mountain. She looked upwards, craning her neck back. The mountain was impossibly high, over a quarter of a mile of sheer rock separating her from the top. There were no handholds, no footholds, nothing.

Jess sagged. She could never climb it in time. She felt herself weakening even as she contemplated the idea, and looked again at her hands, feeling despair creep over her. The skin on them was wrinkled and calloused, as though she were in her late sixties instead of in her teens.

Jess bit down hard on the inside of her lip in fear, and then reached up to her mouth with a grimace. Her teeth seemed to be loose, for some reason. She touched one hesitantly with her tongue, and then gave a yelp as she felt it come loose from her gum. She put a finger into her mouth, pressing it back into place with a jolt of fear.

In her ears, the radiation-style buzzing increased, becoming almost a physical presence.

Really, *really* not good...

Turning around, Jess was struck by a sudden idea. Holding her breath so as not to breathe in the smell, she dashed back to the top of the human ladder, moving as quickly as she dared. Trying not to look down, she began stamping hard on the fingers of those who were holding the ladder in place, crushing the blood-smeared hands holding onto the edge of the rocky ledge. Cries of pain rang out, echoing through the buzzing silence of the void. Perhaps if she could knock the ladder down, she could stop the freaky skeleton creature from reaching her? She had no idea what the creature was, but in her experience, anything that dressed in human skins was usually bad news.

"Hey! Cut it out!"

Jess looked up, bewildered to hear the familiar voice. She looked down at the faces of the first few people on the end of the ladder. They were naked and covered in blood, but after a second, she gave a gasp of recognition.

Charlie.

Amber.

The female cop from the station.

The bouncer.

They were all there, just feet beneath her, the injuries that had killed them revealed in chilling detail. Charlie's body was crushed and mangled, his head listing at a strange angle. Amber was missing an arm, her torso bisected by an almost cartoon-like tire mark. Below her, the cop's skin was white and covered in deep purplish bruising, a bull's-eye-shaped mark showing up starkly on her thigh.

Jess didn't dare look at the bouncer.

"Hi, how're you doing?" asked Amber brightly.

Jess stared at her. "You're dead," she said, eventually.

"Uh-huh. Have you seen my arm?"

"No. I, er..." Jess paused while her brain rearranged itself. "I think they took it to the morgue. Along with the rest of you. There were several bags with you in, I recall." Jess shrugged helplessly, unable to believe that she was having this conversation. "I'm sorry."

"Well, that sucks. None of my clothes will fit me any more. I'll have to get them altered. Do you know how much that costs these days?"

"I haven't a clue." Jess glanced feverishly down the ladder, which was starting to shake with the approach of the huge creature. It was still quite a long distance away from her, but she didn't want to be here if it got any closer. "Listen," she said urgently. "Do you know a way out of here?"

"Out? There ain't no 'out'," rumbled the bouncer. Jess dared to look at him, and instantly wished that she hadn't. The flesh of his face was hanging off in tatters, and one eye was missing, the socket filled with bruised flesh. He peered at her closely through his smashed sunglasses. "Oi. I know you. Do you have your ID on you?"

"Not at the moment, no," said Jess desperately. "Do I need one? This is hell, right?"

"No, just LA. You want to get out of here?"

"That would be nice, yes," said Jess, as the sibilant hissing of the creature below filled her ears. She got ready to run.

"But you don't have any ID?"

"Knock it off, bro," came a voice, drifting up from further down the ladder. Jess inched forward and peeped down to see Tony looking up at her, from ten feet further down. He gave her a little wave, blood tricking down his torso from his crushed skull. "Hey, girl."

Jess fought down a wave of nausea. "Hey," she managed.

"Good to see ya again. We all missed you. Ooh, you wanna see a trick? Look at this," Tony turned sideways and waved a hand through the rectangular hole in his torso. "Ta-da! Great, huh? I'm thinking of adding it to our stage act."

"That's great," said Jess, covering her mouth with her hand.

"Sorry," said Tony, wiping the blood off his fingers. "Had a lot of time to myself recently. It's kinda dull, being dead. There's no TV here, for starters. And very little sex. You gotta get your entertainment where you can."

"I guessed as much," said Jess faintly. She looked down the ladder, beginning to recognize a few faces here and there. Wasn't that the barman from the club? And over there, the naked girl with the interesting eyebrows... wasn't she Charlie's friend from the dance floor?

Jess realized that everyone who had died in the club was part of the ladder, their bodies broken and battered but still very much living.

And Charlie and the others were right at the top.

What kind of a freaky place was this?

Something caught Jess's attention, and her brow creased with concentration as she tried to figure out what it was. She peeked cautiously back at the bouncer. He was the lowest down of the four, with the other three above him. Charlie was at the top.

Jess suddenly realized how the ladder worked. People were placed on it according to the order they died in. The echo of a memory nagged at her, and Jess cast her mind back to her original premonition, trying to remember what she'd seen. She'd successfully blocked the images from her mind up until this point, but now it all came flooding back, in full Technicolor detail...

The bouncer had died first, when the ceiling had fallen on him.

Then Amber and Charlie had gone down, felled by a girder.

The police officer had died next, impaled on a flying drumstick.

Jess realized with a jolt that this was the order they'd actually died in, in real life.

Which meant that...

Macy.

She'd been next to die, in her premonition, when a second girder had fallen on the bar. Did that mean that she was going to be the next one to die, in the real world?

Jess knew that she had to get out of this place, right now, and warn her. But hadn't it started already? The fire in her apartment... the exploding

A/C unit... it was as though the world was out to get Macy.

She had to save her.

But right now...

Jess flinched as a cold, wet hand gripped her calf, breaking the spell. She tore her eyes away from the approaching creature to see Charlie trying to pull himself up onto the ledge, holding onto her leg. His smashed head listed drunkenly to one side as he swiveled his blue eyes in their sockets, attempting a grin. "Yo, Jess. Gimme a hand here. I'll help you out." He waved the stump of his right arm at her, the hand of which was missing. "A hand—geddit?" he chortled, blood trickling from his mouth.

"Dude. That was sick," said the bouncer in a monotone.

Her skin writhing in horror, Jess yanked herself free from Charlie's icy grip, wiping the blood quickly from her leg. "I'm fine—thanks," she said.

Charlie reached out for her as she backed away. "Aw, c'mon. Help me up. If you're gonna die, you might as well have a bit of fun before you go." He leered at her suggestively.

"You what?!"

In reply, Charlie gestured down at his naked, blood-slicked body. Jess tried not to look. Charlie gave a sly grin. "Come on. How about it? It'll be just you and me, baby. Together, till the end."

"Are you crazy? You're dead! And your girlfriend's watching..." Jess stopped. "Why am I even being log-ical about this? Get away from me, you freak!"

Charlie gave an exaggerated sigh. "That's what Amber said. She doesn't want me no more. Can't think why." He tried to scratch his head with his bloody stump, looked surprised, then and gave a short, bitter laugh. "Come on, sugar pie. I've seen the way you look at me. You can't take your eyes off me. I *know* you want me. You always have done."

Jess's expression turned to one of deep revulsion. She started to back away, then looked sharply down at her hand. The blood she'd wiped off her leg was moving, squirming across her hand like a living thing. She shook her hand urgently, trying to get rid of it, and the blood became liquid again and poured off onto the ground.

Jess cried out as it flowed towards her and attached herself to her foot, instantly solidifying and fixing itself to the rock, like an organic shackle.

Jess kicked frantically at it.

Try as she might, she couldn't pull free.

Charlie gave a horrible little laugh and began dragging himself towards her, his eyes fixed hungrily on Jess as she struggled to free herself.

Then he paused as an angry screech came from below them.

"Um, miss? I think you should run now!" called the bouncer.

Jess reflexively glanced over the edge of the precipice. The skeletal creature was nearly upon her, covering the last few hundred yards in a blur of arms and legs, flying up the ladder at an impossible speed. The buzzing noise was almost unbearable now. Jess clapped her hands over her ears, grimacing in pain. The noise seemed to be draining her will to move, to breathe, to do anything other than to stand there and watch the creature approach. A screaming sense of dread filled her, but she couldn't move. Even if she could, there was nowhere to go.

She watched helplessly as the creature flew towards her, the crumbling remains of human bodies falling aside all around it. Approaching the top of the ladder, the creature swung its head around, then suddenly snapped it up towards Jess, fixing her with a knife-like glare. Jess felt her blood turn to ice as its undead gaze pierced her like a thermal lance. Everything else around her faded away. The creature's face was terrifying, all jutting bones and dead flesh. It had no eyes, just two deep, dark holes in the center of its face. To Jess, it seemed as though its eyes were infinitely big, like galaxy-sized black holes in outer space, sucking up everything in their path...

She felt herself start to fall forwards, drawn by their deadly pull. Below her, she watched as Charlie was sucked bodily away from her, his expression turning to one of dismay. Within seconds, he and the others had turned to withered skeletons, crumbling away into the void.

And then the creature was upon her, its black eyes boring into hers. There was only one thing left to do. Summoning up every last ounce of her willpower, Jess clamped her eyes shut and wrenched herself away from the creature, just as it reached out for her. Concentrating, she opened her eyes again and broke into a run, her gaze fixed determinedly on the edge of the rocky ledge. She refused to stay here and die. If she was going to die, she wanted to do it under *her* terms.

Her feet left the ledge, and then she was falling, plunging down through empty air, her body tumbling over and over as she plunged downwards into infinity...

Behind her, the creature screeched in fury.

Jess gasped as she woke up, sticky and sweating, and fought her way out from under the blankets on her bed. She subsided, panting.

Beside her, J-Bo mewed in greeting.

Jess looked at him. "Oh, cat, you're not gonna believe this."

Jess reached a trembling hand towards her cell phone, which glowed dimly on her bedside table. Switching on her bedside light, she began dialing.

ELEVEN

"So remind me why we're here again?"

"I just told you. Crazy Girl called. Said she needed to see us all."

"Urgh." Eric pulled at the white plastic collar around his neck. "You should've just given her the number of my shrink. Why won't she leave us alone? It's the middle of the goddamn night, for Pete's sake."

Ben tittered. "Like you'd be able to sleep in *that* thing. You look like a dog that's just been to the vet." He blew bubbles in his strawberry milkshake, attracting strange looks, then pulled out his straw and sucked the milkshake off it. "Hey, don't scratch."

"I can't help it! It's driving me nuts." Eric let go of the collar and gingerly prodded at the bright blue bruising on the side of his head. The swelling was starting to go down a little, but it still hurt like hell. It throbbed under his touch. He dreaded to think what the hospital bill was going to cost him.

"Hey, loser!"

"What?" Jamie answered, and then screwed up his face in annoyance. *Shouldn't have answered that one so quickly.* He picked the saltshaker off the table and shook it up moodily, glaring at Eric. The top fell off and salt spilled out onto the table. He swept it quickly onto the floor, grimacing.

"How much does it cost to go to hospital?"

"Dunno. Never been."

"What, never?"

"Nah. Don't have health insurance. Can't afford it."

"Dude! How do you live?"

"Very, very carefully," said Jamie. He glanced at his watch. "Where's she got to this time?" he muttered to himself, under his breath.

"*I* think you were very brave." Jamie glanced at Macy as she put a hand on Eric's arm, gazing up at him brightly. She completely ignored Jamie. "If it'd been me that fell down those stairs, I'd be in bed for at least a month."

"That's because you're a gir—" Eric began, then stopped as Ben kicked him hard under the table. He paused, then looked at Macy afresh. "Er, because you're a *great* person." He glanced sideways at Ben for approval.

Macy beamed.

"Sorry I'm late, guys."

"Hey, Jess."

"Hey, Jess," Ben mimicked, then flinched as Jamie threw a handful of salt at him.

Jess threw her jacket down onto the red plastic seat and plucked a menu from the middle of the table. She was wearing black jeans and a sweater, her hair scraped back into an efficient-looking pony-tail. "Do they do coffee here?"

"About twelve different kinds, I think. Take your pick."

"Great. Order me the eleventh kind, whatever that is. Macy, come with me."

"Where to?"

"Restroom," said Jess, marching towards the back of the diner. A waiter laden with four heaped plates of burgers swung to the side as she strode past him in the aisle, then deposited the burgers in front of the others.

"Why? Oh..." Macy turned to Eric. "'Scuse me. I have to get up." She squeezed her way out of the booth past him, doing what Jamie thought was an unnecessary amount of wriggling to get past him.

She trotted off obediently after Jess.

The three guys munched their burgers in silence. Above the table, a neon sign in the shape of a dancing girl with a gun buzzed, casting a flickering red and blue light over them as they ate.

"Why do they do that?" Eric asked, when the two girls had gone.

"Do what?"

"Go to the bathroom in pairs?"

"Who knows? They're girls. They do stuff like that," said Ben, pulling a pickle out of his burger bun. There was no ashtray, so he tossed it onto the floor.

Eric reached for the salt, found that it was empty, and gave Jamie a filthy look. "Dunno about you," he said, "but I always picture them dancing naked around their purses, when they go to the restroom together like that. That takes two. One to hold the purse, the other to do the dancing."

"Nice image," said Ben, gazing out of the sloping plate-glass window at the night. Outside, the bright lights of Hollywood glittered at him, cars streaming past on the packed boulevard. The revelers were certainly out in force tonight, he thought.

He chewed thoughtfully for a moment. "So you don't think they've just gone to have a talk in private?"

"Talk? Nah. Why would they wanna talk?" Eric skewered a load of fries with a fork and stuffed them into his mouth. "There's a whole world of hot lesbo stuff they could be doing in there. Maybe they'll tell us about it when they come out." He stopped as he saw the other two staring at him. "What? Like you've never pictured it. And doesn't that band girl have a pierced tongue?"

There was a brief silence while they all contemplated this.

After a minute, Jamie ordered some more water. With extra ice.

A short while later, Jess and Macy emerged from the restroom and sat back down at the table. Jess was looking grave; Macy was as pale as a sheet.

"So?" said Ben, his head filled with a variety of interesting images. He nudged Eric, who smirked back at him.

Macy looked at Jess, who took a deep breath. "I need to talk to you all," she said.

"Go ahead," said Jamie, clearing his throat sheepishly.

"Yeah. If you wanna tell us anything, we're all ears," said Eric, leaning forwards in his seat. He took a big bite of his burger, munching it excitedly.

Jess and Macy exchanged worried looks. "I'm not quite sure how to say this," said Jess. Macy put an encouraging hand on her shoulder.

"Go on," said Eric eagerly.

"It's just that..."

"Yes...?"

Jess let out her breath. "Well, the thing is... I think that we're all going to die," she said.

"Mmm, die, yes," said Eric, his eyes glassy. Then he blinked. "What?"

"All of us. I think we might be in trouble," said Jess.

"Tell them about your dream," prompted Macy.

"Dream?" Eric threw the remains of his burger down. Ketchup spattered onto the front of his white T-shirt, and he swore. "Is *that* all this is about? Just another of your paranoid little fantasies?"

"Fantasies. Huh huh," said Ben.

"Shut up, dude." Eric turned back to Jess. "So you dragged me all the way out here, in the middle of the night, just to tell me about some stupid dream?"

"It was more than a dream," said Jess. "It was important. Life-and-death important."

Eric gave a deep sigh, resigning himself to his fate. "Go on then, get it over with. Just make it quick, 'cos I've got some major R & R time to catch up on." He glanced down at his T-shirt, and pulled a face. "And some laundry."

"Okay. I know this sounds—"

"Crazy, yeah, thank you, we've been there, got the fuckin' postcards back already," said Eric. He glanced at his watch. "Hurry up. I've got about ten minutes left on my meter."

Jess gave Eric a hurt look. "*As I said,* I had a dream earlier on tonight. No, scratch that, it was a nightmare." She shivered. "A bad one."

"Did you eat pizza before going to bed?" asked Ben. "'Cause I find that when—"

"And," said Jess, ignoring him, "in this dream, I saw everyone who'd died in the club. They were all there. All of them. It was awful. Charlie and Amber were there, too. And so was the bouncer from the club, and the chick cop who died... I mean, *everyone.*"

"Were they naked?" asked Ben, not one to be able to let go of a chain of thought.

"Some of them were."

"Huh-huh."

Jess told them about her dream. At the end, Jamie said, "Hold on. Slow down there. You mean to tell us that you saw Charlie and the other three die in your vision?"

"No." Jess picked at the menu fretfully. "I saw *all of you* die. I even saw myself die. That's what I was trying to tell you."

"We all died in your vision?"

"I'm afraid so. And now people are dying in real life. And they're dying in the exact same order that they died in my premonition."

"Then why didn't you warn us?"

"That's what I'm trying to do now. Warn you, I mean." Jess paused dramatically. "I think my vision might be coming true. In real life."

"Well, that sucks." Eric paused, glancing out of the window. "Hold on a moment. Gotta go put more money in my meter." He fished around in his pocket and pulled out a handful of quarters. "Ben, go feed the meter."

"So," he carried on, as Ben disappeared out of the door, grumbling. "In this *vision* of yours, how did I die?"

"Do you really wanna know?"

"No, but tell me anyway."

Jess looked Eric in the eye. "You didn't want to know back at the club."

"Huh? Oh... Right. You got me there. *You* said you couldn't wait for me to die, or something like that. Cheeky bitch."

"Yeah," said Jess, her voice hard. "I stand by my word."

"Me too. But tell me anyway."

"Okay, fine. You got cut in half, all right? You were trying to climb out of the club window, and it collapsed on you. Splat. Very messy. The end."

There was a moment of silence. Then Eric said, "That couldn't have been me. I don't climb stuff."

"You climbed the fence, downtown."

"And the tree," put in Ben, returning from the car park. "And by the way, there was some old street guy sitting on your car. I chased him off."

"Great, thanks," said Eric absently. He turned back to Jess. "Okay, so I do climb things from time to time. That doesn't mean anything." He turned to Jess, dropping his voice. "Does it mean anything?"

"I'm not sure. The others didn't die the same way they did in my vision. But they still died in the same order."

"So, it's like their deaths were fated," put in Macy helpfully.

"Uh-huh. But I messed up that fate. My vision—I think it wasn't supposed to happen. Seeing the future just isn't normal, right?" Jess took a sip of her coffee, reflecting. "I cheated death, but then death just came along and took the people I saved, using a different method. Death, four. Me, zero. And I think the game's still in session."

"You honestly expect us to believe that horseshit?" asked Eric with a sneer. "Whoever heard of such a thing?"

Ben timidly raised his hand. "I once read in the newspaper that—"

"Did somebody ask you? Be quiet. Drink your milkshake." Eric sat back in his chair as Ben scowled at him. "Okay then, fine." He said to Jess. "If you're so smart, who's gonna die next?"

"Eric!" said Jamie, shocked.

"No, I'm serious. You want us to believe you? Prove it. Go ahead and predict the future. Who is it?" Eric asked. "Is it him?" He jerked a finger at Jamie.

"No, it's not."

"Pity." Then Eric stared at her, realizing what she'd just said. "You mean you actually know?"

"Er," said Jess desperately, exchanging looks with Macy.

"Go on, then. Tell us. Who is it?"

"I... I don't know if I should."

"Because...?"

Beside Jess, Macy reached for an abandoned bowl of fries and began picking at them anxiously.

"Because... it's not a good idea right now. And one other thing. That guy we met the other night, the homeless one. He said that we should look out for signs."

"Signs saying what? Like, road signs?"

"No. *Signs*. Like, things that seem to be warning us that something bad might be about to happen. You know. Ominous stuff."

"What a load of crap. Hey, c'mon. Dish the gossip. If jerkoff over there's gonna buy the farm, I want to be there to watch. With popcorn. And a video camera. I could make a fortune on the internet." Eric sniggered.

"It's not him, I told you. I just wanted to warn you all to be careful. Stay away from sharp objects, if you can. And if you see a lot of, I don't know, pictures of knives or whatever, then for God's sake don't go anywhere near cutlery drawers. Or restaurants. And so on." Jess glanced at Macy, looking deeply unhappy. "That's probably all I should say at this point."

"You can't say that to us!" said Eric, his voice rising. Some of the other diners turned around to stare at him. "You can't drag us out here in the middle of the night, tell us that we're all going to die, and then waltz off back home!"

"I thought you didn't believe me."

"I don't. But I still wanna see you humiliate yourself." Eric picked up the remains of his burger and shoved it into his mouth, chewing rapidly. "Go on, then. Tell us who it is, so we can all have a good laugh at you." He settled back in his seat as a thought struck him. "Is it her?"

Macy dropped her fork with a clatter. Jess turned and put a hand on her arm, glaring at Eric.

"It is! I knew it!" said Eric. "Oh, this is gonna be good. When she gets to ninety-eight and dies in her sleep, are you gonna come banging on the door of my retirement suite, blowing a trumpet and demanding an apology? 'Cos if you do, send me a reminder a coupla days in advance, so I can call everyone I know over to point and laugh at you."

"You know what? I really hope that turns out to be the case," Jess said quietly. Beside her, Macy picked up her fork and continued chewing miserably on her cold fries.

"So," Eric sat forward, his eyes gleaming. "How's she going to die?"

"Eric! That's enough. You don't know what you're saying," said Jamie. He put a protective arm around Macy, who casually shrugged it off. He looked at her quizzically, but she completely ignored him, watching Jess with worried brown eyes.

Jamie frowned.

"I know exactly what I'm saying," said Eric. "And I'm saying that she's full of shit. Come *on*, people, think about it. Are you going to believe her? She's sitting there saying we're all going to die horribly and that there's nothing that we can do about it, and you're just swallowing it? Pur-lease!"

"I didn't say that there was nothing we could do. That's the whole point of me asking you out here. I wanted to warn you—"

"Yeah, right. You wanted to warn us. You know what I think? I think you *don't* want to warn us. I think you want to scare us, so you can feel better about going back to your boring two-bit life and getting ostracized by your loser friends 'cos you've made yourself into a walking freak show, spouting off about all this 'premonition' crap. Right, Ben?"

"Right," said Ben uncertainly.

Eric picked up the remains of his beer and downed it in one gulp. "Why don't you just admit you miss being the star of the show? All that stuff that happened at the club—it was horrible and nasty and we've all gotta deal with that. But first, get over the idea that you're suddenly all high and mighty, just because you think you saved our lives with some whacked-out hallucination. And now what? A couple more folks have died, and now you're suddenly all excited 'cause you see a chance to be the center of attention again?" Eric slammed his empty glass down on the table, making Macy jump. "Well you can think again, little lady, because *we* control our lives, not some whacked out idea of yours about some pre-ordained fate. Take your handbag, and your little drummer-boy, and fuck off back where you came from."

There was a short, ringing silence. Then Ben said, "What does 'ostracized' mean?"

Jamie turned and whispered something in Ben's ear, his eyes fixed on Eric. Ben said, "Oh," then pulled out a biro and wrote something on the back of his hand. He frowned, squinting down at his hand. "I didn't know there were ostriches in LA," he said.

Beside him, Macy snorted, her mouth full of fries.

Then a look of surprise crossed her face. Her head jerked forward, and she put a hand to her throat. She tried to cough, found that she couldn't, and banged a hand frantically on the table.

"See? Even Macy agrees with me." Eric shoved his empty plate away from him and reached for his jacket. "She's got her head screwed on right. She'll probably still be bouncing around when the rest of us are all six feet under. And do you know why? Because she's a tough old cookie. Aren't you, my girl?" He slapped her hard on the back.

Macy spat half a soggy French fry out onto the table and sucked in a deep breath, then began coughing hard. Subsiding, she turned and wheezed at Eric gratefully, unable to speak.

"That's the spirit." Eric smiled at her with affection. "Nasty cough you got there, by the way. Come on, Ben. Let's get going."

He stood up with a flourish, pulling on his leather jacket and motioning to a nearby waiter for the check. Ben stood up, shrugged helplessly at Jess, and stepped out into the aisle.

As he did so, he nudged the cheap plastic table, which jolted and set the glasses clattering. Jess's half-empty coffee cup tipped over, pouring a dark stream of coffee across the table and onto the floor. The waiter chose that moment to walk past the table and deposit their check in front of Jess, carefully balancing an enormous tray of aperitifs and drinks on one arm as he did so.

Jess looked at him with a certain amount of foreboding.

"Look out for the—" she began, but it was already too late. The waiter successfully stepped over the pool of water, but then his foot landed instead on

Ben's discarded pickle. He skidded and stumbled forwards, his tray of food going flying.

Jess watched as the tray flew over their heads and crashed noisily into the wall above them, plummeting to the ground in a din of smashing glasses and clanging cutlery. A shower of sparks rained on their heads as the neon dancing-girl sign above them short-circuited from the impact, then the whole display flickered and went out. Beer dripped down the walls, pooling on the booth's table.

There was a round of applause from the rest of the diner as the waiter pulled himself to his feet. Apologizing profusely, he picked up his tray and began sheepishly scraping the remains of the plates and glasses off their table. People turned back to their food and began chatting again. One or two giggles pierced the general hustle and bustle. The manager came running out of the kitchen and began shouting at the hapless waiter.

"Chill, man, don't worry about it," said Jess, picking a twisty French fry from her hair and examining it to stop her heart thumping. "We were leaving anyway." She paused. "Um, the check...?"

"Forget it. It's on the house." His face said, *Please don't sue us.*

"Cool. And don't sweat it, man. It's not as though anyone di—" Jess stopped, gazing at the crackling neon sign. It was swaying slightly from side to side, getting lower with each swing. She looked down at Macy, who was standing right beneath it, struggling with the zip on her sweater.

A spark fizzed out of a crack in the glass. As Jess watched, the top of the sign detached itself from the wall and started to swing lazily downwards.

Here we go again, Jess thought, as she cried, "Macy! Look out!"

"Hmm?" Macy looked up to see a blur of movement coming towards her. Her eyes widened, and the next thing she knew she was plunging sideways onto the booth seat as Jamie grabbed her in a flying football tackle, pulling her out of the way of the falling sign.

She lay there for a moment, then her head jerked up. She pushed Jamie off her in one quick movement, then stared behind her in fear as the sign twitched and jerked on the seat. There was a strong smell of ozone and burning vinyl, then the seat started to smoke.

Macy scrambled away from it with a cry.

The restaurant manager darted forwards and snatched up a broom from the corner, then used it to pull the sign's plug out of the electrical outlet. The sign buzzed once, then dimmed to a dull glow.

"I think we'll be leaving now," said Jess to the manager. She extended a hand to the prone Macy. "Come on, girl. Let's get you out of here."

The five of them left the diner in silence, watched by everyone in the place.

When they got outside, Eric turned to Jess. "Nice show," he said nastily. "You almost had me convinced, there."

"I'm not trying to convince you of anything," snapped Jess, still wound up. "I was nowhere near that waiter."

"Yeah, but it was your—"

"Look, I don't care what you think, okay? When will you get that through your tiny little mind?"

"Guys, that's enough," said Jamie. "Look at what you've done to Macy."

All four of them turned to look. Macy was standing a little distance away from them outside a nearby gun shop, leaning on a parked car by the busy road. She looked as if she were about to throw up. She noticed them looking at her, and gave a weak little smile, which faded almost immediately.

Puffing himself up, Eric whipped off his jacket and sauntered over to Macy, wrapping it around her shoulders to keep her warm. He leaned back on a big sign that read in big letters *We Buy Guns*," and gave Jess a smug glance. "Yeah. Look at what you've done. You've traumatized the poor wee lassie."

"I was talking to both of you," said Jamie. "You're acting like a pair of school kids. Get over it, and go home. Macy," he said more gently. "I'm taking you home. We'll get a cab." He reached into his pocket for his wallet.

Macy shook her head fearfully. "No thanks. Eric will take me, won't you?"

Jess glanced at Jamie, then back at Macy. She raised an eyebrow.

"I sure will, little lady. You'll be safe with me." Eric glanced up at Ben, who turned away from the others and gave him a big thumbs-up, then made a less polite gesture with his other hand.

"Like hell you will. Macy, come here. We'll drive you back."

"Yeah, and maybe Jess'll see to it that your door isn't shut properly, then she'll take a lot of sharp corners. And then she'll be *right*," said Eric. "I wouldn't put it past her," he added smugly.

"If that's what you think, then you're on your own," said Jess. "At least Ben's on my side." She swung around. "Right, Ben?"

Ben held up his hands. "Don't look at me. I'm just here for the food, folks," he said.

"Come on. You've gotta have *some* kind of opinion."

"Nope. Leave me out of it."

"Tell you what." Macy walked over to the group. "I'll make my own way home. I can't deal with all of this right now." She pulled a pack of chewing gum out of her pocket and absentmindedly unwrapped a stick, then froze with it halfway to her mouth. She took a few careful breaths, then wrapped it back up again. "I gotta get me some sleep. I'll see you all around. Goodnight." She turned her back on them and started walking towards the cab rank.

This time, they all yelled "MACY!" at once.

Macy jumped back as a dreadlocked cyclist whizzed past her on the unlit sidewalk, the metal-tipped surfboard strapped to his side rack pointed right at her.

She stood there for long moment, gazing after the cyclist as he sped off into the night. Then she turned round and walked back to Jess. "So," she said brightly. "Where's this car of yours, then?"

They walked back across the sprawling parking lot in silence, lost in their own individual thoughts. Jess dropped back slightly and walked beside Jamie, who was bringing up the rear.

"So, how's it going with you?" she asked.

"Me? I'm good. Doom, gloom, death and destruction... Same old, same old. Do you want a Tic-Tac?"

"No thanks."

Jess glanced up at him anxiously. There had been no signs warning her of Macy's near misses in the diner. "What do you think about what I said?" she asked.

"I don't know, Jess. I want to believe you, but... you know me. Healthy skepticism and all that. But I'll be careful, all the same."

"Good man."

They walked past a motorcyclist, who was refueling his huge Harley from a can under the light of a streetlamp. The driver glanced up and glared at them as they walked by. He wore a lettered biker jacket and had a dramatic scar running down one side of his jaw. They gave him a wide berth.

Jess glanced sideways at Jamie. "So... what was up with you and Macy tonight?" she asked casually.

"Hmmm?"

"I though I detected a bit of an atmosphere back there."

"You think?"

"Well, yeah. She hardly said two words to you. I thought you guys got on."

"We do." Jamie shoved his hands into his pockets and picked up his pace.

Jess gave a sigh. "You're not exactly helping me out here. Is there something you want to tell me?"

"Nope. Why should there be?"

"You tell me."

They walked a little further on. Jamie glanced at Jess, opened his mouth as if to say something, then closed it again.

"Yes?" said Jess, not unkindly.

"It's just that..." Jamie swigged from his packet of Tic-Tacs, crunching distractedly. He lowered his voice, sounding embarrassed. "I think she kind of has a thing for me."

"So what does that prove? She's not blind," said Jess. She dug Jamie in the ribs with an elbow, raising her eyebrows. "She saw you play, right?"

"Yeah. I guess. She was at the gig last Monday, too. And the one the weekend before that at the Joint. Right at the front, too."

"Well, well well. Looks like you've got yourself a bit of a fan. Oh, it must be hard, being so irresistible..."

"I wouldn't know," said Jamie, a little more sharply than he'd intended. He looked around him, then dropped his voice still further, moving closer to Jess as they walked. "And it's not just that. There was... an incident."

"Oh yeah?" Jess grinned. "Do tell."

"Not *that* kind of incident."

"Pity. Go on."

"I... she... well. It was that night we were all at the police station, after... you know."

"I do. What happened?"

"After you guys left, the cops took me back to the station, and—"

"They caught you?" Jess stopped walking. "I thought you got away."

"Yeah." Jamie sniffed. "So did I. Must be getting slow in my old age. Anyway, Macy came by the station and bailed me out, then took me back to her place for the night."

"That was nice of her."

A thought struck Jess as she started walking after the others. "Why didn't you tell me this?"

"You never asked." Jamie kicked a stone across the parking lot, which rebounded off the tire of a parked scooter. "So anyway," he continued, "I didn't really wanna go back with her, but..." He glanced ahead of them at the others, and put a hand on Jess's arm. "Walk slower."

"That bad, eh?" said Jess, with sympathy.

"I've had worse. So anyway, I knew she liked me, so nat'rally I was a bit apprehensive about going back with her. Turns out I was right. She talks my ear off all the way home, then when we get there, she tells me that oops, all the spare bedding's in the wash because her cats peed on it, and there's no sofa, so would I mind sharing a bed with her?"

"You're kidding! That's so obvious."

"Tell me about it. I nearly turned round and walked out of the place, but I was just so tired, you know? Anyway, it luckily turns out to be a double bed, but it might as well not have been, because now oops, her nightgown's in the wash too, what a shame, and she's tellin' me that she always likes to lie slap-bang in the middle of the bed, in case she falls out... I think you're getting the picture."

"Loud and clear," said Jess, then she stopped again. "Hold on," she said to Jamie. "Eric!" she yelled.

"What?"

"Where the hell are you parked?"

"Over there." Eric pointed to a big black SUV parked in the far corner of the crowded lot.

"Jeez. Okay, go on. So you're in bed with this hot naked girl, and you have a problem... why?"

"Of course I have a problem! I hardly even know the girl, and now she's getting all up-close and personal with me. So I try to sleep, but every time I roll over, she's right up in my face like this." Jamie skipped ahead of Jess and pushed his face right up against hers, grinning maniacally.

Jess stopped walking and grabbed Jamie by the shoulders, pushing him away. She laughed nervously. "All right, I get the picture. Again, you have a problem with this?"

"Sure I do. So after a while, I got out of bed, pretending to need the bathroom, then grabbed my clothes and legged it out of the front door. I couldn't deal with her. I just needed to sleep. She hasn't spoken to me since."

Jess giggled. "I can't believe you bailed on her."

"Neither could she. Hence the not-speaking-to-me thing."

"But you're a guy. Guys aren't supposed to do that."

"Why do you always say that? Jessie, you say it like it's some kind of insult. So I'm a guy. So what? Does that automatically mean I have no standards of behavior?"

"Some would say that's true."

Jamie reached out and tapped Jess gently on the nose. "Then *some* must have a very low opinion of us guys."

"Not low, just realistic."

"Only if you date the kind of men *you* date."

Jess's expression froze on her face. "What's that supposed to mean?"

"Come on, Jess." Jamie's face indicated that he knew he was playing with fire, but he went on, regardless. "What about that doctor guy? The one that turned out to have two other lady friends, as well as a wife and a kid? And then there was that whole football-guy drama... and then the acrobat from the Russian state circus... not to mention that lifeguard you spent all last month chasing after..." Jamie cupped his hands round his mouth, megaphone-style. "Hello, Houston calling Jessica, your time is up, come back in, please."

"It's none of your damn business who I date." Jess tried to walk round Jamie, but he stood in her way. "*Move.*"

"No." Jamie dropped his voice. "You need to take a reality check, girl, or someone's gonna end up getting hurt. Most likely you. There are some bad people out there, and I worry."

"Since when do you care?" Jess stopped as she saw the look in Jamie's eyes. "Oh no. Not this again."

"Come *on*, Jess. You know I'm making sense." Jamie moved towards her, reaching out to cup her face, but Jess took a firm step away from him.

"Hey, don't be like that," Jamie said, looking hurt. "I only want the best for you."

"No you don't, you want... I don't even wanna think about what you want." Jess shook her head firmly. "Jamie, you've gotta stop doing this, 'cos it's freaking me out."

"Doing what? I'm not doing anything."

"Yes you are. You've been like this ever since we..." Jess hesitated.

"Since what?" asked Jamie lightly. "Go on, you can say it. I don't mind. Ever since we—"

"Guys! Come *on!*" yelled Eric, from over by the SUV.

"Coming!" Jess called back, secretly glad of the reprieve. She turned and looked up at Jamie, her face softening. "Look, Jamie." She took hold of his hands. "I really like you. You know that, don't you? You're such a—"

"Nice guy, I know," said Jamie tiredly. He pulled his hands away from Jess and shoved them back into his pockets. "Charlie told me."

"What's Charlie got to do with anything?"

"He said you told him about us."

Jess was silent for a heartbeat. Then she shrugged. "All I said was—"

"It's not important. I don't care what you tell people. The only thing that matters to me is that you take care of yourself. And I don't think you're doing that at the moment."

"So that's your professional opinion, is it?"

"It is."

"Then your opinion sucks." Jess pushed past Jamie, but he grabbed her shoulder and held on tight. "Jess, listen to me. All this stuff since the club disaster, like you hanging around with Charlie? It's just another symptom. You like to feel important, I get that. I'm cool with it. But at what price? I think you're just going to end up getting hurt all over again, and next time, maybe I won't be there to bail you out."

In reply, Jess pointedly tugged her shoulder free of Jamie's grip and turned her back on him, heading over to the SUV. "I'm heading home," she said coldly. "You want a ride? Then hurry up, 'cos it's late and I'm tired."

Jamie watched her go, and gave a deep sigh.

He looked over at the SUV as Eric started unlocking the door.

Something immediately caught his attention. Was it just him, or had someone just ducked behind the car?

Instantly on full alert, he ran over to the SUV, waving his hands. "Guys, wait!" he hissed.

"It's all right, we're not gonna go without you," sniffed Jess, leaning on the door of the car while Eric struggled with his keys.

"No—behind the car." Jamie pointed. "I think there's someone there."

"What? Where?" Eric marched round the front of the SUV. "Hey!" he yelled.

Around the other side, a homeless guy was busy levering one of the chromed hubcaps off the rear wheel. Seeing Eric, he dropped his tire-iron with a clang, backing away quickly. Standing up, he held the freshly-removed hubcap out to Eric, like a begging bowl. "Spare any change, buddy?" he asked with a toothless grin.

"No I damn well cannot! And give that back!" Eric made a grab for the hubcap. The homeless guy whipped it away from him and hid it inside his tasseled jacket. "Sorry, gone now."

Eric started forwards, fist raised, then stopped. His eyebrows did a complicated dance. "Wait a minute— I know you. You're the guy from the other night!"

"Yes. Man from many nights." The man nodded his head sagely.

His supply of relevant conversation exhausted, Eric raised his fist again. "Whatever. Gimme back my hubcap."

"Eric, leave him alone."

"D'you know how much those things cost?"

"Ask him nicely for it back, then."

"What's going on?" Jess ducked her head around the edge of the car. Her jaw dropped. "You!" she said.

"Me," agreed the cowboy.

"I can't believe you're here! You have no idea how badly I need to talk to you."

"No talk. Gotta go. Mother's expecting me," said the cowboy urgently. He swept a hand upwards at the sky.

"Well, good to see that he's still sane."

"Eric, shut your mouth. Now, I really have to ask you—"

"Sorry. Time to split," said the cowboy. He gave Macy a strange look, then scurried off towards the back gate.

"Hey! Come back!" Jess thumped Eric. "Go after him! I need to talk to him!"

"Why are you so weird? I never met anyone as weird as you."

"Just—go! Get him back."

"Screw you. Go get him yourself."

"But he's got your hubcap."

"Oh yeah." Eric's face darkened. "Hey, come back here!" He ducked into the SUV and grabbed a flashlight. Then he set off across the edge of the parking lot, chasing the rapidly diminishing figure of the cowboy, who vanished down a side alley with a whoop of glee.

Jess tore off her jacket. "Stay here, guys."

Jamie bristled. "No way. I'm not letting you go off in the dark with that jerk."

"Come with us then," Jess called over her shoulder, jogging off across the lot. "But move it."

"That woman... eesh!" said Jamie, stamping his foot. He threw an apologetic look towards Macy and Ben. "Guard the car, children. Back in a minute."

Macy watched him run off, then turned and looked at Ben. Ben nodded at her amiably, a huge grin plastered across his face. "How *you* doin'?" he said.

Macy glanced worriedly around her at the busy darkness, then looked back at the diminutive figure of Ben, who gave her a big wink.

She did a swift mental calculation.

"Hey, you guys!" she yelled. "Wait up!" She began trotting off after them as fast as her heels would allow. Within a minute, she'd disappeared down the alley.

"Well. What cheek," said Ben.

A few minutes strolled by. He inspected his nails under the glare of orange light from a streetlamp, then polished them on his jacket. He threw a glance at the alleyway, debating whether or not to go after Macy, then realized that Eric had left the car unlocked.

That meant he was stuck here until they got back.

Well. That really was too much. Why was it always him left holding the baby, so to speak? They didn't even *think* that he might have wanted to go along. Oh no. They'd just gone off and left him, the splitters. Did they not think that he could help? He may not have Eric's looks or Jamie's... whatever it was Jamie had, but he could still make himself useful, in some small way.

He was a man, after all.

Ben puffed himself up to his full five foot six height, and moodily kicked the SUV's rubber tire with his boot. *Stupid car.* It wasn't that he particularly wanted to go running off on some wild goose chase, no. It was just the *principle* of the thing. They'd automatically *assumed* he'd look after the car, and they'd all gone off and left him. There was action to be had, and he was missing it.

He was so sick of everyone taking him for granted.

Ben slammed the car door with considerably more force than was needed, then leaned back on it grumpily, listening to the sounds of the night. Besides the ever-present background hum of traffic, he could hear dozens of voices, talking, laughing, singing. It was past midnight, but out here on the Strip, things were just warming up for the night. A faint rhythmic thumping came from a nearby club, the occasional blast of guitar noise spilling out onto the street as people went in and out. The scratchy sound of a radio came from the valet parking booth on the corner, and the roar of motorcycle engines echoed down the street in the distance. Somewhere in the parking lot, a bottle shattered.

Ben's ears pricked up. A bottle?

Then he leaned forwards, squinting into the darkness. Was it his imagination, or had someone just followed Macy into the alleyway?

He peered closer, then shrank back as a group of dark shapes flitted towards the mouth of the alley and vanished inside. That was a lot of "someones".

Ben tensed, his heartbeat speeding up. He was sure those people were up to no good. He should go warn the guys, just in case.

But who would look after the car? He stole a guilty glance at it. It was brand new, and presumably very expensive. Eric would beat the living shit out of him if anything happened to it.

But on the other hand, if his friends were in danger...

Ah, to hell with it. Ben reached inside his jacket, checking that something was still there. There was a faint click, and he withdrew his hand, closing up his jacket carefully.

Maybe he could be of some use tonight, after all.

Throwing an anxious look back at the SUV, Ben ran off towards the alley, after his friends.

"He's gone. How could he be gone? He just vanished."

"People don't just vanish, doofus. Check behind that car, over there."

"I just looked. He's definitely gone."

Jess put her hands on her hips and peered around her, screwing up her eyes in the gloom. It was dark down the alley and it smelled bad. A row of parked cars huddled against a building to one side of the road, which was covered in tatty builders' scaffolding and wooden boarding. A huge "Site Safety" sign hung loosely from a wire on the scaffold.

There was definitely no sign of the homeless guy.

"Perhaps he went the other way. He can't have gone far."

"He'd better not have. Those hubcaps cost a fortune."

"Look, would you forget about that freakin' hubcap? There's more important things at stake here."

Eric snorted. "Yeah, like your sad little reputation. I'll send out the funeral invites right now, shall I?"

"Look—over there! By that wall! Something moved!"

"That was my shadow. You need some sleep, girl."

Jamie skidded around the corner and jogged over to Jess. "What's happening?" he asked, throwing a sharp glance at Eric. "Is your guy here?"

"Nah. He ran off," said Jess, looking glum. "He came round that corner, but he's not in the street. It's really weird. We looked both ways."

"Maybe he's hiding? I would, at this hour."

"I doubt it," said Eric gloomily. "We checked under all the cars, and that scaffolding's too high to climb." A thought struck him. "Maybe he went down into the sewers?" He shone his flashlight downwards at the nearest manhole, then bent down and tried to open it.

"This is real life, dickwad. People don't go down into the sewers like they do on TV. They're all locked up." Jamie glanced around him anxiously. "Come on, guys. We should get going. It's dark. It's not safe to be around here."

"We're fine," said Jess icily. "You don't have to chaperone us. Go back to the car. We'll be back in five minutes."

"I'm not leaving you. Already said that. I don't think this is a good place to go wandering around in the dark."

"And what would you know?" said Eric nastily.

"More than you, if nothing else. You stand out a mile, in that white collar of yours. You're practically glowing. You may as well paint a bull's-eye on your head. And put that manhole cover back. You're not impressing anyone."

"It *wasn't* locked, liar. And anyway, I was just trying to help."

"Then don't. Just come back to the parking lot, both of you. I'll stay and look round here." Jamie paused, listening, then went on. "He can't have gone far. And even if he did, he can't keep running. I'll find him, if it's so important to you. A person can't just vanish."

"Wanna bet?"

Eric glanced up sharply to see a scruffy, wiry man step out of the alleyway into the light. He had long, matted dreadlocks, and wore a tattered raincoat with expensive-looking trainers. He had a skateboard strapped to his back.

He was holding Macy by the throat.

"What the...?" Eric's eyes narrowed and he swung around towards Jess. "Is this your idea of a joke?"

"Funny you folks should be walkin' round here this time of night," said the man, in a conversational tone. He examined Macy's earrings with his free hand. "Normally vis'ters to these parts don't stop by."

Macy gave a small gasp, and Eric thought he saw something metallic flash under the streetlights. He's got a knife, he thought. Shit.

Out loud, he said, "We were just looking for someone. But now we're leaving. Weren't we, guys?"

He glanced to both sides. Jess's face was ashen, her eyes locked on Macy. Jamie was staring fixedly at the man, his entire body tense. He saw them glance at one another meaningfully, and then slowly begin to edge apart.

He looked back at the man, noticing how white and new-looking his trainers were compared to the rest of his outfit, which looked like it had been washed in a sewer.

"However," skateboard guy continued. He gave a nasty little smile, revealing gold-capped teeth. "I would be willing to help you find your way back home again. Kind of like a public service, that's me. These streets can get very dangerous after nightfall. Spec-taculerilly so, in fact."

He looked down at Macy, who was holding herself very still in his grasp, and sniffed, screwing up his face. "Course, I'd need some kinda funding, for that to happen." He wiped his nose on a coat sleeve.

"We don't have any money on us," said Eric, puffing himself up. Out of the corner of his eye, he saw Jamie shake his head frantically.

"Course you do. I just saw you come out the fuckin' food hall, for Chrissakes. Gimme some credit. I ain't blind." The man straightened up, his eyes glinting. "I figure that at least one of you got some collateral on you. You, Dog-Boy—" he jerked his elbow at Eric. "Roll up yer sleeves."

"What? Why?"

"He wants your watch, dude," said Jamie in a monotone. His lips barely moved as he spoke. "Might be best to give it to him."

"You've gotta be kidding me! Do you know how much this thing cost... me... Oh, damn."

The skateboard man sniggered and stepped forward. "New round here, is he?"

"In a manner of speaking, yes," said Jamie. His eyes still hadn't left the man's face.

"Come on. Soon as we get this over an' done with, sooner we can all be on our merry ways."

"Just do it, Eric," said Jess tensely.

"But my dad gave it to me for my birthday! It's brand new!"

"Then your dad's gotta git you another one, isn't he?" said the man. He yanked Macy backwards, making her yelp. "C'mon. Hurry up. Or your little girlfriend loses a bit off her. An' you ain't choosing which bit."

"*He's* got a watch, too," whined Eric, nodding his head over at Jamie. "Take his instead."

"Eric!"

"Great. I'll have that, too." Skateboard man increased his grip on Macy's throat, making her wheeze. "Quickly please, kiddies. And you too, drama queen. Turn out yer pockets."

Relenting under the heat of Jess's glare, Eric reached up his sleeve and fiddled with the catch on his gold Rolex, muttering to himself. Behind him, Jamie slid off his own battered surf-watch and tossed it down in front of the man, giving Eric a black look. Jess reached into her jeans pockets and threw a handful of one-dollar bills down with it. She stepped back expectantly.

"And your bra."

"Excuse me?!"

"You got anything hidden in yer bra? Credit cards and so on? Come on, you looks like the sort. Don't make me come over there and check."

"I have nothing of the kind!"

"Suit yourself. But you realize there's a no-card fee on this particular transaction."

There was another glint of metal in the darkness, and Macy yelled, "Jess!"

"All right, all right. Fine. Take it." Jess reached inside her top and pulled out a battered debit card. Scowling, she hurled it down onto the pile.

"Pleasure doing business with you folks," said the skateboard man pleasantly, eyeing the pile with satisfaction. "Now, if you would be so kind as to back off, and—"

"Don't move!"

The man's scarred eyebrows drew together, and he glanced backwards, towards the alleyway. There was some short, scared-looking kid standing behind him, both arms raised and pointed right at the small of his back. He couldn't see what the kid was clutching on account of him being so close, but after what he'd just said, there were only one or two things he could be holding.

Judging by the stunned looks on his friends' faces, it was option two.

He sighed. "Drop it, kid."

"No way. Let her go!"

The skateboard man smirked to himself and mentally counted to three, hearing clothing rustle and gravel crunch in the alleyway behind him. Then he tightened his grip on the girl and turned around. He nodded amiably to the five other guys who had just stepped out of the shadows behind the kid. They didn't just stand there. They *loomed*. There was the general crossing of arms and stamping of boots that somehow managed to convey that the newcomers were armed. One of the guys peered closely at the brand-name of the gun Ben was holding and laughed derisively.

In his arms, the girl started to cry.

Sweating, Ben jerked his gun up even higher, the tip weaving crazily from side to side. "Tell them to back off!"

"What makes you think they're with me? P'raps they're just out for an afternoon stroll. Lovely weather we've been having lately..."

"Ben! Put that fucking thing down *now!*" shouted Jamie.

"Yeah, *Ben,*" said skateboard guy. "Guns is dangerous things, you know. They just makes things worse. Might put someone's eye out, if you're not careful. Most likely, your own"

"Just let her go, asshole."

"An' why should I do that? Things just got interesting. Matter of fact, I think I'll grab hold of that other girl over there, see what else you've got up your sleeve."

Skateboard guy tittered to himself.

"Don't you dare go near her," Ben spat. He jerked his head at Jamie. "He's got a knife. He'll slash the shit out of you if you even think about touching her."

All eyes turned to Jamie, inspecting him with interest. The temperature in the alley seemed to drop by several degrees.

"Thanks, Ben," Jamie managed. "And nicely put." He got ready to run.

"Well. More and more interesting."

"Ben! For the love of God, stop jerking around and put the gun down," snapped Eric.

"No way. *He* lets go of her first."

"And then what? We all go and have a drink and a laugh together? Ben, you're an asshole. We were doing fine till you showed up."

"Yeah, looks like you had everything under control." Ben laughed bitterly, unable to help himself. "Oh, and *I'm* the asshole now, am I? I'm not the one who nearly gets himself killed for the sake of a few pounds of drugs, *Eric*."

Eric's mouth dropped open. His hand flew to the brace collar around his neck. "How did you know...?"

"Dude. I'm not stupid. You've been doing it ever since I first met you. Same thing, every time. It's so damn obvious it makes me wanna cry."

"You never said—"

"Sure I never said. I was too busy enjoying the free food and drinks you've been pouring down my throat this last year. Need someone to watch the door? Get old Ben in and set him up with a beer or two. Want a quiet place to deal? Call Ben and get him to rent a room under his name, just in case." Ben gripped the gun tighter. "Why do you think I got this gun in the first place? You think I sleep well at night knowing you're downstairs trading God-knows-what with some hoods from the projects? *They know where we live,* dude."

"I'll have to give you my number," said the skateboard guy, impressed.

"Shut the fuck up or I'll waste you!" snapped Ben. He turned back to Eric, ignoring the sudden warning atmosphere from the guys behind him. "I've had it up to here with you using me. You think it was a coincidence that chick cop was at the club Friday night?"

Eric stared at Ben. Slowly he raised his finger and pointed. "You? You were the one who called the cops on us? I lost eight hundred dollars that night, besides... everything else. It took me *weeks* to set that deal up."

"I didn't want to do it," said Ben, his voice starting to waver. "I just wanted to teach you a lesson. I thought a reality check would do you good. I was so sick of your crap, ordering me around and making me do this and that. Shit, you didn't even turn up in costume!"

"What?" Eric was genuinely puzzled.

Behind Ben, skateboard guy and his pals watched in silent fascination, like spectators at a tennis match.

"It was Eighties Night, jerk. There was me in a tartan kilt and glitter, and you just turn up in jeans. I felt so stupid. You're always letting me down like that."

"Hey, kid—"

"Zip it. And you want your little blue backpack of crack back? You can sing for it, 'cos I flushed it."

"You didn't!"

"I did. You should be grateful to me for even bothering." Ben paused, shaking his head bitterly. "So many people died this week, and you just go waltzing round the edges of it all, singing a happy little song, carrying on with business as usual. You're lucky you've got me to clean up your mess, or you'd probably be in jail by now. I'm the best friend you ever had, and you just treat me like shit, and now I'm sick of it."

"Fascinatin' as this is, I think more pressing business—"

"I told you to be quiet." Ben's eyes blazed.

"Stop it, Ben. You'll get us all into trouble."

"I don't care, Jess. I just want him to let her go, so we can all go home, and go to bed, and forget all this. That's all I want."

"I *said* I ain't lettin' her go. Not till you put down that gun, and your friend loses the knife."

"Not gonna happen, jerkoff. I'll ask you one more time: let her go."

"Oh yeah? Or what?"

"I said I'd shoot you. What, you don't think I will?"

Skateboard guy sniggered. "I'll be surprised if you do, kid."

Much to his surprise, the kid shot him.

TWELVE

Police Officer Andy Adams was driving west on Melrose when a call came in on his radio. Andy swore as his partner answered the call, then swung the car around in a tight and completely illegal U-turn, making him spill horseradish sauce down the front of his clean uniform.

"Spencer!"

"Sorry, man."

Andy reached for the pack of napkins he kept in the glove compartment, tossing the remains of his hot dog back into its container on the dashboard. "This stuff's worse than goddamn ketchup," he said, dabbing the sauce off his shirt. "What's the situation?"

"We got an eleven-six in the vicinity of Mel's on Sunset."

"Meaning...?"

Officer Spencer sighed. "Some idiot let off a gun outside the Hollywood Diner. Or possibly a firecracker. We don't know yet."

"That place with the giant burgers?" Andy licked his lips. "Do you think that by any chance we could—"

"*No*, Andy." Spencer reached over and patted Andy's stomach with one hand. "We can't." He picked up his police radio and switched it on, "Tenfour," he affirmed.

Andy looked at his watch. "What's cop code for 'Going to lunch now'?"

"That's a Code Seven, Andy. You should know that one by now. And no, we're not stopping. Don't make me call your wife."

Andy stared gloomily ahead, loosening his seat belt. "Spoilsport."

Jess ducked as a fist swung over her head, then she darted over to the wall where Macy was cowering. "Come on. Get up. We've gotta go," she said breathlessly.

Macy was staring at the melee behind her, crouched down against the safety of the wall.

Jess turned to follow her gaze.

Ben was just visible beneath the two big skinhead guys who were currently trying to remove his arms from their sockets. His gun lay a short distance from him in the middle of the alleyway. Jamie was battling a third attacker, a huge guy in a green army jacket, trying to keep him away from the fallen gun. One of the remaining heavies was bending over skateboard guy, who lay at an angle across the curb beneath the scaffolding, clutching at his leg and yelling blue murder. Dark blood was streaming out, staining his trainers red in the moonlight.

"I can't get up. I think he cut through my entire neck. Look! I'm bleeding!" wailed Macy, clutching at her throat with both hands.

"Here. Let me see." Jess pulled the girl's trembling hand away from her neck. A tiny line of blood was visible.

Jess breathed a sigh of relief.

"You're fine, girl! He just scratched you. You were lucky."

"Lucky? I don't call this lucky." Macy waved her hand around her miserably. "Jess, I've got to get out of here. I want to go home."

"I know. It's okay. I'll get you out. I... hey!"

Jess turned around and belted the skinny guy in the black T-shirt who had just grabbed her by the arm. The man flinched, then yanked sharply on her arm, knocking her off-balance and sending her plummeting to the sidewalk.

"Eric!" Jess yelled, raising her hands above her head as the guy stalked towards her. "Get over here!"

"In a minute!" shouted Eric desperately. He and the remaining tough guy were playing what looked like a game of tag around a nearby parked car, the man chasing him around and round. Eric shrieked like a girl as the man jumped up onto the hood of the car, growling, then leapt onto the roof and down the other side, making a wild grab for him.

Eric danced away, sprinted a short distance down the road, then disappeared underneath two powerful-looking guys as they jumped on top of him, hurling him to the ground. He curled up into a ball as they started kicking at him. One of the guys reached down and stripped off his leather jacket, holding it up critically against his chest to check the sizing.

As Jess rolled over groggily, Macy hauled herself to her feet and ran over, shoulder-barging Jess's attacker with a kamikaze cry. The guy stumbled, and Macy pulled off one of her high heels and began systematically beating him over the head with it, shouting, "Get away from her!"

Macy hurled her shoe at the man as he ran off. He ducked. There was a fresh howl from skateboard guy as the shoe hit him on the head.

Jess took advantage of the reprieve to roll to her feet. She evaluated the situation at a glance. Macy was holding her own, but the three guys seemed to be fighting a losing battle. Eric and Ben were already down on the ground, bleeding profusely, and Jamie wasn't much better off. As she watched, one of the scary-looking skinheads grabbed him in a headlock and heat-butted him viciously from behind. His legs buckled and he fell forwards, catching himself on one arm before he hit the ground. He grunted as his attacker kicked him hard in the stomach, muttering a stream of oaths that made even Jess blush.

But still, she noted, he didn't reach for his knife.

Despite the direness of their situation, he went up fractionally in her estimation.

Jess stood frozen for a moment, her fists clenched in indecision as she looked around her, trying to decide who to help first. Then a swarthy arm went around her neck and she was pulled backwards. She immediately slammed both of her elbows back, sinking them into the man's stomach, then kicked backwards with all her might. Her heel went through empty air as the man neatly sidestepped and yanked her upwards, nearly lifting her clear off the ground. She yelled out and sank her long nails into his arm, then froze as she felt something sharp and cold being pressed against her ribs.

An instant later, her attacker gave a cry of pain and released her, turning around to clutch at his back. Jess spun away to see Eric standing behind him, blood pouring from his nose. He was holding a Swiss army penknife, the twisty bottle opener attachment open and coated in blood. "Yeah!" he whooped. "Who's the daddy now?" He gave a shout of triumph, then hastily ducked as a huge fist swung at his head.

Jess grabbed the man's other arm and tried to pull him away from Eric, then jumped as a blinding blue light filled her vision. "What the...?"

Jess looked around her, puzzled, then flinched as the blue light flashed again, leaving a black and purple afterglow on the inside of her eyelids. She shook her head to clear it, staring around in confusion. A wave of dizziness hit her, and she went spinning to the floor as the thug shook her off his arm.

Jess hit the ground hard, only just bringing her hands up in time to stop her head smashing on the sidewalk. She lay still for a beat, dazed, her hands stinging, then gasped as a barrage of images filled her mind, overlaid on the street scene before her...

She saw bright lights, neon signs, the flash of passing traffic. A blur of streets zoomed past at high speed, then buildings, squat, gray, ugly, familiar-looking. A white street sign zoomed forwards, quickly blurring out of focus before she could read it, then vanished and was replaced by another, then another. Palm trees swayed crazily behind them in the night-time wind, and the moon blazed down with the intensity of a nuclear furnace, bathing her in its cold white light.

Then she was indoors, running down a brightly lit corridor. Footsteps pounded behind her, and she increased her pace. She frantically scanned the name plates above the doors, driven by a great sense of urgency. Door after door swung open in front of her, and her panic increased as she neared the end of the corridor, fear filling her in a rising tide.

As she ran she heard voices, muted and far away, as though they were coming to her down a long metal tube...

"Someone help me! Macy! Help! I think they got Jess!"

"I can't see anything wrong with her. She's fine."

"Why's she just lying there? Get her up. Oh crap, look out!"

Jess blinked and looked up to see Macy crouched over her, shaking her urgently. Then someone grabbed her, pulling Macy away from her. Confused, Jess struck out blindly as she was dragged along the ground, her mind filled with jumping images as her vision cut back and forth between the alley and the corridor.

Then she cried out in pain as her head struck a brick wall. Black static filled her mind and she felt strong fingers ripping at her clothing, and then the blue fire washed over her again, silencing the voices. Her vision flashed with gray, then jump-cut back again...

...to the corridor, as the end wall sped towards her. With a flash of darkness, she was suddenly on the other side of the wall, moving across the room at great speed. The room was freezing, and dozens of mice darted across the floor beneath her feet, scampering away from her in panic.

Slowing down, she looked about the room. There were dozens of hospital-style gurneys set up in long rows down the sides of the room, the green sheets covering them stained with blood.

They were all empty.

Apart from one.

Jess's nerves screamed at her as she felt herself being drawn towards the gurney, as though she were magnetized. There was a body on it, covered in a similar green sheet. There was no blood on it, but somehow, that was even more terrifying.

Jess knew that whoever was under there was important, but also knew that she wasn't brave enough to look. Beneath her, millions of mice swarmed around underfoot, hopping and jumping over her feet and clambering up the legs of the gurney, squeaking excitedly. Moonlight shone in through the window, bathing the scene in a pale light.

As she stood there, a sharp wind blew through the room, raising dust and making reams of paperwork fly about. She turned around to see the door fly open, but nobody came in. Perhaps it had just been blown open by the storm that was gathering outside?

She fearfully turned back to the gurney, and gasped. The sheet had been blown off. She stared at the person lying on the gurney...

No.

It couldn't be.

But it was. Jess gazed down at the body and felt a single tear trickle down her cheek.

It was her mother.

With a cry, Jess started backing rapidly away, but found herself held tight by some invisible force. She couldn't move. She struck out with a cry and heard someone nearby yell in pain. She blinked as the body vanished and was replaced by a broken guitar, its neck snapped and the strings hanging loosely down onto the floor. Blood was oozing out of the gaps around the pickups.

Jess backed away, then whirled around and began running.

She suddenly knew what had happened to her mother.

But it wasn't her fault, it really wasn't...

She flew down the corridor and reached the main doors to the building, but try as she might, she couldn't open them. She hammered on the door with all her strength, and was surprised as they suddenly blew open, revealing a world filled with blinding bright light.

Jess squinted into the glare, just able to make out the shapes of people running towards her. There was a loud bang and a scream, and the whoop of a police siren. She turned to run, then cracking blue lights exploded on the inside of her retina, and her mind filled with pain.

Then she was falling, falling, falling...

Jess jerked her head up from the sidewalk with a gasp. She was back in the alley again, this time propped up awkwardly against a wall. Eric was bending over her, shaking her much harder than was necessary. Her head hurt and she could taste blood in her mouth.

Jess blinked. Her sweater was torn, and she could feel the rising wind gusting through it. She reached down in confusion to touch the rip. "Get off me. Wha' happened?" she said indistinctly.

A flurry of movement came from nearby. Jess looked over to see Jamie pinning down the guy who'd grabbed her. The man was struggling wildly and growling threats at him as Jamie punched him in the face. Macy gave a shriek, held between two of the skinheads. Ben was lying on the ground nearby, groaning weakly. In the far distance came the sound of a police siren.

"You passed out," said Eric. "You must've hit your head. I—"

"Eric," Jess seized his shirt, suddenly wide awake. "I have to go to the morgue. Right now."

Eric looked down at her. "Jeez, girl, you only bumped your head. It's not that bad."

"No... it's my mother."

Eric looked at her in confusion, one eyebrow raised.

"I think she's dead," Jess managed.

"What?"

"The club. I think she was at the club." Jess felt tears well up in her eyes. "I'm always nagging her to come see me play, but she never shows. This one time, I think she did, and..." Jess took a deep breath, steadying herself. She had to focus if she was going to get through this. "I have to go look for her at the morgue. Dad said she hasn't been home in days. If she was at the club, that's where she'll be."

"Well, that sucks," said Eric, trying to look sympathetic and failing dismally. "We'll go there after we've finished up here..." He waved a hand at the brawl in front of them. Hopefully not in body bags, he added to himself.

"We have to stop this. I need to go. This is crazy..." Jess's voice tailed off as she noticed something lying on the sidewalk, just a few yards from her.

It was the fallen gun.

Scrambling to her feet, Jess ran towards it, darting around the various struggling figures. Reaching the sidewalk, she dived forwards and made a grab for it.

She was too late.

A bloodstained hand snaked forwards and snatched it from under her nose, whipping it away before Jess could stop him. She heard the sound of a trigger being cocked back.

"Ben! No!" cried Jess.

"I *told* you to let her go!"

Ben staggered to his feet and stood there, swaying. The two tough guys holding Jess shoved her in front of them, like a human shield. They started laughing.

"Ben, don't—"

There was an ear-splitting bang that seemed to physically drive the air out of her eardrums. Jess reflexively shut her eyes and slapped her hands over her ears in pain. A high-pitched ringing noise filled her head. She felt as if someone had just kicked her directly in the brain. She was vaguely aware of the sounds of yelling and running, and then everyone went quiet.

Cautiously, she removed her hands from her head and opened her eyes. "Ben?" she said, looking around her. Everything sounded muffled, as though her ears were full of cotton wool.

The she saw Ben. He was staring straight forwards, his hands hanging loosely at his sides. The gun was lying on the ground in front of him. She heard a sharp intake of breath from behind her.

Slowly, Jess turned around.

Macy was cowering against the wooden boarding by the wall, her hands over her head, her eyes screwed tight shut.

There was no one else around.

Her heart hammering, Jess peered closer.

Macy was unharmed.

Jess let out her breath explosively, and she relaxed, a ferocious hope rising inside her.

They'd made it. Macy was alive. If she could make it, then maybe there was hope for the rest of them.

Maybe, just maybe, fate could be beaten.

There was a cry from over on the sidewalk. Jess glanced over her shoulder to see Jamie bending over the skinny skateboard guy, pressing a folded sweater over the man's leg wound. "Someone call an ambulance!" he yelled.

Eric dropped his hand onto Jess's shoulder, making her jump. "Jesus H Christ," he breathed in her ear. "That was close."

"You don't say," said Jess. She stared at Ben. "Did he... Where did...?"

"He missed," said Eric. "Scared the shit out of those guys, though." He reached up and wiped the blood from his nose. "And me." He stepped forward and picked up the gun, clicking the safety catch back on and tucking it into his jeans.

Then he reached out and carefully patted Ben on the shoulder, as though he were a small child who'd just dropped his ice cream. Ben turned around and stared at him, his face completely drained of blood.

"He always was a crap shot, weren't you, Benny boy? I always beat the hell outta him at *Time Crisis*. Do you have a tissue?"

"Here," Jess reached in her pocket and handed him one. There were more important things to sort out. "Macy?" she said.

Macy unfroze and took a timid step forwards. "Can I go home now?" she asked, her eyes huge.

"Sure." Jess gave Ben a hard glare. He noticed her presence for the first time, and started guiltily. Seeing the expression on her face, he dropped his gaze to the ground, hanging his head. The sound of police sirens was getting louder.

Jess waved her hand dismissively towards the noise. "We'll just tell them that we were attacked," she said, nodding at the fallen skateboard guy. "It's our word against his about who the gun originally belonged to."

Turning, Jess started walking over to Macy. "C'mon, girl, let's get you—"

A huge metal panel dropped down from high up on the scaffolding. Before any of them could react, it landed edge-first on Macy's shoulder, cleanly slicing her into two bloody halves.

Jess blinked.

After what seemed like an age, Macy's body collapsed onto the ground, like so much meat dropped from a butcher's van.

Her remains didn't even twitch.

Jess shut her eyes tight, then opened them again and looked at Macy.

There were so many organs inside the human body. Jess knew that because she could see most of them.

She stared, mesmerized.

Jamie ran over and skidded to a halt beside them. The three of them stood and stared at what until five seconds ago, had been a living, breathing human being. Blood gushed out of Macy's hacked-open body, rolling away into the gutter in a bright wave. Inside her truncated ribcage, things glistened.

Eric looked down at his T-shirt. It was covered in spatters of blood.

So much for the damn laundry, he thought, with a touch of hysteria. Numbly, he reached into his pocket for his cell phone, and dialed 911.

Tearing her gaze away from the ruined corpse, Jess's eyes numbly tracked up the scaffolding to the second floor of the building, where the panel had dropped from. A wooden beam hung limply from the scaffold, swinging back and forth. It was still attached at one end, where some kind of brace had obviously given way.

But why?

Jess looked down at the metal panel lying beside the remains of Macy's body. In one corner, by a torn-out bolt, there was a small, incriminating bullet hole.

She glanced up to see that Ben was looking at it, too. He started backing away, a dreadful look on his face.

"Ben," she said, taking a step towards him.

Ben didn't look at her. "I think we should leave now," he said, in a very small voice.

Jess shook her head slowly. "We can't," she said. "This is..." her voice tailed off. She didn't dare say "murder", because it wasn't. "Manslaughter" just didn't say it. What was this? Some kind of twisted fate?

"This is sick, that's what this is. What the *fuck* is going on?"

Jess glanced over at Eric. He was scrubbing hopelessly at his T-shirt with the remains of a bloodstained tissue. He looked up at Jess, a dark expression on his face. "Did you do this?" he asked. "You and your fucking vision? What did you *do* to us?"

"I didn't do anything," said Jess helplessly. "I saved your lives,"

"Yeah, and now we're all getting slaughtered like pigs. How do you figure that one? *Huh?*"

A police siren sounded nearby. A wash of flashing blue and red light flickered over the other end of the alleyway.

Jamie stepped forward. "Where's the gun?" he asked, his voice flat.

"Don't worry, I've got it safe. Why?"

Jamie mutely pointed to the skateboard guy behind him, now lying exhausted and bleeding on the sidewalk, then to the remains of Macy. "Someone's going to be asking some very definite questions, soon."

"Well, fuck that!" Eric pulled the gun from his belt and tossed it down onto the road by Jamie's feet. "You deal with it. Me and Ben are leaving. Come on, Ben."

He turned to go, then stopped.

Turning back, he looked down at the hand on his shoulder, holding him back, then up at Ben. His friend's expression was set, a fine sheen of sweat covering his face. Ben looked terrified, but determined. "We're not leaving," he said quietly.

"Oh yeah? You mean *you're* not leaving. I'm going." Eric paused. A couple of seconds ticked by. "Let go of me, Ben," he said evenly.

Ben took a deep breath. His voice, when it emerged, was emotionless. "No, Eric. You're staying with us. You are not running away, like the big yellow coward you are, because now your fingerprints are all over the damn gun. You'll stay with us, and we will tell the nice police officers exactly what happened, and then I'll probably go to jail for a bit and you can have a nice quiet spell all by yourself to plan your next big deal, because life sucks like that." He tightened his grip. "You are not running away. Do you understand me?"

Eric looked hard at Ben. "Yes, I understand perfectly," he said. "You're a big fat loser, and you have just seriously, severely fucked up. You're wasting your time trying to beat me over the head with morals, because I don't have any. Now get your greasy paw off my shoulder before *I* call the cops."

"Fine. Have it your own way." Ben took his hand off Eric's shoulder. Then he turned his back on him and walked quickly to the end of the alleyway. A police cruiser whirred at the end of the street, cruising slowly up and down. Ben raised his arms above his head and waved at the car.

"Over here!" he yelled. "There's been an accident."

The cruiser's headlights swung around to face them at the far end of the long alley, bathing the scene in pale white light. All four of them shrank back from what the headlights revealed, picked out in unrelenting detail.

The police car started trundling slowly up the alleyway towards them, dipping and bumping over the potholes.

"Dammit, Ben!" shouted Eric. He backed away, running through options in his head. The cops were still too far away to have seen his face yet, but he knew that to run away now would be seriously incriminating, and would probably only get him chased, and definitely onto the evening news. Suspect chasing was the number one regional sport in LA, and he didn't want to have to deal with that, not now.

He knew that he'd done nothing wrong this time, but what if the cops decided to launch an investigation into Ben, once they'd booked him down at the station? The thought of cops searching their shared apartment before he'd had a chance to hide some things brought him out into a cold sweat.

An idea struck him.

"That's fine," he said loudly. "We'll all go back to the police station. Although it won't be Ben who's going to jail tonight."

Jess swung round to glare at him. "Meaning what?"

"Don't you get it? Jess, they're gonna blame you. Every time someone who survived that club disaster dies, you're always at the scene. Don't you think they're gonna put two and two together pretty soon?"

"Those were all accidents," said Jess harshly.

Eric picked up an edge of desperation in her voice, and smiled inwardly. *A-ha!*

"Tell that to *them*," he said, waving towards the sound of the sirens. "We'll all tell that to them. But at the end of the day, you can kiss goodbye to your life, and your job, and your friends, 'cos those kinds of investigations can take months. They usually end up all over the TV. And who's gonna bail you out this time?"

He saw Jess turn pale with worry, and knew that he was onto something. "Yeah," he added. "They suspect you of murder, bail can cost tens of thousands. From what I hear, that could cause you one or two problems."

"Eric, shut your face," snapped Jamie. "She didn't do anything."

"And what about your mom?" Eric went on, ignoring him. "If what you told me is true, do you think they're gonna let you see her before she gets buried?"

Jamie turned to Jess, an unspoken question on his face.

"No," went on Eric. "You might not even get to go to the funeral, as you've now got a history of jumping bail. They'll probably keep you under lock and key for *ages*."

"Eric, you bastard..."

"Wait." Jess held up her hand.

Eric glanced hopefully at Jess. His words seemed to be having some kind of an effect.

She turned to him, ignoring Jamie. "What do you propose?" she asked.

"Come with me. We'll go to the morgue, find out about your mom."

"What good will that do?"

"If she's there, it means your premonitions are true, and we're all gonna die. We can... take precautions, hide you from the police. Plus you get to see your mom, one last time. If she's not there, then it's all been a big bunch of coincidences, and we can all go dancin' off into the sunset." And there'll probably be a furnace there somewhere, to dispose of certain pieces of incriminating evidence, he thought.

"Why don't we wait for the cops? I'm sure they'll take us by the morgue if we ask them nicely."

Eric reached down and took Jess's hand in his. He squeezed it tight, looking earnestly into her eyes. "One reason."

Jess felt something cold in her palm. She looked down, and gasped.

"Because, my dear," said Eric. "Now *you've* got your fingerprints all over the gun. I suggest you join me in running. And quickly, please."

Jess glared at him, an expression of outrage on her face. She opened her mouth to speak, then paused, listening intently. "Do you hear that?"

Over in the road, Ben turned around. He heard it too, a kind of creaking, metallic swinging noise.

It did not sound good.

Acting on a hunch, he glanced up. A look of panic crossed his face, and he jumped to one side as the huge metal "Site Safety" sign from the scaffolding crashed down alongside him. It rebounded off the sidewalk with a sound like metallic thunder.

Trembling, he turned to the others. "Man, that was close," he said.

Then he stepped sideways and disappeared down the open manhole as its cover gave way beneath him.

Eric and the others rushed over to the hole. Eric peered frantically down the ladder, shouting Ben's name, then reached into his pocket and clicked on his flashlight.

They all recoiled from the sight it revealed.

Eric straightened up, licking his suddenly dry lips. "So, Jess," he said. "Tell me again about this vision of yours."

Officer Adams guided his police cruiser down the alleyway. He could have sworn he'd seen someone waving to him at the other end, but by the time he got closer, whoever it was had gone.

"Dammit!" he swore.

He stopped the car as he saw the scruffy-looking guy with the skateboard, lying on the sidewalk and clutching at his leg, which was bleeding profusely. At the other end of the alley, a paramedic van turned in, its red light whirling.

"Spence-man, we've got one down here," he said.

Spencer didn't reply. Andy looked at him. He hadn't moved from his seat inside the car. He was staring out of his window, one hand frozen on the door handle.

"Spencer?" Officer Adams walked around to the other side of the car, looked downwards, and instantly regretted it.

The hot dog he'd just eaten looming hideously in his mind, he swallowed hard and lifted his police radio to his lips. "Send Crime Squad down here, right now," he barked. A thought occurred to him and he clicked his radio back on. "Oh, and guys? Bring a couple of buckets. And a shovel."

Eric reached the SUV first. He was surprised to see a huge guy in motorcycle leathers leaning against the front of the car, whistling to himself. Eric slowed to a jog, and stared at him fearfully. The others skidded to a halt behind him.

"Um, dude?" Eric ventured after a moment, dancing on the spot. "We're gonna need to move that in a minute. Sorry."

The big guy looked down at Eric, unfolding his arms. "You took your time."

"What?"

The man reached up and scratched thoughtfully at the scar running down the side of his jaw. "You left it unlocked. With all the windows open. Just how stupid are you?"

"Well, I, er..." Eric gulped. He screwed up his nerves, aware that time was ticking away. He had to stand up to this guy, and quickly. "You can't have it," he said timidly. "It's mine."

The big man's brow creased, then a look of amusement crossed his face. "That's all you can come up with?" He threw back his head and laughed uproariously. "That's a classic. I don't want it, kid. I just thought I'd keep an eye on it for you, till you got back. You get some weird people round here."

"Really?"

"Sure." The biker scratched his noise with a black-painted fingernail. "Big car like this won't last five minutes out here. I saw you run off from halfway across the car park, and I thought, now there's a guy with a lot on his mind, to leave that nice car alone with all its windows down. So I came and stood here for a bit. I got lots of time on my hands, now I've lost my job. Nobody's been near it, since."

"Are you serious?" Eric thought for a moment, then light dawned. "We don't have any money," he said. "Really, this time." A police siren sounded from the alley behind him, sounding frighteningly loud. He glanced behind him urgently.

"No. It looks like you don't," the biker said. He glanced quizzically at Eric's bloodstained T-shirt. "And it also looks like I didn't see you here tonight." He stood up, stretched expansively, and wandered back across to his motorcycle.

Then he stopped. "Don't s'pose you need a diversion," he said, something that sounded like hope in his voice.

"Erm. That would be nice," said Eric helplessly, shrugging at the others as they leapt into the SUV, yelling at him to hurry up.

The big man winked. "I'm on it," he said, pulling out his cell phone. "There's something I've always wanted to try..."

Trotting back across to sit astride his bike, he kicked the starter, speaking rapidly into his cell phone.

"What was all that about?" said Jamie, as he buckled up his seat belt.

"Beats me." Eric slammed the door and started the car in the same motion. The engine roared. He slammed his foot onto the accelerator and the SUV pulled out with a screech of tires.

Then it stopped. Whirling blue lights filled the car park as the cop car nosed through the alleyway towards them. Jess peered fearfully out of the front windscreen. Eric slammed the car into reverse, then paused, staring through the front windshield. His jaw fell open as they watched five, ten, fifteen motorcycles speed into the parking lot through the main gate.

As the police car skidded to avoid them, they swarmed around it, completely encircling it, corral-style. The car stopped and the cop shouted something threatening-sounding at the bikers, who ignored him, raising fists and bottles of Jack in salute. One of the other bikers jumped off his motorcycle, quickly lying it down on its side, where it rested at a forty-five degree angle.

Almost like a ramp, Eric thought...

Then the cop's eyes widened as he saw the scarred biker approaching on high speed on his Harley. He leapt back into his car and ducked down as the Harley roared towards him, accelerating up the side of the prone bike. It flew through the air, clearing the top of the police cruiser by mere feet as it jumped over it. The Harley pitched downwards and thumped back onto the tarmac, to the sound of cheers and applause from the assembled bikers.

Inside the cruiser, the police officers removed their hands from their heads and grabbed their police radios, barking orders into them.

Jess and Eric looked at one another. "Stunt guy!" they both said, as one.

Eric gunned the engine. "Time to ride," he said.

It turned out to be a lot quicker than Jess had thought getting to the morgue. Their main problem had been shaking off the entourage of motorbikes who had followed them to the end of the Strip, honking their horns and waving regally to passers by. Some of them were even doing wheelies.

"So. Which of us is going to be next?" Eric asked, matter-of-factly, as they turned off the freeway.

Jess didn't reply.

"Go on. There's only three of us left. Who's it gonna be?"

"I don't think she's going to tell you, Eric," said Jamie from the back seat. "Oh, and by the way, I have to say, I think you should get a bigger car, because this one..." he stretched his arms out to either side. His hands didn't even touch the doors. "It's just a little on the small side, you know?"

"You're funny." Eric peered out at the road signs flashing past them. "Jess. I'm lost. Which morgue was it again?"

"It said in the paper that all the..." She couldn't quite bring herself to say "bodies". "The *people* they pulled out of the club were taken to LA County."

"Cool. We're nearly there." Eric glanced into the rear-view mirror. "Are we still clear?"

Jamie peered through the rear windshield. "Yup. Nobody's following us."

"Good."

Jess chewed on her nail. "Don't you think that's a little strange?"

"No, I think it's good. I think that maybe the cops arrested all those motorcyclists, and got us off the hook."

"I hope you're right." Jamie turned his gaze to the city streets flashing past outside. There was a little bit of a summer storm kicking up, wind gusting through the tatty palm trees that lined the residential areas.

A thought struck him. "Jess?" he asked.

"Yes?"

"You said that in your vision, you saw us all die."

"That's right."

"So... if you saw us all die... then you must have died last. Am I right?"

Jess didn't say anything.

Jamie saw Eric quickly glance at him in the mirror, then reach across and put his seat belt on. He thumped his fist on the steering wheel, peering upwards into the sky. "Crap. Helicopter!"

They all looked. There was indeed a helicopter, angling across the sky towards them. As it drew close, its searchlight clicked on, sweeping downwards over the darkened streets.

"Shit. Hang on. We're nearly there." Eric accelerated, dodging around several slow-moving HGVs.

"On your left."

Eric swung the car around and rumbled up the ramp into the parking lot of the sprawling morgue. Stopping by the main entrance, he killed the engine.

Jess took off her seat belt and paused, her hand on the door. "Stay here. I'll be back very soon."

"Again," said Jamie, "I'm not leaving you."

"Suit yourself. Come on."

Breaking into the morgue turned out to be the easy bit. Morgues are not, on the whole, places that people are desperately keen to get into, Jess thought, as she lowered herself in through the open window round the back. It's not like there were huge sums of money left lying about, and they weren't the sort of places you wanted to go wandering around in the dark.

Besides anything else, you don't know what you might go blundering into.

Jamie dropped soundlessly down beside her, with the grace and style of a cat. They both turned and watched as Eric clambered through the window, caught his shoelace on the handle, struggled for a moment, and then fell the rest of the way to the ground.

He picked himself up and glared at both of them. "Don't say a word," he said.

They didn't.

They set off through the darkened corridors, Eric shining his flashlight around nervously.

It soon became apparent to Jess that they were about to have a problem. "What was the name of the coroner, the one on the news?"

"No idea. I thought you knew. This was all your idea."

Jess gazed hopelessly down the long dark corridor. There were at least twenty doors set into it, all with nameplates beside them, just like there had been in her... what was that? A dream? A second pre-monition?

Jess had no idea. She felt her hackles go up as she walked towards the first door. She stopped outside it, staring down at the door handle. An over-whelming sense of déjà vu swept through her.

Trying to brush off the feeling, she tried the door handle. The room wasn't locked. Inside was a paper-strewn room that had the look of an office. She glanced around, then gave a shriek of fright as she found herself nose-to-nose with a dangling skeleton.

She backed off rapidly, yelping in fear. To her relief, she saw that it was just a life-sized plastic one, hanging from a hook. Once she'd started breathing again, she shut the door and tried the next room.

Another office.

"I think we're on the wrong floor," she said, rub-bing her eyes. She was starting to feel very tired. "Aren't they s'posed to keep the dead on, you know, the lower levels?"

"Possibly. Can't hurt to look. Ooh, wait, there's some signs." Eric read the notices dangling down above him. "Autopsy Room... Storage Bay... *Gift Shop?!* What!"

Jamie bounded alongside Jess as she walked towards the stairs at the far end of the corridor. "Are you all right?" he asked her in a low voice.

"I'm trying not to think about it. As long as I don't think about it, then it hasn't happened yet." She wrapped her arms around herself, shivering. "Any sign of that police helicopter?"

Jamie glanced out of a nearby window. "Not yet," he said. "Maybe it wasn't looking for us?"

"There were two, possibly three bodies back in that alleyway," said Jess levelly. "You don't think they'd be the tiniest bit interested in who did it?"

"Maybe they'll assume it was gang related," said Eric. "And by the way, when you guys are done, I *seriously* want to go and look in the gift shop..."

Then he jumped as a door swung open at the end of the corridor. A gruff-looking man in a guard's uniform poked his head around the door, shining a flashlight into their eyes. They squinted in the bright light.

"Here! I thought I heard a noise," he said, reaching for his radio.

"We were just leaving," said Eric automatically. He glanced at Jamie, sharing a thought. The two of them marched towards the guard, Eric opening his shirt to reveal his gun.

The security guard's eyes widened.

Two minutes later, Jess dared to uncover her eyes. "Is everyone all right?" she asked.

Jamie stood up, brushing off his hands. "I'm just ducky," he said. He looked thoughtfully down at the security guard, who had been tied to the radiator with reams of gaffer tape. Two enraged eyes peered out from behind an improvised gag. Eric emerged from the main office, spinning two reels of parcel tape on the ends of his fingers. "This is the last of it," he said.

"Thanks," Jamie took the tape and wound it around the guard's feet in a figure of eight, then stood back critically to admire his handiwork. He turned to Jess, daring to put a comforting hand on her shoulder. To his relief, she didn't move it. "Come on. Let's go look for your mom."

Two floors down, the examination room was every bit as cold as Jess remembered it being in her vision. There was a definite lack of mice, she noted with relief, as she marched across the room towards the steel refrigeration units at the other end. There were no gurneys here either, just bank after bank of stainless steel drawers.

She put her hand on the handle of the first one, trying to pluck up the courage to open it.

"Are we really going to do this?" asked Jamie, staring at the drawers.

"I'm afraid so," said Jess.

"I'm excused," blurted out Eric. "I don't know what your mother looks like, do I?" he said smugly. "Never met her."

Jamie rolled his eyes. He lightly touched Jess's arm. "Let's get started, then," he said quietly.

Jess steeled herself, then rolled open the first of the refrigeration drawers. A white mist of freezing air rolled out. She looked straight ahead for a moment, then quickly glanced down at the contents of the drawer.

She swallowed, then closed it again. "Jamie?" she said.

"Uh-huh?"

"I think I found the club manager."

"That's good, then. At least we know we're looking in the right place."

Jess pulled open the drawer again, getting a little braver. She looked down at the manager, zipped up in his see-through bag. "You know what? He still looks pissed," she said.

"That's 'cos he's dead."

Jess didn't reply. She just concentrated on opening and closing the drawers in front of her as quickly as she possibly could.

Behind her, Eric wandered casually around the room, looking for any door that might be concealing a furnace. He had to get rid of the gun, fast. "So," he said, trying to keep his voice casual. "Where do they burn the bodies, then?"

"Crematorium," said Jamie. "There's one just up the road from here."

Eric swore to himself. Then he wandered out of the door, intent on searching, anyway. All those films had lied to him...

Jess pulled open the thirtieth drawer. The bodies had run out, and now there were just... bits. She shuddered, feeling the bile rise in her throat, but tried to be objective. She was fine in butchers' shops, so why was she having a problem here? After all, it was all just meat, wasn't it?

Her mind rebelled. Screw objectivity, she thought. This meat used to be people.

She opened the next drawer, number 31, holding her sweater sleeve over her nose and mouth. There was part of a corpse inside, the faint image of a snake painted on the pale white skin of its chest.

Jess slammed the drawer closed and backed away, breathing heavily. "I don't think I can do this any more."

"Don't worry. Go and find Eric before he breaks something. I'll look for you."

Jamie pulled open the drawer, said, "Dude," very quietly, then shut it again.

"Guys!" Eric came skidding back into the room. "We've got company."

"What kind of company?"

"Guess."

"Oh, great. Cops." Jamie grabbed the flashlight from the nearby desk. He looked at Jess, one side of his mouth twitching upwards. "Do you want me to stall them?"

"No. Not this time. We're all leaving. Together." Jess ran to a nearby window and ripped the shutter aside. To her relief, it wasn't locked. She slid it upwards with a grunt, then patted the window ledge. "Here," she said.

Jamie scrambled athletically through the open window, dropping down onto the floodlit grass on the other side. The lights outside were very bright. Jess followed him, helping Eric climb up and out after them. She pulled the window shut behind them.

And then they were running again, pelting across the parking lot. There was a police car parked out the front of the morgue. A second police car zipped down the street towards them, sirens wailing and Jess thought, *It's stupid to run. They're just gonna catch us.*

Jess looked down at her feet. They were still running. *You have to try,* said a voice in her head. *That's what it's all about, isn't it?*

The welcome shape of Eric's black SUV loomed and they all tore towards it. Once again, Eric reached it first. He put a hand on the handle, then yelled in fright as the window behind his head shattered in a burst of flying glass shards. He ducked, his eyes wild. "What the fuck?" he managed.

A second later, Jamie yelled something and shoved him aside. Eric stumbled and fell, landing in a big puddle of water that had run off from the nearby garden sprinklers. "What the hell are you doing!" shouted Eric, as Jamie crashed down beside him, covering his head with his hands. "You idiot! I'm soaked! You could've broken my nose, or—"

Above him, Jess gave a muffled scream.

Eric twisted his head around and looked up. The morgue security guard was standing a dozen feet from them, outside the open back door. He was scowling. Long streamers of gaffer tape clung to him, making him look like a newly awakened mummy. He would have looked amusing if he hadn't been pointing a pistol at them.

A wisp of smoke drifted gently up from its muzzle.

Eric looked across at Jamie. Blood was slowly trickling out from between his fingers. He wasn't moving.

"Dude?" Eric reached out and nudged Jamie with a foot. Jamie rolled over slightly, his hands falling away from his head. Blood welled in a gush from an open wound in his chest.

He didn't seem to be breathing.

Eric looked up at Jess as she ducked for cover. "I think he's dead," he said stupidly. He stared down at Jamie. "He saved me. Why the fuck did he save me?"

Jess blinked, tears starting to well in her eyes. "Because he's a nice guy," she whispered.

Eric saw two police officers run down the steps of the morgue towards them, reaching for their weapons. "Throw down your gun. Now!" shouted a voice.

To Eric's surprise, the security guard didn't move. "Yeah, drop it, you bastard!" he yelled.

"He's talking to us," said Jess, her voice barely audible.

"What?"

"The gun. Ben's gun. He saw it, right?" she nodded at the furious guard. Eric looked at her. She was trembling with emotion. "I'd throw it to him, if I were you."

"No way!" Eric rose to his feet, with a blatant disregard for his own safety. "You killed my friend! I'll get you for that, you fucker!" he yelled.

He started to reach into his shirt.

"Eric!" yelled Jess desperately. There was a sudden flurry of movement from the police officers. The next moment, Eric gave a yelp of pain and collapsed to the ground, his body twitching and jerking.

Jess leapt away from him with a cry, fearing the worst. She looked down to see a silver two-pronged dart sticking out of Eric's hip. A long steel wire connected it to a blocky black gun held by one of the policemen. There was a stylized logo of a mouse on the barrel of the gun.

Tazer, thought Jess dazedly as she ducked back down behind the car. When did those become standard LAPD issue?

"Come out from behind the car!"

Jess hesitated, peering around the car at the two figures lying in the dirt. Ben's gun lay between them, having fallen from Eric's shirt when he'd hit the ground.

She peered closer. Blood was pulsing from the wound in Jamie's chest. Did that mean his heart was still beating? Jess strained her eyes, trying to see if his chest was moving at all. She thought she caught a faint flicker of movement.

Before she even knew what she was doing, she was running towards him, hoping against hope that he was still alive. She landed on her knees in the puddle of water and started crawling over towards Jamie, desperately calling his name.

There was a faint hiss on the periphery of her hearing. Jess glanced up, then cried out as the twin tips of a Tazer dart thunked painfully into her ribcage. Her body convulsed as a wave of blue fire shot down the high-voltage wire, snapping her head back and contracting all her muscles at once. She fell to the ground, screaming soundlessly. Flashes of blue light filled her vision as electricity crackled off her skin, fizzing down into the water surrounding her, amplifying the power surging through her.

Within seconds, the water started to boil.

She heard frantic shouts from above her. A moment later, the power cut out and the pain stopped, but by then it was too late.

Jess lay on the concrete, steam drifting up from around her. Her body jerked as her heart gave a sickening lurch, and then another, jolted out of its rhythm by the electricity.

Then a wave of darkness hit her, and her vision started to fade.

That wasn't good, Jess knew. She stared up at the sky as the world cut in and out all around her, the night creeping in around the edge of her vision.

She really was so tired...

Bizarrely, the last thing Jess thought about before her heart stopped was that now she'd never get to play at the House of Blues.

That really sucked, she thought.

Then it all faded to black.

THIRTEEN

Darkness.

More darkness.

Then...

Light. And then there was pain.

Sound soon followed, and then there were voices, far away and muted-sounding, as though heard underwater. "What's her BP reading?"

"One-twenty over eighty."

"Heartbeat's back. Stabilizing."

"Janine, get over here now. We need to get all these guys moved."

"Roger that, John."

The doors slammed on the paramedics' van, which then drove off into the night, siren wailing.

In the bushes behind the SUV, a scruffy figure peered through the shrubbery, and waved at the flashing lights.

* * *

It was just coming up to ten pm on the Santa Monica shore. The surf boomed and hissed in the darkness, the light breeze whipping the froth off the tips of the waves. The full moon shone down onto the ocean, broken into a thousand tiny reflections on the surface of the lapping water.

Despite the lateness of the hour, the beach was alive with hundreds of young people and families, camped out on the sand on blankets and deckchairs. Each miniature territory was staked out by dozens of candles set in multicolored glass holders, which dotted the beach like a colorful reflection of the night sky above. Some had brought iced coolers full of food and drink; others had just brought drink. A young man with an acoustic guitar and a harmonica wandered amongst the blankets, serenading the picnickers and drawing admiring glances from the young ladies. In the water, close to the pier, a solitary surfer cruised the swell on his board, enjoying the night tide and hoping to catch one last wave before bed.

Jess stood leaning over the railing at the end of the pier. Behind her, the bright lights of the pier's fun park whirled and flashed, the giant Ferris wheel slowly turning, its bucket-style seats swinging gently. Shrieks came from above her as the gaudily painted rollercoaster car soared up and down along its track. On shore, late-night rollerbladers hissed past on the concrete path that wound its way between the palm trees on the beach.

"And here she is. The lady of the hour."

Jess looked up to see Eric lean over the rail next to her. He was wearing black jeans and a red linen shirt, which was hanging open on one button. The bruising on his face had faded somewhat, although he still walked with a slight limp. His hair was shorter, and he had a brand-new leather jacket draped over one arm.

He would have looked almost presentable, if it wasn't for the electric blue, glowing gig necklace he was wearing, which he'd wrapped around his head like a misplaced halo.

He reached into his pocket and brought out a second necklace, this one unlit. Jess watched as he cracked it between his hands, shaking it up to mix the chemicals. It lit up with a bright blue glow. "Here. I got this for you."

"Gee... thanks." Jess took it, holding it between thumb and forefinger as though it were a dead fish. "It's what I've always wanted."

"I dunno how they work, but they're really neat, aren't they?" Eric said, completely missing her sarcasm. "Look—put it over your eyes, like this. It looks like the mothership's come for you."

Sighing, Jess tried it. Her expression changed. "Hey—that *is* kinda cool," she admitted.

Eric gave a little smile. "You know, Ben always liked these. He'd buy a dozen whenever he saw 'em for sale, then he'd cut them open and try to use the chemicals to dye his hair with. Had to take him to the hospital twice last summer, the jerk."

Jess shrugged. "People do silly things," she said, meeting Eric's eyes.

"You're telling me," Eric said.

He held her gaze for a moment, then turned and looked down into the sea, watching the waves lap around the legs of the pier.

After a while, Eric said, "So what did it feel like, being dead?"

Jess thought for a moment. "Kind of peaceful," she said. "Although the waking-up bit wasn't fun. I've still got a huge fucking bruise on my chest."

Eric laughed. "Dude. Compared to living in LA, anything's peaceful." Eric turned and gazed out at the crowded pier behind him, teeming with life. "But we love it here, don't we?"

"Wouldn't be here if we didn't," replied Jess. She gazed out at the scene before her. At the other end of the pier, a giant live music stage had been set up, surrounded by van-sized speakers. A huge crowd had gathered around it, watching eagerly as the next act set up their gear. Onstage, the band members tuned their instruments, laughing and joking with one another. The smell of hot dogs and popcorn drifted in on the sea breeze.

Jess glanced at her watch. She still had plenty of time, but it might be an idea to start making her way back, now. The crowd was getting pretty excitable, and she didn't want to get stuck at the back, especially not tonight.

"So when's your mom's funeral, then?" Eric asked awkwardly, kicking at a broken surfboard that was propped up against the rails. It had a big bite taken out of one side, almost like a shark bite. Eric shivered. He hated sharks.

"Tuesday."

"I'll be there." Eric hesitated. "So, that was like, the first time she ever came to see you play?"

"Yeah. The first and the last. Fate's a bitch."

They stood for a moment in contemplative silence, while the world went on around them.

"Um, Jess?"

"What?"

Eric pointed at her chest, looking hopeful. "I know that maybe now's a bad time to mention it, but I don't suppose I can see the, erm..."

"No."

"Fair enough."

Jamie proved fairly easy to find, being the only person in the crowd who was facing away from the stage. His face relaxed when he saw Jess approach, and he stopped scanning the crowd and turned back to the show.

Jess stepped up beside him and poked him in the ribs.

"Go on. Admit it," she said, after a minute had passed.

"No."

"You were worried, weren't you?"

"Not at all. I knew you'd show." Jamie turned and looked at her. "Eventually."

Jess slid her arm around his waist. "You know I'd never let you down, baby."

Jamie just smiled.

"So are you sure you'll be all right tonight? Playing, I mean?"

"I'm sure." Jamie reached up and scratched at the heavy white bandage that covered the side of his neck and shoulder. "At least I've got the feeling back in my arm now. I'm told that's a good sign."

Jess shrugged. "The drummer in Def Leppard's only got one arm. If he can do it, I'm sure you'll have no problems."

There was a pause as they all considered this.

"What, really only one arm?" said Jamie.

"Yup."

"How'd he lose it?"

"Car crash, I think."

"Brave guy," Jamie said pointedly. He gave Jess a sidelong glance. She still hadn't removed her arm from around his waist.

Inside him, something did a little dance of joy.

Eric pushed his way through the crowd and joined them, a giant hot dog clutched in each hand. "Here you go Je... oh," he said, looking at Jamie.

"And now we're all here," said Jamie, his eyes fixed on the band.

"Yeah. We are." Eric hesitated, then grumpily handed a hot dog to Jess.

Up on stage, the band walked on and picked up their instruments, to be greeted by a chorus of cheers and wolf-whistles. The shirtless drummer waved to a group of girls in the audience, then turned and picked up his sticks, adjusting the pad-locked chain that he wore around his neck.

Eric turned to Jamie. "How's the shoulder?" he asked, trying to refrain from adding, "*loser.*"

"Fine," Jamie said, looking faintly embarrassed. He opened a can of soda and took a sip. "Thanks for helping out with the, um, you know. The hospital bill."

"Yeah, whatever," said Eric quickly. "Hey Jess, could you pass me that tub of ketchup, if you've fin-ished with it?"

They watched the band warm up, munching on their dogs.

"So," said Eric, trying to keep his voice casual. "You think we're gonna be okay now?"

"I hope so," said Jess. She took a bite of her hot dog and chewed thoughtfully. "I died, right? And so did he. Even though it was just for a minute, I have a feeling that it satisfies the conditions of the premonition. Fate got what it wanted, and moved on."

"You think?"

"That's what I'm hoping. I was supposed to die after you two, and that didn't happen. It messed up the order, and now hopefully you guys will be spared. Although I'm told Jamie's heart stopped twice during the surgery."

Jamie shivered, rubbing at the bandage on his neck. "Does that even count as dying?" he asked.

"Depends on who's asking," said Jess. "Anyway, it's been over a month now, and nothing bad's happened to us. No more signs, nothing. I'm assuming that means we're in the clear."

Eric snorted. "Or maybe death took one look at you guys and went 'Eek! Not having those two freaks cluttering up my nice clean eternity'."

"Anything's possible," said Jamie, winking at Jess.

Onstage, the lights dimmed and the first notes of the show rung through the night air. The crowd cheered. Onstage, the lead singer stepped up to the mike, a gorgeous blonde dressed in a skimpy outfit made entirely of rubber gloves. She playfully waved to the crowd, generating a fresh chorus of cheers.

Jamie blinked, pointing at the stage. "Who're these guys?"

"Oh, that's Powder," said Jess. "They're awesome. I saw them last summer on the Strip. Been to every show since. Best live band in LA, by all accounts."

"Is there any band you haven't seen?" asked Jamie.

"Not many." Jess watched as the lead guitarist marched onto the stage to the accompaniment of wild applause, a charismatic young guy dressed in a tight black T-shirt and PVC pants. His hair was spiked up crazily into gravity-defying points, and he had a stickered white guitar slung around his neck.

He raised a fist to the crowd in salute, then plunged straight into the opening chords of the first song. The crowd went wild as he bounced across the stage, leaping and jumping and slamming out wave after wave of heavy-duty rock riffs. The drummer kicked in with some high-energy beats, grinning and theatrically spinning his drumsticks around his fingers as he played. He was joined by the funky tattooed bassist, laying down some killer turbo-rock grooves. The band picked up its pace as it hit the first chorus, the swirling music blasting out across the water of the bay like a sonic storm.

The crowd on the pier roared its approval, joined by a chorus of whoops and cheers from the growing audience on the beach below.

This, thought Jess, was what it was all about.

Jess, Eric and Jamie watched the show together for a while.

"So," said Eric, shouting over the music. "I guess you'll be going on a little late tonight."

"Yeah," shouted back Jess. "Still no sign of the new bass player. We'll give him till half past eleven, then go on without him."

"Suit yourself." Eric glanced back up at the stage. The band was now setting up three strip-poles in the center of the stage. Eric watched, his mouth hanging open, as the lead singer was joined by two other rubber-clad girls dressed as Fem-Bot clones, leading them in an intricate and graceful pole-dance routine. Behind them, an eight foot-high alien monster on stilts sprayed colorful streams of Crazy String into the audience.

Eric shook his head in wonder.

Tearing his eyes away from the band, Eric glanced around him at the gathered crowd on the pier. Beyond them, the dark ocean gave way to the distant lights of celebrity mansions on the mountains that ringed the bay. Down on the beach below, a fire-eater juggled with flaming knives.

Eric looked back up at the stage, a wry grin spreading across his face. The horrific events of the last month had started to fade away, and life seemed to be slowly settling back down into something approaching normal, if there was such a thing around here.

Jamie finished his drink. "Jess—you ready? I'm gonna go get my gear out of the van."

"Gimme a minute," said Jess, still gazing at the stage. The lead singer had done a lightning costume change, and was now dressed in a futuristic outfit consisting of small strips of PVC tape, a platinum-blonde wig and very little else. She was liberally dousing the crowd with a giant pump-action water gun, laughing delightedly as the audience cheered her on.

She looked as if she was having the time of her life.

And on that note...

Jess turned and looked at Jamie, who was watching the show with a kind of rapt fascination, unconsciously nodding his head to the beat.

She tipped her head on one side. That bandage *did* kind of suit him...

And hey, at the end of the day, he *was* a nice guy.

Perhaps that was as good a place as any to start.

Shrugging, she reached out and touched him lightly on the shoulder, giving him her brightest smile. "Ready to rock?"

After a while, Eric left the stage and wandered back through the cheering crowd, a strange sense of melancholy settling over him. Crowds did that to him, sometimes. There was nothing like being around a lot of people being very happy to make you feel just the opposite.

He walked past the display stands full of tourist junk and ambled across the wooden boards towards the end of the pier. Leaning on the rail, he watched the solitary surfer riding the waves for a moment, then reached into his bag and pulled out a bottle of beer. There was a logo of a shark on the label, which he found faintly amusing. He twisted the cap off, then raised it in a silent salute to the starry night sky.

After a while, the world started to seem just a little bit better.

Eric gazed up at the moon as he drank, turning things over in his mind. Funny thing about fate, if you could call it that. Just when you thought you were home dry, it could turn on you and bite your head off. He wondered whether Jess was even thinking about him at all. Somehow, he doubted it.

Beneath him, the moonlit water sparkled.

Finishing his beer, he noticed a pretty young Filippino girl leaning on the rail a short distance from him. Eric perked up a bit. She was wearing a miniskirt and an improbably small top, and was hugging herself as if she were cold. It was a warm enough night, but the damp ocean air combined with the light sea breeze probably weren't doing her any favors.

At least, not in that outfit, anyway.

Eric opened his mouth to whistle at her, then stopped. In the back of his mind, he saw Ben giving him a disapproving look. A new and interesting thought crossed his mind. "Excuse me," he said.

The pretty girl looked up, studying him cautiously.

"I couldn't help noticing you looked a bit cold. Would you like to borrow this?" he asked, holding up his jacket.

The girl looked at him suspiciously, then shivered. "It *is* a bit cold tonight," she admitted. She unfolded her arms and leaned back on the railing. "What's your name?" she asked, brushing her long hair out of her eyes.

"Eric."

"I'm Jocelyn. Nice to meet you."

"So... do you want the jacket? It's nice and warm."

"Are you hanging around here for a while?"

"Uh-huh."

A smile touched the girl's lips. "Go on, then." She took the jacket from Eric and pulled it on. It was way too big for her, but Eric thought she looked kinda cute in it.

He jumped up and sat on the top of the pier railing, trying to look cool, and grinned down at her. A sudden sense of happiness welled up in his chest. The night was still young, and maybe, just maybe, things were looking up for him.

As he gazed down at the girl, smiling, the blue glowing necklace around his head slipped down over his eyes, making him jump. He'd forgotten he was wearing it. Reflexively, he reached up to push it out of his eyes.

Using both hands...

If it wasn't for the bottle of beer he'd just drunk, Eric might have recovered his balance a little quicker. As it was, he wobbled briefly on his precarious perch, then spun over backwards before he could catch himself.

With a yell, Eric plunged down thirty feet into the ocean.

He hit the water hard, winding himself, struggled for a while in the black, pounding depths, then resurfaced with a splutter and an oath.

The wind picked up, blowing the increasingly large waves towards him.

Above him, boots pounded across the wooden pier. A circle of faces peered down at him anxiously, backlit by the fairground lights. "Are you okay?" shouted the girl.

Eric spat out a mouthful of salty seawater with a gasp, treading water. "I'm alive!" he shouted back.

Then a dreadful thought struck him. *Look out for the signs,* Jess had said. Eric looked down at the dark water, a memory replaying itself in his head...

"Sharks!" he yelled. "There might be sharks!" He started doggy-paddling frantically towards the shore, staring at the water around him in terror. He hated sharks. And now, in his mind, the ocean became full of them.

He was so intent on watching the water for invisible sharks that he failed to notice the solitary dreadlocked surfer bearing down on him at full speed, riding on top of a wave on his metal-tipped surfboard...

A little while later, a lone figure walking along the edge of the beach stopped and peered down at the surf.

There was a glowing blue ring floating around in it.

The man gave a toothless grin.

Reaching down, he scooped it out of the water and held it up wonderingly. It was the same shape as the moon, although he wasn't so keen on the color.

Still, you had to work with what you were given.

Shrugging, he put it on like a space cadet and turned to salute the night sky.

Then he turned and walked away, whistling a little tune under his breath.

ABOUT THE AUTHOR

Natasha Rhodes is an author and screenwriter from the south-east of England. She is the author of the novelization of the hugely successful *Blade: Trinity*, and is also working on several other movie-based titles for Black Flame. She is currently living in various coffee houses in London and LA, and trying to put off getting a real job for as long as possible.

Also available from Black Flame

FINAL DESTINATION:
DESTINATION ZERO

by David McIntee

Jim Castle and Tony Chang emerged onto the roof of the LA field office of the ATF. A dark blue Blackhawk helicopter was flaring in towards the roof, where ten men in blue jumpsuits, black body armor and ATF patches were waiting. They all wore "Fritz" style Kevlar helmets and carried a variety of weapons. There was roughly a fifty-fifty split between MP5/10s and FN P-2000s. There were two Remington sniper rifles with scopes and everyone also wore at least one pistol, either a SiG or M92F.

Flak vests and Fritz helmets were waiting for Jim and Chang on the seats in the chopper. They started to pull them on as the armed and armored men mounted up. The Blackhawk was back in the air within fifteen seconds and banking west.

"Where are we going?" Jim asked, checking his SiG 226. "Van Nuys?"

Chang, doing likewise but with a Walther P99, shook his head. "Not quite. Burbank airport. We'll rendezvous with the FBI and LAPD SWAT there before heading to Van Nuys."

Although most people thought of LAX, Los Angeles International, as LA's airport, there were actually several airports in LA. John Wayne Airport down in Orange was capable of handling large domestic jets, while other airports at Van Nuys, Malibu and Burbank all catered for executive jets, helicopters and private planes. Van Nuys and Burbank airports in particular were quite close together, a little over five miles apart.

The flight from South Figueroa to Burbank took a bare twenty minutes, a fraction of the time it would have taken to drive, even in the best possible traffic. Through the open door of the chopper, Jim could see a second Blackhawk in formation with the ATF bird. The other Blackhawk sported police markings. Since most police choppers tended to be smaller machines designed for lighting up suspects on the ground with spotlights and cameras, and the Blackhawk was more of a troop carrier, Jim was certain that it was ferrying an LAPD SWAT team. The local Van Nuys team would be en route in a truck or van.

On approach to what was more properly called Burbank-Glendale-Pasadena Airport, Jim could even make out Van Nuys airport in the distance, with the two stubby towers of its attached hotel, the Airtel Plaza, on the southwestern corner of the field. The tiny dots of commercial and private helicopters floated around the airport, while colored flecks that were light aircraft came and went along the main east-west runway. Then the Blackhawks were descending into Burbank, and slipping over towards a cordoned-off hangar as far as possible from Burbank's small terminal.

Several police vans were waiting a safe distance away, alongside various unmarked cars. About a hundred yards further away, a Learjet was waiting, its steps lowered, and the engines already turning.

Ducking under the spinning rotors, Jim and Chang hopped to the ground and ran across to the hangar. The bulky shapes of a couple of planes loomed in the darkness at the back of the hangar, draped with protective tarpaulins for some reason. Jim wasn't an aviation engineer so he had no idea why they did that.

A series of lightweight metal tables had been set up in the front part of the hangar, with powerful PCs and communications equipment on them. Freestanding frames held aerial photos of Van Nuys airport and flipcharts with hastily scribbled notes and diagrams that looked more like football plays than strategies for assaulting part of an airport.

Chang shook hands with his opposite numbers in the FBI and LAPD SWAT, and introduced Jim, who did the same. "How are we doing?" Chang asked.

The SWAT captain looked to the FBI suit, who nodded. "Van Nuys units are on scene already, as are the FBI. They're keeping an eye on each other to make sure everybody keeps their head down until we're all set. We don't want to spook these guys and scare them off."

"Here's how it's going to work. Assault teams in choppers will come in low and drop onto and around the suspect warehouse. There are choppers coming and going from the airport all the time, so the noise shouldn't spook them. However, we don't want them to look up and see what kind of helicopters are coming in, so we'll give them something else to watch."

"The Lear?"

"The Lear. We recommend you guys go in that. By the time you reach the bad guys' hangar, they'll be bushwhacked by airborne SWAT and ATF teams."

Chang nodded, and Jim could tell he approved. Jim could see a problem, though. "Shouldn't we evacuate the airport and the hotel there?"

"We do that, and they'll suspect that we're onto them. Unless of course we were to include them in the evacuation, which would kind of defeat the purpose. Van Nuys PD will be mounting an evac op as soon as the assault teams make their move, but in any case we're lucky that the terrorists have picked a fairly remote warehouse to hole up in. There's two hundred yards of open ground between them and either the airport proper or the hotel. No cover; they're screwed."

"What sort of resistance will the assault teams—and ourselves when we get off the Lear—be up against?" Chang asked.

"Fully auto assault rifles and subguns. Pistols, maybe hand grenades. No rocket launchers as far as we can tell."

Chang and Jim exchanged glances. "Here's hoping your people have good eyesight."

"They're the best," the SWAT captain promised.

With barely time for a sip of bottled water, Jim and Chang were aboard the Learjet, and hurtling into the sky. They had both strapped themselves into comfortable seats, along with a couple of members of the ATF assault team. The rest would be going in the Blackhawk.

This wasn't the first time Jim had flown, but it was the first time he would spend the whole trip with his safety belt fastened, since the flight—if it was even worthy of the name—was just a couple of minute turnaround, the takeoff and landing coming back to back. The plane began to descend almost as soon as the thought had crossed his mind.

Sean Reilly glanced up at the sound of helicopters overhead. Helicopters flew over the little airport all the time but there was something about this sound that set his teeth on edge. One chopper could easily be innocent, but two, in formation? That was suspicious. He walked to the bonded warehouse's side door and peered out. The sound of rotors was louder, though the only chopper he could see was a two-man job floating over the Airtel.

A Learjet had just touched down on the runway and was taxiing towards the small terminal and airport office, a route that would take it past the warehouse. Reilly ignored it, craning his neck around to search for the helicopters. To be so loud and yet impossible to see from the doorway, they must be very low, he realized.

Low enough to almost land on the roof, in fact. "Ah, crap," he muttered. "Khalid! We're going to have company!"

"Let them come," Khalid shouted back, unshipping the AK74 from his back and cocking it.

The Blackhawks kicked up sand and dust and soot from the warehouse roof as the SWAT teams leapt from them.

Skylights were blown with sharp cracks, and SWAT men swarmed inside. Jim was first out of the Lear when it stopped, and already he could hear shooting. The terrorist's had already seen the SWAT teams, and engaged. The game was up; the authorities' cover blown.

The door Jim was making for was a side door. Observers had reported vehicles parked inside the bonded warehouse's main door, and those would be guarded. The side door offered a better chance of penetrating the building without running into any of Reilly's group coming the other way.

No battle plan, however, survives first contact with the enemy, and Jim walked almost straight into Leon Khalid.

Khalid's eyes widened and he let rip with an AK. Jim dove keeping his face down so he wouldn't be blinded by shards or splinters. Inside the warehouse, the terrorist gunmen were giving it all they had, blasting away on full auto from their AKs and MP5s, but they didn't seem to be aiming true. The SWAT teams, highly trained and disciplined, were firing fewer shots, but better aimed and more effective.

The barrage of terrorist fire blew sparks and chips of concrete from the walls and floor, and occasionally clipped a Kevlar helmet. A three-round burst from a SWAT MP5 dropped a terrorist in his tracks when he let himself creep a little too far out of cover.

Jim glanced round the side of the doorjamb and saw Khalid pulling the banana clip from his AK74. Without waiting for the man to reload, Castle popped out from cover, gun arm straight and support arm crooked, and let him have four rounds in the chest. The terrorist fell and didn't get up. Either he wasn't wearing body amour, or he had taken the hint and decided that discretion was the better part of valor.

Chang grinned at him. "Well done, kid," he said, and moved into the warehouse. Like most bonded warehouses, it was a vast space filled with crates and containers of various sizes, with several sections of the floor area partitioned off by chain-link for storing more sensitive goods, or one on which duty would have to be collected. This forced both SWAT and terrorists to break down into smaller units, each fighting separately from the rest.

Wooden and metal catwalks lined the interior walls, and there were several large wooden crates on a high platform in the center. Suddenly, with a thunderous crack, a flimsy office halfway up one wall, used for controlling the cranes that lifted cargo around the floor, exploded into fragments. Its windows disintegrated into a hailstorm of glass shards. No one in the warehouse, terrorist or lawman, could resist the impulse to look up, squinting and holding their hands up to protect their eyes against the razor-sharp blizzard.

Almost impossibly, a motorcycle was at the heart of the glittering storm, its rider standing in a half crouch on the footrests, an Uzi in each hand and a flaming red ponytail peeking out from under his helmet. It was Sean Reilly.

Before anyone on the ground could get off a shot, and before the bike dropped to earth, Reilly opened up with two outward arcs of automatic fire. Jim, Chang, and everyone around hit the cement or took cover behind crates or the two pickups that were parked near the main doors.

Sirens were getting louder and a police cruiser nudged its way in between the pickups just as Reilly's jump came to its natural end, unfortunately for the cops inside.

The gunman's bike bounced when it hit the
cement floor and leapt like a salmon, thumping
onto the hood of the black and white, and speeding
for the runway.

Jim Castle rolled to his feet and let off a couple of
shots at the back of the fleeing biker, then the slide
on his SiG locked open, the clip empty.

There was another bike parked nearby, chrome
and scarlet, wearing the logos of a Triumph Day-
tona 650 with pride. Like the bike Reilly had just
fled on, Jim supposed it was an import machine
waiting for duty to be paid. Hoping that being outside its shipping crate meant the terrorists had
illegally fuelled it, Jim ran for the bike, swapping
magazines on his SiG as he went. A SWAT man was
standing next to it, and Jim snatched the "Fritz"
Kevlar helmet off his head and leapt onto the bike.

More cops were heading towards the warehouse
from the main part of the airport, so that was not
an option as far as Reilly was concerned. He spun
his bike, a BMW K1200S, on a dime, and started for
the chain-link fence that separated the airport's tie-
down spots from the Airtel's parking lot.
Something snapped and whined from the tarmac
nearby, a sniper round. He was glad he wasn't
trying to cross the two hundred yard kill-zone on
foot.

Reilly weaved the bike, zig-zagging slightly to
throw off the cop snipers. When he approached the
fence, he risked straightening out, aiming for a half-
forgotten crate that lay there. The wood was just

strong enough and at just the right angle. The BMW
leapt the chain-link fence with ease, and Reilly held it
steady until it was confident enough in its grip on the
blacktop to gain speed in a straight line. That line was
taking it across the parking lot, and straight for the
glass double doors of the Airtel's north tower
entrance.

Reilly let rip with the Uzi, all but disintegrating the
doors in an instant before he would have hit them,
the bullets taking out the glass at the other end of the
corridor.

Jim held onto both grips as the Triumph leapt the
fence between the airport and the hotel parking lot.
The man he suspected to be Sean Reilly was easily
within shooting distance of him, but Jim didn't dare
spare a hand to pull his gun.

The Airtel north tower's ground floor corridor flashed
past Sean Reilly in a couple of seconds at over one
hundred and fifty miles per hour.

Reilly gunned the BMW across the lobby, sending
people, most dressed in strange science fiction cos-
tumes, diving over the plush sofas. The Uzi loosed a
burst down the main building's ground floor corridor, removing the glass from another pair of double
doors at the far end.

Then Reilly was out, bursting through the hedge
that separated the Airtel from Sepulveda Boulevard.
The BMW skidded across both westbound lanes. The
tire of a small hatchback just clipped the rear wheel,
sending a jolt through every bone in Reilly's body.

He managed to recover from the slide, pulling the bike upright despite the pain in his back and shoulders. Then he was off again, eastbound.

Jim Castle hit the ruined north tower door at about fifty miles per hour, and jerked right to avoid slamming into the kink in the corridor.

The occupants of the lobby were still under cover when Jim reached it. At the far end of the corridor on the opposite side of the lobby, he could see another wrecked door, and a torn hedge. Movement out of the corner of his eye to the left was traffic on Sepulveda, and he just registered Reilly's helmet in the eastbound lane.

Jim sideslipped left, out the hotel's main doors. The doors weren't fast enough to open for him, nor did he shoot out the glass. Instead he hunched down, pulled a low wheelie, and hoped for the best. The Triumph's front wheel pulverized the glass, and he burst through it. He could feel his sleeves and pants' leg tear, and hear the screech of glass scratch across his helmet. There was a sudden line of red pain across his cheek.

Then he was out of the hotel's driveway and onto Sepulveda, accelerating into the oncoming traffic in the westbound lane. Cars whipped past, their blaring horns lost behind him, drowned out by the Triumph's engine and the wind in his ears.

Jim threw his bodyweight this way and that, darting the bike between oncoming vehicles at such short notice that half the time he thought the blasts of wind pummeling him was the impact of his own death rather than just a wall of slipstream trying to swat him from his mount.

Jim tried not to let his mind dwell on the fact that he was speeding into traffic on the wrong side of the road. There just wasn't time to be scared, because the time it took to imagine a fiery crash would be more than the time it would take to have one.

He had to get to his right, across to the eastbound lane. Doing so, however, was like attempting a slalom in which all the markers were moving at least as fast as he was. Slipping and hitting a car or truck would be a lot more likely to end his run today than hitting a flexible plastic pole did on a downhill slope in Aspen.

There was a crossroads up ahead, letting traffic out from both sides. Jim took advantage of the gap, cutting across in front of an SUV that clipped a sedan when it swerved to avoid his near-suicidal dash. A chorus of horns erupted behind him, but Jim ignored them. He was now eastbound in the right lane and he could see Reilly's bike ahead of him, just passing the big post office building.

Abruptly, the sound of sirens became audible, and police cars appeared in the westbound lane, probably coming in from Burbank. A police chopper swooped in overhead and Jim felt overwhelming relief that he was no longer alone. Tony Chang must have got the word out. Jim waved at the police helicopter, pointing the observers aboard in the direction of Reilly's fleeing bike. Immediately, the various police cars, a mixture of

State, LAPD and Highway Patrol, started making U-turns, closing in on Reilly.

Reilly glanced back to see CHP police cruisers and an LAPD 4x4 behind him already. Above, a news chopper was jostling with an LAPD bird for the best view of the chase. Behind his visor, Reilly grinned. He'd give them a show worth watching, all right.

Ahead, a tanker was in the center lane. Reilly reached inside his jacket pocket, and pulled out a smooth green sphere about the size of a small apple: a hand grenade. Grinning, Reilly slid his bike closer to the rear of the tanker truck.

Once he had matched speeds with the tanker, he got in tight by its rear wheel. He doubted the driver could see him from here. The cops following could see where he was, but they wouldn't be able to quite make out what he was doing... which was unfortunate for them.

He managed to pull the pin on the grenade, lifting his index finger off the handlebar just long enough to do so, but kept his fingers firmly down on the safety lever. Then, carefully, he stretched out his arm and shoved the grenade snugly into a gap between the wheel arch and the container tank itself. When he took his hand off the grenade, the safety lever sprung off, disappearing into the air.

Reilly immediately grabbed the bike's throttle and opened it up all the way. The BMW surged forward under him, leaving the tanker behind.

The grenade went off with a sharp crack that was audible over the roar and rumble of the traffic. The blast blew out the left rear tires of the tanker trailer and punched a hole in the tank.

The trailer jackknifed, sending smaller cars scrambling out of the way as it slewed across the lanes, and began to roll. In a matter of instants it was tumbling, spilling out hundreds of gallons of gas across the highway. The cops in pursuit all stepped on their brakes as the exposed wheel rims struck golden and white-hot sparks amidst the flowing gasoline. The bloom of flame that erupted from the tanker was inevitable.

The steel tank momentarily inflated like a balloon and burst. Liquid fire hit the freeway like red and gold breakers on a blacktop beach. The choppers wheeled away as a fireball seared the sky and turned to a roiling black cloud so thick that it looked as if the choppers would dash themselves to pieces on its surface.

A white Ford sedan, one of the police cruisers, and a pickup with three surfboards propped against the cab, didn't manage to stop in time. The sedan and cruiser hit the tanker head on, while the pickup overturned, spilling the surfboards amid the wreckage. The other cruiser dug its nose to the ground and stopped in time, blowing out both front tires in the process.

Jim almost crushed the Triumph's brake levers in his hands as he hurtled toward the burning wreckage that completely blocked the highway, but then saw a way through. It was a surfboard, tilted against the hood of the cruiser with the two front flats.

Ignoring the part of his brain that was screaming at him to think rationally, Jim Castle gunned the Triumph's four-cylinder engine for all it was worth, aiming it at the sloping board. As he hit the board, he leaped up off the seat as he took to the air. He had no idea if doing so would really make the bike any lighter or help it fly any easier, but at least he felt he was doing something to make a difference, and that was better than just trusting to fate.

The Triumph soared. For a moment the world turned hot and black, and Jim had the uncomfortable suspicion that he knew how it must feel to ride across the plains of hell. Unseen flames cloaked in the black smoke slid around his legs, tantalized by the prey that was so close to falling into their loving embrace. Even through the helmet, he couldn't breathe, and the smell of burning gas made him want to puke.

All thoughts of Patricia Fuller, Will Sax and the other Metroline survivors had gone from Jim's mind as if they had never been. Instead he was thinking of the dead in the train, now passengers in an electrified Metro transit rail system belonging to a Twenty-first century Charon. The only name he could think of to hold on to was Lauren's. She would keep him not just safe but also victorious, just by being in his heart.

Then he was through, dazzled by sunshine that was suddenly brilliant in spite of the tinted visor, and falling towards the blacktop.

Having a jackhammer slam into the tailbone, driving the spine into the base of the skull, could hardly be worse than the impact Jim felt. For a gut-churning second he thought the bike's aluminum frame was coming apart under him, to the sound of shattering metal and plastic, but then it bounced back to life and sped after the fleeing Reilly. Jim wished he had a police radio on the bike so that he could know whether more cops were on the way. From the way things had been going so far, he half expected the National Guard to be the next wave, maybe with an air strike.

If wishes were horses, he reminded himself, beggars would ride. He'd just have to stay in pursuit and hope that somebody in charge was smart enough to not just leave the situation to him. At least he himself wouldn't have to break off anytime soon; the terrorists seemed to believe in keeping their bikes well fueled, if the gauge in front of him was actually working and hadn't been fried by the jump he had made.

Reilly kept his attention in front now. The wrecked tanker should have put a stop to the police who were chasing him. If he could just work out where he was, he could figure a way to slip away to some safe area and lie low until things settled down a little. Then he could get out of California for a while. He had plenty of friends—or at least friends of his former cause—on the Eastern Seaboard. Boston or Baltimore, he thought to himself. Either of those places would provide a good measure of sanctuary for him.

First things first: get onto the freeway. A turn on to Highway 170 should be coming up soon; he had seen a couple of signs for it already. As he throttled back a little—save the gas for when it was most needed, he thought—he caught a flash of blue in his mirror. For a moment he thought it was the light on top of a police cruiser, being guided by the chopper that still floated above and behind him, out of pistol range but within camera range. When he could see the blue more clearly, he realized it was a motorbike. It looked like the Triumph that Khalid had bought, but it certainly wasn't Khalid riding it. From the blue windbreaker and Kevlar it was a cop or a Fed.

The guy must be good to have made it past the tanker, and Reilly appreciated that. At the same time, he had no intention of being caught, whether by a worthy adversary or anyone else. He opened up the throttle, speeding for the turn on to the highway.

He got there in seconds, and swept up onto the 170, which headed southeast, back towards LA. His elation was short-lived, however. Two armored cars, ex-military Greyhound wheeled tanks adapted for police use, blocked the road ahead. From behind, sirens screamed at him. It was a trap.

Reilly wasn't beaten yet. Still three hundred yards from the tanks, he tipped the BMW forward into a nose-wheelie, and spun, almost on the spot, so that it was now moving back towards the pursuing black and white cruisers that had come along the highway behind him. Reilly hooked the toes of his boots under the footrests and leaned back against the rising seat. For an instant he looked almost as if he were crucified on the nose-down bike, arms akimbo. Then he squeezed off a whole clip from the Uzi in each hand just as he passed between the cars' noses.

The windshields and side windows on both police cruisers disintegrated, metal craters erupting in the doors. Red puffed out onto the shattered glass, as the heads of one car's driver and the other's passenger took direct hits.

Then the terrorist was past and behind them, his rear wheel returning to the ground at high rev, the spent Uzis clattering to the road as he gripped the handlebars. By this time, the car with the dead driver slewed across, ramming into the other car, whose driver was too shocked to react in time. Metal screeched and tires exploded as both police cruisers crumpled into the concrete center divide, their sirens dying into sad wails.

Jim Castle powered onto the highway just in time to see Reilly trash the police cruisers. The Irishman was now heading straight toward him. Jim gave a moment's thought to getting out of the way, but didn't, for three reasons. Firstly, Lauren didn't marry a man who would quit. Secondly, the terrorist needed to be taken down. Thirdly, Jim realized that his opponent had no way to reload. He was out of ammo and, in effect, weaponless.

Speeding towards the oncoming bike at a combined velocity of over a hundred miles per hour,

Jim risked steering one-handed and drawing his gun with the other.

As the two bikes closed like medieval knights on the jousting field, Jim fired again and again at the oncoming terrorist, until he had emptied the gun and its slide locked back. Jim's "Fuck!" was lost to the winds of speed, and he dropped the gun so that he could grab the Triumph's handgrip again.

Then Reilly was upon him, reaching towards his boot for some kind of weapon. With no weapon at his disposal, Jim leaned left and twisted the throttle, toppling the bike into a power slide. Sparks coruscated past his leg and hip, as the bike hurtled belly-first towards the oncoming motorcycle. Sean Reilly tried to lean back, bringing his BMW up on its rear wheel in the hope of getting over Jim's Triumph. It was a big mistake, as the belly of the Triumph caught his rear wheel and tripped the BMW. The front wheel smashed down into the ground almost to the forks, and the whole bike flipped forward. The terrorist was thrown clear off his bike, slamming head first into the tarmac. His BMW, completing its own forward revolution, crashed down upon him, tail first.

The sudden silence, bar distant sirens, was a jarring shock to Jim's system. He rolled onto his back, which felt like it was on fire, and roared with rage and pain. As if that sated the fire on his back, he felt a little better and managed to stand. He limped over to where his SiG had fallen, retrieved it and loaded a new clip. Working the slide to jack a round into the chamber, Jim approached the wreckage of the BMW. He approached cautiously, keeping his pistol trained on the sprawled body that lay a few feet from the mangled bike.

Reilly was having difficulty breathing, but he was still alive. He looked at Castle dazedly and then seemed to remember where he was. "Ah," he said tightly. "So much for that, then."

"You're going down, Reilly."

Reilly forced a laugh, then his face contorted in pain. "Don't be so sure. For once the Good Friday Agreement comes in handy. You'll have to hand me to the Brits, and under the deal your Mister Clinton helped set up, they'll have to let me go as soon as they've sentenced me."

"They might have to wait a while. You'll be tried for your crimes here first."

"That's true, but we have quite a lobby here. Politics always gets in the way of a fair trial, one way or the other."

"You're forgetting that your 'lobby' isn't best pleased with you. A rogue agent isn't their favorite kind of man. There's no 'I' in team, Reilly, even if there's one in IRA."

The story continues in
FINAL DESTINATION:
DESTINATION ZERO
by David McIntee

Available from Black Flame
www.blackflame.com

FINAL DESTINATION

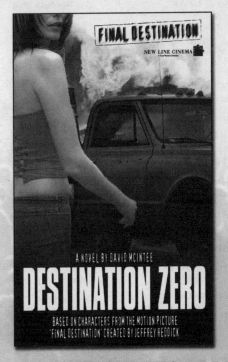

DESTINATION ZERO

1-84416-171-4   £6.99/$7.99

WWW.BLACKFLAME.COM
TOUGH FICTION FOR A TOUGH PLANET

CHECK OUT THESE FANTASTIC TITLES AVAILABLE FROM BLACK FLAME!

JUDGE DREDD

Judge Dredd #1:
Dredd vs Death
1-84416-061-0
£5.99 • $6.99

Judge Dredd #2:
Bad Moon Rising
1-84416-107-2
£5.99 • $6.99

Judge Dredd #3:
Black Atlantic
1-84416-108-0
£5.99 • $6.99

Judge Dredd #4:
Eclipse
1-84416-122-6
£5.99 • $6.99

Judge Dredd #5:
Kingdom of the Blind
1-84416-133-1
£5.99 • $6.99

STRONTIUM DOG

Strontium Dog #1:
Bad Timing
1-84416-110-2
£5.99 • $6.99

Strontium Dog #2:
Prophet Margin
1-84416-134-X
£5.99 • $6.99

ROGUE TROOPER

Rogue Trooper #1:
Crucible
1-84416-111-0
£5.99 • $6.99

NIKOLAI DANTE

Nikolai Dante #1:
The Strangelove Gambit
1-84416-139-0
£5.99 • $6.99

ABC WARRIORS

ABC Warriors #1:
The Medusa War
1-84416-109-9
£5.99 • $6.99

DURHAM RED

Durham Red #1:
The Unquiet Grave
1-84416-159-5
£5.99 • $6.99

NEW LINE CINEMA

Blade: Trinity
1-84416-106-4
£6.99 • $7.99

Freddy vs Jason
1-84416-059-9
£5.99 • $6.99

The Texas Chainsaw
Massacre
1-84416-060-2
£6.99 • $7.99

The Butterfly Effect
1-84416-081-5
£6.99 • $7.99

Cellular
1-84416-104-8
£6.99 • $7.99

THE TWILIGHT ZONE

The Twilight Zone #1:
Memphis/The Pool Guy
1-84416-130-7
£6.99 • $7.99

The Twilight Zone #2:
Upgrade/Sensuous Cindy
1-84416-131-5
£6.99 • $7.99

The Twilight Zone #3:
Sunrise/Into the Light
1-84416-151-X
£6.99 • $7.99

BLADE
TRINITY

A novel by Natasha Rhodes
Based on the motion picture written by David S Goyer

THE UNQUIET GRAVE

PETER J EVANS

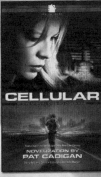

CELLULAR

NOVELIZATION BY
PAT CADIGAN

JUDGE DREDD

THE FINAL CUT
MATTHEW SMITH

NEW LINE CINEMA

THE **TEXAS**
CHAINSAW
MASSACRE

A novelization by STEPHEN HAND
Based on the screenplay by SCOTT KOSAR

Hard-hitting action
from the war-torn
future!

CRUCIBLE
GORDON RENNIE

ISBN 1-84416-106-4 $7.99/ £6.99

The vampire apocalypse looms as a desperate battle unfolds to end the
secret war between the vampires and the few humans who know of their
existence. The only person who stands between the ultimate vampire and
the enslavement of humanity is the daywalker, Blade!

WWW.BLACKFLAME.COM
TOUGH FICTION FOR A TOUGH PLANET

EVIL GETS AN UPGRADE

JASON X
1-84416-168-4   £6.99/$7.99

WWW.BLACKFLAME.COM
TOUGH FICTION FOR A TOUGH PLANET

TERROR WITHOUT END

JASON X:
THE EXPERIMENT
1-84416-169-2   £6.99/$7.99

SUFFER THE CHILDREN
1-84416-172-2 £6.99/$7.99

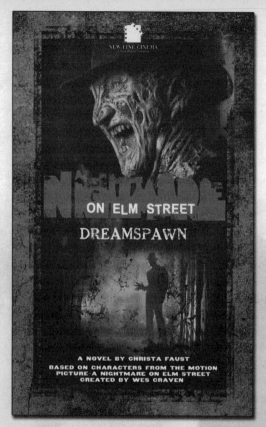

DREAMSPAWN
1-84416-173-0   £6.99/$7.99